SHADOW WALKER COMPLETE TRILOGY

TIFFANY SHAND

DEDICATION

For Mum

ACKNOWLEDGMENTS

Editing by Dark Raven Edits
Cover Design Rainbow Danger Designs

SHADOW WALKER

PROLOGUE

Charlie McCray looked at her watch for about the thousandth time and glanced down into the gloom on the floor below. The warehouse felt cold and smelt of dampness. Cracks of light shone down through the splintered glass windows casting eerie white pools onto the floor. Hell, she couldn't wait to catch these guys in the act, find out what illegals they were trading and get the hell out of there. Her best friend and her fellow enforcer, Natalia, grinned at her.

What's taking so long? Nat groaned in thought.

Tell me about it. I want this over with so I can have a drink and we can give Simon a proper retirement send-off. Charlie shifted in an effort to get her stiff limbs more comfortable.

Natalia's smile widened. *Sure it's not because you're dying for your promotion?*

Charlie rolled her eyes. Yes, the big promotion where she'd become a lieutenant at just twenty-four years of age since their team leader, Simon, was retiring. She finally had the chance to lead their team and get to where she'd been wanting to be for the past six years. Running her own team. But first, they had a gang to deal with.

Working as an enforcer often meant waiting around and working undercover. But Charlie loved the good she could do enforcing justice. She kept a close watch on Simon as he waited for his contact to arrive. Catching one of the Tears, a gang of ruthless criminals who liked to trade illegal artefacts and drugs had been something her team had been working on for months.

Be patient, Charlie told herself. *You can't afford to blow this.*

She glanced over at their fellow teammate, Louis, who flashed her

3

smile from where he perched on the other side of the upper floor of the warehouse. *Ready to celebrate, lieutenant?*

I'm not an LT yet, she reminded him.

I could kill for good beer! Lou turned his attention back to their boss.

Shush, we need to focus.

Aye, aye, LT. He gave her a mock salute.

Charlie just shook her head, tried to focus on the job. Hell, she couldn't wait to celebrate but the job hadn't been completed yet. They'd spent months setting up this operation. Plus, her boyfriend, Scott, was coming home too, so she had even more to celebrate. Everything was coming together. She'd finally oversee her own team and had her boyfriend home. After weeks apart it would be great to finally spend some time together. But she knew she'd have a lot of work to do after her big promotion.

The sound of the warehouse door creaking open made Charlie grip her gun tighter. A man dressed in a black hoodie came in with Simon's informant. She couldn't make out the man's face. *Lou, do you have a visual?*

Not yet.

Nat?

Negative, her partner replied.

Charlie crawled along the floor, feeling the cold metal against her skin. She had to be careful, quiet or she risked giving them all away.

Simon, his informant, and the newcomer gathered, talking in low voices. She tried to listen in on them through the comm link in her ear but couldn't make out much of their conversation.

Charlie, that's him. That's our guy, Lou said.

Her heart started to beat faster and she aimed her rifle at their target. The man pulled a small wooden box out of his jacket. *Lou, can you see what that thing is?* she asked.

Nope, nothing showing up on my scanner.

Charlie held up her own scanner with her free hand and searched for what might be inside.

"This is the device," Simon's voice echoed in her ear.

Charlie bit her lip. This was it. The moment they'd been waiting for. She stared through her rifle scope, making sure her recorder was working.

The man flipped open the box. A brilliant burst of blue light blinded Charlie as a roar of thunder shook the air. The floor beneath her gave way. She screamed as she felt herself falling through space. Then darkness swallowed her up.

CHAPTER 1

Charlie tucked a lock of brown hair behind her ear. "I thought transferring to a new unit would mean less stake-outs." She glanced over at her new partner, Kaz. Kazia Snowden. With her flaming red hair and sharp green eyes, she looked and acted the opposite of her former partner, Natalia.

"It's not a stake-out, we're waiting for the artefact to be handed over to us," Kaz replied. "Of course, you could always go back to the office and get through that pile of paperwork you've been avoiding."

"Hey, that's your job, officer."

Kaz rolled her eyes. "What's the matter, McCray? Grunt work too much for you?"

Charlie snorted. "No, I just can't believe the Arts, Antiquities and Collectables Division involves so much damned paperwork."

"You could always go back to Major Crimes. I heard the chief left the position open for you, right?"

Charlie winced. Yes, she could still become a lieutenant and lead a team the way she'd always dreamed of, but how could she lead any team when her own was dead now? Deep down, she knew she couldn't do it. It had even forced her to turn down her coveted promotion.

She felt a familiar ache rise in her chest and fought to stay calm. It had been six months since she'd lost them, and the pain still felt just as raw. "No, I told you I don't work with Major Crimes anymore. That part of my life is over." Hell, she'd only been working with ACC Department a couple of weeks. She had to give it a chance.

Charlie knew Kaz, an Ashrali fey, back from her days at the Enforcers Academy and decided it might be fun working with her again. She spotted a man in a black hoodie striding towards them. Her mind flashed back to the man standing next to Simon. Charlie gritted her teeth. *Not now! Stay calm.* She took a deep breath. *One, two, three. Breathe.*

"Hey, are you..." Charlie started to ask.

The man's dark eyes widened, and he pulled out a gun. "Bloody hell!"

Charlie knocked it away with a sharp kick. He lunged at her; she blocked and shoved him to the ground. "Stay down," she snapped, pulling out her cuffs and yanking his arms behind his back. "Jeez, Little. What the hell are you doing here?" She knew the low-level street thug from her early days of working in Setara City. She hadn't expected to bust him while working in ACC.

"God, McCray, why the fuck did it have to be you?"

Kaz only stared. "Nice moves, McCray," her partner remarked. "Does he have the painting on him?"

Charlie patted down Little's body and pulled a piece of parchment out of his jacket.

Kaz examined it. "It's fake."

"Jeez, McCray, I heard you'd gone soft, but I can't believe you're working in ACC," Little remarked as she dragged him into the station. "Aren't you bored out of your freaking mind?"

"No, it's peaceful. Catching you reminds me how much I don't want to go back to my old job." Charlie took him through booking. *Plus, my new job doesn't get people killed.*

Walking through the small station brought back memories too, but she forced them down. The small red brick building had been used as a school before the country's revolution but had since been turned into an enforcer's station. Kaz and Charlie took Little through the security scanner, showing their badges for ID then took him through to booking.

Little fiddled with his cuffs then stared at Charlie. "Seriously, McCray, I used to enjoy seeing you around. You're cool, well, cool for a cop anyway," Little said with a grin.

She flinched; she really didn't want to be reminded of the old days. "That was a long time ago, Little."

Charlie handed him over to the desk sergeant and headed back to the cluttered office she now shared with Kaz. She slumped into her rickety desk chair and scowled at the pile of paperwork.

"You did good out there, sarge. Doesn't it make you miss Major Crimes?" Kaz asked.

Charlie sighed. She knew Kaz had just been biding her time until she could join Major Crimes herself. It was the dream for a lot of enforcers. She hadn't had an office when she'd worked in her old unit and this looked more like a cupboard than an office. With its skinny window, desks that looked like they'd been through a war zone and the endless piles of books and paperwork, it was a far cry from her old life.

"Look, no one really wants to work in ACC, I'm only doing it because the experience looks good for when I tried to apply Major Crimes," Kaz told her.

Charlie tried not to wince. She'd been just like Kaz a few years earlier. Young, eager to join the newly formed Major Crimes Unit. Setara hadn't had much in the way of law enforcement before and the city had needed a lot of help. "It's not all it's cracked up to be," she muttered and gulped down the station's foul coffee.

Kaz slumped into her desk chair, shoving paper to one end of her own desk. "I still don't get why you want to be here. I mean you're a Denai witch, for crying out loud." Denais were immortal witches who used their gifts to enforce and ensure justice with their powers of telepathy, empathy, compulsion, divination and being able to sense the truth. Charlie had been born Denai medium, her powers worked on the dead, not the living.

"I'm a medium," she corrected. *Or at least I was.*

A gangly looking man with a mop of brown curls tapped on the door. Charlie smiled when she saw Nigel with his chequered shirt and cargo pants. The third unofficial member of her new team. He'd joined ACC like Kaz—for experience.

"Hey, sarge, the chief wants to see you in his office," he told her.

Charlie groaned. *Now what?*

"Thanks."

Charlie headed up to Chief Whitely's office. She still had no idea why the chief had decided to work in Setara City after the country's revolution. Maybe he had felt pushed out after the Excalibar team— her aunt's investigation team—had moved to Elaris years earlier. Setara City wasn't the place it had once been. She took a deep breath as she knocked on the door. If he wanted to talk to her about moving back to Major Crimes again he'd be wasting his time.

Charlie opened the door and saw Jason Talbot there instead of Chief Whitely. He had short dark hair, and silver eyes, towering over her at six-and-a-half feet. "Uncle Jason," she gasped. "I mean, er, chief. What you are doing here?"

Jason smiled, moved around the desk and wrapped his arms around her. *Goddess, I hope no one sees this!* One of the reasons she'd come to Setara in the first place was to get away from her family's influence in Elaris.

"Hey." He gave her a warm smile.

She groaned, closing the door behind her so no one else would see the exchange. Her cheeks flushed with embarrassment. *What's Chief Whitely gonna think with the commander being here? Well, Jason is his boss so I suppose he can't object.* "Please tell me Aunt Cate didn't send you to check up on me again."

"No, but she still worries about you—we both do."

She'd spent a few weeks with her family after losing her team, although she loved them, and they knew the downsides that came with being an enforcer it hadn't helped. "I'm fine," she insisted, resting a hip against the visitor's chair. "Is that what you came all this way for?" *Please don't ask more questions about how I'm feeling, I just want to get back to work.*

"No, I came to talk about your case." Jason leant back against the desk and folded his arms.

Charlie's heart skipped a beat. After the bombing Excalibar Investigations, the team of enforcers led by Jason and her aunt, Cate, had investigated but hadn't found the people responsible. "Have you found something?" she asked, wringing her hands together.

"Maybe. I know someone who can help you get close to the Tears, but—"

"Tell me," Charlie snapped. She'd do whatever it took to find the people responsible for killing her teammates. *Come on, just tell me, I didn't expect you of all people to keep things from me.*

"You don't have the clearance to work with Major Crimes' files now and you broke all ties with them."

Charlie gritted her teeth and shoved her hands into her pockets. "This had better not be a trick to get me back with them," she hissed. "Since when does clearance matter? You're the chief, plus the Grand

Master. You and Aunt Cate are the highest legal authority over Magickind. Why wouldn't you just give me the clearance?"

"Charlie, you know I'd never trick you. I won't force you back either but there are rules in place..."

"Ha, since when do you care about rules?" Cate and Jason were famous among the enforcers for breaking the rules and forming their own investigations team separate from the traditional enforcer's constabulary.

Jason sighed. "I can't hold out on reforming your team. I've left the position open because I know how much you wanted to lead them."

Charlie looked away and felt the sting of tears but held them back. Crying did nothing. "I told you, I don't want that. I don't care about any of it." Charlie folded her arms, hugging herself. "Reform the team. I know there's a lot of enforcers who'd kill to join."

It had been her dream too. Once.

She turned to face her uncle. "Tell me about the lead."

"It's not much to go on, I think he can help you find some answers."

"Give me the details. I'll go right now." Paperwork could wait a little longer. Finding her team's killers trumped everything. "Who is it?"

"You're not going to like it."

CHAPTER 2

Charlie pulled up outside the club Nocturne, a large red brick building with darkened windows and black double doors. *Unbelievable!* She couldn't believe Jason would send her here of all places. She sat staring at the club for several minutes, gripping the steering wheel so hard her knuckles turned white. Maybe Drake wouldn't be there. Hell, his main club was in Elaris so there was a good chance he wouldn't be around. She'd spent the past six years trying to avoid seeing him again and had hoped this day would never come.

Get a grip. You're here because of your case—okay, not officially my case, but they were my team. Nothing will stop me from getting justice for them. She took a deep breath, pulled on her leather jacket and glanced at herself in the rear-view mirror. With her brown locks pulled back in a loose knot and only a tinge of makeup, she wondered what Drake would think of her now. She'd been just shy of eighteen when they'd last seen each other.

Her deep brown eyes had dark circles under them from lack of sleep. *Why should I care what Drake thinks?* She clipped her badge onto the belt of her dark black jeans and strode towards the club. She wasn't an awkward teenager anymore; she was a woman, an enforcer. Plus, it wasn't as if anything would happen between her and Drake. She was only here to find out what he knew, then they'd go their separate ways again. Besides, she had Scott.

Charlie took a deep breath, pushed the doors open, and stepped inside. She put on her Denai face to show a neutral expression. Denais never gave away their true emotions and she didn't want him to see hers either.

Bright glaring white lights broke through the dark interior of the club with its black and white chequered floor and black and white tables and stools.

Definitely Drake's style. If demons have style.

She spotted a giant of a man with a spattering of ginger hair and a short beard by the door. His dark eyes fixed on her she walked in, eyeing her badge. "Hi, I'm..." she said.

"I know who you are. The boss is expecting you, he's in his office." He motioned to a door at the back of the club. Her eyes widened. Expecting her? How had he known she'd come? Had Jason told him?

Ah hell, no backing out now. Part of her wanted to turn around and run back out. If she walked through that door, she'd be inviting Drake into her life again and she didn't think she was ready for that. Charlie took another breath, counted a few times to stay calm. *Here we go.*

She hesitated when she reached the door. Should she just go barging in there? She knew how to handle people, even criminals— but Drake? Nope, no amount of experience or training could help with that. What was she supposed to say?

"Hi, long time no see; is there any way to break the connection you created between us when you saved my life?" Or, "Hi, have you gotten over your ridiculous idea that we're supposed to be life mates yet?"

No, she was here for work, for her team. Nothing else mattered but that.

As she reached the door handle, her senses tingled, feeling the warmth of his presence. Charlie shook her head to shake off the feeling, then pushed the door open. Inside a large desk took up one corner of the room with a console unit stacked high with a neat pile of paperwork.

Behind the desk sat the man himself. He rose and moved around the desk when he saw her. "Charlotte." He made her name sound exotic.

She didn't know what she'd expected but he looked different from what she remembered. His rich long black hair was now cut short, but his jet-black eyes looked the same. Same strong masculine body that looked damned good in his sharp grey suit.

Despite only being a few inches taller, he dwarfed over her, his massive body seeming to take up the entire space. Damn, the man looked good.

"Drake." Charlie felt her heart beat faster. Goddess, she would not feel any kind of insane attraction to him, even if he did look like sin itself.

"How are you?"

She blinked, surprised by the question. His face remained neutral; she'd never been able to read his expressions. "Er—I'm fine."

"It's been a while."

"Yeah." She tucked a lock of hair behind her ear, biting her lip with uncertainty. "I'm an enforcer now." She brushed her hair back, struggling to find the right words. The strange magnetic pull tugged at her senses. *Bloody connection!*

"So I've heard." He folded his arms. "I'm sorry about what happened."

"About what?" She stared at him, losing herself in the dark pools of his eyes. *Demon,* she reminded herself. *You can't have lusty thoughts about a demon, but hell, who am I to judge? I'm part demon.*

"About the loss of your team."

"Oh, that." She'd almost hoped he'd apologise for the damn link between them. "I mean, that's why I'm here. Jason said you have info about the Tears."

"Please, sit." He motioned to the leather visitor's chair.

Charlie shook her head. "This isn't a social call. Just tell me what you know," she insisted. "I have to get back to work."

"Very well. The Alliance is interested in the gang suspected of killing your teammates."

The Alliance was an organisation created after the revolution of Setara to deal with the aftermath. Setara had gone to hell for a while after the downfall of the tyrant who once ruled it. So together the Alliance made up of five leaders of the original races of Magickind. Together the Alliance became a separate entity from the United Magickind Council, their main goal was to ensure justice and make sure a group like the infamous Covenant never came to power again. Along with the council, they created new laws to make sure each race was treated equal and no one had the power to control others. From what she'd heard Drake had joined the Alliance too and become a representative of Demonkind.

"Why is the Alliance interested in the Tears?" Charlie asked, folding her arms.

"We have our reasons." His face remained cool and calm, not betraying any emotion.

Right. There it was. Somehow she doubted she'd ever get the whole truth from him. "Which are?" She arched an eyebrow.

"Look, if we work together, I believe we can bring down the gang," Drake said. "The Alliance has suggested we work together to find the gang's true leader."

She scowled, wondering what kind of game he was up to now. "You're civilian; I'm an enforcer. The two don't go together." *Hell, that's an understatement.*

"I'm not a civilian. I run my own private black-ops unit for the Alliance. If you agree to work with me, I can make you a Division agent."

Charlie's mouth fell open. Of all the things she'd been expecting him to say, that hadn't been one of them. "Drake, look. I appreciate you trying to help me, but..." She'd heard of the elusive Division before but had never had any encounters with them. She hadn't been interested either. Being an enforcer had been all that mattered to her, but Division went way beyond normal law enforcement.

"I'm not just doing it for you, little witch. The Alliance believes the gang is using ancient weapons and that they were after one the day your team was killed. Ancient tech is dangerous in the wrong hands. I'll do everything I can to stop them."

She shook her head. "I work alone now on my team's case. It's personal for me."

"It would only be for a few weeks at most. I'm sure we can solve this together."

Charlie sighed. Maybe Drake could prove to be a valuable source of intel, but she had other reasons for not wanting him around. "You know nothing has changed between us. I still won't be your life mate," she said. "We should break the link between us." She saw something flicker in his dark eyes but couldn't read what.

Drake shook his head. "The link between us can't be undone, little witch. I brought you back from death; that kind of connection can't be broken." He reached out to touch her, but Charlie took a step back.

"Fine, just so you know where we stand." Charlie turned back to the door. "I'd better go."

"Will you work with me or not?"

She groaned. What could she say? She'd do whatever she had to do to find her team's killer, even if it meant working with Drake.

"Fine, like I said, nothing is going to change between us. I'm with Scott. He's my future," she insisted. "Come by the station later. We can go over details then."

"Very well, we'll meet again tomorrow morning."

Have this all planned out, don't you?

"Fine, see you then." Charlie turned and left. She had to get out of there. Just being near him made her feel uncomfortable. It had awoken the connection she'd spent years ignoring. *I'm not attracted to him,* she told herself as she headed back to her car.

Once at home, Charlie poured herself a beer and settled in front of her computer. Stacks of paperwork covered her living room with its wooden floor and whitewashed walls. A board sat in one corner pinned with all the info she'd managed to gather about the case and boxes were scattered in every room from where she'd moved in the year before. She'd never gotten around to unpacking. Her mind wandered back to Drake again. She swore she could feel his presence too—something that both annoyed and confused her.

What had changed? The link between them had been something she'd put to the back of her mind over the years. Had seeing him again brought it back to the surface?

Her laptop chimed and she clicked on to see the grinning face of Scott there. "Hey, babe." Scott waved.

Charlie's lips curved when she saw him. His goofy grin always made her feel better. "Hi."

"God, I've missed you!" Scott's job as a tech consultant meant he travelled a lot, but she'd grown used to his absences.

"I miss you too." She touched the screen, part of her wishing he'd teleport back right now. She needed a distraction from all thoughts of Drake. "When are you coming home?"

"Not sure yet. Maybe another week. How you've been?" he asked. "Still having nightmares?"

She winced. She hated the nightmares, being forced to relive her team's last moments. Damn, he knew her too well, and it made her uncomfortable. He'd only learnt of the nightmares by accident when she'd woken up screaming. "Not so much."

"See, the therapy is helping."

Right. Therapy. She'd had a few sessions with Marina Talbot— Jason's mother—since the bombing but had stopped going. Therapy hadn't helped; only justice would. Only that would bring closure.

"Char, are you still listening to me?" Scott's voice brought her back to reality.

She shook her head, trying to clear it. "Yeah."

"Maybe we should take a holiday when I get home. It'd be good for us to get away for a while and finally spend some quality time together."

She tried not to cringe as a familiar panic set in and gripped the arms of her chair for support. "Scott, you know I can't. I just started working in a new department. Plus you have to work too."

He frowned. "ACC is just a side gig, right? I thought we agreed you were going to retire?"

Charlie looked away. Despite what happened, she couldn't imagine ever walking away from the job. Being an enforcer was in her blood; it's what she'd always wanted to be. "I didn't say that, and I can't walk away. Not until I find out who did it."

"It's not your case, right? We agreed we'd talk when I get back, remember?" he said. "About moving in together."

Charlie tried not to wince. Despite dating for a few months in college and then hooking up again a year ago, their relationship had been long-distance for most of that time. The idea of taking the next step by moving in together felt like a big deal and one she didn't think she was ready for. "We'll talk," she promised.

"Great, it's a date. I love you, Char."

She opened her mouth to say the same as an image of Drake popped into her mind again. "You too." The screen went black.

Charlie grabbed a bottle of sleeping potion, gulped it down. She hated the stuff, but it was the only way to avoid the nightmares. She glanced through her case notes, found nothing new. Scott sent her a text wishing her goodnight.

She smiled. She'd be glad to have him home, but it wasn't Scott who came into her mind as sleep took over.

CHAPTER 3

Charlie walked into Chief Whitely's office the next morning, relieved to see Drake not there. "Morning, sir," she said. "We need to talk about..." She touched her Denai pendant for comfort. Even just mentioning the case brought back a heavy pit in her stomach.

Whitely stared at her. His hair had turned white over the past few years, unusual for an immortal but she guessed it was from years of rank. "You remind me so much of your aunt, sometimes it's disturbing."

"I'm not as sarcastic as her," she pointed out.

The chief's lips curved into a smile. "True, but you McCrays seem to think you're above the rules."

"Sir, I don't believe that. Have I done something to offend you?"

"No, but we need to discuss your situation with Drake Dumont. Talbot suggested you two should work together and I'm not one to disagree with him."

Charlie slumped into the worn-out visitor's chair. "I've never worked with Division before; hell, what do we really know about them?"

"True, but Division are the best of the best when it comes to getting the job done. They may not have the red tape we enforcers must contend with, but they are damned good," Whitely said. "Drake is a leader of the Alliance and has quite the influence among Demonkind."

"But Division are more than just enforcers. They're more soldiers, aren't they?" Charlie ran a hand through her hair. She'd been debating all morning whether to go through with this or not. "I'm an enforcer, despite the six months I spent working in special ops a few years ago. Division are supposed to be…"

"Division is similar to your aunt's team Excalibar, but they work much more high-risk cases. But I want to know if you can do this. Division may have the resources and have taken over the murder case, but I won't force you to join them."

Charlie nodded. "I can do this. Maybe Drake will prove to be a good source of intel."

"This will only be a temporary assignment. After this case, I want you back at the station. The promotion to lieutenant is still on the table if you want it."

She gripped the sides of the chair so hard she thought they'd break. "Sir, I already told you, I can't work in Major Crimes anymore."

"McCray, I hate to see your talents going to waste in ACC, of all places. They'll always be a place for you in Major Crimes if you still want it."

Charlie felt the familiar ache rise in her chest. She couldn't break down in front of her chief, so she looked away. "I can't go back," she whispered.

Whitely nodded, understanding in his eyes. "Very well. Drake will be here soon. You're only on loan to Division, but from now on you'll be known as Agent McCray. You'll be working undercover on this assignment. Our ultimate goal is to find what the Tears' ultimate goal is."

Charlie met his blue gaze then. "Why are you letting me do this?" she asked. "Be straight with me, sir. Enforcers aren't allowed to work on cases where they have a personal involvement."

"I can't answer that. The Alliance controls Division and they requested you. You'd have to ask them that," Whitely answered. "Perhaps because you were there, or perhaps of your shadow demon abilities."

Charlie hadn't found out she was part demon herself until six years earlier and still didn't like the idea now. "I'm only part demon. I have fey and Phoenix DNA too, but I'm a witch first and foremost. That doesn't mean I have any of those abilities though." No, her strongest abilities had been her Denai and demon powers—at least up until the bombing. Charlie hesitated as Whitely put the paperwork in front of her to sign. "Unofficial, right? If I change my mind, I can walk away, can't I?"

The chief nodded. "Of course, but honestly, McCray, I think you're wasting yourself in ACC. You're too gifted for grunt work."

"I appreciate that, sir, but I'm not the enforcer I used to be."

"Fine. Drake will be here soon, I'll—"

"I'll go and grab my case files from my office." She headed to the door.

"Drake requested to use space here at the station so I told him he could use the old bullpen your team used. No one is using it right now and you know how short we are on space here," Whitely told her. "You should also know Kazia Snowden and Nigel Monroe are Division agents."

Instead of heading to the office, Charlie drove home after telling Nigel and Kaz the news, insisting she had to pick up her case files first. She could have shimmered there, but teleporting wouldn't give her time to clear her mind. She didn't know how she'd be able to face going back to her old office. After the bombing and transferring to another department, she'd sent Scott to pick up her stuff.

But she could really go back there? There wasn't enough room to work in ACC and limited resources of the station meant she had little choice but to go back to her team's old workspace. Why the hell did Drake want to work at the station anyway?

She pulled up outside her apartment block, took a deep breath. *You have to do this,* she told herself. *For the team.*

Jumping from the car, she headed up the street to her block of apartments. The huge stone tower had seen better days, its white paint had long since vanished and graffiti covered some off the walls in artwork of various colours. Charlie knew this was a rougher part of the city and she could've got somewhere better, but she liked it here. It was unpredictable and no one bothered her there. No one knew who she was, and she liked it that way. The small apartment had only a small lounge/dining room with a kitchenette, a double bedroom and a smaller room that she'd turned into an office. Scott hated the place, but it suited her with its simplicity. He'd no doubt insist on moving somewhere else if she did agree to move in with him.

Her phone chimed. Kaz.

"Hey, I'm on my way back. I just need to get my stuff," Charlie answered as she moved down the cobblestone street with its array of cars and transpos.

"Nigel just told me." Kaz cried. "Excited to be joining Division?"

"Don't get too excited, we're only working one case," Charlie insisted. She'd been surprised to learn Kaz and Nigel actually worked for Division already and had been sent to watch over her when she'd joined ACC. Drake's plan, no doubt. "Do you know his lordship well?"

"Do you mean Drake? No, he's the boss. He created Division and he works his own cases. You should be honoured he's asked us to work with him. Well, you mostly. You'll be his new partner. Weird, I don't think he's ever had a partner before."

What a shock! That bastard really has this all planned out. If he thinks he's going to win me over to become his life mate, boy is he mistaken! "Drake is an Alliance leader and they're worried the Tears might become a new big bad. That's the only reason he's joining us." *That and some deluded belief he has about us being life mates.*

"He's the demon who helped during Denai Storm too, right?"

Charlie snorted. She didn't understand why some people called the revolution *Denai Storm*; there had been more Magickind than Denais involved. "Right. He's a friend of the family."

"He's pretty hot too, right?"

She laughed. "If you like tall, dark and demon, yeah."

"Brilliant, it'd be better than looking at Nigel's ugly mug. When——"

Someone grabbed her, pulling her backwards, clamping a hand over her mouth and wrenching her arms behind her. Her phone clattered onto the pavement. *I don't need this today!* He pulled her gun from its holster, out of her reach. She tried to yank her arms free, but his grip proved too strong for her.

A flash of Nat's smiling face then the burst of blue light ran through her mind. Charlie threw her head back, knocking into his jaw, then slammed her boot down on his foot. The man grunted but didn't loosen his grip.

Charlie drew in a breath, reached for magic. Light shimmered over her as she phased out of his grasp. She hit the ground hard as her body became solid and rolled away as her attacker made another grab for her.

"Come here, witch!"

Charlie took another breath, vanishing into the concrete beneath her. A world of grey swallowed her up, she could see every inch of dirt and cement surrounded her like tiny molecules of darkness. Her heart thundered inside her ears as panic took over. *Light flashed, the roar of the bomb going off.*

Her body started to reform, her lungs screamed for air as the concrete enveloped her, trapping her beneath the pavement, the darkness swallowing her whole. No light penetrated the inky blackness around her. Charlie took one choking breath and burst back into the world of above, light burning her eyes. She coughed up dust, taking gulps of air.

Her attacker flew at her.

Still coughing, she blocked his blow and raised her hand. Nothing happened. No magic came to her. She hit the ground when she tried to phase, pulled out her clutch piece weapon from her ankle holster and fired. A stream of blue energy shot out, knocking the man to the ground.

His hood fell back, revealing his bald black head, his dark brown eyes widened in shock. It was the man she'd seen that day in the warehouse. The one who haunted her nightmares. She'd recognise his face anywhere.

"You," she gasped. "What..."

He fired an energy ball at her. It hit her in the stomach, sending shock waves of pain jolting through every nerve ending.

Charlie's weapon fell from her hand. She couldn't breathe, couldn't think as blackness threatened to drag her down. Blue light flashed through her mind, the roar of the explosion tearing through metal and flesh.

Light shimmered as Drake appeared, clad in his usual dark suit. Her attacker looked to him then vanished. "Little witch?" Drake knelt beside her, putting a hand on her shoulder. "Are you alright? What did he do?"

Charlie blinked. Hell, there was no way she'd pass out front of him. "What—are—you—doing—here?" she said between gasping breaths.

"I sensed your panic."

She brushed off his hand, scrambled up. "I'm fine." Her voice came out stronger than expected.

Goddess damned connection! Did he sense everything she felt now? Having Drake feel her panic was too humiliating. She bent, grabbed her fallen weapons and clipped them back in place. Her magic had failed again. She couldn't understand it. She'd spent years learning to master her powers. Discipline and control were something all Denais learnt from infancy. She'd never struggled with them before. Marina had said the disconnection was caused by the emotional trauma, but Charlie doubted that.

"Charlotte—"

She gritted her teeth. No one ever called her Charlotte and she didn't like the name either. "Enough with the Charlotte and the little witch crap!" she cried, feeling tears prick her eyes. Goddess, she would not break down in front of him. "I'm fine. Just go away."

"Are you hurt?" he demanded. "Yell at me all you want to; I just need to know you're alright."

"I'm fine." Charlie ran a hand through her long hair, brushing it off her face as sweat covered her brow. Why wouldn't Drake just leave? "How the hell was he still alive?"

"Who?" Drake asked.

"No one. You can leave now."

He cupped her face, making her look up to meet his dark eyes. Damn, those eyes were sexy—like pools of darkness, yet they shimmered from blue to black again. It should have frightened her, but she saw only concern there. "Who attacked you?"

The memory of Scott's smiling face made her tear her gaze away as she pulled away from him. "That guy is supposed to be dead. He died that day in the warehouse."

CHAPTER 4

This witch was going to drive him to distraction, Drake was sure of it. Why the hell fate had chosen her to be his life mate he'd never know. He'd never met such a stubborn creature in his eight thousand years of existence or one more beautiful. Even with her auburn hair a ruffled mess and her chocolate brown eyes tight with anger she still looked like the most beautiful thing he'd ever seen.

With her petite lanky form, she'd blossomed into a woman from the girl she'd been when they first met. She still looked young, but her eyes held a sadness that made his heart ache. It made him want to drag her into his arms and hold her close in a way he'd never felt.

The loss of her team still haunted her. That was why he'd insisted on helping her now.

When her panic had flooded through him earlier, he hadn't been able to stay away as he had on previous occasions over the past few years. Since he'd seen her the day before everything in him demanded he go to her, make her his. Yet, Drake knew if he did, Charlie would never forgive him.

But there was more than grief at work here. Something else had happened, he was sure of it. He just needed to gain her trust enough to get her to talk. But would she?

She was a Denai after all.

After Charlie calmed down, Drake convinced her to head back to the station with him after she grabbed a box of files from her tiny apartment. Despite her protests, he wanted to keep an eye on her. Sooner or later she'd have to deal with her grief, and he'd be there for her when she did.

Drake said nothing while she drove there, and she seemed grateful for the silence. The groan and snarl of city traffic made him miss the old city in some ways but Setara was much better off now than it had been. The glistening silver towers shone like diamonds as Charlie cut through the cobbled streets.

His mind went back to the conversation he'd had with one of his own informants just before he'd gone to help Charlie.

"There's a hit out on your witch," Val had told him.

"A hit? By who?" he demanded. "Why?"

"Looks like your girl messed with the Tears. They want her, and they're gonna be gunning for her."

"I don't understand why they'd come after me now," Charlie muttered, seemingly more to herself than to him. "It's been six months!"

He tore his attention away from the cityscape and glanced at her as she clutched the steering wheel. "Perhaps because of the hit the Tears' leader put out a hit on you."

Charlie's gaze snapped towards him. Her deep brown eyes had turned a hazy green. He guessed that was a sign of the Ashrali fey in her. Or perhaps her demon side. Demons' eyes often changed with strong emotion like his own did. "What hit?" she hissed.

"Their leader wants you."

She swung her car into an empty space and cut off the engine. "Why? Is it because I survived?"

Drake leaned closer, breathing in the sweet scent of her. She smelt of chocolate and coffee. Damn, she looked even more beautiful up close. "You tell me. What happened in that warehouse?"

Her eyes turned bright red with anger. "My friends died, that's what happened."

"But why were they there in the first place? What were you after?" He raised a hand when she started to protest. "We're partners now, little witch. You need to be honest with me."

Her eyes whirled with an array of colour.

"Do your eyes always do that?" He stared, watching the colours change.

"What?" She ran a hand through her hair and clutched the small seven-pointed star pendant at her throat, the symbol of the Denai.

He stroked her cheek, no longer able to resist the urge just to touch her. "Your eyes keep changing colour."

Charlie gritted her teeth, flinching at his touch. "Crap!" She waved her hand, conjuring a glamour spell to hide her eyes.

"Don't, I like it. I've always found the Ashrali fascinating, the way their hair or eyes change colour with emotion."

"I'm only one-part Ashrali. Plus, it freaks people out." She pulled the spell in place, but it shattered. "Look, there's nothing to talk about. We went to bust a gang member who was selling illegal weapons. I don't ask questions; I followed orders," she said. "Enough with the little witch stuff."

Drake bit back a smile. She was his little witch whether she liked or not.

Charlie flung the door open, grabbing the box. "Hey, maybe I need a nickname for you. How about Vlad?"

His lip curled. "What kind of name is that?"

"Vlad, like the famous vampire who crossed over here once from the human world." She grinned.

"Vampires aren't even real demons, they're parasites," Drake snarled. Why she'd want to call him that he couldn't fathom.

"I didn't say you were like that, but Vlad was tall, dark and probably annoying so Vlad it is. Let's roll, Vlad." She flashed him another smile and headed inside.

Seeing her smile was worth the ridiculous nickname.

They were stopped when they reached the security scanner in the lobby. Charlie held up her badge to be identified but Drake walked straight through. Charlie frowned at him. "How'd you do that?"

He only smiled. If only she knew. He was more than just the club owner and they both knew it. As a Division agent, he didn't need to use any form of ID.

Charlie gave him another glare.

He sighed. Winning this witch over was going to be damned harder than he thought. But he'd do it.

Drake followed her into the lift, noticed her avoiding his gaze. She seemed lost in thought. What he wouldn't give to know those thoughts. The link between them felt ever-present; he could feel her surface emotions when they were close or strong emotions if they were heightened, but no thoughts. Not the way a true bond would work.

"What about your club?" Charlie said, leaning back against the rail. "Don't they need you there?"

He shrugged, watching the numbers moving on the panels as the lift ascended. "My people can take care of it; my businesses are used to running without me being there."

"How many clubs do you have?"

"Twenty all over Setara, more in Britannia. They're not my only businesses."

"That's what I mean. You're a businessman, not an enforcer. Why help me?"

Drake chuckled to himself. Yes, he knew business well, but they only provided a distraction between assignments and provided a good cover. *Because you need me just as much as I need you,* he thought. No, those weren't the only reasons. Drake had his own for wanting to be part of this case.

"I still don't see how this is gonna work between us. I know you've worked with Excalibar, but this is different." Charlie shifted the box under her other arm. "Why do you want to work here? Don't Division have their own HQ hidden away somewhere?"

"Indeed, but the Alliance suggested I work here, and I'm inclined to agree." He thought Charlie would be more comfortable here in her own environment. Plus, the Alliance hadn't been keen to have them at their headquarters.

The lift doors dinged open, revealing a small bullpen of three desks and the door to a small office.

He felt Charlie stiffen next to him when she saw a red-haired Ashrali woman with sharp green eyes sitting at one desk while a scruffy haired man sat playing with a consul on the other. Agents Monroe and Snowden, he recognised them from their profiles. He'd chosen them to watch over Charlie when she'd gone back to work.

"Charlotte." Drake touched her shoulder; waves of pain rushed through him like a thousand knives through their link. Touching her must've deepened the psychic connection between them.

She shook her head, brushed him off and the wall between them went back up. "I'm fine." She turned away from him and stared at the others. "What the hell are you two doing?"

Both of them stared at her. "Sorry, Charlie. The chief told us to come up here," Kaz said. "There wasn't anywhere else for us to set up."

Nigel joined in and said. "I know this must be hard for you." He squeezed Charlie's shoulder.

Drake let out a low growl. He should be comforting his witch, but he stifled the growl with a cough. He couldn't show jealousy, they had a job to do.

"It's fine." Charlie dropped her box onto the empty desk and pulled off her jacket. "The guy from the warehouse attacked me. Now we need to find out why and how he's still alive. I'll grab a board so we can go over what we have so far." Drake watched her go into the office and felt another wave of sorrow.

"Hey, you must be Drake. I'm Kaz." The woman held out her hand. "That's Nigel over there."

He grasped it with a faint smile. "A pleasure to meet you both." He strode past them into the office where boxes had been stacked in one corner, no doubt things belonging to her former teammates. Charlie stood staring at them, unmoving.

"Little witch?"

Charlie blinked. "Right, work." She pulled out a board. "Do you need a desk?"

"I'm sure we can both fit in here."

Drake pulled out his own files of the case on his PDA and called them up on the team's flat screen. "Vincent Moret," he announced. "That's the man who attacked you today and was there at the warehouse when the explosion went off."

Charlie frowned. "How did you—oh, never mind. You're full of mysteries, Vlad."

"From my own files he went there to trade weapons with your team leader, Simon Drummond," Drake continued. "Who used an informant to make the connection with Moret."

"Right."

He noticed the surprise and couldn't hold back a smile. He knew this case just as well as she did, if not better.

"Right." Charlie pulled up the photos on screen. "Moret is a suspected member of the Tears, has convictions for theft, weapons and drugs."

"What about the informant?" Kaz asked. "It doesn't mention his name in the files." She glanced at her own PDA.

"That's because no one has ever been able to identify him. There wasn't anything left of him for testing," Drake replied, and Charlie winced.

Nigel looked over from his comp unit. "What were the weapons they were going to trade?"

Charlie shook her head. "Again I—"

Drake rose and pulled an assortment of strange-looking weapons onto the screen. "Here are some examples of Ashrali and ancient weapons recovered after the revolution. Many were never seen or used outside of Setara," he explained. "Some you may be familiar with already." Crystals, twisted sticks, staff weapons, jagged knives and odd-looking guns were among them.

"The Alliance has done everything it can to recover such weapons since the revolution, many of them were acquired by Oberoth and other Ashrali members of the Covenant, but some had unknown uses even to them. After the Cosgrave incident, you know how important it is that we recover such weapons."

"You must've seen a lot of cool stuff in all your years leading Division." Kaz grinned and batted her eyes lashes. "Bet you could tell me—I mean us—some great stories."

He spotted the way she looked to him, with the hunger of desire in her sharp eyes. Once he might have taken her up on it, but he was bored of meaningless sex; he wanted something real. A real relationship; a life with the stubborn, gorgeous witch sitting next to him.

The Cosgrave incident occurred when an unsuspecting family had purchased a weapon that destroyed an entire street after being turned on. Now gangs craved such devices.

"If the weapons were so important, why the bomb? Why blow everyone up in the first place?" Nigel asked. "Was it just a cover to make off with the weapons?"

"That was my guess since nothing was found," agreed Charlie. "But there were bodies there too." She shook her head. "It doesn't make sense."

"There has to be more to it. Moret escaped the blast as we know when he came after you today." Drake said.

Both Nigel and Kaz's eyes turned on Charlie who shrugged.

"Why didn't you tell us?" demanded Kaz, crossing her arms.

"Yeah, Charlie. We are your team now." Nigel scowled.

"I was going to." She sighed. "Focus on the case."

"This is part of the case," said Drake. "Why would the gang leader come after you now? He has his weapons."

"Maybe because I can ID Moret. He must be tying up loose ends." *You're really annoying, Vlad.*

The sound of her voice in his mind made him grin like an idiot. Finally, she'd acknowledged their link. *Just asking the right questions, little witch,* he replied.

"There's not much else in the file to go on," Kaz observed. "What did you pick up from the warehouse, Charlie?"

"Huh?" She frowned at the fey.

"I mean when you went back there, what did you pick up?" Kaz glanced at her file again. "It doesn't mention anything."

"Yeah, you're Denai, what did you get?" Nigel prompted.

"I'm a medium, not a seer." She shuffled her papers. "I didn't get anything." Charlie shifted in her seat. Drake knew she'd just lied. He doubted she'd gone back to the warehouse.

"I say we should all go back there," said Kaz. "I know my area of expertise is ancient artefacts and testing weapons, but I think I could run a few more forensic tests to see what went on. The place has been sealed since the explosion, right?"

"Er—right." Charlie looked at the screen, showing pictures of the crime scene.

"We'll all go. You shouldn't go anywhere alone now there's a price on your head," Kaz insisted.

CHAPTER 5

Charlie insisted on driving to the warehouse instead of shimmering there in an effort to wrap her head around going back. She hadn't been able to bring herself to return there again, despite knowing she might pick up certain things. She'd only gone back once but her powers hadn't worked, and it'd been too hard to return again.

Kaz and Nigel bickered over something, but Drake remained silent for which she was thankful for.

Charlie didn't know what to say. Instead, she tried to think of an excuse not to go. This was her team, her case. She couldn't let emotion get in the way. Nor could she admit the truth. "Gee, sorry my powers don't exactly work very well now. No one can figure out why."

Marina's suggestion of psychological trauma seemed like a load of rubbish. Hell, she'd lost people before, been traumatised before. She'd been kidnapped, and even blown up when she'd first met Drake.

Charlie glanced over when she felt Drake staring at her. "What?"

"Nothing."

"Then stop with the creepy staring thing, Vlad."

His eyes narrowed. "Are we really going to carry on with that stupid nickname?" he asked. "I'm not a vampire."

"Are you going to stop calling me little witch?"

He smirked at her. "You are a little witch."

For some reason, she couldn't stop smiling back. "Not that small—well, compared to most my family I'm short since most of them are six foot or over," she said, turning her attention back to the traffic. "What kind of demon are you anyway?"

Like Magickind, Demonkind had different races and species too but she'd never found out what Drake was. She hadn't given it much thought either but now felt curious. He was powerful, and she guessed more important than he let on. He had to be to become a member of the Alliance. "I'm a long story," was all he said.

One she'd like to know more of. "Come on, Vlad. We're working together, I deserve to know more about you."

Drake's eyes shifted to the back seat and he leaned closer. "You can find out whatever you want to know, little witch."

She felt him then, a lingering presence at the edge of her mind. The ever-present link seemed so much stronger now. Charlie gripped the steering wheel, tearing herself away from that gorgeous gaze as the warehouse loomed into view. The cold steel building seemed untouched since the explosion had been contained just inside. Her heart pounded like a drum as she stared at it and pulled the car to a halt. The building looked the same, with its slanted roof and broken glass windows that looked jagged in places. It loomed like a glowing beacon, a memorial to those who'd died there.

"McCray, are we going in?" Kaz asked, opening the car door and climbing out.

"Er—right, you head on in. I'm just going to check something." Charlie flipped the boot open and rummaged around in it. Anything to avoid going in there just a bit longer.

Drake moved to her side. "Are you alright?"

She jumped to the sound of his voice, not realising he now stood beside her. *How the fuck does he do that?* "You sure you're not a vampire? Because you sure do sneak around like one," she snapped. "Go in. Do whatever is you're here to do."

"I'm not leaving you alone," Drake insisted, grabbing a box. "Do you need this inside?"

Charlie stared daggers at him. "I don't need a bodyguard. I can take care of myself." She waved a hand. "Just take the box to Kaz."

He leant back against her car. "You're avoiding going in there."

"Gee, a few thousand years really has made you highly observant." She scowled. *Why won't he just leave me the hell alone? I wonder if he can read my mind now.*

"Charlotte." He set the box down and put his hands on her shoulders.

She took a deep breath. Maybe some of those breathing exercises would help her cope with having him around. "Just give me a minute, okay?" She pulled away from him.

"I lost my family too."

Charlie blinked at him, surprised. "What?"

Something flashed in his eyes, pain perhaps. "My family, they were killed a long time ago. I haven't set foot in my former home since then."

She stared at him, feeling a pang of sadness for him. "Oh, I'm sorry—why are you telling me this?"

"Just thought I'd share something. To let you know understand what it's like to lose people you love."

She didn't know how to respond to that, so she slammed the boot shut. "Let's just get this over with."

Kaz and Nigel had already gone to work. Nigel used a scanner while Kaz had a field kit out.

The concrete floor still had remains of debris, along with patches of dark stains. Was that blood where her friends had passed or leftovers from the sweepers?

Charlie felt her stomach recoil as her throat filled with bile. She couldn't throw up on her first day back in front of Division agents—or Drake. Instead, she bit her lip, hard, the pain proved a welcome distraction. "I'm gonna check around, see if I can pick up any psychic remnants."

To her relief, Drake didn't follow her; instead, he seemed to be looking around. Charlie retreated to the back of the warehouse, ducked behind a few stacks of old boxes. Just being back there brought everything to the surface. *Okay, you can do this,* she told herself, taking a few calming breaths. Next, she called on her Denai powers, then cast her senses out. As a medium, she'd always been able to detect the feeling of spirits around her. She felt nothing, no trace of spiritual energy. Her heart pounded, all trace of magic drained away.

"Ready for that drink, lieutenant?" Nat grinned. "I can't believe you got promoted before me."

A brilliant burst of blue light, then falling, the ground swallowing her up. Charlie sank to the floor, trying to gulp in air, her lungs burning.

"Charlotte?" Drake appeared at her side, kneeling next to her. "It's alright. Just breathe."

She shook her head. "No, it's not. They're gone, they're all gone."

"Charlie, you need to breathe." He placed his hands on her knees. "Look at me."

But she couldn't meet his gaze. "Drake, I can't do this. I can't be an enforcer anymore," she babbled. "I'm not a real Denai, my powers don't work."

"Look at me." He cupped her chin, tilting her head up.

She met his eyes then noticed they'd changed to pale blue and felt her breathing return to normal.

"It's alright," he repeated, taking her hands in his.

She slumped back against the cold stone wall. "Why are you here?" His touch felt strangely comforting.

"Because you need me."

"That's not what I meant."

"I have my reasons," Drake replied. "What did you mean about your powers?"

"They're gone. I can't sense much anymore. I haven't even phased again until today." She gripped his hand tighter glad for the comfort his touch seemed to bring. "I told you I couldn't do this."

"It isn't magic that makes an enforcer, little witch." Drake pulled her to her feet.

Charlie noticed they were still holding hands. Strange, it felt oddly natural. "We should get back to the others, they'll—"

"They won't notice anything." Still clutching her hand, Drake led her back out to show Nigel and Kaz frozen in place.

Her mouth fell open. "What did you do? Freeze time?"

Drake shook his head. "I have no power over time. They're just suspended like this."

Charlie blinked. He'd done this for her. She reluctantly pulled her hand away. *Maybe I hit my head during my panic attack.* Her cheeks flushed with embarrassment. "Sorry you had to see that," she muttered, avoiding his gaze.

"Don't be, I know what trauma can do."

She looked into his intense gaze. Damn, the man was too gorgeous for his own good. Part of her wanted to reach up and run her fingers through that silky hair. *Great, first a panic attack, now weird lusty thoughts.*

"It's probably why you're disconnected from your powers," he continued.

She pulled her hands away from his, feeling her skin still tingling from his touch. "Now you sound like Marina."

"Jason's mother is a wise woman—she's helped me too in the

past."

"With your family?"

He nodded. "Sometimes talking can help."

Her hands balled into fists. "I've talked—it hasn't helped. Only justice can do that."

"Try to focus. Your senses and abilities are still there, little witch."

Charlie took another breath and sent her senses out. "I don't remember much," she admitted. "I fell when the floor exploded but…" She moved to where Simon had stood. "I never understood why the bomb only damaged the inside of the warehouse. Any type of explosive would have blown this place apart—unless it wasn't a bomb." She raked a hand through her hair, pushing it off her face. "Whatever was in that box must have done it." She reached for magic again; this time felt it building up inside her chest.

Drake slipped his hand into hers, their fingers entwining.

"What are you doing?" Charlie frowned.

"Helping you to concentrate. Skin to skin contact can help."

"Are our powers linked too?" Powers could become linked between life mates. *But we're not bonded,* she reminded herself. *Not yet.*

Drake touched the edge of her mind. His presence there felt warm, comforting as did his hold on her hand. She felt more warmth build low and deep inside her. With him there, her fears seemed to melt away. Would her powers even work?

Charlie glanced around. "Simon? Nat? Louie?" she said. "If any of you are still here, come forward. Show me what happened that day."

Light blurred before her eyes as the scene around her changed. *Simon walked over and spoke to Moret. He opened the box; brilliant blue light burst out followed by the roar of thunder.* Charlie stumbled backwards as the world started spinning.

She groaned, feeling her head pounded like a drum. Glancing around, she saw she was lying on the leather sofa in her cluttered living room. *What the hell? What happened?* She'd been a bit out of it after the dizziness had kicked in and Drake had shimmered them out.

Drake. She could feel his presence close by at the edge of her mind. She wanted to block it out, but their link seemed stronger now. "What happened?" she asked, sitting up.

"I brought you home." Drake appeared, handed her a glass of water. "How are you feeling?"

"Why?" she demanded, eyes narrowing.

"You almost passed out—it must've been the shock of using your powers after so long."

She put the water down, groaned. "Damn it, what did the others—"

"They didn't say anything, they didn't see. I told them you were called away."

Again he'd protected her, this time from embarrassment. "Drake, listen—" She tried to find the right words to get him to leave, to make it clear nothing could happen between them but couldn't. Not yet. "I haven't had a vision like that before. Did you cause it?"

"It wasn't a vision. You saw the last moments of the dead—it's part of your gift."

Charlie's eyes narrowed. "How do you know about my gift?"

He only gave her one of those smiles again.

"This doesn't change anything. I'm grateful for you helping me today, but—"

"Why do you keep pulling away from me?" Drake asked, sitting on the arm of the sofa. "What are you so afraid of, little witch?"

Afraid? Of him? She snorted. "I'm not afraid of you."

"No, not me. Of what we could be." His fingers traced along her wrist, making her skin burn from his touch.

She liked the feel of his touch, wanted more. What would it be like to really touch him? To taste him?

The sound of the front door opening broke through her thoughts. Charlie shot to her feet and felt a wave of nausea as her stomach recoiled. But happiness overcame panic at the thought of Drake and her boyfriend seeing each other. With Scott, things felt cool, normal. Everything just felt confusing with Drake around.

Scott came in. With his floppy blonde hair, pale skin and grey eyes, he looked the complete opposite of Drake. Scott glanced between them, frowning. "Charlie, what's going on?"

"You're home." She threw her arms around him and drew his mouth down for a kiss. Scott blinked, still confused. "You remember Drake, don't you?"

He nodded, glaring at Drake. "Yeah, been a while. Why are you here?"

Charlie blinked, surprised. He'd never acted jealous before. She noticed his jaw clench as he glared at Drake.

"I helped Charlotte home," Drake answered, his expression cool.

"We are working together on a case."

"Yeah," Charlie agreed, sounding calm. Goddess, she didn't want them to meet like this. "Drake was just leaving, weren't you?"

Am I? he asked. *Will you be alright?*

Of course. Go! she insisted.

"I'll see you at work tomorrow," she added.

Scott froze in place, just as Kaz and Nigel had.

"What are you doing?" she demanded. "You can't freeze Scott."

Drake moved closer to her. "About what you saw—I saw it too."

Her mouth fell open. "How?"

"We're connected, whether you choose to like it or not." He grazed his knuckles over her cheek.

Her skin tingled. He really needed to stop touching her! "Do you know what it was?"

Drake shook his head. "No, I didn't see enough but it had to be some type of weapon—one with its own protection."

"Drake, we—" She glanced at Scott.

"He can't hear us."

Thank the goddess! "Good, because nothing has changed," Charlie said. "I'm still with him."

"For now." Drake stroked her cheek one last time. "I'll see you later, little witch." He vanished in a blur of light.

"What the hell, Charlie?" Scott fumed.

She'd almost forgotten he was still there as she stared at the empty space where Drake had stood. "What?" she muttered, feeling dazed.

"Why didn't you tell me he was back, or that you're working with him?"

Feeling weary, she turned to meet her boyfriend's angry gaze. "It's not a big deal."

"Not a big deal, bollocks! He's the guy you're bound to, for god's sake." Scott threw his bag across the room.

Charlie sighed. This hadn't been the homecoming she'd wanted him to have, but Drake didn't seem to be going anywhere any time soon. "We are linked, not bound. He saved my life, remember? I wouldn't be alive if it weren't for him."

"He wants you now though, doesn't he?" Scott dumped his pack on the floor, crossing his arms. "I knew this would happen one day."

"Scott, it's not a big deal," she repeated. "I'm with you, not him." She slipped her arms around his neck. "Don't let him come between

37

us."

Scott pulled away from her. "You've gone back to Major Crimes, haven't you?"

"I didn't have a choice. The chief…" She couldn't tell him about Division that work had to remain classified.

"Ha, you're a Denai, you never follow someone else's orders unless they come from on high," he snapped. "Did Drake put you up to it?"

She ran a hand through her hair. "No, we're just working on one case together. You know how important finding my team's killer is to me."

That seemed to deflate him a little. "Oh, that. I'm-I'm sorry, Char."

"Good, because Drake isn't going to come between us." She took his hands.

He gripped her hands, lips curving into his usual grin. "Will you move in with me then?"

Her jaw dropped. "What?"

Scott's eyes flashed and he let go of her hands. "You said you'd give me an answer when I came back, and I'm back now. Will you move in with me or not?"

Charlie hesitated; she'd been avoiding this conversation for weeks now. "You can't put me on the spot like this." She bit her lip, trying to think of a reasonable excuse, but found none.

"It's a simple question. Do you really want us to be together?" he demanded. "Am I the one you see having a future with?"

She opened her mouth to say yes, but words faltered. She couldn't deny the attraction to Drake. "Maybe we need to take a break for a while to sort things out."

"I guess that answers that question." Scott swung his backpack over his shoulder. "I love you, Charlie, but I'm not going to wait around for you forever." He turned and walked back out the front door.

CHAPTER 6

Charlie strode through a magnificent hall with its red carpet, beautiful marble statues and rich colourful tapestries that made her feel out of place in her black jeans, red leather jacket, black vest and boots. Typical great-grandma and her lavish opulence. But then the Ashrali liked colour, the brighter and bolder the better.

Niara, the head of the United Magickind Council and leader of the Ashrali, sat in her office with its view looking out onto the shimmering spires of the city. The ocean looked a deep turquoise synchronising with the pale blue of the sky.

"Hey, GG." Charlie loved calling her great-grandmother "GG" for short, and went over to hug her.

"Charlotte, I wasn't expecting you." With alabaster skin, electric blue eyes and long hair that changed colour on a whim, Niara had the ethereal beauty of the fey. Power rolled off her like waves lapping at the shore. Hugging Niara felt like hugging sunshine.

"Sorry I haven't been by to see you in a while," Charlie muttered.

Niara was the only family she had living within Setara City.

"That's alright. How have you been? You look..."

"Like crap, you can say it. I haven't been sleeping well," she admitted. Though last night's bad sleep hadn't been because of nightmares. She'd been plagued by dreams of Drake. Damned demon wouldn't leave her alone in sleep now either, but it hadn't been from the link. Her mind had enjoyed playing out every part of him.

"Losing your team still haunts you," Niara said.

"I wanted to talk to you about that."

"Come sit." Niara led her over to two overstuffed armchairs and a tray of tea appeared. Charlie didn't like tea; she preferred coffee, but she sat and drank it anyway.

Niara's hair turned a shade of light blonde, though any colour suited her. "Have you made any progress with the case?" She sipped her tea, then poured more milk into it.

"Maybe. Yesterday I saw something. Do you know of a weapon that could cause an explosion but not destroy a whole building?" She told Niara what she'd glimpsed at the warehouse.

"It could be anything. I'm no expert when it comes to weapons."

"You know things about the ancients." Charlie sipped the tea. It tasted sweet, maybe it wasn't too bad.

Niara stirred her own tea as she poured cream into it. "Some things, but the best person to talk to would be Helga."

"Helga? The crone who is on the council with you? She creeps me out with her beady little eyes." She shuddered at the memory of the old seer.

Niara chuckled. "Helga is both old and wise."

"Yeah, and from what Auntie Cate has told me, she likes to be cryptic and speak in riddles."

"She may know more. She's the only immortal left alive who knows about our ancestors," Niara replied. "How is Scott? You should come to dinner this week. It'd be nice to see you both."

Her cheeks flushed and she bit her lip. "We're er—taking a break. He got so jealous when he saw Drake and me together—speaking of which, did you know we are working together?"

Although not an official member of the Alliance, Niara knew what went on in their world. "Yes, he comes to visit me on occasion."

Charlie gaped at her. "Why?" She couldn't imagine why Drake would visit Niara, they had no connection to each other outside of him being a friend of the family as far as she knew.

Niara shrugged. "I've known Drake a very long time. I helped him to get to Britannia after his family was killed."

So Drake had been connected to her family longer than she'd imagined. "What's his deal?" She wondered, almost to herself.

"He's a good man. He's helped many people over the centuries."

"I hear he runs Division, I thought he just ran nightclubs."

Niara laughed. "Oh, he does much more than that. His businesses are sanctuaries, places of neutral territory for demons and other Magickind to go when they need refuge."

Funny, he'd never mentioned that. Not that she'd asked.

"How—how can I break my connection to him?" Charlie asked. "I know he thinks we're meant to be together, but I'll be back with

Scott soon, and Drake is... He's not who I imagined my future with."

"You think he's wrong about the bond?" Niara sipped her tea, her hair flashing in a rainbow of colour before settling back to blonde again.

Charlie nodded. "Yes, I want the link gone. I can't think straight when he's around."

"Charlie, he couldn't have saved you from death if he wasn't—"

"Enough with the soulmate stuff, GG. I want it gone, can you do it or not?" She gripped the sides of the armchair to rein in her anger.

Niara hesitated, hair darkening. "I can try, are you sure this is what you want?"

"Never been so sure of anything." She needed her shit together on this case, not Drake creeping into her mind or her dreams. It'd be better for both of them, they could both move on. Although working together would feel more awkward, but she'd put personal feelings aside to get the job done.

Niara sighed, rose and raised a glowing hand.

Charlie felt warmth radiate through her body, seeping through her. It tugged at her link to Drake, then pain tore through her so hard she doubled over. It radiated through her, cutting into her very soul. She felt Drake's pain too, heard his shout of agony as their minds opened to each other. "Stop," she gasped.

Light blurred around her as Niara's office faded. Charlie landed on a shiny black floor, skidding across it. The pain still tore deep inside her, both physical and mental.

Drake sat hunched on the floor in front of his desk, face contorted in pain. "What did you do?" he growled.

"I..." She couldn't get the words out. Damn, this hurt like a mother! She crawled over to him, being near him seemed to lessen pain.

"You tried to break the link," he snarled, eyes black pools of obsidian.

"Can you blame me?" she hissed, clutching her chest. "Goddess, why won't the pain stop? You said we were only linked psychically."

"Our souls are still connected, Charlotte, bond or no bond."

She moved closer, resting her head against his shoulder. She felt him tense at her touch as she clung to him. After a moment's hesitation, he wrapped an arm around her. There were both breathing hard as the pain faded.

Charlie snuggled closer, glad for the warmth of his body. "Don't do that again," she muttered.

"I did nothing." Drake tried to shove her away, but she held on.

"I'm sorry," Charlie murmured against his chest. "This thing between us scares me. I just needed a break from it. Please don't be mad at me." She didn't know why his anger hurt so much.

Drake muttered something in a language she didn't understand but she felt his body relax as he sighed. "You're impossible."

"But you like that about me, don't you?" She grinned and scrambled closer, climbing onto his lap as she leaned closer and ran a hand along the hard plane of his jaw.

"Drake?" called another voice.

That brought Charlie out of her lust-filled haze and she scrambled up, cheeks flushing. "I should go."

Drake shot to his feet, muttering a curse. "No, don't."

But Charlie shimmered out before she could do anything else.

Shit, shit, shit! What had she been thinking? Charlie glanced around, expecting to find herself back at Niara's instead she found herself in woodland. Thick trees spanned across the horizon like green giants guarding the way to another world. "Ah, hell!"

Her demon powers had always been unpredictable at times. She had no idea where the heck she'd shimmered to. *Great, now I'm in the middle of nowhere. Argh, damn Drake and his sexiness!*

It must have been sexual frustration. That must be it. She'd convince Scott to come around. He was safe, normal and she didn't have to control her feelings around him. Now she had to figure out where the hell she'd shimmered to. Niara had mentioned Helga and Charlie had thought of her just before she'd left. Right, a crone would be much easier to deal with them rampaging hormones or stubborn boyfriends and sexy demons.

Light blurred as Drake shimmered in beside her, scowling. Her heart skipped a beat and she took off in the opposite direction. "No way," she muttered, stalking through the trees. Branches caught at her clothes, covering her with leaves which she brushed off as she stalked through the treeline.

"You can't just almost kill me and then leave." Drake caught up with her faster than she could blink.

Damn, she'd never been able to outrun him. "I didn't try to kill you and I'm not the one who did it, Niara did." *Because I asked her to.*

She felt a sharp pang of guilt. *I didn't know it'd hurt so much.*

"Why do you keep running away from me?" Drake moved in front of her, blocking the way.

"Because I want you gone!" Charlie cried, glaring daggers at him. "I want you out of my life forever."

"Do you?" Drake loomed over her, backing her up against a tree trunk. "Is it so hard to admit there might be something between us?"

Her breath caught in her throat, feeling the heat from his body. "Yes, how many times do I have to—"

Leaning down, his face so close they were almost touching. "I know part of you wants me just as much as I want you."

She hated how her body shivered in reaction. "That's just the stupid link between us." She placed her hands on his chest and tried to shove him away, but he wouldn't budge.

"I could have you, make you mine, and you'd let me. I feel your desire." He ran a finger down her jaw.

Charlie felt her heart beat faster. Yes, she did want him, and that freaking scared her. "You said..."

Drake pulled away, breathing hard. "I know why you're shutting me out, why you're shutting everyone out. You're afraid of getting hurt," he said. "You blame yourself for what happened that day."

"Yes, I do. They died, and I survived." She felt tears sting her eyes. *Oh crap, I can't cry in front of him!* she thought and said. "I should have died. I don't know how I got out. I don't know why I survived and they didn't."

"Sometimes people die, Charlotte. We lose the people we love; we can't stop that even as immortals."

She rubbed her eyes, refusing to let the tears fall. "That's why I can't do this. I can't be what you want me to be."

"I don't want you to be anything," Drake told her. "I just want you."

"Are you done with the shouting?" another voice rasped. "You're spoiling my tranquillity."

Charlie turned to see the hunched form of Helga with her straggly white hair, leathery skin and piercing eagle eyes. "No, we're just— he's leaving," Charlie replied. "I need to talk to you."

I'm not leaving when you have a price on your head, Drake insisted.

I can take care of myself. She folded her arms and raised her chin. *Go away! Go work on the case while I can't be there.*

We're partners, I'm not letting you go anywhere without me, he said then broke off the connection. "Helga, it's been a long time," Drake said. To her amazement, Drake bowed his head to Helga. A sign of respect. The demon surprised her more and more.

"Drakon," Helga said, eyes brightening. "Come, let's go inside." She motioned for them to follow.

Charlie glanced at Drake but the expression on his face told her he wasn't going anywhere. "Fine," she muttered, stalking after the old woman.

CHAPTER 7

Drake fought for control of his emotions as he followed Charlie and the crone through the thicket of heavy leaves. Something trying to break their link had felt like someone trying to tear through his soul. The pain had been unimaginable. He knew how resistant Charlie was, but he hadn't expected her to do that. Yet it hadn't mattered when he held her in his arms as he longed to do so.

They'd almost kissed and she'd fled. Again.

The anger and frustration had taken over during the argument. He'd been tempted to give in. Bond on her. She'd finally be his and have no choice but to be his mate. But no, he wouldn't do that to her.

Why fate had given him such a god damn stubborn, infuriating creature as his life mate he'd never know. Every time they drew close, she pulled away. But he forced his emotions aside as he stalked after her. Despite his frustrations, nothing could make him walk away from his little witch, not even her.

He had no idea why she'd shimmered to Helga, of all people. What good would the crone do? Helga was both feared and respected for the true seer she was, but she never gave up answers easily.

Charlie didn't seem up for answering questions either.

Part of him wanted to get the hell out of there but the need to protect his mate wouldn't let him leave.

Helga led them inside her tree dwelling. The house itself was carved into an enormous oak tree. Thick branches covered the walls and ceiling, crisscrossing in places. The air smelt of fresh leaves and morning dew as they stepped into a larger room. "Why are you here?" Helga hobbled over to a high-backed chair. An enormous eagle perched on top of it, its golden eyes so like its owners.

He heard Charlie's gasp at the sight of the huge predator, and she grabbed his hand. He squeezed it, reassuringly.

"Don't you know?" Charlie retorted, pulling her hand away from his again. "I thought you were all-knowing?"

Drake's lips thinned into a smile. He missed the feel of her touch but said nothing.

"I can't see everything, little Denai," the crone rasped. "But I guess it's because you want something."

"You're a seer, right? I need to know what happened the day my team died."

Ah, he should have known that was why they'd come.

"What was the weapon that caused the explosion?" Charlie persisted.

Helga sighed. "The stubbornness of youth. So young and impatient. A true McCray."

Charlie scowled. "Can't you just give me a straight answer?" She crossed her arms, flopped into the other high-backed chair. Drake stood next to her, draping an arm over the back of the chair. The closeness eased some of the tension between them.

Helga fell silent, her eyes turning an eerie white then she shook her head. "That is unclear. Strange, something cloaks against my sight."

Charlie and Drake glanced at each other. *What does that mean?* she asked.

He felt her mind open to him again, reinforcing the connection. She still felt irritated by him, but it had lessened.

The Tears really don't want us to find that weapon, she said.

I doubt the gang has that kind of power, Drake remarked.

Helga shook her head. "I cannot see." Her eagle eyes fixed on Drake. "What did you see that day?"

Charlie's brow creased. "What does she mean?"

He froze, feeling his heart pounding. Damn it, he hadn't planned on telling Charlie that, not yet. He'd only just begun to gain her trust. The truth would shatter it.

"Drake, what's she talking about?" Charlie asked.

He scowled at Helga, pleading with her not to say anything else.

"He saved you," Helga said. "Yet you resist the life bond. Stubbornness." She cackled.

Charlie shot to her feet, grabbed Drake's arm and pulled him outside, muttering, "Excuse us." She rounded on him when they were far enough away from the tree. "What the hell?" Charlie demanded. "Why didn't you tell me?"

"Would it have mattered?" he retorted. "You've made it clear how you feel about me." He didn't keep the bitterness of his voice. Gods, how could he want her and hate at the same time? Sometimes he wondered if the connection was just a trick, a cruel twist of fate.

Something flickered in Charlie's eyes. "I-I don't know how I feel about you," she said. "Why didn't you tell me you saved me? How did you—"

"You called for me. I heard you whisper my name, I felt your pain, so I came, pulled you out of the carnage and got you to safety," Drake told her, crossing his arms.

Charlie shook her head. "I don't remember."

"Well, it happened. Now you know."

"What about the others?"

His mind flashed back to that day. The feel of her pain, the terror of losing her. He'd heard her call and had almost lost his mind when he'd seen her lying crumpled on the warehouse floor, blue light blazing around the building. "They were already dead. Only you were still breathing."

He felt the shock of pain and found himself tugging her to his chest. To his surprise, she clung to him. The feel of her so close sent a rush of desire through him. He needed to leave, to get away. Being around her felt comforting and torturous at the same time. "I'll go." He ran a hand through her soft, silky hair. "I won't burden you with my presence. We'll go back to the way we were." The thought of staying away, of never seeing her again felt worse than the pain Niara had caused.

"No! Stay." She rested her head against his chest.

"Charlotte, we can't keep doing this." He tightened his hold on her. "I can't pretend I don't want you anymore. I thought we could..."

She sniffed, meeting his gaze. "No, I need you with me even if you're over protectiveness irritates the hell out of me. We have to see this case through, and we will."

"What then? What happens after the case? We go back to our normal lives? I can't do that."

Charlie shrugged. "I don't know," she admitted. "Maybe we just need to figure this thing out."

"Have dinner with me tonight."

"You mean like a date?"

He smiled. He didn't date women. He'd never had a serious relationship. He fucked them and that was it. He quickly grew tired of them—except this one.

She sighed. "Okay, but just dinner. Nothing else." She pulled away, glanced at the tree. *Do you think she's telling the truth?*

Drake shrugged. *I see no reason why she'd lie.*

Still, she creeps me out. Why wouldn't she see what happened? Charlie shuddered. *Niara said she's one of the most powerful seers in the world. Maybe she's just hiding something. Let's find out.*

Helga said nothing when they came back in.

"Why can't you see anything from that day?" Charlie persisted.

"Wise one, we need your assistance," Drake said to Helga.

Helga shook her head. "This is a dangerous path you're both treading. You should walk away from this case. Both of you."

"We can't. I need to know what happened." Charlie leaned forward. "Please, Helga."

Drake touched Charlie's shoulder. He knew Helga wouldn't say no unless she had good reason to. Yet he thought he glimpsed fear in the crone's eyes. *Perhaps we should leave. She seems afraid.*

Charlie scowled. *I need to know. We're so close, I can feel it.*

Helga stroked her eagle's wings and sighed. "No one ever listens to my counsel anymore."

"Can't you just try?" Charlie asked.

"If there is a risk of a new Covenant, you should help us," Drake agreed.

The crone snorted. "I don't interfere in the affairs of other Magickind. It's not my place."

"You were there the day my aunt killed Raven," said Charlie. "I remember—I was there too. You acted like you were on Raven's side, but you helped Cate."

"I didn't do anything. I was only there to see Raven finally die." Helga patted her eagle.

Charlie rose. "Maybe you're just not as powerful as they say. Let's go, Drake."

Helga's eyes flashed.

Wow, I think I pissed her off. Charlie stifled a laugh.

I'd say that wouldn't be wise, little witch.

The old woman's lips thinned. "Fine, I'll see what magic cloaks my sight," she hissed. "Give me your hands, girl."

Drake hesitated, something didn't feel right, but he could do nothing as Charlie grasped Helga's outstretched palms. Helga's eyes blurred to white again. Charlie gasped, her own eyes snapping shut. Both women's bodies trembled as energy surged between them.

Drake stumbled backwards as the entire tree began to groan and vibrate.

Helga's eagle squawked, flapping its great wings.

What the hells? he wondered. "Charlotte?"

At the sound of her name, her eyes shot open, radiating bright blue, similar to the light he'd seen that day he pulled her from the warehouse. She gripped Helga's hands so hard Drake heard the crunch of bone. Helga shuddered, falling to her knees, gasping.

"Charlotte, what you are doing?" Drake demanded.

Charlie rose, hands outstretched as black shadows shot out like smoke billowing around Helga. The crone choked as the smoke wrapped around her throat in a vice-like grip.

Drake stood there, dumbfounded. Whatever this was, it wasn't his witch or even the demon side she refused to acknowledge. "Stop, you're killing her!"

The blazing azure eyes narrowed at him but continued the assault.

Drake knew he had to do something, but what? If he used his powers, he risked hurting Charlie, something he'd never be able to live with. "Charlie, listen to me." He wrapped his arms around her from behind, pulling her away from Helga.

She snarled at him with a flash of fangs. "Stay away." The harsh voice sounded nothing like his witch.

"No, you're inside my woman. Now whatever you are, get out before I force you out." He tried forcing his mind inside hers through their link but felt an impenetrable shield there.

The creature laughed. "You have no idea what you're dealing with."

Helga coughed, gasped for breath. "Drake, get away..."

Charlie sent Drake flying with a blast of blue light. Energy jolted through him, pain wrenching through every nerve ending but the only thing that mattered to him was Charlie.

Charlie turned her attention back to Helga, speaking in a language he didn't understand. But Helga seemed to as her eyes widened.

Drake scrambled up, ignoring the pain. "Charlie, come back."

She can't hear you, Helga told him.

What's wrong with her? he asked. *How do I stop this?*

We've triggered something old and very dangerous—ah, help me! Helga clutched her head, face creasing with pain.

Fire formed in his hand. *Don't make me do this, little witch.* But Charlie ignored him. He threw it, hitting her in the chest. Charlie didn't even flinch.

Not that way. Use your other power, Helga snapped.

No, I can't do that.

Do it or we'll both die.

Drake raised his hand, dropped his mental shields and let his power roam free. "Stop," he snarled.

Charlie's burning eyes widened. He let his power out, power he hadn't used in centuries. Charlie grunted, forcing her way through the compulsion.

"Stop," he repeated. "Whatever you are, you won't harm anyone here. Now get the fuck out of my witch." His eyes bled black as he let his inner demon's true nature show.

Charlie laughed. "You have no idea what she is, do you?"

"I know you're harming an innocent woman—two innocents. Now go!"

The creature snorted. "You won't harm this body. You love her; I can sense it."

Drake flinched. No, he wouldn't give into that feeling, he wouldn't admit to it. "Then you know I'll do whatever I can to save her." He felt the link with Charlie, the mental link between them, ordered it to break.

Charlie screamed, and blackness swallowed them both.

CHAPTER 8

Drake groaned as the echoes of soul-wrenching pain shook him for the second time that day. He forced himself to stay awake. A glance across the room showed him Charlie's sprawled unconscious form lying there. His heart ached at the sight of her. He'd done that to her.

"Blessed spirits," Helga muttered as she scrambled up, leaning on her walking stick for support. "I'm too old for this."

"What was that?" His entire body ached but he forced himself to crawl over to Charlie. Their link hadn't broken, and it had been enough to force out whatever had possessed her.

"Something old and very dangerous. I warned you not to tread this path." She hissed in pain as she pulled herself into her chair.

"What path?" He brushed Charlie's hair off her face, felt for the pulse in her neck. He breathed a sigh of relief. "I'm part of this. I have been since the day I dragged her from that warehouse." Drake pulled Charlie against his chest, carried her over to the chair where he slumped down, cradling her against him.

"What did you see that day?" Helga asked.

His mind flashed back to that awful day, seeing Charlie lying among the debris. "My worst nightmare."

"Think, Drake, what did you see? It's important."

His dark eyes narrowed on her. "Why?"

"Because when I touched her, I touched something ancient, powerful."

"Why did it possess her? Did you let in?" Charlie's eyes remained closed, but her breathing was steady.

Helga shook her head, her hand trembling as she poured herself something to drink. "Spirits, no." She stared at Charlie. "That was no possession, there's something strange about that girl."

"Maybe she has unusual power from her mixed heritage."

The crone snorted. "Whatever it is, it didn't come from her father's family."

"Steve mentioned her mother was half Zexen."

This time Helga cackled. "Either he is lying or he didn't know what she was. That was no Zexen, and it's linked to whatever caused the explosion."

"What do you mean?"

"I don't know all the details, but I sense she and the weapon are connected to each other," Helga replied. "How was she when you found her? Uninjured?"

Drake frowned, remembering that fateful day. "Unconscious. She had some bruises and scrapes from the fall but yes, otherwise unharmed. Everyone else was dead."

"Exactly."

"Are you saying she did it?" Drake gasped.

"No, but maybe—oh, I don't know." Helga sighed. "There are things in this world far older than I am."

"Do you know what that weapon was?"

She let out a breath. "The ancients had artefacts and weapons that had their own intelligence. It could be anything, but I do sense it's connected to her." She pointed to Charlie. "She doesn't know what breed of demon you are either."

"No," he admitted. "We don't know each other that well."

"No, but she was right when she said you love her. That scares you."

Drake looked away. He lost everyone he'd ever loved. That was why he'd never let anyone get too close. He had few friends, only a couple of close ones like Jason, but that had changed. The McCrays had become his friends too. "Does it matter?" Drake muttered. "She won't have me and I won't force the bond on her. I couldn't, no matter how much of me wants to."

"She'll need you," Helga said. "Your destinies are intertwined."

"How can I love someone I barely know?" he said, muttering a curse. "It's just the link."

"Is it?" she demanded. "You've watched over her for years."

Drake rose, still clutching Charlie. "What else do you see for us?" *Will she ever accept me?*

Helga shook her head. "The future is conflicted. An outside power—strong, old—will stop at nothing to find that weapon."

"Are you saying the Tears don't have it?"

"Ancient weapons can have a will of their own, you should know that."

"I shall leave you now. Will you be alright, wise one?"

Helga let out a shaky laugh. "Oh, it will take more than that to kill me. Peace to you."

"And to you."

Drake shimmered home, placed Charlie on his bed and wrapped a blanket over her. He thought of calling a healer but doubted it would do much good. Instead, he called the only other person he knew who might be able to help.

Niara appeared in a swirl of gold orbs. "What happened?" she demanded.

He explained, not leaving out any detail. "Whatever it was almost killed Helga."

Niara's sapphire blue eyes widened. "I feared something like this would happen." She touched Charlie's cheek.

"What do you mean?"

She sighed. "My family are all powerful, you know that especially since most are descended from the five elder races and have mixed blood," she said. "But Charlie is different. Just like her mother."

"I thought her mother was half Denai, half Zexen." His brow creased in confusion, remembering what Jason had told him of Charlie's history.

Niara shook her head. "Helena was—strange. I have met many different Magickind over the past ten thousand years but I could never tell what she was. She appeared Denai and Steve believed her story about being part demon, but…" She glanced at Charlie again.

"You don't believe it." He folded his arms, frowning at the Serenity. "How is Charlie connected to all of this?"

"I wish I knew. Charlie has always been unreadable to me. I can't sense much about her." She played with a strand of her hair, something Drake had noticed she always did when she got nervous. Did she know more than she was letting on?

He sat on the edge of the bed, brushing Charlie's hair off her face. "Will she be alright? I never would have…" Guilt washed over him so hard it hurt.

"You did the right thing." Niara rose and a scroll appeared in her hand. "I looked into weapons. Perhaps this will help with your search."

"Maybe we shouldn't let her work this case. If the Tears—or the one orchestrating them—uses her to try and…" He looked at Charlie as her brow furrowed and knew that would be pointless. His witch would never give up a fight.

She let out a harsh laugh. "Do you think you can stop her?"

Drake's lips thinned. "No, she's too headstrong for that."

"Let her rest." Niara kissed Charlie's cheek. "Will you stay with her?"

"Of course."

Niara turned to leave, hesitated. "It will be safer if you didn't seal the bond."

"I wouldn't…" he started to protest, then thought back to their earlier kiss. He'd wanted nothing more than to make her his, and would have too, if Cate hadn't interrupted them.

"I know, but heed my advice. We don't know what that force was. If you connect with her, it might kill you too." She turned to leave, her long robe flaring as she spun around.

Drake grabbed her arm. "Wait, you know something, don't you?" He searched her eyes for answers but found none.

Niara tugged her arm away. "Perhaps, but I can't discuss it now. It's not my story to tell." She vanished in a flash of gold orbs.

Drake sighed, wondering why the woman he'd worked for centuries would suddenly keep secrets from him. He watched Charlie sleeping. Still feeling drained after the battle, he lay down beside her and gathered her up in his arms.

***

Charlie groaned, head pounding. Every bone in her body ached as memories flash to her mind of Drake being thrown across the room and Helga choking. She bolted up, feeling a wave of nausea. "Drake!" She glanced down and saw him lying beside her, eyes closed. She breathed a sigh of relief when she saw his chest rise and fall.

Seeing the sun streaming in through the arched windows, she wondered how long she'd been out for. Glancing at her watch, she realised it must've been at least a couple of hours. Damn it, what the hell happened?

Her phone buzzed on the table beside her. She grabbed it and saw Scott's name flashing on the screen. She bit her lip. How could she answer with Drake right there next to her?

Taking a deep breath, she answered, "Hey."

"Hey, are you okay?"

She frowned, letting the breath out in a whoosh. "Yeah, why?"

"No reason. I just miss you."

She winced, feeling a pang of guilt. Drake had kissed her, and she'd not only let him, but she'd enjoyed it. "I-I think we should break up." She checked Drake, prayed he didn't overhear them.

"What?" Scott gasped. "Char—"

"I mean it, Scott. We can't pretend I don't have feelings for Drake because we both know I do. I'm sorry it had to end like this, but this is how it has to be," she blurted out and hung up. Guilt twisted in her stomach but when she looked at the demon beside her, relief washed over her. Better to end things with Scott now rather than give him false hope.

Charlie opened her mouth to wake Drake, but hesitated, trying to decide whether she wanted to talk or just get the hell out of there. The room around her with its plush cream carpet and red walls hadn't been what she'd imagined his room to look like. Silk covered the enormous four-poster bed with soft linen sheets. Great, of all the ways to end up in his bed.

Charlie leaned closer, taking in every feature. Beneath his suit was a body of hard muscle. Damn, the man was gorgeous—and irritating as hell.

But whatever he'd done had saved her. Maybe she should get to know him better. Deep down, she knew he wasn't bad. The damned link pulling at her mind, making her want to be close to him. Charlie rose and took an unsteady step.

"Where are you going?" The sound of Drake's voice made her jump

She groaned. "Work—or maybe home. Is your room spinning or is that just me?" She touched her head, trying to make the swaying sensation stop.

Drake moved in a blur, wrapping his arms around her from behind. "You're still weak. You need to rest."

She sighed, enjoying the feel of his warm body. "What did I do? I don't remember much—did I hurt you?"

He let out a harsh laugh. "All in a day's work, little witch."

"This isn't funny, Drake."

He pulled her back down onto the bed and made her sit down, then propped some pillows up for her. "I don't know what it was," he admitted. "Something overtook you. You weren't yourself. Helga thinks you and the weapon are somehow linked. That it sensed a threat when she tried to see what happened."

She shook her head, then shoved her hair off her face. "That doesn't make any sense. I'd never hurt my team. Never." She wrung her hands together. If she had, she knew she wouldn't be able to live with herself.

"Whatever it is, it's dangerous. We need to be extra careful which is why I think you should stay here with me."

Charlie shook her head. "I can't. Scott—"

Drake scowled, bared his teeth. "He can stay too, if he must."

Her eyes widened. "You'd do that for me?"

"If it's what you need, yes."

She bit her lip. "I can't stay here, but I'll still go to dinner with you."

CHAPTER 9

Drake shimmered into his club after leaving Charlie at the station. A scruffy haired man in the long brown trench coat stood by the bar, slugging a pint of beer. "I hope you intend on paying for that, Val."

Val coughed, splattering beer all over the bar. "Jeez, Drake, why do you have to sneak up on me like that?" he muttered, wiping his face with the sleeve of his coat. "Yeah, yeah. You know I'll pay for the beer."

Drake arched an eyebrow. That would be a first. He pulled out the scroll Niara had given him from his jacket. On it were a few ancient weapons and rough drawings of them. Drake laid it out on the bar, avoiding the splashes of beer. "Have any of these come up on the market recently?"

Val peered down at the scroll. "The good market or the underground one?" Val scratched his beard, took a nervous gulp of beer. "They're all ancient tech. Get a good price for all of them but no; I haven't seen or heard any of those items."

"Are you sure?" he persisted. "It's important."

"Well, that one you'd want to steer clear of." Val motioned to an orb-shaped crystal.

"Why?" He frowned at the scroll, trying to place the image but didn't recall anything.

"That thing has some bad juju, mate." Val shuddered, gulped down more beer. "It's called the Srimtar. No idea what it can do, but anyone who tries to use the thing winds up dead."

"I need you to find anything you can about it. Anyone who is looking to acquire ancient tech, you contact me." Drake rolled up the scroll and slipped it back into his jacket.

"What's got a bee up your behind?" Val eyed the beer, scowling when he saw he'd almost drunk it all.

Drake gripped the bar, feeling the familiar anger rise at how someone dared to hurt his mate. "This weapon hurt someone I care about. I need to know where it is and who wants it."

"This wouldn't have anything to do with that witch who has a price on her head, would it?" Val smirked, eying another beer bottle.

Drake's eyes bled to black as his inner demon raged. His hands fisted but he fought to keep his emotions under control. "What do you know about that?"

Val scratched his chin. "Not much. Just that it's a pretty big price and a lot of demons—"

"A lot of demons will die if anyone dares to harm her," he snarled.

Val took a step back, raised his hands in surrender. "Whoa, easy, mate. I didn't mean nothing by it."

"Good, see that everyone else knows that. Now go."

Val vanished in a puff of smoke.

Phil, his bouncer came over. "You gonna be around today? Had a lot of folks passing through. Some wanting your attention."

Drake sighed. It was part of his job to help demons in need, but his only concern right now was keeping Charlie safe. "Deal with it," he muttered.

"Boss, you can't put your life on hold for the witch."

Drake growled a warning. "I'll do what needs to be done."

He shimmered out, moving through the different planes of existence. He felt weary of it all. Weary of the club, weary of being guardian of the sanctuaries. Everything. Only Charlie seemed to bring him real joy—and utter frustration. He hovered in the ether as he headed back towards his witch, pausing for a moment to watch her as he stayed incorporeal.

Charlie sat at her desk, scanning her computer screen. Kaz's chair slid over to hers. "Hey, what's up with you and the hunky demon?"

Charlie's eyes narrowed. "Hunky demon? That's not what I'd call him. No deal, he's a friend of the family."

"Really? He seems more than that. So you're not sleeping together then?"

"Goddess, no." Charlie laughed.

"Good." Kaz licked her lips. "You won't mind if I go for him then?"

Charlie choked on her coffee, sending drops of dark liquid over her paperwork. "What? You want to go for Drake?"

"Yeah, who wouldn't? That guy is hot and there's a gorgeous body under that suit I'm dying to get my hands on."

Drake cackled and had to hold back from materialising with laughter. Instead, he watched Charlie's reaction. After having dinner together the other night, he hoped their relationship would start changing.

She scowled. "I have a boyfriend, why would I care?"

Ah, yes the damned boyfriend again. Although he wondered why he hadn't seen Scott around so much since the other night. Hell, Charlie had gone to dinner with him, not Scott. He wanted to ask her about it but thought better. He wasn't sure he'd like the answer. His amusement turned to frustration. Would she ever want him the way he longed for her?

"Great, just checking. I didn't want to mess up anything if you had something going on." Kaz slid back to her desk. "Plus didn't you say you and Scott were taking a break?"

He watched Charlie for a moment longer, but her expression remained unreadable as he shimmered in beside her, a smile on his face.

"What are you grinning at?" She glared up at him.

"Nothing, little witch." He placed the scroll in front of her. "Niara gave me this. I may have a clue on the weapon. I believe it might be the Srimtar."

"The shrimp-what?" Kaz asked.

"It's an ancient weapon. Not much to go on, but it's a lead. Better than anything else we've come up with so far."

The sound of bells chiming through the room made everyone jump.

"What's that?" Kaz shot to her feet.

"It's a call from the Alliance, I must go now. They'll want to discuss this new development." Drake backed up and checked his phone to see if they'd sent any messages.

Charlie rose. "Sounds like they want to see me, too. I'll just go tell Nigel." She wandered off.

Kaz sidled up to him. "Hey, Drake, I—"

"No." He leaned back against Charlie's desk and crossed his arms.

Her brow creased. "No, what?"

"No, I'm not interested in you in any sort of romantic way."

"Oh." Her smile fell. "I was only going to ask you for a drink."

"I'm sorry, Kaz, but I belong to someone else." His eyes trailed after his witch.

She frowned. "I thought you were just friends?"

He smiled. "For now." One way or another he'd get Charlie to see they were meant to be.

Kaz snorted. "Good luck with that one. She's not easy to get close to."

He chuckled. "No kidding!"

"Ready to go?" Charlie reappeared, giving him another glare.

Drake shimmered them to the corridor leading to the Alliance's meeting hall. He missed the contact when Charlie let go of his hand. The oak floor gleamed and the russet walls held a flag of each race of Magickind.

"What did you tell the Alliance about me?" she asked.

"The truth. I can't lie. If someone is trying to use you then we need to be prepared."

She groaned. "What if they think I'm too dangerous to be on the case?"

"This is our case, little witch. We'll see this through no matter what."

He thought he saw a faint smile on her face. "Thanks, Vlad."

He grinned and shook his head as they headed inside.

Inside the meeting hall sat Sirius McNab, an Ashrali; Lana, a Phoenix elemental; and Jason and his wife, Cate, the Grand Mistress with her sapphire eyes, pale skin and long brunette locks. She commanded an air of power benefiting her rank. Drake had come to like the strong-willed witch in the years he'd known her. As she often said, she didn't take crap from anyone.

Cate smiled when she saw her niece and Charlie ran over to hug her. "Hey, kid, how are you?"

"Okay, I guess." Charlie shrugged.

Cate gave her another squeeze. "We'll talk more after the meeting."

Drake took his seat at the table.

"Thanks for coming, everyone," said Jason. "Today we're here to discuss a case led by Drake and Division agent Charlie McCray. Agent McCray's team was killed in a bust gone wrong when a gang known as the Tears tried to trade in illegal weapons."

"It's come to our attention that weapon may be ancient in nature," Cate continued. "Drake has discovered a potential lead that may be connected to some type of orb." She glanced at the screen in front of her. "Drake, why don't you tell us more?"

Drake straightened, explained what had happened the day before. He felt Charlie's unease from where she sat between him and Cate. "The Srimtar, as it's called, seems to be the only weapon we found so far that matches what we suspect caused the warehouse explosion."

"What is your connection to this weapon, Agent McCray?" Lana spoke up, brushing her silvery hair off her face.

Charlie shifted in her seat. "I don't have a connection to it other than it killed my team."

"But an outside force possessed you when Helga tried to see the day's events, correct?" Lana arched an eyebrow and picked at her nails as if bored by the whole meeting.

"Whatever it was, it wasn't me. I'd never hurt Helga or Drake."

"How did you break her out of the possession, Drake?" McNabb prompted. "It doesn't say in your notes."

"He used our link," Charlie spoke up.

"What link?" Lana asked, giving Drake one of her seductive smiles.

She was lovely with her lithe body and purple eyes. They'd slept together once, but her ethereal beauty and fiery energy did nothing for him now. "We have a telepathic link," Drake answered. "Now—"

"You never mentioned you were life mates." He thought he saw a flash of fury in Lana's violet gaze.

"We're not bonded," Charlie added. "Besides it's none of your business what we are."

"Perhaps you are not the best to work on this case then," McNabb agreed. "Personal feelings..."

"Ha!" Charlie motioned to Cate and Jason. "They're married, and they work together every day."

The conversation droned on for the next hour as they discussed the ins and outs of the case.

"I think this venture is a waste of time," Lana said. "You have nothing but theories to go on. If I'd known your reason for pushing this so hard was personal, Drake, we—"

Drake opened his mouth to speak, but Cate beat him to it. "Enforcers died. People trained and chosen by us," Cate snapped. "I won't let this go either. There's much more to this case, I can sense it."

Jason spoke up. "I think we should all join powers. Charlie, would you be willing to show us what you remember from that day?"

Charlie turned pale but nodded. "Okay."

CHAPTER 10

Charlie shifted in her seat as Cate and Drake both took her hands. Electricity jolted through the circle of joined hands. Reliving her team's final moments was her worst nightmare.

Relax, little witch. Drake's voice soothed at the edge of her mind.

Shit, would everyone else be able to hear that? She'd noticed Lana giving Drake the eye all the way through the meeting and had felt a smug sense of satisfaction when Lana had realised she and Drake were linked. Good, the bitch was pissed off. Drake was her demon. That thought scared her. Maybe it was because he'd been so nice after what had happened, or because he'd saved her life again. Or maybe she'd started to warm to him.

"I don't remember much about that day," she told them.

"It's okay, Charlie. Just let the vision drag you in," Cate said.

Charlie squeezed her eyes shut, heart pounding as the room faded. She found herself back in the warehouse, lying on the floor, gun in hand.

Getting excited for the big promo, huh? Natalia chuckled.

"Nat?" Charlie said, frowning at the image of her former partner.

"Focus," Lana snapped.

Goddess, that bitch really needed a slap. *This is my fucking memory!*

Ignore her, Drake said. *Concentrate on what you saw.*

She clutched her gun, felt the familiar weight of it in her arms. *I can't do this.*

Yes, you can, little witch. I'm right here with you.

So are you and Scott going to have your own celebration? Natalia grinned.

Or are you still arguing about moving in together?

I could kill for a drink. Charlie had thought. *And Scott…that's complicated.*

Come on, Charlie. You've been doing the long-distance thing for over a year now. You can't keep leading the guy on.

"Ladies, I hate to interrupt the chitchat, but we have a job to do here," Simon's voice echoed in her ear and made Charlie's heart skip a beat. She missed that voice, the one who'd trained her, been almost like a second father to her.

"Aye, aye, captain." She gave him a mock salute, causing Nat to stifle a snort.

"You know how important this deal is, guys."

"Yeah, the big one before retirement," Lou muttered.

"Incoming," Charlie said as the door groaned open. In walked Moret and Simon's contact carrying the box.

Target in position. Charlie stared through the scope of her rifle, zeroing in on the box, then glanced at her scanner.

That thing's giving off some weird energy, Nat remarked. *Watch yourself, boss.*

So do we know what's inside?

Negative, Lou answered. *Scanner's readings all over the place.*

Charlie so wanted to cast her senses out to scan the box's contents, but she couldn't risk anyone detecting the team's presence.

Opening the box, Simon told them. *Be ready for the takedown.* Simon flipped the lead. Blue light exploded around them with a roar of thunder.

"Shit!" Charlie squeezed her eyes shut, feeling the floor give way. Then she was falling. She let out a scream as her body hit the ground, hard. Her ears rang, her eyes blinded by the blazing blue light. Blackness pulled under as she lay there, gasping for breath.

"Focus, what else do you see?" demanded Lana.

Charlie could still feel herself lying on the floor, the cold concrete beneath her but her thoughts were only of her team. "Simon? Guys? Are you there?" She rolled on her side, vision blurred from the blinding explosion. Her ears continue to ring as she crawled, seeing Natalia's blank eyes staring back at her. "Nat," she choked out her friend's name. Charlie crawled over, touching her arm. "Nat?" She glanced over and saw Lou lying a few feet away. She felt his spirit leave too.

"Grab it," said another voice.

She looked up through half-closed eyes to see Moret and his contact standing by the still intact box. Moret reached into it, then yelped when a blast of blue light sent him staggering backwards. "Fuck, it won't let me touch it." Then she squeezed her eyes shut and slowed her breathing. *Play dead, and you might just get out of this alive.*

"Damn it, Goodridge needs that orb."

"What about them?" He motioned to the bodies of her fallen teammates. "Make sure they're all dead."

Charlie closed her eyes. She was going to die. She thought her family, her little brother, then Drake came into her mind.

"Enough!" Charlie wrenched her hands away then ran out of the room. Tears spilled down her cheeks as the memories came flooding back. She hadn't thought of Scott, she'd thought of Drake. She remembered muttering his name when she lost consciousness. She slid down the wall, wrapping her arms around her knees. All her grief had bubbled to the surface again. *Get a grip, Denais don't cry. You have a job to do.*

The door opened and closed. She didn't need to look up to know who it was. She could feel him. "I'm sorry you had to relive that. If I could have—" She shot up, throwing herself into his arms. "Can you just hold me?"

Drake wrapped his arms around her, pulling her tight to his chest. He ran his hand through her hair, muttering something she didn't understand.

Being in his arms felt comforting. "I called for you," she muttered against his chest. "I remembered. I thought I was about to die and I thought of you. Why do we always seem to come together during death and destruction? First, the bombing at your club when we first met, me almost dying during that lab explosion, the revolution, now this..."

He chuckled. "You do have a tendency for trouble, little witch."

She nudged him in the ribs. "Thanks."

"For what?"

"For being there."

"I told you a long time ago I'd always be there for you." Drake stroked her hair.

"Bet you'd prefer someone like Lana, huh?"

He scowled. "No, I only want you."

Suddenly his presence didn't feel so unwanted; instead, she enjoyed the feel of his arms around her. Charlie wiped her eyes. "It hurt seeing them like but I know I can see this through—we can see this through." She pulled back. "Let's go back in."

"Are you sure you're alright?"

"Yes." She reached up and gave him a quick kiss on the cheek that surprised them both.

As she turned to go, Drake caught hold of her wrist and kissed her again. This kiss was hot, demanding. She clutched at his shirt, pulling his hard body closer. This wasn't like any other kiss she'd felt before, she needed him like she needed the very air to breathe.

"Guess you're okay then," said another voice.

They pulled apart, saw Cate standing in the doorway. Damn! Charlie felt her cheeks burn. She couldn't believe Cate had seen that. She glanced at Drake and then headed after her aunt when she headed back inside the meeting room.

"I sensed something while we were witnessing Charlie's memories," Cate said. "I saw a flash of something. It looked like an orb."

"What do we know of the Srimtar?" asked McNabb. "What power does it have?"

"Not much. Just a lot of myths and legends around it," answered Jason. "No one knows what its true power is."

"Most legends have some grain of truth in them," Drake pointed out.

Charlie glanced at the data on the screen.

"Why were you unaffected?" Lana gave her a questioning look. "Why did they die and you survive?"

Drake glowered at the Phoenix. "Lana."

"What? At least I can be objective on this matter. I'm not blinded by emotion." She glared back at him.

This bitch really needs a slap. Yet the bitch did have a point. Charlie had asked herself that same question every day.

"Moret and his contact had shields on. Did you activate your own shield, Charlie?" Cate asked.

"No, protocol states we don't turn on our shields until after we're announced a presence or we engage our weapons," she answered. "As you saw, we didn't have time for either."

"I think I should use my powers on you. I have visions too and I know to be careful." Cate held out her hand for Charlie to take.

"What if you get hurt too?" Charlie gripped the sides of her chair.

"I'll be careful."

Charlie glanced to Drake.

I can pull you out again, he said.

Yeah, but I'd rather not experience mind-numbing pain again. Charlie held out her hands to her aunt. Cate's eyes turned bright silver and Charlie closed her own eyes. *Please don't hurt my aunt!*

She waited for something to happen then felt a violent jolt. The same feeling she'd had when Helga had tried to use her power on her. Her eyes snapped open and blue light shot from her hands, sending Cate hurtling across the room.

Not again! Charlie thought, shocked to feel the presence of something else at the edge of her mind. *What's happening to me?* She wouldn't let it take her over this time. She focused on her power and tried to reach for Drake's hand, but her fingers only twitched in response.

Jason swore, static flaring between his fingers.

"No!" Drake snapped.

"What is that?" McNab rose from his seat and backed away.

"Yes, you should fear me, for I am power." Words came out sounding nothing like Charlie's voice.

Whatever the hell you are, get out of me! Charlie snarled. *This is my body, not yours.*

More words came out of her mouth.

Fool, I am you. We are one and the same.

Charlie felt a rush of panic. What the hell did that mean?

Blue light exploded as the strange entity knocked everyone across the room. She felt her legs moving as she stalked across the room towards the double doors. *No, stop!* Charlie cried. Something tugged at her senses, like a rope being pulled. Her body spun around to see Drake. Blue light flared again.

No! Charlie screamed, trying to use every ounce of strength she had left to fight for control. The blue light shot out, hitting Drake in the chest. His head slumped forward, eyes closing. *No, no, Drake!* Her body continued moving, pushing open the double doors.

"Oh, no you don't," Cate said. "Whatever the hell you are, get out of my niece!"

Charlie's body froze as if held by invisible bindings. Charlie knew

Cate must be using her GM power which allowed her to control all witches. *Ha, take that!* Charlie cheered. *Now get out of me.*

"Fool, your powers are no match for mine." Another burst of light sent Cate crashing to the ground, and then light exploded around the room.

Everyone in the room fell unconscious—at least Charlie hoped they were. If anyone else died, she wouldn't be able to live with herself. *Seriously, whatever you are, you better get out of me right now.*

I am you, the voice hissed. *You are me.*

Charlie snorted. *Right, how the heck is that possible?* Her body continued to move down the hall. *Where are we going?*

To find it.

Find what? Light blurred. Charlie felt her body becoming incorporeal. Next, she found herself back in the warehouse where it had all begun. Her hands raised, blue light surging through the barren building.

What are you doing? demanded Charlie. She tried to move her limbs, but the invading force overpowered her every attempt at regaining control.

Blue light bathed the building in an eerie glow as more words came out. Metal groaned and vibrated from the force.

"Hey!"

Her gaze flickered to a figure in the corner. One of the Tears, Charlie guessed. Or someone eager to cash in on the price on her head. *Great, just great. Now would be a good time to use your mojo.*

The man drew a gun, pointed her, but the entity didn't feel bothered by it. "Get down on the ground, witch," he ordered.

Don't kill him, he can—

Another burst of blue light and the man hurtled across the room.

More light pulsed and burned until a dark room came into view.

"Minc," the entity hissed.

Out! Charlie screamed. What would it take to control her own body again?

Strong arms suddenly wrapped around her.

"Forgive me," Drake murmured, and the world went black.

CHAPTER 11

Charlie glanced at her board again. After making sure everyone was okay and losing her only potential lead, the gang member had escaped. After that she'd returned home, refusing to talk to anyone—even Drake. Although he'd called by phone, doorbell and telepathically over the past couple of days, Charlie was determined to figure out what the hell had taken her over and how it connected to her case without anyone's help. It was safer for everyone if she stayed away from them.

Cate and other family members had tried calling, but she felt too embarrassed to speak to anyone. Damn it, there had to be a connection somewhere. *What am I missing?*

Silver orbs sparkled as Cate appeared in the armchair.

"Don't you have more important things to do? Like council meetings or running your own cases?" Charlie groaned.

"No, I came to make sure you're okay." Cate gave her a quick hug.

"I'm fine, I'm working," Charlie replied, shrugging off her embrace. "Are you alright?"

Her aunt grinned, rubbing her forehead. "Fine, but my head hurt like a bitch after you knocked me out."

Charlie flinched. "I said I was sorry."

"It wasn't your fault, and you and I are going to chat," she said, squeezing her arm. "I know you're hiding away because you think you're a threat—"

"I am a threat," Charlie snapped. "I attacked you and everyone in that room."

"We know it wasn't really you," Cate said, shaking her head. "Plus you've seen me at my worst. Look how I reacted when I almost lost Jason."

"How do you know it wasn't me?" she retorted. Hell, she hadn't even wanted to look in a mirror since then for fear she wouldn't see her own reflection staring back "That thing said it was me, that we're one and the same."

"Look, whatever it is we'll figure it out." Cate sank down in the armchair.

She snorted. "No, go home, Aunt Cate. Don't you have your own cases to deal with?"

Cate's eyes narrowed. "Charlie, shutting everyone out won't help. Maybe you should come home for a while."

"I tried that, remember?" She couldn't deal with everyone fussing over her again.

"I know losing—"

"Yeah, losing my team sucks. I'm done with the feeling sad all the time stuff. I need to work, so go." She waved her hand in a shooing motion.

Cate crossed her arms, leaning back in the chair. "What's going on with Drake?"

Charlie froze, remembering the kiss. "Nothing. He comforted me and I—" She shook her head. She didn't want to think about him.

"You like him, don't you?" Cate grinned.

"Maybe when he's not being irritating as hell."

"The link you have will make things more difficult, but I think you care about him," Cate said. "I sensed you and the orb are connected. How, I don't know, but you shouldn't ignore it."

"We've only been working together a few weeks. I'm not in love with him. Scott and I are just taking a break." She felt a pang of guilt at the mention of Scott, she hadn't spoken to him once since their last encounter and he hadn't called either. Maybe their relationship was truly over now.

"It's your choice, not mine." Cate rose. "You know where I am if you need to talk. Get yourself out of this place. Shutting yourself in here won't help." She vanished in a swirl of silver orbs.

Charlie slumped onto the chair, sighing. Okay, maybe she'd been avoiding Drake, confused by their kiss and what had happened. Her phone buzzed again. This time it was Kaz. "Hey," she answered.

"Finally! Where have you been? Drake told us what happened. You don't have to lock yourself away," Kaz said. "If you go postal on us I'll just stun your arse."

She snorted. "Good to know. I needed a break from—everything."

"Drake's been worried. I don't know why you don't jump on him. I'd kill for a hunky demon to care about me that way."

She rolled her eyes. "Is that all you called for?"

"No, I got a lead. I think I found a potential witness who was close to the warehouse that day. I tracked him down and got a number. He's a junkie though."

"Great, that's doesn't make him reliable, but hell, any lead is better than nothing. What's the number?" Charlie pulled up the notes tab on her phone. "I'll talk to him. Have you told Drake about the lead?"

"Not yet. He's been at his club most of the day."

Thank the goddess for that! "Okay, don't tell him." The address appeared on screen.

"We're supposed to be working together, remember?"

Charlie sighed. "I know. I just can't face him—yet."

"So there is something going on between you—wait, he's the demon, isn't he? The one you're connected to?" Kaz demanded.

Charlie's eyes narrowed at the phone screen. "How'd you know about that?"

Kaz chuckled. "Nigel and I saw you two kissing."

"How?" Her heartbeat skipped a couple of beats, cheeks flushing.

"The Alliance building has cameras; we watched the footage of what happened after you attacked everyone."

"Right." Her cheeks burned hotter. "Damn it!"

"On the recording, Drake said you're life mates. Why didn't you tell me? I'd never hit on your man."

"He's not my anything. It's complicated."

"Well, I'd grab onto him while you can. That Lana bitch has a big thing for him," Kaz said. "You're not going to talk to the witness alone, are you? The Tears are gunning for you."

"I've already proved I can handle them. I'll call if I need backup."

After a quick chat with the witness who called himself only Andre, Charlie drove to a small cafe outside the city to meet him. Her phone chimed, signalling another text from Drake.

Are you alright? Answer my damn messages!

She grinned; she liked it when he lost his cool demeanour. *Fine,* she texted back. *We'll talk later.*

When?

She sighed, knowing she could no longer avoid the inevitable. *How about we have dinner tonight?*

Fine, I'll pick you up at seven. We need to talk.

We will.

The cafe was a small building that had seen better days with grimy walls that had once been white, paint peeling off the windows and bins overflowing with rubbish. A perfect place for a junkie to hang out. Charlie checked her weapon, clipped on her badge and covered both with her jacket.

Seeing an enforcer often made people uneasy and she didn't want to scare the potential witness away. She knew the others would have wanted to come but it was easier to go alone. More than one enforcer, or having Drake there, would spook Andre even more.

There were only a couple of people sitting at one of the tables. She sat down and ordered a coffee. Her eyes took in everything from top to bottom. The bells on the door jingled as a man in torn jeans and a black anorak came in. His brown hair fell over his eyes and his beard needed a trim. He glanced around, uneasily until he spotted her.

"Andre?"

He nodded and stalked over. "You the girl who was there that day?" he whispered.

I'm a woman, not a girl. "Yeah, I'm the one. Would you like some coffee or something?"

His eyes scanned the room again, darting in every direction. "No, listen, kid..."

Her lips thinned. Hell, she was twenty-four, hardly a kid. "Agent," she corrected. "What did you see that day?"

"I saw Moret and another guy going in there."

"You know the name of the other guy?" She pulled out her PDA to start writing notes on. The team still hadn't been able to identify him.

"He's bad news. Saw him run out after a loud bang went off. Lots of blue light came out of that warehouse."

"Do you know his name?" Charlie paused when the waitress bought her coffee over. "Did you see them carrying anything?" *Come on, Andre, give me something to go on here.* She took a closer look at his eyes. *No signs of being high.*

"Yeah, they were carrying a wooden box. It had blue light coming out of it." Andre shuddered.

She sipped the coffee and almost gagged. It tasted like boiled swamp water. *Bet this is gonna burn a hole in my stomach.*

"Listen, I was only by the river guarding my stash. I sleep there sometimes," he said. "I didn't do nothing."

Charlie sipped more of the foul coffee then shoved it away. "Then why didn't you come forward before now? It's been six months." She drummed her fingers on the table.

Andre flinched. "I was scared, kid. You know what them Tears would do to me if they found out."

"Names," she persisted, tapping her PDA, ignoring the kid comment. "Did see anything else? How did the men leave?"

He chewed on his bottom lip. "I can't tell you. He'd kill me."

She put down her PDA and reached over the table to touch his arm, making him flinch as if she'd just scalded him with fire. "Andre, I promise I'll keep you safe, but you need to give me that name and tell me what you saw." She stared into his washed-out eyes. *Please give me something, anything!*

Andre continued to tremble even as he gulped down his own coffee, sloshing it over the table and leaving brown puddles. "Goodridge. That's his name.

"What else?" She tasted a bitter aftertaste in the back of her throat and pulled up her case notes to make sure she hadn't missed anything.

"One of them pulled out a ball."

Charlie's eyes narrowed. "A ball? What kind of ball?" She wondered if this was a dead end and the guy had just come to tell her nonsense after getting strung out on his drug of choice.

"You know, a glowing blue ball thingy. Never seen no bomb like that."

The cafe faded as her mind went back to the warehouse. *She crawled along the cold concrete. Blue pulsing lights came from a wooden crate.*

"Stay back," Moret shouted, aiming his gun at her.

She glanced over at the fallen box. The orb seemed to call to her. The Srimtar. She'd seen it.

Light exploded from it, knocking the men away from her before she passed out.

Charlie blinked, feeling a wave of dizziness wash over her. Three people now surrounded the table. Moret, Andre and another man. "What the hell?"

A sharp pain hit the back of her head as something struck her from behind. Her vision blurred as blackness took hold, threatening to pull her under but Charlie fought to stay conscious. She reached for magic. Someone yanked her hands behind her back. Her powers wouldn't come. She'd been drugged, she realised too late. But she'd be damned if she'd go down without a fight.

She jabbed the man behind her in the ribs and heard a grunt of pain. With a shaking hand, she grabbed her gun and fired. A blue stream of energy shot out.

Andre screamed.

Figures faded to colours. Damn it, she couldn't see a bloody thing. Using her free hand, she dropped her badge on the floor as someone grabbed her, hitting her again.

Charlie blurred in and out of consciousness as they threw her into a van. She blinked from the impact. They tied her hands and feet and then gagged her mouth. They'd taken her gear too, even her comm link ring. Her head pounded like a heavy drum as she heard an engine start.

She moaned, trying to call for help but only muffled sounds came out. *Drake!* She tried to call him in thought. But their telepathic link only worked with magic, he wouldn't hear her.

She closed her eyes as oblivion took over.

A sharp pain across her face brought Charlie back to consciousness. Her vision swirled in a blur of shapes and colours as she found herself in a dark room. The windows had been boarded up, the crystal lamps on the walls cast eerie shadows around the room. It contained nothing but the chair they'd tied her to.

"Welcome back, witch," said an unfamiliar voice.

She tensed, realising she wasn't alone.

They yanked off her gag. "Don't bother calling for help. This place is shielded. No one will hear you."

"Who are you?" she demanded. "Where the fuck am I?"

"I'll ask the questions. But you might as well know my name. I'm TJ, one of the Tears."

She closed her eyes, trying to get her body to focus. Her magic still lay just beyond reach. *Drake!* she called again.

Still nothing.

"Where's the Srimtar?" TJ demanded.

She shook her head, trying to clear it. "I don't know what you're talking about."

The response to his question earned her another blow to the face. Charlie felt blood drip from her nose, her head pounded harder and her stomach recoiled as she spat out vomit. It left a nasty taste in her mouth. She hoped she'd brought up some of the drug too.

"Don't think being related to the Grand Mistress will save you. No one's coming to rescue you, witch. Now, where's the Srimtar?"

CHAPTER 12

Drake paced up and down the office area. "Gods above and below, where is she?" he thundered. Fire formed in his palm, but he snuffed it out.

"Would you please calm down?" snapped Kaz. "We don't know she's in trouble."

"I know!" he snapped back. "I can't sense her presence. Gods, I should have forced that damn bond on her."

"Calm down," Nigel intoned. "Losing it won't get you anywhere."

Drake muttered a curse in his own language and balled his hands into fists. His inner demon demanded blood as rage burned hot in his veins. He hadn't lost control like this since he lost his own family eight thousand years earlier. That was why he'd never grown too close to others, except his oldest friend, Jason, then the McCray family.

He'd come close to losing Charlie once before when she died six years earlier; forming a link had been the only way to revive her. A link he no longer felt. What had happened? She'd been a presence at the edge of his mind since that day. Where had she gone?

If she were dead, he knew he would have felt it.

"Got it. I found her phone," Nigel announced, holding up his PDA. "I know where she is."

Drake grabbed the screen, peered at the location, started to shimmer out. One he got there he'd find his witch. If anyone had hurt her, he'd burn them from the inside out then send them to spend eternity in hell.

Kaz jumped up, grabbing his arm. "Hey, we're coming with you. Charlie is our friend too."

He muttered another curse, grabbed hold of them and shimmered out. Stars and planets swirled around them in a riot of colours as he moved through the different planes of existence. Light blurred as they reappeared in a small car park. He didn't see Charlie's little blue car anywhere in sight and wondered if she'd shimmered there. If so, he would've sensed her magic, yet he felt nothing. Not a good sign.

"This must be where she was meeting Andre," Kaz remarked. "He's the witness I mentioned."

"Convenient having a witness come forward after all this time," Drake muttered, scanning the cafe in front of him. He felt no trace of his life mate anywhere, but he sensed she'd been there. He could feel the lingering energy. He sniffed, spotted something burning in a nearby bin. "Investigate that." He stalked into the cafe, eyes alert.

There was only one customer there staring into a coffee mug. The man's body shook. Drake smelt fear. Something glinted on the floor. He held out his hand so the object flew over to him and he flipped the case open. A gold shield glittered there, and on the other side was a photo of Charlie. Drake let out a growl, picked the man up by the throat. "Where is she?" he snarled, shoving it in the man's face. "Where's the woman who came here?"

The man squirmed, trying to break free. "Don't know, I—"

Drake sensed he was a low-level demon with negligible power. He could squash him like an insect and the little weasel knew it. "Where is she?" he repeated, shoving the badge into his jacket. The walls trembled as his eyes burned with red fire, letting the feel of his power roam free.

"They—they took her," the man cried. "I was only paid to meet her."

The door flew open as Kaz and Nigel rushed him. "Drake, we found Charlie's gear in the bin," Nigel announced. "I think the cafe's camera might show us more. Maybe we'll be able to get a lead on how they took her out of here."

Drake ignored them as he forced his mind into the other demon's. *Tell me what you know.* Power he hadn't used in centuries bubbled to the surface images as flashed by. He saw Charlie being grabbed, then dragged away. The name Myles Goodridge came to him.

"Drake, put the guy down. He's just a lackey." Kaz grabbed his arm. "We don't kill people out of personal revenge."

Drake threw the man across the room. His inner demon growled but he had no time for revenge. Oh, people would pay he'd make sure of it, but vengeance would have to wait for now.

Drake shimmered into his club. "Val?" he yelled. "Val, get your arse over here."

Vale appeared. "What now?"

Drake gave him a look, eyes flashing amber. "Tell me where to find Myles Goodridge."

"Goodridge? That's impossible. That guy moves around so much no one can find him."

"I will find him. Give me every address you have connected to the Tears."

"I said it's not possible, mate. He…"

Val vanished as Drake sent him away. He felt power burning through him; the entire club trembled around him. "Silas!" he boomed.

An old man with a long, pointed chin, a long beard and white hair the made him look like he'd been electrocuted appeared. His blue robe glittered with stars and his amethyst wise leaned and swirled. "You're losing control," the old man cackled. "I haven't felt the power of a true Akaran in millennia. It's about time you started using it, boy."

"You're a seer—so see. Tell me where to find Myles Goodridge." He grabbed Silas by the collar of his robe and shook him.

The tremors turned more violent, glasses and bottles fell from the shelves shattering around them. Silas grinned and shrugged him off. "Temper, temper, boy."

Drake made a grab for the old man again, but Silas vanished in a puff of smoke, then reappeared behind him, still laughing.

"I warn you, I'm not to be trifled with." Drake spoke in a rough harshness of his own language.

Silas still smirked. "I've missed seeing you like this, Drakon. Reminds me of the demon you should have been."

"TELL ME!" The walls rattled as every object within the bar exploded, glass crashing to the floor.

"I can't sense him. Myles is an elusive bastard," Silas replied. "What vexes you, boy?"

His hands clenched into fists, his patience wearing thin. "He took my life mate. I want her back. If you can't find him, I'll search myself. Even if it means shimmering all over creation."

"Life mate? Gods below, you always let that silly notion prevent you from seeking dominion over all Demonkind." Silas scratched his beard.

"I never desired to rule. I never will, I just want my witch back." His eyes flashed, his inner demon clawing at his mind, rage heating his blood as power hummed through his veins. If Silas didn't start talking he'd give in and use his powers.

"A witch? Even better." Silas's chest heaved from silent laughter.

Fire formed in Drake's palm; he wanted to kill someone. Anyone. It didn't matter who. He started to shimmer out.

"You can't take on Goodridge on your own," Silas snapped. "Even you're not that powerful."

Drake's fangs came out. "Why not? If he's a demon, he won't be able to resist my power."

Silas's lips thinned. "You'll find out soon enough." The old man's eyes blurred to white. He shuddered. "The witch you seek is connected to the Srimtar. You need to stay away from her."

"I'd never do that. I've waited too long to have her. What does that bloody orb even do?"

Silas shook his head. "It's a curse, that's what it is."

"Can you tell me where she is or not?"

Silas rambled off a list of addresses and locations used by the gang. "Don't say I didn't warn you," Silas muttered as Drake shimmered out.

CHAPTER 13

The room shifted into focus when Charlie opened her eyes. Her face throbbed from where she'd been punched repeatedly. But her eyes cleared enough to see the gloomy windowless room around her. The door creaked open as a man with reddish-gold hair came in, pushing a device on wheels. The machine had a small screen connected with wires.

She gulped. A mind-reading device. She'd seen them before, but they had been banned since the revolution. Charlie felt for her mental shields, prayed they would still hold despite her powerless state. She'd spent an entire year learning how to protect her mind. *You can do this,* she told herself. *You trained for this.* It didn't mean it wouldn't hurt like a bitch.

Damn it, how long had she been there? Power blockers only lasted a few hours, but they hadn't dosed her up again—that she knew. Goddess, she longed for her connection to Drake. Pathetic as it was. The link had been comforting over the years even though she often chose to ignore it.

"It won't work on me," she insisted. "I already told you I don't know what happened to the orb. Last thing I remember you and Moret were carrying it out of the warehouse. You're Goodridge, right?"

He smiled. "Clever little witch."

She scowled. Only Drake got to call her that.

"It will work. The more you resist, the more it will hurt." He stabbed a needle into her arm, making her wince.

"You're going to be damn sorry when I get loose," she told him. Her heart thundered in her ears. If she came close to death again, would it finally bring on the ascension? "I'll kick your arse, then there's my demon side that gets pretty pissy."

He laughed. "Are you going to tell me your auntie will come after me too?"

"Maybe. My family is very overprotective. Then there's my life mate, he's even worse. You'll have a lot of people after you." She hoped he'd leave her alone soon. She had to figure out a way to break loose.

"Drake? How is he? Still trying to be good?"

She frowned. "He is good."

"Is he now? You don't know who or what he really is, do you?" Myles snorted.

She glanced up at him. "What's that supposed to mean?"

"Nothing. Just he's not what he seems. He's not good, he's pathetic. How he threw away all his power I'll never understand." He chuckled. "But then he never deserved it."

Charlie wanted to ask more but he stabbed another needle into her arm and then hooked electrodes to her aching scalp. He injected something into her and pulled her into a vision. Charlie found herself back inside the warehouse, crouching in position.

Boom, blue light exploding.

Not again! She felt herself falling, next she stood in front of the box.

"Where is the Srimtar?" Goodridge demanded. "Tell me where it is."

Charlie gritted her teeth, wondering why he wanted the orb so much. "I told you I don't know. I passed out before I was rescued." She paused, unsure if more questions would earn her another beating. "Why do you want it so bad?"

He responded by sending a wave of dizzying pain through her brain. Charlie gritted her teeth. *Focus,* she told herself. *Take control.* Damn, she would have welcomed a visit from that blue light demon just then. Sending the thing postal on this guy would be good.

She felt her mental shield still in place, despite her lack of power it still remained. She thought back to her training as she tried to figure out a way to gain control. Her brow creased.

"Hey, McCray, you can treat us all to drinks tonight." The sound of Natalia's voice made her feel a sharp pang of sadness.

Pain jolted through her, rolling down her neck to her back.

"Show me where the orb is. What did you do with it?"

More pain followed, but Charlie retaliated by showing different memories of her team. The torture seemed to go on for hours as they poked, prodded and jolted her with pain.

When Myles finally stormed out of the room, Charlie let her head slumped forward. Her limbs felt like dead weight, her head felt like a jackhammer was hitting her brain. Blood dripped down her broken nose. She had to get out of there.

Her magic still felt out of reach. *Guess I'll have to improvise.* She saw nothing but the machine and a few pipes behind her. No windows or any objects that could be of use.

"Drake?" She tried calling for him again. *Drake?* she called in thought. *Can you hear me?*

No response.

Leaning forward, she examined the machine, searching for anything that could break her bonds. Her blood wouldn't do much good as she still had the blocker running through her veins. The machine looked old judging from the style of it. Maybe a few centuries. Which meant it had no communication capabilities.

Charlie glanced at the bonds around her wrists, chains made of infused Silveron, not the usual cuffs. She moved her wrists around, trying to pull them free. That didn't work; she felt the silver ring on her left index finger still there. Great, they hadn't stolen it. They wouldn't have even noticed one of Steve's inventions since it wasn't magical. She turned it, pushing it to turn on the laser.

The door burst open as TJ and Goodridge came in.

Weird, she couldn't sense what Goodridge was.

Myles gave her a bright smile. "Hello, McCray. Nice to see you again."

"Wish I could say the feeling was mutual," she replied. "I told you, I have no idea where that damned orb is."

"No, but you are the key to finding it. You weren't harmed by it."

Charlie shook her head. "I can't find it. I don't even know where it went."

Myles came closer, muttering words of power she didn't understand but thought she heard the word "Srimtar."

Something jolted through her, making her body straighten and her eyes burned with light. In her mind, Charlie saw the glowing blue orb. It sparkled, whirling with stars inside it. *No,* she thought. *Don't show them where you are. Come on, demon thing, come and get me out of here.* The other presence took over. Charlie felt energy surge through her. The chains fell away as the strange entity phased her body free.

"Guardian," Myles murmured.

Charlie's lips curved into a smile. "You're trying to find what doesn't belong to you." A harsh voice came out in a strange language. Charlie found she could understand it. *Don't kill them, just get me out of here,* she told it.

"Avna!" Myles shouted, sending a burst of blue lightning.

Charlie's body slammed back into the wall, knocking the air from her lungs. *I'm gonna be so bloody bruised!* The entity snarled, firing back with her own lightning burst.

Myles dodged it and TJ ran from the room.

Okay, now kick his arse!

The entity formed a glowing ball of energy in her palm and hurtled it at Myles.

Why can't you just knock him out like you did with the Alliance? Charlie demanded.

He's like us, the voice replied.

What does that mean?

His powers can match ours. Another blast sent Charlie crashing across the floor. She felt the other presence in her mind flicker. She grunted with pain, back in control of her own body again. She dove through the nearest wall, body blurring as she phased into an office with a console and a scattering of paperwork.

No, we must stop Goodridge! The entity screeched.

She grinned. *Ha, not nice being stuck at the back of my mind with no control, is it? Now you know what it feels like.*

The entity let out a harsh laugh. *I've been trapped for years. First, I remained dormant until you came of age, then you repressed me.*

Excuse me? What the hell are you on about? Charlie demanded. *Goddess, I'm arguing with myself.*

I'm you, the part of you that you refuse to accept. The part you ignore.

Okay, I've clearly lost my mind now. I must have. She glanced around, searching for an escape. Again no windows, no phone either.

Charlie scanned through the piles of paperwork hoping she'd find something of use or an object she could use as a weapon. She flipped open the file and saw her name and picture inside. Skimming through it she saw mother unknown, marked next it was race unknown.

What the hell? My mum was a Denai—okay maybe part demon too. Thanks for that surprise, Mum. Another file caught her attention which was marked "Srimtar." She stuffed it in her back pocket.

"Where do you think you're going, witch?" Myles demanded as he appeared in the doorway.

"Getting the hell out of here." She dove through the next wall. This time it ended in a corridor.

Two guards opened fire on her; she dodged the bullets by ducking around the corner. *Great, just freaking great!* If her phasing power worked, would her others?

Let me have control, said the voice.

Not bloody happening.

I can save us.

No, you can get the hell out of my head. Taking a deep breath, Charlie peered around the corner, raising her hand. The bullet bounced off her palm as her psychokinesis took hold.

Myles rounded the corner, and then threw another energy ball. She cried out as it struck her in the shoulder. Blood seeped from the open wound. Another blast had her crashing to the ground. *Come on, demon. Fight back.* The other presence took hold again; she blasted Myles with her own power.

"Avock!" he screamed.

The other presence in her mind vanished. Gone.

Drake? Charlie called.

Light blurred as Drake shimmered in, his eyes burning. Power rolled off him in violent waves, making the air around them sizzle. He hurled a fireball at Goodridge, striking the other man in the chest.

Myles chuckled, undeterred by the blow. He pointed at Drake and a bolt of blue lightning shot out.

The blast sent Drake staggering as Myles turned and fled.

An alarm rang out, flames appearing all around them.

Charlie clutched her injured shoulder as she stumbled over to him. "Drake, come on, shimmer us out of here." She grabbed his hand.

His eyes still burned red. It reminded her of the blood rage, a state Denais could enter to use the full dark side of their gifts to kill if they lost someone they loved. The heat from the flames seared against her skin but it didn't burn her. Orange flames licked at the walls, engulfing everything in their wake. "Drake, please, you have to get out of here before this whole place blows. I'm too weak to use my powers."

Light blurred around them.

Charlie grunted as they landed in a heap on the floor, both breathing hard. Drake held onto her tight. "Ow!" She winced from the pain. She watched his eyes change back to normal as he released her.

"Where are you hurt?" He ran his hand over her, checking for wounds.

Charlie rolled away from him, clutching her bleeding shoulder. "I don't think there's part of me that doesn't hurt right now."

Drake pulled her hand away, placing his palm over the wound. She felt a warm rush of energy pass between them. The wound on her shoulder closed over and her nose stopped throbbing. "How did you do that?" She frowned. "I didn't think you could heal people."

He shook his head. "I can't. I just gave you some of my own power. I've seen Jason do it with Cate."

"I don't feed off living energy. I've never really needed any energy," she admitted. Most Denais needed to feed off living energy in order to survive, but mediums took their energy from other sources.

Drake wrapped his arms around her, pulling her tight against him. "Thanks for coming for me," she murmured, returning his embrace.

"Always, little witch," he said, kissing the top of her head. "I swear you're taking centuries off my life though. Stop doing that to me."

She snorted. "I'll try. Can't make any promises though."

Drake brushed her hair off her face. Charlie reached up and kissed him again, slow and tender. She smiled. "Let's just take things slow for now, okay?"

He nodded. "I want you to stay here with me. It's safer and you can have your own room."

"Okay." Charlie pulled away from him. "What was that back there? I've never seen you like that before." Drake hesitated. "Come on, Vlad. If you want this to work between us we can't keep secrets from each other."

He rubbed the back of his neck. "That was part of my true demon self. I come from a very old, very powerful race of demons. I haven't used my power like that for centuries."

"Why?"

"I don't like what I become when I do. Besides, that's not who I am," he said.

She sat down and told him what happened. "Why do you think that thing keeps taking control of me?" she asked. "Do you think it's the demon part of me? If so, why?"

"Have you explored the demon part of yourself?"

"No," Charlie admitted. "I guess I don't acknowledge it. I'm a Denai, that's who I was raised as. I'm an enforcer, that's I choose to be. But there's more to me than that." She remembered the file she'd seen and pulled it out. "Drake, can you sense what kind of demon I am? I mean, part demon?"

Drake shook his head. "No, I assumed Zexen and I can sense what any Demonkind is—it's one of my gifts."

She shot her feet. "I have a way of finding out if that voice in my head was telling the truth. Let's go." They shimmered into her apartment and saw items scattered all over the place.

"Shit! I thought I had this place shielded," she gasped. "Damn it, we need a lab." She opened the wall where she kept her most important items and pulled them out.

"I can help with that."

Drake opened another door when they returned to his house. Inside was wall-to-wall computer equipment, plus a countertop for lab testing.

"Wow," Charlie breathed.

"I created it when Jason and the team were here during the early months after the revolution. I thought it might come in useful again someday. What do you need a lab for?"

"To test something. I told you about a file I saw, I can't do this at the station without raising any red flags."

Charlie found her way around the equipment with ease thanks to her dad and Uncle Ian's teachings. She pulled out a scanner, pricked her finger, placed her blood on a slide and waited. "This will tell me what races I have in my DNA. I know what some of them will be, but even my dad didn't know much about where my mum came from."

Drake frowned. "What do you want it to tell you? DNA can give only basic answers."

"I need to know what I am."

The scanner bleeped. Charlie, heart pounding, pressed a few buttons to pull up the results on screen, thankfully the tech was connected to the databases back in Elaris. Lines started appearing as the computer threw out the names.

Charlie began interpreting the results. "Denai, there's Ashrali fey like my dad, there's a strand of Phoenix. The other strand is black and blue." The screen read 'race unknown.' "How is that possible? If my mum was part Zexen that would show." She stared at him. "What am I, Drake?"

CHAPTER 14

Drake and Charlie shimmered into the foyer of Cate and Jason's house. A beam of light shot down from the ceiling, roamed over their bodies and scanned them, then blinked out.

"Hey, I'm home," Charlie yelled as she passed into the massive hallway where a blue Denai star had been engraved into the marble to match the pale blue walls. "Dad?"

A blur of colour shot towards them and leapt straight at Charlie. "Char!" screeched a delighted voice.

"Whoa. Hi, Tom-Tom." She wrapped her arms around her six-year-old brother. "Wow, you're so big now." She ruffled his mop of unruly dark hair.

Tommy grinned. "You bring me presents?"

"Indeed, we did." A toy car appeared in Drake's hand.

"Thanks, Uncle Drake." He grabbed the toy and ran down the hall. They followed after an excited Tommy as he chatted away as he led Charlie upstairs.

A redheaded woman appeared. "Hey, I didn't know you were coming home." Jade, Charlie's stepmother, wrapped her in a warm hug.

"Hi, Jade. Where's my dad?"

"Upstairs in his office, working. You know what he's like," Jade said, rolling her green eyes. "We're just about to have some lunch, want to join us? Maybe you can drag Steve out too."

Charlie smiled. Only Jade understood her workaholic father the way Charlie did. "I need to talk to him. It's important. I'll see you guys later."

"I'll join you," Drake said to Jade. "Tommy, I don't believe we finished building that castle last time I was here." Charlie watched Drake walk away. Weird, she hadn't expected him to be great with kids. But she learnt there was much more to him than she could have imagined.

Steve stared at his numerous computer screens when Charlie walked into his office. He spun around and wrapped his arms around her. "Goddess, I've missed you. Why were you holding hands with Drake?"

"Hello to you too, Dad," she said with a wry smile as she pulled away from him.

Steve ran a hand through his unruly dark curls. "I saw you come in on the house screen. You've come to tell me your bonded, haven't you?" Steve had always been wary of Drake too.

She shook her head. "No. Dad, Drake's a good man. I care about him. Like it or not, he's part of my life now. I—"

"So you are a couple now?" Steve expression remained neutral.

"Not exactly." She bit her lip. She hadn't come to talk about Drake and knew it wouldn't be easy getting Steve to talk about her mother.

"What about Scott? He rang me a couple of weeks ago, asking for my blessing."

Charlie's heart skipped a beat. *Goddess, I'd better talk to him. Tell him it's over. I can't lead him on, not when I'm starting to have feelings for Drake.* Scott planned on proposing? Shit, she hadn't seen that one coming.

"Scott and I aren't together anymore." She sighed. "Look, I need to talk about Mum." She saw the familiar pain in his bright blue eyes. Despite being married to his true soul mate now, she knew he lost part of himself when her mum had died in childbirth.

"What about her?"

"Things have been happening to me recently. I think my demon side is emerging. Do you know what kind of demon Mum was?" She perched on one of the stools and waited for his response.

"She told me she was half Zexen but she never liked talking about it. There's not much to tell," he told her. "Your mum never spoke of her past, she said it didn't matter because her future was with me."

"How long did you know each other?" She rested her elbow on the worktop, realising how much she'd wanted to know all these things.

"We saw each other on and off over the centuries but we started dating about thirty years ago, married a couple of years later which was two years before she got pregnant." He rubbed the top of his nose. "Four years—that's nothing to an immortal. I loved her, part of me always will. I knew we weren't soulmates—not like life mates are—but we were happy."

"Didn't she tell you anything about her past? How old was she?" She'd tried asking things before but Steve had always been reluctant to tell her much.

"She was over three thousand. I know age doesn't matter much after a few centuries," Steve said. "Why are you asking so much? You could call your mum in spirit and ask her all these things yourself."

"I tried to before we left, she wouldn't come." Charlie shook her head. "Dad, I did a DNA test back at Drake's lab. There is no trace of Zexen in my blood and from the look of it my Denai powers were passed on through you, not her. Did you ever do any tests on me?"

Steve frowned, turning his attention back to the numerous screens. "You're my daughter, why would I?" Charlie touched his arm and he sighed. "Okay, yeah I did, but it was to test me, not her."

Her mouth fell open. "You thought you weren't my dad?"

He looked away. "For a while, yes, but the result wouldn't have mattered anyway."

Charlie hugged him again, feeling a tear drip down her cheek. "The test said there is no match on what kind of demon I am." She pulled up the results on screen to show him.

Steve tapped a few keys to search the databases but no match came back. "From the looks of it, Helena wasn't a Denai at all but a full blood something. Maybe not even a demon," he observed. "Goddess, I had no idea."

Charlie nodded; she'd suspected as much. "Oh, I'm half demon—of some kind. I can sense it."

After leaving the manor, they headed back to Drake's house. Charlie still felt weak from the beating the day before but Drake's energy had taken the edge off.

Drake came back in carrying a mug of coffee. "What is it?"

"I think I found something, come look." He sat beside her but she noticed him keeping his distance.

"What's wrong? Why don't you want to be near me?" She frowned.

"Not you. That." He motioned to the book.

"Why?" She glanced between him and the book.

"I know the legends of that book. It can electrocute people."

"Only people it views a threat, which you aren't." Charlie shoved the book closer to him. A picture of a blue orb had been drawn on a page. "Said to be a weapon of great power. It will protect itself from any who try to search for it. Only one can control it, one it uses to be its guardian," Charlie read.

Drake peered at the page. "That's it? Does it mention who the guardian is?"

She flipped the page. "Only the guardian shall be unaffected by power." She bit her lip. "That fits me."

"It would make sense. The blast killed everyone in that warehouse but you. You weren't even burned when I found you."

"If I am its guardian, why can't I find the damn thing? We have no idea where it went after it was at the warehouse."

Drake rubbed his chin. "What if it never left?"

"What do you mean? My witness—okay, maybe he wasn't a real witness, but no one saw it afterwards."

"That doesn't mean it's not still there. Magical artefacts are notorious for their stealth abilities."

Drake shimmered them into the warehouse. "Do you really think it's still here?" Charlie let go of his hand. "If it is, why would it stay here? The book said it moves and stays with its guardian."

"Maybe you have to call for it first."

Charlie took a deep breath, let it out. Being back here made her want to run but she wouldn't let fear best her. "How do I summon it?" She hesitated. This thing had killed her team; did she even want to find it? Yes, if it helped bring the killers to justice.

"Personal feelings aside, we can't let the Srimtar fall into the wrong hands," Drake pointed out, clutching her hand. "I know this will be hard for you, but Goodridge must want it for a reason."

Charlie sighed, glancing around the concrete floor with its weeds and bits of broken debris. "Okay, Srimtar, come out. Appear, or whatever it is you do."

Drake's lips curved into a smile; he wrapped an arm around her shoulders. "I don't think it works like that, little witch."

She groaned, closed her eyes. *Okay, demon, do your thing, find the damn orb.*

Blue light flashed, casting an eerie glow around the room as a small glowing crystal sphere appeared at her feet. "Wow, it's so little." Charlie bent down, picked it up. It fit into her palm and seemed to swirl with stars when she examined it. "So much death for such a small thing." She rolled it in her hand and felt power hum against her skin. So much power in such a tiny object.

Drake tensed and pulled away from her. "Someone's here. Don't let that orb out of your sight." He stalked away.

"Hey, you're not leaving me here." She grabbed his arm.

"Protect the Srimtar." Drake vanished in a blur of light.

Charlie muttered a curse and then glared at the orb. *You better be worth it.* She opened her bag to shove it inside but then noticed it glowing again. An image of Drake appeared in the desert with golden sand covering the horizon. He glanced back, then walked away, disappearing into darkness. "What the hell does that mean?" she muttered to herself.

Outside a loud explosion went off. She stuffed the orb into her bag and carried it outside. Moret stood hurling fireballs at Drake, then he opened fire with an automatic. Charlie grabbed Drake's arm, their bodies blurring as she phased, causing the bullets to pass straight through them. "We need him alive," she hissed.

She turned on her new comm link. "Kaz, Nigel, we could do with some backup here."

"On our way," Kaz said in her ear.

Charlie ducked, feeling her heart pounding. Goddess, now wasn't the time for a panic attack!

Focus, Drake told her. *You can do this.*

She felt her back pulsing with energy but she ignored it. Somehow she knew she was meant to protect it. *You keep him busy; I'll go from behind.* She ducked out of sight, phasing into the concrete. Moving through the hard ground, she glanced up and saw where Moret stood. Leaping back up, she kicked him and knocked the gun from his grasp. He blocked the next blow, punching her in the face.

She stumbled back and blocked his next attack.

Drake grabbed hold of him, trying to wrench his arms back. Moret elbowed Drake, sending him crashing to the ground. "Where's the orb?" Moret snarled at Charlie, aiming a gun at her head. "I know you have it, I can sense it."

Charlie kicked, spun around and punched. She was surprised by her sudden strength. She didn't know if it came from the Srimtar, her emerging demon side, or both. As they fought she knocked his gun away.

Drake grabbed Moret again; instinctively Charlie grabbed his throat. Power surged from her into him. He fell to the ground, unconscious.

"Phew!" She breathed a sigh of relief as Drake hugged her.

"We did it, little witch."

She pulled away as Kaz's car drew up. "There's something I have to do."

Charlie went straight back into the warehouse. The fear she'd felt had passed; instead, she felt a strange calm settle over her as she held the glowing Srimtar. "I won't let your deaths mean nothing," she murmured. "I won't walk away from the job. I'll carry on fighting in your names until I bring down Goodridge." She sniffed, feeling a tear drip down her cheek. "I miss you all." More tears started flowing.

Orbs of white light appeared, falling into the billowing form of her former partner. Nat grinned. "Knew you had it in you, girl."

Charlie wiped away her tears and half laughed as relief washed over her. "I'm sorry I blocked you out. I was scared you'd blame me."

"It's not your fault, McCray. We all know that," Nat said. "Don't ignore your power either."

"I miss you—all of you."

Nat shook her head. "You know we'll always have your back, even in the spirit world." Nat held out her hand. Charlie gripped it, making contact with solid flesh thanks to her medium abilities. "Keep that demon around too. He's hot."

Charlie laughed. "Yeah, he is."

CHAPTER 15

After Moret had been taken into custody and charged, Drake took the team to the club to celebrate the victory. Charlie sat with Kaz and Nigel at the bar. Strangely, he found he rather liked working with all of them.

"Here's to our first case together." Kaz held up her beer.

"I'll drink to that." Drake raised his own glass.

"Hey, does that mean you're leaving us now?" Kaz asked him.

Charlie glanced at him too. *Are you?* she asked.

The club became silent as Drake suspended everyone in time. "You found the orb," he pointed out.

"Yeah, but we still have to find and capture Goodridge. I doubt he'll stop coming after me just because we caught Moret and charged him with murder," she remarked. "Besides, you're not so bad to have around." She reached over and squeezed his hand. "Hey, how about we get out of here? Go and have a real date?"

He smiled. "Where would you like to go?"

Her grin turned mischievous. "How about we go home? I'm sure we can celebrate there."

"You're staying with me then?"

"The threat's not over yet, is it? I could stay longer." He leaned over the bar to kiss her.

"Drake?" Phil called as he came into the room. "There's a message for you in your office."

Drake muttered a curse. "Leave it there," he growled. He wanted to finally spend some time with his witch, not worry about the club.

Nothing was that important.

Phil shook his head. "It's urgent. Trust me, boss, you'll want to see this."

He sighed, moved around the bar and kissed her cheek. "I'll be right back."

"It's okay," Charlie said. "Just don't take too long."

As the club unfroze, he walked to his office and cast his senses out when he saw a familiar face walking to the bar.

Scott.

What the hell is he doing here? Drake closed his office door but kept his senses on alert as he listened in. Damn it, he finally had Charlie to himself, and now Scott had reappeared.

He spotted a folded piece of parchment on his desk. How archaic. No one used parchment any more except some of the very old immortals.

"What are you doing here?" He heard Charlie ask.

"I heard you arrested someone in connection with your team's murder," Scott said. "I came to see if you're okay."

"I'm fine. We should talk." Her tone sounded neutral. Drake wasn't sure if he wanted to hear more but forced himself to listen.

"I miss you, Char. I know it's been a rough few months, but I want you back."

"Scott…"

"Char, we're meant to be together. Drake's lying. He only created a connection to you because he's tired of being alone," Scott insisted.

She sighed. "Look, we can't talk here. Meet me outside in a few minutes."

Drake stopped listening, not wanting to hear more. He pulled the parchment open and saw the words written in spiralling scrawl: *come home.*

No, that was impossible. He wouldn't contact him, not after all the centuries. *I have to go; I have to find out.*

The door opened as Charlie came in dressed in a short black dress and heels, she looked beautiful. His heart ached just staring at her.

"Is everything okay?" she asked. "You look—different."

"I'm fine." He shoved the scroll into his jacket. "Ready to go?"

Charlie hesitated. There it was. "No, I need to take care of something first."

"Scott."

"I need to talk to him." She tucked her hair behind her ear, something she did when nervous.

"Fine, go. I have more important matters to take care of anyway." He waved a hand. Damn it, he needed a way out of there, without her asking any questions.

She grabbed his arm. "Drake, don't be like that."

He shrugged off her touch. His heart twisted but he knew what he had to do. "I have to leave. You need to choose. Me or Scott, which is it?"

Her dark eyes widened. "What's that supposed to mean?"

"I mean choose, Charlotte. I won't share you and I don't think he will either. So choose, right now."

She bit her lip, hissing out a breath. "I need to—"

"I'm tired of waiting for you to choose me. Perhaps we should just end things now before we go any further."

Charlie shook her head. "Drake, I… Things were going great between us. I thought we agreed to take things slow."

"I'm not asking you to bond with me but I at least expected…" He sighed. "You've made your choice. There's nothing more to say." He pushed past her.

She ran after him. "You can't just leave like this. I need time to—"

He pulled her head up, kissed her hard. This kiss was filled with years of longing and unresolved tension. She returned the kiss with just as much passion. Her eyes widened as he pulled away, muttering words of power. Something inside him snapped, leaving an empty void. It might not last long, but it'd be enough to make his escape. He didn't want to leave her, but knew he must now.

She gasped, clutching her chest. "What have you done?"

"I broke our link. You're free—just like you always wanted," he told her. "Goodbye, Charlotte."

"Drake, wait!" she cried as he shimmered away.

The emptiness became replaced by physical ache as he moved through the different planes of existence. Miles of desert stretched in front of him as he materialised. He pulled the parchment out of his suit jacket. The demon he'd been before was gone now. He thought about shimmering back to the house of supplies but the only thing that truly mattered to him he'd already left behind. He'd never see her again. But at least he'd had her, even if only for a very short time. He loved her too, even if she didn't know it. He never thought he'd love anyone again. *Goodbye, Charlotte.* He strode along heated sands, wondering what lay for him on the other side

***

Charlie felt numb as she muttered an excuse to the others. Her plan had been to talk to Scott and break up with him properly. She needed to do it, knew she should have done it a long time ago. Then Drake had given her an ultimatum. Him or Scott. What kind of question was that? Him. It had always been Drake.

And now he'd broken their link.

She moved through the streets, feeling an ache in her heart and an emptiness that went much deeper. Scott had gone off to a restaurant so she'd reluctantly agreed to meet him there. Scott sat waiting for her as she walked inside, smiling his goofy grin. "What do you want to eat?" he asked, grabbing her hand. She stared at the table, wanting to cry but no tears would come. It hurt too much to even do that.

"Char, are you okay?" He squeezed her hand.

"Why are we here?" she muttered more to herself than him.

"I thought we were going to talk." He kissed the inside of her palm. "Look, I know things have been rough, but I love you…"

The emptiness started to fade. "I'm sorry, Scott, it's over between us."

His mouth fell open. "What? You don't mean that."

"Yeah, I do. We haven't been happy for a long time," she said and relief washed over her. "You're not the one I want to be with." It felt good to finally admit how she really felt. She'd wanted him to be the one so much, to ignore the attraction to Drake but that had all changed. *If I only I'd realised sooner just how much Drake meant to me.*

Scott grabbed her arm, his expression darkening. "You can't just leave. You might think you have feelings for Drake, but I know he's lying to you. He's already left you, hasn't he?"

Her eyes narrowed. "How would you know that?"

"I know more about you than even you do. Please, Char, he's using you because you're different. Listen, if you come with me I can tell you what that means, what—"

"Just stay the hell away from me." She shimmered back into the office, relieved to get away from Scott. For a moment he hadn't looked anything like the man she'd thought she'd known and it hadn't been just jealousy either. "Drake?" she called. "Drake, come back here. We need to talk." She waited but no reply came. Warmth flooded her chest. Their link was back, but where he was nowhere to be seen.

"I choose you," she whispered into the empty room.

One way or another, she would get Drake back.

SHADOW SPY

CHAPTER 1

Charlie McCray ducked down by her car as a fireball came at her. This was not going according to plan.

"I thought you said this guy would help us?" Kaz muttered, drawing her gun.

"I don't think he was happy when he found out we're enforcers." Charlie grabbed her own weapon, wincing as her wing mirror exploded. "Time for this guy to go down." Her body blurred as she vanished into the ground below. She moved through the concrete, using her phasing power which allowed her to become incorporeal and pass through solid matter. She jumped back up, pointing her gun at the man's head. "Now, I don't like to use this unless there's a problem. We don't have a problem, do we, Val?"

The demon, a scruffy looking overweight man with a balding head and shaggy brown bead, froze. "You said you were Drake's mate, not a fucking enforcer!"

"I'm both. Now, are you gonna stop throwing fireballs at me or do we have to go and chat at the station?" She brushed her long brown hair off her face.

Kaz moved out from behind the car, sunlight catching on her strawberry blonde locks. "Yeah, attacking Division agents gets you at least three hundred years in prison," Kaz said, her emerald eyes flashing. She grinned. "You'd get bored."

"Yeah, and if my aunt hears about this well, you know what the Grand Mistress is like when it comes to punishment." Charlie holstered her gun and crossed her arms. She didn't think he'd attack again if he had any sense.

Val sighed, raising his hands in surrender. "Fine, but I'm not talking to you out in the open like this. I have a reputation to uphold."

"Okay, we'll meet you back at the club. You'd better be there," said Charlie.

After calling their teammate Nigel to get her car towed, Kaz and Charlie shimmered into Drake's club, Nocturne. With its red walls and black and white décor, it had a cool, dark racy feel about the place. Just walking in there made her heart ache. This was where she last saw Drake—where he'd ended their relationship.

Val stood at the bar waiting for them, gulping down a beer. "What do you want now, witch?"

Charlie tried not to groan. It hadn't been easy getting Drake's informants to trust her, especially since she was a Denai and enforcer but she'd brought most of them around. "Have you found anything out about Drake?" She kept the desperation out of her voice. No demon would respect her if she showed any sign of weakness.

"Nothing. No one's heard from him since the night he left." He scratched his beard. "I did hear something about him dumping you though."

She snorted and leaned against the bar, casting her senses out. As a Denai she could sense when someone lied—even demons. "You sure about that?"

"Yeah, and if you want me to keep looking I expect payment."

Charlie glanced over at Drake's bouncer; a giant named Phil. He'd been great since Drake's disappearance and helped her with all the contacts in an effort to find Drake.

"Drake doesn't pay you, does he?" asked Kaz, hopping onto a bar stool. "You trade info, right?"

"Drake keeps the demons in this city—hell, this country—in order. You haven't taken his place, little witch."

Charlie winced. Drake always called her "little witch." No one got to call her that but him. "How about you carry on searching and I don't tell everyone you're a snitch?" she offered. "For the record, I'm his mate. He'd never dump me."

Val scowled, gulped down the rest of his drink. "Maybe you should accept the fact he might not want to come back or be found."

"He has obligations here too." *Plus, I need him here. I never got the chance to tell him how I really feel about him.*

Val shimmered out.

Charlie slumped back against the bar.

"It's okay, don't give up." Kaz touched her shoulder. "Drake wouldn't have left you without good reason."

"Yeah, then why did he break up with me?"

"Relax, McCray, the boss is crazy about you," Phil said. The giant towered over her at over seven feet tall, with a bald head and a shiny ginger beard.

"Then where is he?" She shook her head, eyeing the alcohol behind the bar. "I know he's in trouble, I can sense it. Why won't he tell me where he is?"

"Still having dreams about him?" asked Kaz, holding out her hand so a bottle of water flew into it.

"They're not dreams, they're too vivid for that. They're more like a telepathic meeting of minds." She felt her cheeks flush.

"Have you asked him?"

"Yeah, but he tells me to stay away." Besides they didn't exactly talk much during their dreams.

Bells chimed, making her groan as she realised the Alliance was calling for her. Now she'd have to go to one of their stupid meetings again. "I'd better answer that."

"I'll meet you back at the station." Kaz gave her a quick hug. "Remember that demon wouldn't just leave you because like baldy over here said, he's crazy about you."

Yeah, so crazy he left me.

Kaz headed back to the station.

"Phil, is there anyone else I can talk to?" Charlie asked. "I don't care who they are or what they might be involved in. I need to find him."

Phil's brow creased. "There's only one contact you haven't met yet and that's Silas. He is a slippery bugger—the boss wouldn't be happy if you talk to him," he told her. "Silas comes with a price. A steep one too."

"Good, contact him for me. I have a meeting to get to. I'll swing by later." Charlie him a smile. "Thanks for helping with everything."

Phil shrugged. "You're his life mate. That makes you the boss too. Still, Silas is—"

"I've handled worse believe me."

Charlie headed for the Alliance's meeting hall. The Alliance was made up of different leaders of Magickind, their sole purpose was to ensure law and justice to all Magickind.

Charlie's aunt and uncle were among the leaders. Drake had worked as leader of the demon clans and Charlie had unofficially taken his place because she was half demon herself, as well as his life mate. Though, she suspected Cate had suggested she become the official replacement.

Lana, the leader of the phoenixes, scowled when Charlie walked in. "I thought we were going to discuss hiring a new demon leader?" Lana asked. With her long, lithe body and piercing grey eyes, Charlie tried not to feel jealous of the other woman for being Drake's former flame.

"We did. We agreed Charlie could remain in Drake's seat until he returns." Cate gave Lana a smile that showed too much teeth.

"She's a Division agent. That hardly makes her impartial, does it?"

Cate's sapphire eyes flashed silver. "Do you have a problem with my niece being here?"

Charlie bit back a smile when she saw Lana flinch. Even she seemed scared of the Grand Mistress.

"No, I just—do we have any news on Drake?" Lana brushed her long silvery blonde hair off her face.

Charlie knew Drake had slept with the gorgeous woman once and afterwards Lana hadn't taken his rejection well.

"That's partially why we are gathered here today," Jason answered.

Charlie sat down beside her aunt. She hated politics but at least the Alliance wasn't as political as the council.

"There's been a sudden rise in demonic crimes lately," Jason continued. "Demons fighting demons, clans—"

"Since when do we care about the affairs of demons?" asked McNabb, the Ashrali representative. "They've always fought among themselves."

"It's different now. There are reports that some demons are planning to overthrow the Akaran—the leader of all demons," said Cate.

"I thought the Akaran lived in the demon lands and hadn't stepped out in centuries?" Charlie spoke up. Since Drake's disappearance and the emergence of her own demonic powers, she'd learnt everything she could about Demonkind.

"He hasn't but there are reports that there is a war brewing between two very powerful demon clans—the Amargens and the Illuminari. Although no one seems to know much about the Illuminari or if they even exist," Jason remarked.

Charlie straightened. Drake was an Amargen demon, she'd found that out from his associates.

"Reports suggest the Akaran is either weak or losing power somehow. If the tribes start warring together it could be chaos. Not just for them, but for all Magickind," Jason said. "The last time the demons had an all-out war thousands died."

"I agree with McNabb. Unless the demons pose a real threat, I see no reason why we should get involved," Lana said, drumming her fingers on the table.

"The council and I have agreed we need to know more. I believe this sudden surge in violence may also be why Drake left us," Cate continued. "I sense they're connected. Charlie, what have you found out about so far?"

All eyes fixed on her, making Charlie flush. "Not much. Just that Drake received a message from someone. He was last seen travelling towards the Amana desert that borders Kyral. After that, I haven't been able to find anything."

"Maybe you just grew tired of you," Lana remarked, smirking.

Charlie gritted her teeth. This bitch really needed a slap. "I'm his life mate, you know the whole destined thing. You—"

"Charlie," Cate warned.

Charlie glowered at her aunt, but she shut her mouth, reminding herself Lana wasn't worth it.

"We need to know more about what's happening in Kyral," McNabb remarked. "Do we have any contacts there we can use?"

All eyes turned on Charlie once more. Drake would have known someone. "I'm friendly with his contacts, I'll see what I can find out from them," she said. "Or better yet, let me and my team go to Kyral. We can find out what's going on. We've all done undercover work before; I know we could get in there and find out what's happening."

Lana snorted. "You? Be trusted with such an important mission?" she said. "No, I don't think it's worth the risk. We need more information."

"I see no reason why Charlie isn't up to the job," Cate said, glaring at Lana. "But I have to agree, we don't have enough information to warrant you going to Kyral."

The meeting droned on but Charlie only half listened as she stared at the small map of Kyral. In the end, she still hadn't made any progress on finding where Drake had vanished.

After the meeting, she headed home to Drake's house. She'd felt like an intruder there at first, but now she felt closer to him by being there. As she walked into the living room with its plush cream carpet and silver walls, she found a wizened old man with a pointed white beard and thin straggly hair sitting on the black leather sofa.

He gave her a toothless grin. "So you're Drake's witch. You're nothing like his usual women."

Her hand went to her gun, the other drew magic. "Who the hell are you?"

"Phil said you wanted to see me. Come along, I don't have all day, little shadow walker."

She let go of her gun. "You're Silas, right?"

"Indeed. How can I be of service?"

"I need you to help me find Drake." She cast her senses out to find out what he was.

Silas shot to his feet, his eyes bleeding to black. "Didn't your mama ever teach you not to scan people without their permission?"

Charlie shrugged. "She died giving birth to me so no, she didn't. I was raised a Denai. We scan first and ask questions later."

He cringed. "Never did like Denais. Too damned powerful, the lot of you."

She snorted. "Why? Because we can sense when someone lies and make them tell the truth?" She folded her arms. "Look, can you help me find Drake or not?"

"He's your mate; why can't you sense him?"

"Because we're—never mind. Can you do it or not?" An icy feeling prickled over her skin, making her back up a step. "Hey, keep your creepy senses off me too, pal."

Silas chuckled. "You're a feisty one. I like that. Despite you being a Denai bitch, you're better than all the other bimbos he's had."

Charlie scowled. She knew she wasn't Drake's usual tall, blonde and gorgeous type. She just reached five and half feet, brunette with brown eyes and a curvy body.

"No, I can't help you." He shook his head.

"Can't or won't?" she demanded.

"Both. If Drake doesn't want to be found, I can't help you."

Charlie slumped into the leather armchair. "Look, I'm getting sick of people saying that. He wouldn't just leave me. I know him."

"Do you?" Silas arched a thin eyebrow. "I've known him almost eight thousand years and that man doesn't give away his emotions easily."

Tell me something I don't know. "You're some kind of seer, right?" Charlie said. "Find him for me. Name your price."

Silas stroked his beard. "Why do you want to find him so much?"

"Is that your price? Answering stupid questions?" Her lip curled.

His lips curved into a smile. "No, but indulge me."

"I'm his life mate." She clenched her teeth to keep control of her anger. Why did some immortals have to be so damned cryptic? Did they just do it to be annoying? Maybe they ran out of things to do after a few millennia.

"True, but you've been resistant to him for years. How he didn't claim you before now I'll never understand. It's rare for demons to find their mates at all."

If they'd sealed the bond he'd still be here with her. "I know someone has him, I need to find out who."

Silas continued to stroke his beard. "I might be able to show you something but my visions don't come with guarantees, witch."

She leaned forward. "What's your price?"

"I want the Srimtar."

How the hell did he know about that? She laughed, rising from the chair. "I don't know what you're talking about." She would never let on that she had the legendary orb. Hell, no one, not even she, knew what it could do. She wouldn't let anyone know she was its guardian.

His eyes flashed. "Denais are bad liars, witch. I know you're the guardian of the orb."

She glared at him. "Then you know I'd never give it to you."

"I don't want to keep it—just take a look."

Her brow creased. "Why?" Phil had been right; Silas was a slippery bugger.

The old man chuckled. "Just like a Denai to ask questions. Why I need to look isn't important; do you want to find your man or not?"

Charlie slumped back, sighed. *If I don't this I might not find Drake before it's too late.* She held out her hand, blue lightning crackled as the glowing orb appeared in her hand. She was meant to protect this thing even though she didn't know what its true purpose or power was. It had already proved to be a dangerous weapon when it had killed her enforcer teammates.

"You can look but I won't let go of it," she warned.

"Fine." Silas reached out, placed his hand over the orb.

Energy vibrated between them, the orb pulsing with an eerie light. Charlie gripped it harder, feeling it beginning to slip from her grasp. *No!* she thought.

Her eyes glowed azure blue as she felt her inner demon awaken. *Oh no, not again!* The last time her demon had taken control it had attacked and tried to kill people. Their hands shook as the orb trembled, turning a violent shade of red.

Her inner demon clawed her mind, demanding to take control. *Let me out,* it told her.

Not bloody likely! Charlie gritted her teeth, refusing to let it gain control of her body again.

He threatens the orb, I must protect it.

Light exploded from the Srimtar, sending Charlie and Silas crashing across the room. The orb hummed and throbbed with power leaking from it. Charlie gripped it, knowing it wouldn't harm her. "Don't say I didn't warn you," she muttered.

Silas lay there, breathing hard.

Charlie made the orb vanish, sending it back to its hidey-hole in the spirit world where it could harm no one. Scrambling up, she moved over to Silas. "Are you okay?"

The old man shot up with unnatural speed. "Well, fuck me with a lightning bolt." He laughed. "That thing has power. I see now why Drake's been so keen to keep you safe over the years. Dangerous artefact you have there, girl."

She brushed her hair off her face. "Tell me something I don't know." She held out her hand. "Come on, show me Drake now."

Silas shook his head. "No can do."

"What? I let you use the orb; you hold up your end of the deal or you'll get more than just a jolt of energy!"

His eyes narrowed. "Visions won't work on you, you never mentioned you're a shadow walker demon."

People had called her that before, she still had no idea what it meant. "Bollocks! I've had visions shown to me before by my aunt."

"Have seers been able to use their power on you since then?" Silas asked.

She bit her lip. "No," she admitted. "My demon side doesn't react well to it." Hell, she didn't understand her demon powers, much less how to control them.

"Well, well. I haven't met one of your kind in a millennia, but then you're a slippery lot, aren't you?"

"One of my what?" Charlie demanded. "What am I?"

Silas turned to leave. "I've answered enough for one night. Be seeing you."

"Hey, you're not leaving until you show me a damned vision. You've got to give me something," she said, grabbing his arm. "Please, I can't lose him."

Silas rubbed his beard. "I can sense he's being held somewhere. He was on his way to Kyral, then he vanished."

She groaned. "Thanks for nothing."

"You'll find him, I can sense that, but he might not be the same man he was when he left."

Silas took her hand, and to her horror, kissed it. "Pleasure meeting you, little shadow walker. Never thought Drake would find a mate with power to match his."

He vanished in a blur of light.

Charlie slumped onto Drake's bed. Another dead end. She called for the orb and looked at the glowing Srimtar, feeling its energy pulsing like a heartbeat between her fingers. It had shown her Drake would leave, why couldn't it show her where he was now?

"Show me Drake," she murmured. The orb flickered then darkened again to nothing. "Come on, I know you can show bits and pieces of the future. Show me Drake now."

Still nothing.

She threw it on the bedside table in disgust. "Worthless thing. I don't know why so many people want to possess you." She sent it back to the spirit world before grabbing one of Drake's shirts. Pathetic, but the only way she could sleep was by clutching it. It smelt like him and brought a little comfort.

CHAPTER 2

Charlie blinked, finding herself back in a strange room where the walls were made of purple mist and the floor looked like glass. Her own little place in the spirit world where she could retreat to, where Drake would appear in dreams. She could come and go there both in dreams and physically. But she hadn't seen him there in over two nights now which made her even more worried. "Drake, where are you?" She felt the presence behind her and spun around to see him standing there. "Oh, thank the goddess!" She threw her arms around him, hugging him tight.

"I missed you, little witch." Drake ran a hand through her hair, holding her like he never wanted to let go. "What's wrong? I felt your panic." He leaned down to kiss her but Charlie pulled back.

"Don't. You're not gonna distract me with kisses this time." She put her hands on her hips. "Tell me where you are. Right now."

Drake shook his head. "We've been through this, Charlotte. I won't put you in danger."

She laughed. "I'm already in danger. Myles still has a bounty on my head and wants the Srimtar. I'm an enforcer; danger comes with the territory," she snapped. "What won't you tell me?" She saw his form flicker. "Goddess, your growing weaker, aren't you?"

He nodded. "This might be the last time we see each other. I'd rather not waste it by arguing."

Charlie's eyes flashed. "Don't be stupid, of course we'll see each other again. Come on, tell truth. I never believed that crappy story you gave me. Things were going great between us, then you just left.

Why?"

Drake slumped onto the sofa, made from the same misty material and ran a hand through his short black hair. "I had to go to Kyral to see my brother." His skin looked paler than usual and there were black circles under his eyes.

Charlie tried not to wince at his haggard appearance. "I know that, but why did you pretend to break up with me?"

His dark gaze met hers. "Because I can't drag you into it. My brother is the Akaran," he told her. "I was on my way home when—"

"When what?" Charlie demanded.

His form started to flicker again. Charlie grabbed him, crushing her mouth to his. He returned the kiss with just as much hunger.

"You can't go." She clutched his shirt then wrapped her arms around his neck, the other hand caressing his face. "I won't let you. Not this time."

"You know I'd stay if I could. That's why I want to enjoy whatever time I have left with you."

She pulled away. "You sound like you're just giving up. Don't you want to be with me?"

"More than you'll ever know."

"Then why the fuck won't you tell me where you are?"

"Charlie—" Drake's body flickered in and out of existence.

Charlie grabbed onto him, feeling something yank her out of the misty room. She blinked, suddenly surrounded by darkness, surprised to find herself back in the physical world. The only light came from a machine that buzzed and whirred in the corner. Hooked up to it was a man, his hair fell over his gaunt face, wires were hooked along his arms, his wrists and feet were chained in place.

Goddess, Drake! Her heart skipped a beat.

"Drake? Drake, wake up!" Charlie reached up to touch him only to have her hand pass straight through. Glancing down, she saw her feet hovering to feet off the ground. *Bloody hell! My phasing has gone to a whole new level.*

She glanced around, knowing she wouldn't have long before this connection ended. She knew she could do nothing to free Drake in her incorporeal state. But she could try and figure out where the hell they were. Maybe this was an astral projection.

She moved through the closed door into an empty hallway,

surprised she could stray so far from Drake. She hurried through, finding nothing but empty rooms. *Come on, there must be a clue here somewhere.* She passed through another wall and came face-to-face with a huge man with a shaggy red beard.

"What the hell?" He gasped when he saw her.

Damn, he can see me! "Who are you?" Charlie demanded. "Where the hell are we?"

He hit the desk; an alarm sent out a loud wailing sound.

Charlie shot back out through the wall, hurrying towards Drake. "Drake, please wake up." She reached out; her form shimmered, making contact with solid flesh for an instant.

Drake groaned, his eyes blinking open as he stared up at her. "Char—" he tried to say her name.

"It's me, I'm here. Somehow." She smiled.

"No, you—have to go."

"Listen, I'm gonna get you out of here. You have to help me." She stroked his cheek. "Do you know where we are?" The sound of running footsteps echo down the hall. "Drake, please!" Charlie begged.

"Desert—Lochlyn, he's..." He turned his head towards the closed door. "Go!"

Charlie gasped, head spinning as she found herself falling from the ceiling to the floor of Drake's bedroom. But she smiled; she finally had clues. Though, who the hell was Lochlyn?

Charlie headed inside Niara's sitting room. "GG, do you know—whoa!" She stopped dead when she saw Niara with her arms around a man, kissing him.

Niara and the stranger pulled apart. Niara's hair turned a shade of flaming red to match her cheeks. "Charlie, what you are doing here?"

She covered her face. "Losing the will to live!"

"Hello." The man said. "You must be Charlotte."

"Yeah." She gave him an awkward wave.

"Damon was just leaving." Niara squeezed his hand.

"Right." Charlie fell her cheeks burn as Damon gave her great-grandmother a quick kiss, then left with an awkward bow.

"Would you please knock in the future?" Niara hissed.

"Jeez, GG. Aren't a bit old for that?"

"I'm an immortal. Many of us have lovers over the centuries.

Don't I deserve a private life?"

"No, because you're very old and it's very gross." Charlie cringed, trying not to gag. Although an eleven-thousand-year-old immortal, Niara looked no older than thirty with her ethereal beauty of the fey, sapphire eyes and long hair that changed colour on a whim.

"Your partner is only three thousand years younger than me, and you're not even twenty-five yet."

Good point. "So who's your special friend?" Charlie asked, grinning.

"He's an old friend. We knew each other when I was young."

"Before you married a psycho?"

"Yes." Niara sighed. "What did you want?"

"I can come by later if you want Damon to come back."

"No, tell me."

Charlie told her about her dream, the strange astral travel and what she'd found. "It felt weird. It was like I phased, but different."

Niara poured some tea. "It sounds like your power is escalating."

"Escalating to what? No other medium in Denai history has ever been able to phase or pass in and out of the spirit world." She sipped the sweet tea. "Do you know anything about it or what Drake told me?"

Niara shook her head. "I'm sorry, dear. I still can't sense what your demon side is. Have you tried calling your mother's spirit again?"

Charlie scowled. "She never answers—not even when I command her to come to me."

Niara's hair turned back to its natural shade of pale blonde. "Perhaps it would be worth a visit to the Kyral Desert."

"The Alliance won't give me clearance without solid proof." She shook her head. "Silas said I'm shielded from visions. Is that true?"

"Yes, I've noticed that."

"What does it mean?"

"I can't answer that. Perhaps Helga or Cate could help. They're both far stronger seers than I am."

"Cate's already tried and Helga is a bad idea. I almost killed her last time she tried to get a vision for me." She fiddled with her silver Denai pendant. "Drake's not around to stop me this time. GG, I've got to figure out what my demon half is and how to control it too. But first I need Drake."

Niara sipped her tea. "You care for him, don't you?"

"Of course I do, more than I thought possible." She put her head in her hands. "Now I might lose the one person I could see having a future with."

"We'll find him." Niara patted her hand. "Besides, I can't see Drake giving up so easily. Go see Helga."

Charlie nodded and rose. Despite hating Helga, she'd do whatever it took to find Drake. "So what's with you and Damon?"

Niara's hair flashed red again. "Like I said, we're friends."

Charlie laughed. "Right."

A door slid open as Charlie approached Helga's tree and found the sitting area inside empty. Vine covered the gnarled walls, filling the air with the scent of fresh leaves and wood. "Helga?" Her heart raced. She found this place creepy and its owner even more so.

A quick scan of the tree revealed no sign of the crone.

Charlie retreated outside, leaves crunching under her feet. She slumped down onto a tree stump and closed her eyes, trying to shimmer or phase to the place she'd seen Drake. Nothing. She buried her head in her hands.

"Giving up, are you, girl?" a voice rasped.

Charlie looked up and sniffed when she saw the hunched old woman with her straggly grey hair, wrinkled face and sharp eagle eyes. "No. Niara told me to come see you," she replied. "Listen, I'm sorry about what happened the last time I was here. It wasn't me—it was something else."

"Yes, your demon side. So yes, it was you."

Charlie folded her arms. "It's not like I can control it. I don't even know what it is." She brushed her hair off her face. "Can you help me find Drake?"

Helga cackled, leaning on her walking stick. "I won't help you again."

"You don't have to, and I'm pretty sure that was because you were trying to see the Srimtar."

Damn it, what would she have to do to convince Helga to help her? She couldn't make a deal like she'd done with Silas.

"Why should I help you?" Helga asked, shoving leaves out of her path with her stick.

"Because you have nothing better to do. Plus you've got to admit your kind of curious about what I am, aren't you?" she asked. "As long as you don't ask to use my orb."

"Definitely a McCray and, no I'd rather steer clear of that damned orb." She shuddered and motioned for Charlie to follow. "Come."

Charlie ducked inside, breathing in the heady scent of fresh leaves falling.

Helga slumped into her high-backed chair. "I can't offer any guarantees."

"I don't expect any."

Helga's eyes turned white as she called on her sight.

Charlie waited, telling her demon self to behave.

Helga shook her head. "I see conflicting images."

She sighed. "Thanks for trying."

"I do sense you'll find answers in Kyral—but I warn you, you might learn more than you bargained for."

Kyral it is then. Now she just had to convince the others to let her go.

CHAPTER 3

Drake slumped onto the cold steel bunk, exhaustion washing over him. The stench of sweat and waste-filled the tiny space but he ignored it. His arms and chest ached from being stabbed by needles, from the machine meant to drain his powers. Despite his body's ability to regenerate, the constant strain had taken its toll. He was becoming weaker and didn't know how much more he could take. Still, draining his energy wouldn't give them the power they sought. Closing his eyes, he willed his body to heal, but he needed sustenance for that. Lochlyn wouldn't keep him alive much longer.

He had to get out of there but somehow Lochlyn had managed to block his powers and attempts of escape. Not much could do that. He hadn't survived over eight thousand years by power alone. He'd learnt how to stay alive and shield himself from his enemies. Nor could he figure out what Lochlyn had been using.

Drake's thoughts drifted to Charlie again. Gods, he hoped she stayed safe. Despite their dream encounters, he'd ended their relationship, pretending like she meant nothing to him. He still worried about her, but knew he had to find a way out of there and get to his brother and find out why Daron had called him home after all these centuries. But first he had to see Charlie, apologise and try to win her back. She was the only thing that kept him alive here. Not that this was the worst kind of hell he'd been in. He'd been through worse, much worse.

Drake wondered if hearing Charlie's voice the night before had been real. Strange, he felt like she'd been there with him. *Maybe I am losing my mind.* He heard the outer door creak open, signalling the guard bringing him food and water.

He sat up, filling a wave of dizziness. He needed more than a few scraps of bread could offer. Only energy could replenish him now.

The guard unlocked the door, static flashing over the bars. The guard was a low-level demon with a mop of dark hair, grey eyes and a skinny figure. Young too, with little power. He dropped the plate and plastic tube on the floor.

Drake shot to his feet, grabbed the man by the throat. The guard gasped, his eyes widening. He pulled out an agron, a small metal rod that caused intense pain. Drake knocked the weapon aside. His eyes turned black as he squeezed the demon's throat, snapping his neck. Light shot from the demon as his body exploded. Drake took a deep breath, feeling a surge of energy pass through him, giving him temporary strength.

Charlotte, he thought as he closed his eyes.

The room around him faded as he reappeared inside another room. His home office with its huge desk made from dryad oak covered in maps and files. Charlie had her head slumped on the desk.

She was still here in his house.

"Charlotte?" Gods, he wanted to reach out and put arms around her, show her just how much he missed her. But he had little time left. "Wake up, little witch."

Charlie looked up, eyes still half-closed. "Drake." She bolted up. "Goddess, you're here. Am I dreaming again?"

"No, listen—"

She wrapped her arms around him, burying her face against his chest.

He blinked, surprised when she made contact with solid flesh. He pulled her closer, breathing in her familiar citrus scent. "We don't have much time. I am—"

She pulled his head down to capture his mouth in a rough and hungry kiss. He groaned, fingers tangling in her hair he returned the kiss. He missed the taste and feel of her, but then he pulled back. He couldn't waste time.

"What's wrong?" Charlie asked, disappointment showing in her eyes.

"No time; I'm not really here. I came to tell you where I am."

"Finally, about time you put your damned pride aside and came to me for help." She breathed, hands on hips. "Where are you?"

"I don't know the exact location but—argh, not enough time." He felt the tug, knew he'd soon be dragged back to his body.

Charlie grabbed his hands, he felt energy tingle against his skin as she held his spirit in place. "No, you can't leave. I can lock your spirit here if I have to."

His lips curved at his determined little witch. "My body is too weak to survive that."

She gripped his hands tighter. "Maybe I could shimmer to you. I came there last night—though I'm not sure how. I can't lose you again."

"You won't. The only way to show you where I am is through my memories. I should be able to do that through our link." He stared into her warm brown eyes, watching them shift colour from her emotions. "Are you ready?"

Charlie nodded.

"Good, because you have to initiate it. I'm too weak."

"How?" Her brow creased.

Drake touched her cheek. "Close your eyes."

She did so.

"Good, feel our link with your mind then open yourself up to it." Drake felt her presence at the edge of his senses. He closed his own eyes and let the memories drag them both in.

Drake blinked as he found himself at the edge of the border between Setara and the Kyral desert where he had stood the last time he'd been free. The sun beat down on him, its ray making the sand shine like tiny diamonds. His heart ached at the memory of leaving Charlie behind.

Charlie appeared beside him. "Nice to know I wasn't the only one hurting."

Drake frowned. "How are you here? I only meant to show you."

"We're linked, remember, Vlad?" She smiled despite her scowl. "When this is all over, remind me to kick your arse. You should never have left me behind."

"I needed to keep you safe from that."

"Drake, we're partners. We need to trust each other if we ever gonna have a future together."

"I know that now." He sighed. This wasn't the time to talk. He walked into the desert and felt a sharp pain on the back of his skull.

Fire flared in his palms, he lashed out, sending flames shooting in all directions.

A scream echoed as someone blew up.

Drake spun around, seeing a demon with a bright red beard. Lochlyn.

"That's the guy I saw last night," Charlie gasped.

"It's been a long time, Drakon." Lochlyn grinned.

"Why are you here?" Drake growled.

"Because you've harboured your gift long enough. It's time for it to be passed on to a new host." Lochlyn raised his hand, an emerald flashing on his finger.

Drake sank to his knees as an invisible force took hold. His limbs felt like dead weight; his power slipped from his grasp.

"What is that thing?" Charlie asked.

"An old artefact. It's called the Jewel of Antat. It can control any demon—even me to an extent," he told her. "Lochlyn has been using it, trying to get me to relinquish my powers."

"Why?"

Drake looked away, feeling the familiar shame but knew he had to tell her the truth. If he didn't, they'd never have a future together. "I'm the real Akaran," he admitted.

Charlie fell silent then nodded. "I suspected that."

Not the reaction he'd expected. He'd expected shock, horror, disgust at his omission of being the leader of all demons. "I…"

"I don't care what you are, Drake. You're my life mate." She took his hand. "All that matters is you come back to me."

The desert flashed by as he was dragged away and ended up back in a cell. "This is all I remember about how I got here," he told her. A stabbing pain made him clutch his head. The images around him blurred as his body started pulling his spirit back.

"No." Charlie grabbed his hands again.

"Charlie, I have to go." He gasped.

"No, you need to show me more. There has to be something else."

Drake pulled her into his arms. "If anything happens to me, I need you to know you're the only thing in this world I care about."

She touched his cheek. "Don't talk like that," she snapped. "We'll get through this. We've survived worse."

He smiled, clutched her hand. In all his eight thousand years no one had made him feel anything so deeply.

Drake allowed himself to be dragged back. He gasped as he sank to his knees, the energy surge faded. The cell door still lay open. He had a way out.

Scrambling up, he staggered out into the passageway, the light from the crystal torches stinging his eyes. He reached the power and try to shimmer but failed. The wards around the building were too strong for him to pass through in his weakened state. He leant against the wall for support to guide his way.

Drake? Charlie's voice at the edge of his mind. *Drake, answer me, please.*

Charlotte. He blinked, surprised at feeling her there.

Are you alright?

I'm—alive. For now. He winced as more pain followed. The connection cost him more energy. *I can't talk now, love.* He moved down the passage, turned left instead of right. That was where they had dragged him for the law the rounds of pain and torture.

I can see what you see, Charlie remarked. *I knew how weak you are, so don't talk. Just keep moving. I'm on my way.*

How? You don't know where I am—neither do I for that matter. He looked around, unsure where to go next and doubted he could take down a bunch of guards if they appeared.

I know you were in the desert, where you last vanished. I'll go from there.

Drake passed into another corridor and another two passageways lay beyond. Any could lead him to potential danger.

Left again, Charlie said.

How do you know? Drake frowned.

Just a guess. We need to reconsider that bond thing when this is over.

He stopped dead. *You'd bond with me? You've never wanted that.*

Keep moving, you big lug. You're wasting energy. If we were bonded, maybe you wouldn't be in the mess.

Drake only grinned like an idiot. The thought gave him strength. He opened a door and found a room stacked with boxes.

You need to find a way out. Keep moving, she said.

Drake chuckled. He loved her bossiness. The other door revealed another empty room full of boxes. He ducked inside and pulled open one of the boxes to search for a possible weapon. It was full of explosives.

Wow, that's a lot, said Charlie. *But don't get any ideas. Blowing yourself up isn't an option.*

Fire can't hurt me.

Given how weak you are right now, it might. Don't cause yourself any unnecessary harm—that's the number one in the life mates' rulebook.

There's a book? He moved through the room, looking for a potential weapon but found none.

Yeah, I'm writing it. What else do you see?

Drake glanced around, spotting a barred window. He gripped the bars made from reinforced Silveron. They wouldn't break without some serious magical force. He peered outside, seeing miles of desert outside.

"Where do you think you're going?" Lochlyn appeared in the doorway with a huge grin on his face.

Drake, run! Charlie's panic made his own heart beat faster.

Where? He glanced around. There was no way out.

Shimmer to me—we're connected. Mates can teleport to each other no matter where they are.

We're not bonded, Drake reminded her.

Wait, why can't you bond with me now? We could sense each other and—

"You can't have it," Drake said and straightened. "You should know by now I'll never relinquish my power."

"I thought of that. That's why I sent men to go after that witch of yours. Once I have her, you'll have no choice." Lochlyn raised his hand.

Drake doubled over as pain tore through him. *Charlie, wherever you are, go to my safe. Get the ring from inside it.*

His last thought was of her.

CHAPTER 4

Charlie let out a scream of frustration as her connection to Drake ended. She scrambled up, stuffing clothes and gear into a small holdall. Drake needed her now. She had to reach him before she lost him. Grabbing her phone, she called Kaz. "Are you and Nigel ready to leave?"

"No, we were working on tracking down some leads," Kaz replied.

"I know where Drake is. I need to leave now." She hitched her bag over her shoulder, hurried back to Drake's office and dialled the code when she found the safe.

"We can be ready in twenty minutes," Kaz told her.

"We don't have that long." Charlie pulled out a small wooden box, shoved into her bag.

"Be there in five then. Are we teleporting or taking the car?" A banging sound echoed in the background as Kaz moved.

Charlie stopped as she shoved in some protein bars and tubes of water. She doubted they could carry all their gear and weapons by themselves and they'd need to make a quick getaway. Her car was too small and ill-equipped to cope with the desert. "Drake has a garage full of cars—I'll find something. Hurry!"

Charlie rushed down to the lower level of the house where Drake kept an entire fleet of cars. She still felt surprised when the security system let her wander all over the mansion.

Cars of every make and model and size sprawled through the underground basement. They all gleamed as if they'd just rolled off a showroom floor. It put even her family's collection to shame. Cars occupied one level, on the next were transpos, a minibus and even a mini copter.

She let out a low whistle. *My demon likes his tech.* She scanned the different vehicles. "Goddess, it could hours to find something in here." She went over to the house screen that controlled the mansion's security and computer systems.

"Hello, little witch," a too pleasant voice chirped as the system came online. "How may I help you?"

She tried not to grit her teeth at its perkiness. Machines shouldn't sound so damn happy. "Now that's just plain weird. Are there any jeeps in this maze?" Charlie scowled at the screen.

"Indeed, little witch. What make, model..."

"Just a jeep that can withstand a desert and has weapon capabilities," she snapped, tapping her foot.

A sleek 4x4 slid out in front of her.

"Nice." She loaded her bag, weapons and gear inside the boot, then pressed the start button. The engine purred to life as she guided it outside. Kaz and Nigel appeared with bags and packs.

"Let's move."

Charlie ordered the car to teleport to the desert to the spot where Drake had been taken and stopped the car.

"Wow, this car is gorgeous," Kaz breathed.

Nigel sat in the back seat, staring at one of the mini comp screens. "God, have you seen this system? It's mag!"

"Kaz, take over. I need to concentrate." Charlie phased out, allowing Kaz to slid over into the driving seat. Charlie shifted onto the other seat, pulled out the Srimtar. "Come one, show me Drake." The orb flashed then clouded over with a veil of mist. Nothing. Damn it, she'd sensed him before. *Drake?* She reached out to him with her mind, only to be greeted by silence. "Nige, you're a shifter, can you smell anything?"

Nigel got out of the car and moved around in a small circle. "Char, it's been over a month. There are too many smells out here for me to track anything."

"Damn it, I've got to get to him." Her hands clenched into fists.

"How'd you connect with him earlier?" Kaz asked.

Charlie shook her head. "I didn't. He connected with me—like in astral form. He killed a guard and took his energy. They'll kill him too if we don't get there in time."

"If he's connected with you, why can't you do the same?"

Three men approached dressed in black uniforms, surrounding the jeep.

"Oh boy." Kaz pulled out her gun.

"Car, shield," Charlie ordered. A glowing blue bubble formed around the vehicle. All three demons started hurling energy balls at them.

"Who are they guys?" Nigel tapped away on the mini comp.

"They look like Goodridge's guys. Damn, I wondered when they'd come after me again."

Goodridge was a gang leader responsible for killing her former enforcer teammates when her team had unknowingly tried to bust him as he tried to get a hold of the Srimtar. He'd had a price on her head and had been gunning for her ever since.

They all rolled their windows down and returned fire, both with bullets and rounds of static. Energy and bullets zipped through the air, batting against the car's shield. Charlie saw the energy level had already gone down to half.

Four more demons appeared. They looked different from the others; Charlie guessed they were Lochlyn's men.

"We're sitting ducks here!" Kaz yelled over the blasts of gunfire and exploding energy.

Charlie leapt from the car. "I'll draw their fire!" She dropped and rolled, shooting the first demon in the chest, then sending a second hurtling into one of Lochlyn's guys. Fireballs came at her. The ground swallowed her up as she phased out, grains of darkness whirled around her, passing straight through her incorporeal form.

Kaz and Nigel jumped from the jeep, returning fire.

Charlie grabbed the feet of two demons, pulled them down into the ground too, then leapt at and punched another in the face. Four down, three to go. One of the demons grabbed her from behind, she elbowed him in the gut then faded away.

Srimtar, she thought and the glowing orb flew into her hand. "Now I think we all know what this thing is so I'd back the hell off if I were you."

Goodridge's lead demon laughed. "You can't hurt us with that, witch. Our master cast a spell to protect us from it."

Charlie snorted. "You're bluffing."

"Am I?" he asked. "We know the power of the Srimtar better than you do."

"I'm its guardian. You can't and won't take it from me." Charlie felt her inner demon clawing at the edge of her mind, itching to get out.

Let me have control, it said.

Not flipping likely! I— Charlie gasped as her inner demon took hold. Her eyes flashed a bright blue and the Srimtar hummed with power. A blast of blue lightning shot from her hand. The other demon exploded in a fiery blast.

She spotted Lochlyn's only remaining demon as he started to shimmer away. *No!* Charlie screamed. *He is our only lead to finding Drake, stop him!* She raised her hand, energy reverberating through the air like thunder without sound. *Wow, I can compel demons—when did that happen?*

Charlie gasped as she regained control of her body again. "Listen up, you're going to take us to Lochlyn right now," she ordered. "Get in the car." The demon blinked, dazed and nodded as he climbed into the jeep.

"Kaz, let's move."

CHAPTER 5

Drake groaned as two guards pulled him into the interrogation room. One shoved and bound him to the chair whilst the other pulled out the machine that drained his powers. He wanted to put up a fight but his body felt too drained.

"Not yet," Lochlyn snapped. "He killed one of my men, punish him."

The guards held him down on the floor while they punched and kicked him.

Drake closed his eyes. He'd become numb to all of it. Hell, he suffered far worse than this in the past. They continue to punch, hit and kick at his head and torso. His head spun, his stomach recoiled, but he ignored it.

Where was Charlie? He missed the feel of her presence at the edge of his mind. She'd vanished after their connection had ended. At least he'd seen her again. He focused on that.

Another jarring pain almost broke him out of his thoughts as he focused on the memory of her. They stabbed him. He felt the cold steel of the knife ripped through his flesh again.

Drake gritted his teeth, moved past the pain, let memory drag him in. His thoughts drifted from Charlie to another time.

He stood outside on the steps of his family's castle in the heart of Kyral. Its great stone walls glistened like gold rising out of the desert in the morning sun. He smiled. He'd been happy here with his parents and his two siblings.

A scream sent a chill down his spine.

He ran inside, hurrying into the living room and found his mother, her beautiful dark hair matted with blood. Her cold eyes stared up at him, empty, almost accusing.

"Mama," he gasped.

His father lay feet from her, blood gurgling from his mouth. "Drakon…"

Drake grabbed his father's big hand. "No, Papa," he cried in Demonish. "You can't die, you can't leave me."

Take my power, his father told him.

Drake shook his head, tears spilling down his cheeks. He was only twenty. He couldn't lead their people, he wouldn't.

Daron and Arya, keep them safe, his father said before his hand went limp in Drake's.

Arya. Gods, where was his little sister? He dropped his father's hand, his mind on finding both his brother and sister. "Daron? Arya?" he called. "Answer me!"

Drake raced through each room, finding guards either dead or dying, but he left them there. Their bodies were covered in burns as if they'd been hit by some kind of blast. All that mattered was finding his sister. Who had done this? What had done this?

He called for his siblings, flinging open doors as he ran. When he reached his sister's room, he gasped when he saw her standing by the window. Her back to him. "Arya, something's happened—"

"Drake," she whispered.

He ran over, catching her as she fell. She'd been hit too. No, not her. Not his sweet little sister with her mop of dark curly hair and ice-blue eyes that sparkled when she laughed. "No!" he screamed. "Sister, tell me who did this." He cradled her in his arms.

"Didn't see, no one there. Hidden in shadows," she rasped. "Drake, you must listen."

"I'll get you to a healer. You won't die, do you hear me?"

"Drake." She clutched his arm. "I'm dying. Soon I will pass from this world."

"I'll find whoever did this, kill them and everyone whoever knew them. I don't care how long it takes," Drake vowed, tears stinging his eyes.

"No—vengeance. You must find—your mate. She's the light to the darkness. Find her," she said. "Never stop. It will take many

125

centuries but you'll find her when you least expect." She let out one last rasping breath. "Witch who walks in shadow."

"No, you can't die!" Drake sobbed against her shoulder, feeling his heart break. A thick mist filled the room, crackling with lightning. Drake shot up, letting go of his sister as he backed away. "No!" he screamed. "Stay back. I don't want you. I refuse!"

He ran from the room but the mist followed, wrapping around him like a cloak. Lightning flashed, sending a thousand volts of electricity surging through his body. Fire glowed all over him as pain shot through every nerve ending. His eyes turned black as the power of the Akaran took hold. Drake blinked, feeling stronger, more powerful than he'd ever felt.

"Drake?" Daron appeared in the doorway. "By the hells, what have you done?"

Drake looked down at his sister's lifeless form. "I didn't do anything." His voice sounded harsher than before. Gone was the boy, now a man stood in his place.

"You did this, you murdered our family." Daron's blue eyes, the same as their mother's, stared at him full of accusation.

"No!" Drake growled and fire formed in his hand. "I'd never do that. Brother, we only have each other now." His hand clenched into a fist, snuffing out the flames.

"You're not my brother; you're a murderer. Get out and don't ever come back." Daron raised his hand, a jewel of Amit flashed as an invisible blast of power sent Drake hurtling across the room.

He winced as pain tore through him, both from the past and present as the knife cut into him, needles stabbed into his arms, trying to pull away what little power he had left.

"Get up, Drakon." His father's voice boomed. "The Akaran doesn't cower like a dog. You are the leader of all demons now. You fight, not cower." He'd heard those words when he'd run away from his home without looking back.

He blinked, the memory faded as he found himself back, imprisoned and powerless

"Ready to give up your power now?" Lochlyn's voice echoed through the blackness.

He looked up through blurred eyes as Lochlyn sneered down at him. "You're dying, Drake. You won't last more than a couple of hours," the other demon said. "Why not die like a true demon with dignity. Give me your power, make me the Akaran."

"Power must be earned," he muttered.

His father had always said that, but what had Drake done to deserve any? He'd watched his family die then ran away from his true home and the people he was meant to lead.

Blackness took him under again and back into memory.

Drake walked through the desert, the sun burned his skin like the very fires of hell and glistened like a million diamonds. He'd never travelled this far from Kyral before, but he knew he couldn't go back. Not until he found those responsible for killing his family. He'd prove to Daron his innocence. They had never been close but it pained him to think his brother thought him capable of such a thing. Drake had loved his mother, his sweet little sister, even his ruthless father and jealous brother. He sank to his knees, weak from hunger and exhaustion. What good was this power if it couldn't save him?

He collapsed, feeling the heat of the sand burn through him as he lay there, the sun burning like a golden orb above him. He'd die here but his new immortality would revive him. He wanted to die, to be with his family again. To hear his mother's songs and Arya's gentle laugh.

"One who walks in shadow." Arya's voice echoed in his ears. "Your mate. You must never stop looking for her."

What mate? Demons rarely ever found their life mates; many went mad then had to be put down. *I don't care,* he thought. *I just want to die here.*

"Would you leave your mate alone in the world, Drakon?" Arya asked inside his head. "She needs you as much as you need her."

Strange he could almost feel her there with him yet he saw nothing. Drake blinked, pulled himself up and summoned power. *I need help. Send someone to help me.*

Nothing happened.

He tried again.

This time an old man with a bald head and a long pointed white beard appeared. He cackled, showing sharp pointed teeth, some missing in places. "You look too young to be the Akaran, boy."

Drake frowned, wondering if his new power had failed, but in truth, he had no idea who to ask for assistance. All demons had no choice but to answer the Akaran when he needed them so he guessed he had to trust his unwanted power knew best. "I need help. You must assist me."

The old man laughed again. "Do I now? And how will I do that?"

Drake frowned. He needed a place to stay, food, water. But where would a demon on the run hide? Daron had said he was the Akaran now and if people knew he'd lied Daron would tell everyone Drake was a killer. Where could he go?

He couldn't be around his own kind, not with his unpredictable powers. He remembered one of his mother's stories of a beautiful woman called the Serenity who'd come and brought some of the Magickind races together. The Order she'd called it.

"I—I want you to take me to Elaris to the Serenity," he said. "I command you."

The man gave a toothy grin. "Why would the Akaran want to see the Serenity? The other races are no friend to Demonkind. They'll kill you."

Drake shook his head. No, he didn't believe that. The Serenity was said to be kind and just. He had to see her, beg for her help.

"Now," he ordered.

Drake blinked as the memory faded. He thought he felt Charlie's presence. *Gods, let me see her again.* He watched the screen, saw his energy drain away and felt blood dripping from the numerous wounds in his chest. "You haven't won, Lochlyn," he hissed. "My power's mine and it will die with me."

The echo of gunfire sounded from somewhere close by.

Drake frowned and wondered if he'd started hallucinating, but then he felt her presence. Charlotte. His lips curved into a smile. Drake reached for the power. *I am power. I am the Akaran.* He gritted his teeth, pulled his hands free from his bonds.

"Impossible!" Lochlyn raised his hand, the gem on his ring flashing.

Drake fell to his knees in force, too weak to fight. He would die here, but he'd be damned if he went before he saw his witch one last time.

The door flew off its hinges, clattering to the floor as one of the guards fell on top of it.

Charlie bounded in, gun raised.

"You!" Lochlyn raised his hand, the gem flashed as its power extended. She gasped, gun falling from her grasp as she was forced to her knees.

No, Drake thought, forcing himself up. "Stop," he snarled, eyes burning with fire. It broke Lochlyn's hold.

Charlie spun into a roundhouse kick, knocking him backwards and delivered another kick to his head. "Guard, help Drake," she yelled.

To his amazement, the guard caught hold of him. Drake grabbed the man's arm, making him scream as Drake took his power. The guard vanished in a burst of flame. "The ring, Charlie. Break the ring!"

Charlie and Lochlyn blocked, hit and blasted each other. The room vibrated from the force of their fight. Drake hated standing by helpless but Lochlyn's control of the ring still forced him to stay back.

Charlie's body blurred as she phased, gripped the ring and smashed it.

"No!" Lochlyn screamed.

She dodged a fireball, then grabbed the demon by the throat. Her eyes turned black as she unleashed her touch, thunder without sound shook the air. "Tell me who sent you to kidnap him," she said.

"I don't know. I never saw his face. He gave me money—said there would be more once I took his powers," Lochlyn murmured.

Drake sagged against Charlie as she wrapped her arms around him.

"Goddess, you're bleeding. Come on, let's get out of this awful place." She put an arm under his shoulder to support him.

Drake moved away from her and caught hold of Lochlyn, watching the other demon's eyes widen in shock as Drake pulled magic from him. Lochlyn's body burst into flame too. He glanced at Charlie, expected to see disgust on her face. "I'm sorry you had to see that."

She shrugged and hugged him. "You beat me to it."

He let out a hiss of pain but didn't care. It felt so good having her back in his arms. "The energy won't sustain me for long."

She wrapped an arm around his waist. Light blurred around them as she shimmered outside. Kaz and Nigel appeared.

"Jeez, you look like hell," Kaz remarked. "What did they do?"

"Nothing I can't handle." Drake grimaced, knowing he could no longer hide the pain or weakness.

"Nice to see you again, mate." Nigel put a shoulder under his arm and helped Charlie to get him into the back seat of the vehicle.

His vehicle.

"Kaz, program the car to take us straight back to Setara City." Charlie rummaged around, grabbed a med-kit. "Nigel, help me bandage up those wounds."

"No!" Drake gritted his teeth when she pressed a cloth to his stomach. "I need to go to Kyral."

"You're in no fit state to go anywhere. You need time to heal and recover," Charlie insisted, eyes flashing. "We're going to Setara."

Kaz glanced between them, unsure what to do.

"I still run Division—I still have rank," Drake said.

Charlie snorted, rolling her eyes. "Now you choose to pull rank, unbelievable!"

Drake shoved Nigel away and sat bolt upright. "Charlie, I will get to Kyral one way or another. Are you coming with me or not?"

Charlie bared her teeth. "Of course I am, I'll be damned if I let you leave me again."

"Good, my body just needs time to heal—I won't die." He slumped back against the seat, sinking into unconsciousness as he gave into oblivion.

CHAPTER 6

Charlie scowled, wrapping up the last of the bandages. "Guess we're going to Kyral. Bloody stubborn demon!" she said, glaring at Drake. "We're making a pitstop first though. Are there any other towns or villages or civilisation nearby?"

Kaz glanced at the map on the car's screen, pulling up the local areas. "There's a small town about fifty miles from here. It's inhabited by demons."

"Good, they should have a healer. I don't know enough about demons to know how to help him much." She bit her lip. *Maybe in all my recent study of Demonkind I should've read more about healing.*

She and Nigel bandaged and cleaned Drake's wounds the best they could while Kaz drove. Charlie watched Drake as he slept, relieved to finally have him back. It would take at least a day to get to Kyral. Neither they nor the car had enough energy to teleport there. Charlie decided teleporting would be a bad idea anyway since they had no idea what they'd be walking in to.

Darkness had fallen by the time the town came into view. Charlie breathed a sigh of relief when she saw the stone houses with their tiled roofs and latticed windows. She made sure the Srimtar had returned to its hidey-hole in the spirit. The last thing they needed was anyone trying to track that.

"Kaz, keep an eye on Drake. Nigel and I will take a look around." Charlie made sure her gun was secured beneath her jacket.

"Why aren't you taking Kaz?" Nigel asked, running a hand through his mop of blonde hair.

"You're a shifter. You can smell danger. Let's move."

They headed for a pub called the Grey Dragon. The smell of ale and stale smoke hit them as they walked inside. Dark wood covered the walls and a worn-out green carpet looked almost threadbare. Every man and woman there fell silent when Charlie approached the bar. *Guess my looks screams enforcer. Hell, it's in the blood. Can't change it.*

"Hey," she said to the massive giant who stood behind the bar. "We're looking for—"

"Get out," he barked, glowering at her. "Ain't no enforcers welcome here."

"I'm a Denai. Denais can enter any town and demand custom."

"No witches allowed here either. You ain't the GM, you have no authority. Out!" He banged his fist on the bar and pointed to the door.

"Hey, we're—" Nigel started to protest.

"We're outta here," Charlie grabbed his arm. She wanted to pull rank, demand bed, board and a healer; but instinct told her not to. It wasn't worth starting a fight with these people and drawing more unwanted attention, not even for Drake. Plus she thought he'd be okay for tonight, at least, and wouldn't have welcomed a healer.

"Why didn't you argue back?" Nigel demanded once they were outside. "Drake needs a healer."

"I know." She sighed. "I won't force my way into somewhere we're not welcome. If they found out about Drake they might attack us. There's no structured law and order in this country. It's every demon for himself." Charlie hurried back towards the jeep. There was no moon out tonight so she hoped no one would've spotted their vehicle. But still, she wanted to make a quick getaway just in case anyone from the pub tried to follow them.

"What happened?" said Kaz, straightening up and lowering her gun.

"We'll have to set up camp in the desert." Charlie climbed in next to Drake, touching his neck to make sure he was still breathing. To her relief, his pulse felt steady. She climbed into the driving seat.

"Are you serious? Drake doesn't look good." Kaz stared back towards the bar.

"We have tents and camping gear." She engaged the jeep into drive. "We'll head out again at dawn. There's another village about forty miles away. Let's go a few miles away from this place first. I didn't get a good vibe from those people."

Kaz and Nigel got to work setting up the tents which sprang up while Charlie set up a perimeter of crystals around them to warn of any unwanted visitors.

Kaz lit a small fire to brew some of their food on whilst Nigel carried Drake onto one of the makeshift camp beds.

"Why do I have to share a tent with Nigel? He snores." Kaz grumbled. "Stupid question, we know you want to jump Drake's bones."

Charlie snorted. "No chance of that happening. He's too injured."

"What was he like before that?" Kaz arched an eyebrow. "I'd kill to get my hands on that body."

Charlie shrugged, cheeks flushing. She didn't want to talk about her sex life, or lack thereof.

"Are you serious? You dated and lived together for over two months and you never—"

"Shush!" she hissed, checking to make sure Nigel hadn't heard them. "No, we didn't have sex."

"Why?"

"It's complicated."

"Again, why? Scott's out of the picture."

Charlie gritted her teeth, not wanting to think of her ex-boyfriend either. "If we sleep together our link becomes stronger. We both wanted to wait until it's the right time."

"When he's healed, make it the right time. I know how much you care about him."

"Yeah." She sighed. "I never thought I could care for a demon but that doesn't matter. He's a good man. I do know it'll be more than sex between us, I just want—"

"There's no right or wrong time for sex." Kaz grinned.

"What about you and Nigel?"

Kaz burst out laughing. "Nigel, are you joking? Gods, he's like my brother." She clutched her stomach as she tried to breathe. "No, I wanna find my own hunky demon to hook up with. I'm not ready for the life mate thing yet."

"No one's ever ready for the life mate thing—it's just something that happens."

Nigel came out of the tent. "Drake's fast asleep. I'll take the first watch."

After what was meant to be a meal of roast chicken potatoes and vegetables, Charlie settled on the makeshift bed next to Drake. She sat reading through maps of Kyral. The country looked much larger than she'd imagined, and most of it uncharted too since demons weren't big fans of mixing with the rest of Magickind.

A glance over at Drake showed him still sleeping. She pulled off one of the bandages, relieved to see it has started healing.

Putting her PDA on the floor, she snuggled closer, careful not hurt him as she wrapped an arm around his waist. Closing her eyes, she let the dream draw her in until she reappeared in her room in the spirit realm. "Drake?" She didn't know if he had the strength to find her now but she hoped he could. "Drake?"

Drake flashed him beside her.

Charlie threw herself into his arms and kissed him hard. "I missed you," she murmured against his lips.

"I missed you too." He ran a hand through her hair and hugged her again. "I can feel your anxiety."

"Can you blame me after what those bastards did?"

He shrugged. "I've been through worse, believe me. They can hurt my body but they couldn't touch my mind."

"Promise you won't leave me again. I mean it. If you want this to work between us we have to be honest with each other."

"I promise, little witch. I thought—" Drake shook his head. "I thought I had to face my past alone."

"I saw your memory of how your family died. I can't believe your brother blamed you." They sat down on a misty sofa together. "Does he still…"

"I don't know," he admitted. "I tracked down and killed every demon involved but Daron refused to see me. I still don't understand why he summoned me."

"Guess we'll find out when we get there." She clutched his hands. "I think we should seal our bond, or at least take the next step, so we have more than a telepathic link." She didn't know when the idea of being bonded had stop terrifying her but now it didn't seem to matter anymore. She wanted it more than she ever thought possible.

Drake shook his head. "I can't."

Charlie's mouth fell open. "Why not? I thought it's what you wanted," she said. "I want it too. I care about you."

Drake stroked her cheek. "I do want it, but with you possibly being in transition, I won't risk triggering your ascension."

Charlie scowled. She hadn't expected him to react like this. He'd wanted them to become bonded before; what had changed? "My ascension might not happen for months yet. The sooner I'm immortal, the better."

He laughed. "We have time, little witch."

"Good, because if you leave me again, I will kick your arse."

Drake laughed and kissed her again.

Charlie woke to cracks of light creeping through the tents closed flat. She glanced over Drake, relieved to see sleep had done him some good now he had more colour back in his cheeks and hoped he'd be healed soon. When she tried to roll over, an arm snaked around her. "Where are you going?"

"Getting up. We're still got a long way to go before we reach Kyral."

"We can stay here a little longer." His lips travelled down her neck, making her giggle.

"As fun as that would be, you're hurt and the others can hear us," she whispered. "Speaking of healing, how long before you're fully healed?"

"A few days, perhaps less. Lochlyn took a lot of energy."

Charlie leaned up on one elbow. "Do you feed on energy? I saw you drain that guard, and Lochlyn, of power."

"Not feed in the way Denais do. I can take power but I only did it because I've lost so much my own energy."

"What happens when we reach Kyral?" Charlie asked. "I have a bad feeling things are gonna change."

"Indeed they will. I don't know how Daron will react to my presence."

"He must've called you back for a reason."

Drake reached up and kissed her tenderly.

She opened her mouth to speak but Drake cut her off by putting a finger to her lips. "I'm not going back to Setara," he said.

She scowled. "I still think it'd be safer for all of us, but okay. If anyone tries to hurt you, they'll have to go through me first."

He chuckled. "I do love it when you go all warrior."

135

The sound made her smile, making her heart skip a beat. She wrapped her arms around him, reached up to kiss him.

Drake hissed in pain. "As much as I want you, I suggest we wait."

"Sorry." Charlie bit her lip as she pulled away. "Are you sure you're okay? I mean you can talk to me about what happened."

He shook his head. "I know and I don't need to. The torture hurt, but I didn't notice much of it when it happened."

She knew he'd been trained to withstand torture, but no amount of training could protect the mind from everything. "Repressing emotions isn't a good idea either," she pointed out. "You taught me that." She sat up, ran her fingers through her hair, muttered. "I look a bloody mess!"

"You look perfect, little witch."

"You're just being nice now."

"I'd never lie to you, Charlotte. Not again. I promise you that."

"I'll hold you to that." She gave him a nice quick kiss. "Even though you look like crap, you're still hot." Charlie grabbed some clean clothes from her pack.

"Charlie?"

She glanced back.

"You kept me alive there. My only concern was for you."

"Well, you better take care of my demon from now on." She wondered when she'd started to think of him as "her demon" but decided it didn't matter.

After a quick breakfast and checking Drake's wounds, they set on the road again, seeing nothing but rolling hills of golden sand stretching out before them.

"After we got turned away from that town last night, what can we expect by way of a welcome in Kyral?" asked Nigel.

Drake leaned back against his seat. "I say we should come up with a good cover story," he remarked. "Don't tell anyone you're enforcers."

Charlie snorted as the car bumped over the uneven ground, ignoring Kaz and Nigel as they started bickering in the front of the car. "We look like enforcers. The guy in the pub last night spotted it straight away."

"Pretend to be bounty hunters then. I'll be your captive. Whatever you do, don't mention you're my mate."

Her eyes narrowed. "Why not?"

"I'm the Akaran. Anyone associated with me will be seen as a weakness, especially my mate. You're still mortal, little witch, and we are not bonded," he said. "They'd see you as an easy target."

Charlie laughed. "Then I'll give them a shock."

"Please, Charlotte." He clutched her hand.

The look in his eyes made her heart ache. "Fine." She folded her arms. *That doesn't mean I have to like it.*

It's not forever. Drake kissed her hand. *I don't know who I can trust there. I need to know who my enemies are.*

I still say we should do something about the bond thing. But you're stuck with me anyway now. She grinned. *Try to get away and I'll just follow you.*

Likewise, little witch.

The day passed in a blur of desert sand and seeing the occasional cactus.

"You sure you programmed this thing right, Charlie?" Kaz grumbled, who'd now taken over the driving. "We should have seen that other town by now."

Charlie leaned over the seat and touched the screen. "We're going the right way. The town should be close by."

"What maps were you using?" Drake asked, peering at the screen.

"Ones from your office, plus Phil got me updated ones. Carry on heading east, Kaz." Charlie settled back in her seat as a chill ran over her senses. Unsure what it meant, she cast her senses out further.

"What's wrong?" Drake frowned.

She shook her head. "I feel—something." She observed the surrounding desert again. Miles of sand surrounded them with no sign of any building in sight. "Kaz, turn the shield on."

Kaz and Nigel glanced at each other. "It's not fully recharged yet," Kaz pointed out.

"Do it!" Blue light shimmered out from Charlie's bag. Damn, she'd forgotten to send the Srimtar back to its hiding place after looking at it the night before.

A burst of blue light bounced off the shield. The engine stuttered as the car stopped, dead.

Kaz and Nigel raised their weapons.

"I don't see or smell anything," said Nigel, rolling up his window.

Charlie pulled the orb from her backpack, drawing magic as she tried to open a portal to the spirit realm. Light flashed then faded with no portal forming. "What the…"

Blasts of blue lightning came at them from every direction, battering against the shield.

"I can't sense anything," Nigel said. "Where are they?"

Charlie scanned, saw only brief flashes of light.

Drake sat up, wincing. "I sense something too."

A face appeared next to Charlie's window.

"Kaz, hit the gas!" Nigel yelled.

"I can't, the engine is dead."

The face blurred into a figure that passed straight through the car, its hands made a grab for Charlie's glowing pack.

Nigel fired a shot, a bullet ripped through the air, pinging off the car.

Charlie yanked the orb out, clutching it to her chest. "You're not taking this." More figures appeared, hands reaching in through the car. Nigel's body blurred as someone yanked him through the door, dragging him onto the ground. More hands grabbed Kaz and Drake, pulling them from the car. "Charlie, what do we do?" Kaz cried.

Charlie glanced around, bewildered. She'd never seen any Magickind who could pass through solid matter—except herself. How could she fight them? They weren't spirits, that much she could tell.

She drew in a breath, phased, shot out the car, about to fling the orb back into the spirit realm, then stopped. What if these strange things could pass into the spirit realm too?

Drake hurled a fireball at his assailants, Kaz fired both this kinetic and gunshots. Nigel shifted into his black panther form, snarling at them and trying to attack the invaders.

Another glowing figure came at Charlie. She dodged it, raised her hand to force a portal open. She felt her magic tearing through the fabric of the world as a glowing portal formed. She shoved the orb inside, letting out a breath as it vanished.

It didn't stop their attackers.

Drake, do something! she cried as hands locked around her.

I can't, I can't grab onto them long enough, he replied.

She phased again and kicked one in the stomach, surprised when the figure fell backwards, becoming the solid form of a man with blue tattoos covering half his face and most of his arms and upper torso. His eyes widened in shock.

"What are you?" Charlie demanded. "Tell Myles he's not getting my orb."

Both the man and the glowing figures all vanished in a blur of light.

CHAPTER 7

Drake scrambled back into the car, wincing from his aching wounds.

"What the fuck were they?" Nigel asked after he shifted back into human form.

"God only knows," Kaz muttered. "Why couldn't you scent what they are?" She grumbled, glaring at Nigel. "Oh, forgot you're a lousy shifter."

Nigel shook his head. "I couldn't smell anything from them—which is weird. All Magickind have a particular kind of scent."

Drake felt something wet and saw blood seeping through his shirt. "Ah, damn!"

"I thought you were healing?" Charlie wrapped an arm around him.

"The fall must've reopened my wounds." He slumped into the backseat, wincing from the throbbing pain. Seeing the pulse at Charlie's throat, he felt the magic flowing through her veins, making him want to take it. Gods, he hadn't needed to feed on magic since he was a lad. After he'd become the Akaran, he'd had no need for it. Had Lochlyn drained him that much?

Kaz and Nigel got to work on the car whilst Charlie re-bandaged his wounds. "Do you know what those things were?" Charlie asked, pulling out another bandage.

Drake frowned. They reminded him of something, but it was impossible. He'd wiped out that race off the face of the earth. "They reminded me of another Demonkind but they're extinct," he told her.

"Their powers seemed like mine. I've never met anyone he could phase before." Charlie covered over the wound, making sure it stuck and stemmed the flow of blood. "Do you think they're like me?"

Drake shook his head. "No, I'm not sure what they were."

"It's weird, I don't think they were trying to hurt us," Nigel said, his head peering underneath the bonnet.

"Yeah, right!" Kaz snorted. "Can you fix this?"

"Let me work, woman," Nigel muttered. "I didn't smell anger."

"You didn't smell anything because you are lousy shifter," Kaz replied.

"They came for the orb. Goodridge won't stop until he gets it. Too bad Charlie is the only one who seems to have any effect on them." Kaz pulled her rifle out of the boot.

"That guy looked just as surprised as I was," Charlie said, closing the med-kit. "Can you fix the car?"

"Working on it," Nigel grunted.

"I'll scout around, make sure there's no one else stalking us." Kaz hooked her automatic over her shoulder.

Charlie settled on the seat beside Drake. "Goddess, I hope they can't get into the spirit realm." She'd never met any other Magickind who could enter the spirit realm as she could and it worried her.

"They won't, it's your domain, little witch."

"Are you okay?" She touched his cheek. "I'm not used to you being like this."

"I'll be fine." It would take more than a few stab wounds to kill him. He clutched her hand and felt the call of her power grow stronger. Everything in him demanded he make her his, say the vow, make her his mate. Instead, he pulled her to him, capturing her mouth in a long, searing kiss.

Her eyes widened but she returned the kiss.

"Argh, I'm not going to have to put up with that, am I?" Nigel grumbled.

"You're just jealous," Kaz muttered. "Because no one wants you."

Drake and Charlie pulled apart, both laughing.

Sure you don't want to seal our bond yet? she asked.

Drake brushed her hair off her face. Yes, he wanted that more than anything. His heart swelled just looking at her with something he hadn't felt in almost seven millennia.

Love.

The shock of that made him stumble out of the car.

"What's wrong?" Charlie said, alarmed.

He shook his head. "Nothing. Nigel, stand aside. Let me look at the engine."

Realisation dawned on him. He felt his heart starting to beat harder, faster. He hadn't truly loved anyone since he'd lost his family. He had Jason's friendship and that of the McCray family, but this went so much deeper than that. Drake forced the feeling aside as he stared at the engine. He muttered something and it sputtered to life.

"How did you do that?" Nigel arched an eyebrow.

He shrugged. "It's my vehicle. Come, the village is close. We should rest there for the night. We've only got a couple of hours left before it gets dark."

The village contained nothing but a half dozen houses with tiled roofs, a small shop and a pub which also served as an inn. The innkeeper did nothing to refuse them and Drake ordered three rooms for the group.

Drake slumped onto the bed, after yanking off his jeans while Charlie had a shower. He couldn't decide whether it made it easier or harder having her close but she'd refused to share a room with Kaz.

He pulled his brother's message out. It still said the same words: Come home. Now.

Nothing else.

Drake still couldn't understand why Daron would call him home. But he had to go there and find out the truth for himself.

Charlie came out wearing nothing but shorts and vest with her long hair loose around her shoulders. Drake forced his gaze away from her luscious curves. "I've been thinking of a cover story. You and the others could pose as bounty hunters," he mused. "You liked having me in chains as I recall." He remembered their trip to Setara years earlier before the revolution where he'd acted as her prisoner.

Charlie giggled as she slipped into bed beside him. "That sounds like fun." She rested her head against his shoulder. "I still think we should seal our bond soon."

"Why so eager, little witch?" He ran his fingers through her hair, playing with the silky strands. "You've been dead set against bonding since the day I formed our connection."

"It's different now. I know you. I care about you a lot." She leaned up on one elbow. "Don't you care about me?"

"You know I do."

"Show me," she challenged. "Don't you remember the dreams we shared?" She brushed her lips over his. "What we did?"

He remembered every detail and it made him want her even more.

"It's not nice to tease an injured man, little witch,"

"You wouldn't be injured if you'd just say the damn joining vows."

"The ascension—I'm too weak to help you through it. It could kill us both."

Charlie rolled her eyes. "You really know how to kill the mood, Vlad." She sighed, turned away from him. "But you're right. We can't."

Drake brushed the hair off her neck. "I never said I didn't want you." But he knew if he gave in, he'd never be able to let her go. His lips trailed down her neck, one hand roaming down her stomach until he found her wetness.

Charlie's breath caught as he stroked her. "Who's teasing who now?"

"I want you," Drake growled. "Never doubt that."

The vein on her neck throbbed, begging him to bite down in and take her power. Oh, how he wanted to.

"Drake," she gasped, thrusting her hips against his fingers.

He continued to stroke, harder, faster, feeling her close to climax. She cried out his name as she went over the edge.

Drake turned her over, crushed his mouth against hers. Charlie pulled him closer, wrapping her legs around his waist.

She tugged at his shirt and a searing pain burned across his chest. He bared his teeth, fangs coming out as he muttered a curse.

"Goddess, I'm so sorry." Charlie pulled away. "I shouldn't have—"

"I'm alright." He moved away from her, clutching his stomach.

"You don't look alright, you're turning white." She touched his face. He rolled away from her, breathing hard. "I'll see if the landlord has a healer or knows one." Charlie rose, pulling her clothes back into place.

"No, no healers. They won't do me any good." He caught hold of her wrist. "I can't risk anyone finding out what I am. Do you remember that box I asked you to get from my safe?"

Charlie nodded. "Yeah." She reached into her bag, pulled out a small wooden box.

"Open it."

Charlie pulled the lid to open it. Inside lay a large ring made from black gold with a huge amethyst stone. "Wow, it's beautiful. You're not…"

Drake chuckled. "No, I'm not proposing—if I were I'd give you something much nicer. Besides, demons don't wear wedding rings."

She looked almost disappointed. "What is it?"

"One of my few weaknesses. With that ring, you can control me. It's a safeguard of sorts in case I—or any other Akaran—lost themselves to our darkness then that can stop us," he explained.

Charlie's brow creased. "Why are you giving it to me?"

"Because there is no one in this world I trust more." He winced as he sat up. "I spent eight thousand years holding this power inside me. If I ever lose control, you must promise me you'll use it." He took her hand. "No matter what."

"No, I wouldn't control you. You can't ask me to do that." She shoved the box closed.

"Charlotte, you know how demons can lose themselves. You have to promise."

"You want me to promise to kill you after everything we've been through?" Her brown eyes flashed an icy blue. "No! I won't do it." She threw the box on the floor. "Is that why you won't bond with me? Because you're afraid something might happen to you?"

Drake suppressed a groan. Damn, this girl knew him better than he'd imagined. "It's possible, yes."

"I still don't understand why you want to go back when your own brother vowed to kill you." Hands balled into fists, she rose from the bed. "You're unbelievable!"

Drake felt his own temper rising. "Just promise me," he snapped, in a tone he used when he told others they had no other choice but to obey him.

She folded her arms, shaking her head. "I don't get you. I thought you wanted us to have something real. That's what you said. A relationship built on trust. How can we ever have that when you keep things from me?"

"I'm telling you now." But he knew she was right.

"Only because you don't have another choice," Charlie snapped back. "Would you have told me if we weren't going to Kyral?"

Drake looked away, unable to answer. He wanted to keep her away from all of this. That was why he'd ended their relationship. But she'd come right long after him. "Yes," he said finally. "I would've told you everything in time. Use the ring or don't. I just thought you should know. In truth, I have no idea what kind of danger we'll face in Kyral—I wanted you to go home but you chose to come. So we do things my way."

Her eyes flashed, turning the same shade of amethyst as his ring. "I'm your mate, not one of your lackeys who you can boss around."

Drake let out a breath in frustration. "You're the most bloody stubborn woman I've ever known."

Charlie snorted. "You're just not used to people saying no to you."

"I'd do anything to keep you safe," he growled. "Even if it meant giving up my own life because you're the only thing in this world that matters to me."

Charlie sighed. "How do you do that?"

"Do what?"

"Make me mad, then say something to make me melt inside."

Drake smiled, rubbing his knuckles over her jaw. "I'm your mate."

Charlie sat down beside him. "Yes, you are. I'll use the damn ring if I have to, but I want you to know I want a relationship with you— not anyone else," she told him. "I want something real. If you can't give me that you need to tell me now before we get any deeper."

Drake caressed her cheek. "I want that too—but know that I can't give you any more than this right now."

"This is enough." She snuggled against him as they let sleep claim them.

CHAPTER 8

Charlie awoke to the feel of claws wrapped around her throat, piercing through her skin in sharp pinpricks of pain. Her eyes flew open to see a skeletal face looming over her, its hollow mouth open like a black hole of emptiness, its black wispy form floating above her like a giant hooded cloak.

A Mija, great! Charlie tried to draw in breath to phase out but she couldn't. Her lungs burned from lack of oxygen. She gritted her teeth, wrapped her fingers around the creature's bony arm and let her magic loose as she unleashed her touch.

The Mija let out a bloodcurdling screech as her power burned through it. Drake shot up beside her as Charlie phased out and fell onto the floor, landing in a heap. He hurled a fireball at it. Mijas were skeletal beings that hovered between life and death. They needed to feed on magic to survive, but most had been wiped out after the revolution. Only the touch of the Denai could kill them.

The screams grew louder as flames engulfed its body but it soon shook off the flames.

"Does Goodridge ever give up?" Charlie muttered.

Drake threw another fireball.

Charlie scrambled out. "Come on, Mija, come and get me. We both know it's me you want. My demon doesn't have much magic."

The Mija flew at her, its claws slashing her arm. She ignored the pain, grabbed its throat and let her power out. Her eyes burned red as she let out her touch. The creature exploded in a burst of light.

Blood seeped from Charlie's arm and throat. "Gods." Drake hurried over to her, igniting the lamps as he went. "You're bleeding." He grabbed her med-kit, pulling out bandages.

"Bloody Goodridge," she cursed as Drake held a cloth to her neck. "Why do I get the feeling he's not trying to kidnap me?" She winced as he pressed harder. "I think he's testing me."

Drake's jaw clenched, his ice-blue eyes bleeding to black as they did when he felt strong emotion.

"I'm alright." She touched his cheek.

"Sometimes I forget how fragile you are," he muttered.

Fragile? Me? She snorted. "There's nothing fragile about me, Vlad."

Charlie's skin began to tingle. She looked down to see the blood flow ebbing. Had she started healing on her own? That meant only one thing: transition. She backed away, seeing the slashes close over. Drake looked too, frowning. "My ascension must be getting close," Charlie mused. She didn't know whether to be excited or terrified. She'd become immortal soon, and that came with its own risks.

"We'll need to be extra careful then." Drake wrapped an arm around her, hugging her against his chest. Charlie melted against him, knew he worried.

"You're right, Goodridge does seem to be testing you," he said, running a hand through her hair.

"For what?" She pulled back, running her fingers over her throat to feel the slashes fading and wiping the dried blood away. "The Srimtar is somewhere he can't reach it—unless he's trying to figure out a way to weaken me." She slumped onto the bed, feeling too wired to go back to sleep.

Drake sat up beside her. "We are already weakened. Your powers will be unpredictable now you're in transition and I'm still injured."

"Why do I get the feeling you're hiding something from me?" She looked him right in the eye.

He flinched and had the same guilty look on his face. She'd started to read her demon well now. "Drake, we agreed no more secrets."

He sighed. "There is one way to speed up my healing."

Charlie brightened. "Good, are we finally going to be bonded?"

"No, I can take power from other demons."

She nodded. "Yeah, I've already seen that."

Drake hesitated. "It's more effective if I take it from blood."

Okay, that part she hadn't expected. "Like a vampire?" Charlie grinned. "Guess my nickname is more fitting than you let on, huh, Vlad?"

Drake scowled. "I need blood to survive, it strengthens me. Blood drinking was outlawed by my clan centuries ago. I've never drunk blood from anyone before," he said. "I have no need for it, but…"

"But you're weak." Realisation dawned on her. "Oh." Her cheeks flushed. "You need to drink from me, don't you?"

"No, I won't." He moved away from her. "I'll be healed a few days."

"Drake, you're the Akaran. You can't be weak like this." She grabbed his arm, forcing him to face her. "You don't know what your brother will do either. So just do it."

His eyes shifted from blue to black again as his jaw set. "No," he growled.

Stubborn demon! "Why not? You wouldn't have told me if you need my help." Charlie held out her wrist. "Go ahead."

His eyes narrowed. "You trust me that much?"

"Of course I trust you—more than anyone."

Drake's fangs shot out and sank deep into her wrist. She felt a stab of pain, then pleasure shot through her entire body. "Wow, I may have to get you to do that," she said when he pulled back.

Drake pulled off one of his bandages, saw the wound had vanished.

"Feel better?" Charlie raised an eyebrow.

He answered her by pulling her in for a deep kiss.

The team set out again the next morning on the road for the city. Charlie felt relieved to see Drake looking more like his old self but she sensed how uneasy he felt.

Strange, she seemed to pick up on his emotions now—the sign of a bond. She could tell he held back but she'd get him to seal that bond soon. She was in this for the long haul now and nothing would change that—not even him.

Cate had said to her once, "The trouble with us McCrays is when we fall in love, it's forever."

Charlie pondered that thought. She'd thought herself in love with Scott, her ex-boyfriend too, but he'd never been able to stir the kinds of emotions in her that Drake did.

"We should reach the city in the next couple of hours." Charlie glanced at the SatNav as she drove. She felt Drake tense in the seat beside her. *You don't have to do this,* she said.

His jaw tightened. *You know I must.*

"So we're bounty hunters, your brother is the fake Akaran and we've got to pretend you're our prisoner," Kaz stated.

"Why?" asked Nigel.

"Daron blamed me for our family's murder, I don't know how he'll react to my presence," said Drake.

Kaz raised an eyebrow. "Then why the hell are you going back?"

"Because he sent for me and I've already wiped out the demons who were responsible."

"If you're the Akaran, why don't you rule demons?" Nigel wanted to know.

Drake didn't answer, instead continuing to stare out of the window. Charlie glanced over at him then noticed the stone walls of buildings up ahead. Had they reached the city already? No, it looked too small for that.

The map on the SatNav led straight through it. When Drake didn't protest, she guided the car forward. Wooden shutters hung from windows, doors were missing and bodies lined the streets. Some were hanging from trees.

Charlie slammed on the brakes. The team exited the car to investigate. Drake knelt to examine the bodies.

"Are they demons?" Charlie asked. She assumed demon's bodies vanished in death, but maybe not.

"Yes," Drake growled. "Not all demons vanish."

"What killed them?" Charlie knelt beside him, touching his shoulder. She spotted a black symbol burned onto the forehead of the bodies. It looked like a Griffin—half lion, half eagle.

Drake muttered something in Demonish, stalked off without saying a word.

"What's up with him?" Kaz asked.

Charlie shrugged, glancing after him. "I don't know, he's trying to pull away from me again. I can feel it."

"Well, don't let him."

"I don't have a good feeling about going to the city either."

"Let's not go and drag Drake's fine arse back to Setara instead." Kaz smirked.

Charlie's lips quivered. "No, he'll go back there one way or another. Let's look around while we're here." She kept a hand on the butt of her gun as she moved. Drake disappeared but she sensed him close. Best leave him alone for a while.

Charlie sent her senses out, scanning for any signs of spirits. She'd never encountered demon's spirits before. Given they had souls too she didn't see a reason why they wouldn't have them or some kind of remnant of their former selves.

Inside the houses contained old furniture. Bread and meat were laid out on the table and all of it had turned rotten with flies buzzing around. She guessed everyone had been killed at least a month ago. She didn't much like working among the dead despite her medium powers.

Nothing triggered her senses, no trace of spiritual energy. Strange. Victims of violent deaths often hung around waiting for justice. Yet she found nothing.

Charlie moved to the next house, furniture had been toppled over, with scorch marks covering the walls. She reached to touch the mark, wondering if her transitioning powers might include visions.

Nothing happened.

She decided she could do without that gift but wondered why she didn't send something. Her Denai powers often let her sense how someone had died.

Light shimmered at the corner of her eye.

Charlie turned and saw a girl there. Her dark curls fell past her shoulders, her pale blue eyes looked sad as she stared at Charlie.

Charlie cast her senses out but they gave her no reading. Weird; this had to be a spirit. The girl's robe glimmered white in the pale light.

"Hi, did you live here?" Charlie asked, grimacing. She never developed a tact for talking to the dead, despite years of practice. "I'm Charlie, what's your name?"

The girl blinked, those cool blue eyes seeming to stare straight through her. "You must save him."

"What? Save who?" She frowned, releasing her gun that hung over her chest.

The girl motioned her to follow.

Charlie hesitated. She hated when she couldn't sense anything from spirits, which meant they weren't ghosts or they were big trouble. *Get a grip, you're a medium. You can control spirits and stop demons.*

She found herself moving forward as the girl vanished through the wall.

Drawing in a breath, Charlie phased after her, passing through the wall.

No, you must go back! A voice echoed in her mind.

Mist whirled around her, a haze of swirling purple.

What the hell?

The girl stood there. "Save him. You must save him from the darkness."

Charlie let out a breath again in a whoosh, lungs burning. "Save who?" she gasped. "Where are we?"

This didn't feel like the spirit realm; it was something else, yet she didn't feel afraid of it all the girl.

She took a step closer but the girl seemed further away. "Who do you want me to save?"

"Beware those who hide in the light. They will try to distract you from your past," the girl said. "Only you can save him."

Blurs of light moved around her, ghostly, a blur of hands and faces. It reminded her of the strange beings who'd attacked them the day before. Had they followed her or had she entered their space?

Charlie clutched her gun then let go. It wouldn't do any good. This wasn't the physical world. She didn't know what it was. One of the figures moved towards her. She raised her hand. Blue orbs flared to life between her fingers. *That's new!*

"You're not getting my orb," she snapped. "It's not yours to have."

"We do not want the orb," the voice sounded female but Charlie couldn't be sure.

Where the hell had the girl gone? How could she get back to the village?

"Charlie, listen," the voice continued. "You must get away from the Akaran. He deceives you."

It sounded so ridiculous she burst out laughing. "Yeah, like I'm gonna leave my demon."

"Lies," the voices echoed. "He deceives you. You are not his."

"I've heard enough." Charlie tried to phase but nothing happened. Her heart started pounding. Why couldn't she go back? "Let me go!"

The figures closed in around her, swirling like a circle of enveloping mist around her, blocking any possible way out.

"Drake is not your mate. If you stay with him, you will die."

Her fists clenched. "He'd never hurt me." She'd heard enough of this crap, but couldn't get through them.

"You barely know him," another voice said.

Her hands clenched into fists. "I know he's my mate. What we have is real."

"He left you," the voice reminded her. She felt a stab of pain at the mention of that, but ignored it. If they thought they could play on her fears and doubts, they'd be damned wrong. The mist swirled around her. "All Akarans die; he'll take you with him unless you leave now."

Charlie gritted her teeth, shivering as the mist tingled against her skin. *I need to get the hell out of here.* "I am leaving now. Let me the hell out of this place."

Blue lightning shot from her hand, hurtling one of the figures away from her. She let out a breath she hadn't known she'd been holding.

She did have power here.

"Charlie…" A glowing hand reached for her.

"No!" she screamed.

The purple haze around her blurred as she felt herself being dragged backwards. Charlie hit the ground as she landed on the floor of the house. What the hell had that been? First a strange girl, now creepy mist people telling her she had to break up with Drake. *As if!*

"Charlotte." Drake appeared behind her, yanking her up. "Where were you?" He shook her shoulders and she saw fear in his eyes. "I couldn't sense you anywhere in the world." He crushed her against his chest.

"I don't think I was in this world," she admitted.

"You went into the spirit realm?"

Charlie opened her mouth to tell him what happened but then hesitated. Should she tell him the truth?

"I saw a girl—I went somewhere else." She shook her head. "I guess I passed over without meaning to."

"What girl? What does she want?" Drake asked.

Charlie hugged him, resting her head against his chest. "It was just a lost soul trying to get some closure. I'm sorry I couldn't help her— her message was too mixed up for me to understand." Holding him eased some of the uneasiness away. "Did you find anything?" she added.

His expression darkened. "The mark and the bodies are the symbols of the Akaran."

Charlie frowned. "You didn't kill them."

"No, it must have been my brother."

"Maybe we shouldn't go there." She clutched his jacket. "I don't have a good feeling."

Drake touched her cheek. "I can't ignore my past any longer."

Charlie sighed. "I know, and I'll be with you no matter what."

Drake gave her a quick kiss.

She glanced back at the wall, remembering the girl stare. "You think you know what you are, what's to come. You've not even begun," a voice whispered.

Drake didn't seem to hear or sense anything as he wrapped an arm around her. Charlie shivered, checking again, half expecting the strange figures or the girl to reappear. But nothing happened.

"What's wrong?" he asked.

"Nothing, this place just creeps me out." Somehow she didn't think they were connected to Goodridge. Weird, they'd felt almost familiar to her. Though she had no idea how that could be possible. But she didn't want to stick around to find out more.

CHAPTER 9

The great stone walls of the citadel loomed into view as they approached Kyral city. Charlie stared in awe. Seeing it again gave Drake mixed feelings. But he couldn't afford to let any emotion get in the way being back here. He had to think and act like an Akaran.

"Wow, this place is huge," Kaz breathed.

Drake had remained silent on the rest of the drive but Charlie hadn't said him about it.

"How long do we have to be bounty hunters?" asked Nigel.

"Until I know what my brother's plans are," Drake replied.

Charlie's strange disappearance had made him all the more uneasy. But he tried to brush his concern aside. Just seeing his former home again brought back a familiar pain he'd thought had long passed.

He'd spent millennia controlling his feelings, he'd had to in order to keep his true power hidden. Drake glanced over at Charlie; she'd been quiet on the way over too. He felt like she was hiding something but he had no idea what.

Kaz and Nigel became motionless as he froze them.

"Hey." Charlie frowned. "Why'd you do that?"

"So we can speak privately."

"We could do that in thought."

"Did you see anything else when you vanished?" He studied her expression, trying to see if it betrayed any emotion. He had no idea why she'd need to hide anything from him.

She bit her lip, hesitating. "I saw a girl. She told me I had to save someone," she answered. "I don't know who she meant. Like I said, she's just a lost soul—I can't save everyone."

He took her hand. "You can't tell anyone in Kyral you're my mate, either. We aren't bonded nor do you bear my mark to show you're mine. I have enemies here and they'd see you as my weakness," he said. "This place is very different, another world almost compared to what happens elsewhere."

Charlie scowled. "Why not just bond with me then?"

Because if I die here, I won't risk you, he thought. *You are my weakness—the only thing I'd give up everything for.* "We don't need to rush—you said you wanted to take things slow, remember?"

She folded her arms. "I changed my mind."

He kissed her hand. "Why does it matter? I'm already yours."

Charlie smiled. "I'm yours too. If we can't tell anyone we're mates, does that mean we can't even hold hands in public?"

"Maybe not for a while." Drake stared up at the looming walls. "I can't be seen to have any weakness."

"This spy stuff sucks sometimes." She sighed. "Maybe I can find some clues to my own heritage here." Drake kissed her then watched his former home edge ever closer.

Two Zexens stood guard outside the gates. Strange, his clan would never have let them anywhere near the citadel when his father was the reigning Akaran. But a lot would have changed in almost eight thousand years. Though Drake was surprised. Although Zexens were strong and made the perfect guards due to being able to hide in shadow most of them had worked for the Grand Mistress who in exchange for their service, who had protected them from the other demon clans.

"State your business," the first guard snapped.

Charlie leaned out the window. "We're here to see the Akaran. We're bounty hunters." She motioned to her gun. "Heard there is a bounty for his brother." She inclined her head towards Drake.

Drake allowed the guards to place cuffs around his wrists. "Are you going to let these people treat me like this?" he snapped. "I demand to be taken to my brother at once."

Charlie rolled her eyes, hit him over the back of the head with her sidearm. "See what I have to put up with."

Drake winced. Damn, his witch could put on a show. He would have felt proud if it hadn't hurt so much.

"How do we know it's him?" The second guard asked.

"I am Drakon Damrus—son of Thaddeus and Liliana Damrus, brother of Daron—"

Charlie let out a breath. "Oh, it's him alright. Will you let us through? We're eager to get our money and be rid of this guy." The guards exchanged a look then the gates swung open.

Did you do have to hit me so hard? Drake asked, rubbing the back of his head.

Charlie smirked. *I had to make it look real.*

They were stopped inside a cobbled stone courtyard by four demons armed with staff weapons.

"They look like Ashrali weapons—old tech," Kaz murmured.

"My clan would have traded during the wars. But don't expect much in the way of tech here," Drake told them. "My brother is a great believer in the old ways. Power means everything to my people."

"What if your brother tries to kill you?" asked Nigel.

Drake shook his head. "He won't—at least not outright. He knows he doesn't have the power to do that." Charlie climbed out of the car, cuffing Drake to her left wrist.

Drake recognised another Amargen demon called Seth who'd been one of his father's sentinels.

"Drakon, so you've finally returned." Seth towered over six-and-a-half feet with a long red braid. He had deep green eyes and his black leather uniform bore the Akaran's mark.

Who is he? Charlie asked.

An old friend. Drake replied.

Can we trust him? She frowned at Seth.

Perhaps. He shrugged, wishing he could use his powers to try and sense Seth's thought. But he had to limit all use of power now.

"We're bounty hunters," Charlie said to Seth. "We want to see the Akaran."

Seth's gaze roamed over them. "How did bounty hunters get their hands on you?" he asked Drake.

"We're the best," Kaz added. "This guy stood no chance."

Seth frowned. "The Akaran has been informed of your arrival, we're to take you to him but you must relinquish all your weapons first."

Charlie snorted. "All? You've got to be kidding me."

Do it, you can't risk raising suspicions, said Drake.

Now I'm glad I moved all our gear into the spirit realm.

Charlie, Kaz and Nigel handed over their stunners and knives. They left only their supplies in the jeep after Charlie had moved their gear into her secret place in the spirit world.

The guards herded them past a market full of people selling their wares. The smell of cooked broth and wood smoke reminded Drake of being a boy and stealing things from the stalls.

Remember not to use your witch powers, he told her. *You're a demon, don't make anyone question that.*

What kind? Since I don't even know what my demon half is.

Say you're part Zexen, part fey. That's believable enough. Zexens and Ashrali have been around each other centuries.

As they walked, Drake's mind wandered.

Drake woke up in the room Silas had dumped him in. The bed felt soft and warm. It gave him the feeling of security—until everything came flooding back. He bolted up, sweat dripping down his body. He was the Akaran now and his family was gone.

Power hummed through his blood, so strong he felt like he could rip the world apart. He never thought he'd become the Akaran; his father had been so powerful, Drake had thought he'd live forever.

He splashed cold water onto his face and grabbed his shirt which still had bloodstains covering it. He couldn't meet the Serenity like this.

Light whirled around him as new clean clothes appeared on his body. At least this power can be good for something. He ran a hand through his short, cropped hair. He had no idea how to act or live in this country. Kyral had been his only home.

"Silas?" Drake barked. "Get over here." His voice sounded stronger than expected.

The old man appeared, giving him a toothy grin. "The Akaran can summon any demon at will—there's no need to shout."

Drake's lips thinned. "Where would be the fun in that?" He felt his palms grow sweaty, but he couldn't show fear in front of this demon or anyone. His father had always warned him fear was a weakness. "Did you get my message to the Serenity?"

Silas chuckled. "The Akaran doesn't send messages. If you want something you take it."

Drake thought of his father, how he'd done just that and now their clan had almost been destroyed because of his lust for power. Drake knew that wasn't the way to do things here, nor was it his style. "What did she say?"

"She agreed to meet you—seemed surprised since your father despised the fey."

All Magickind always seemed to be at each other's throats and what good did it do? Nothing.

Drake stood outside the huge foot double doors of the Serenity's office, heart pounding. Facing a demon horde felt less terrifying than facing this woman said to be so powerful she was a goddess in her own right, but kind and benevolent, unlike her former husband who ruled Setara.

He knocked once then went inside. The air seemed to crackle with power, rolling off the woman in front of him. Long blonde hair fell past her waist, her skin looked like alabaster and her sea-blue eyes seemed to sparkle. This was a woman who deserved respect.

"Serenity." Drake bowed, hoped it was a sign of respect here in this new land. "I'm Drake the—the Akaran." He winced at saying it out loud.

The Serenity rose, her long white robe moving like seafoam as she walked around her desk. She stood almost as tall as he. His senses reeled as she stared at him. "What brings you to Elaris, Drakon?" she asked.

"I-I need your help." He flinched at the tremor his voice. "My family were killed. My brother and I were the only ones to survive."

"My spies tell me your brother Daron has assumed the role of Akaran." Her cool eyes felt like they were scanning him as his skin tingled. "I sense that is wrong."

Drake's gaze dropped to the tiled floor. "He blames me for their deaths, but I'd never harm them. I can't go back there—not until I find those responsible."

"Why come here? Elaris is such a new city."

"I heard people are free here no matter their race. I'm tired of war, I've seen so much already," he told her, now meeting her gaze. "I believe you can help me."

"To do what?" Her face looked calm, like a silent lake betraying no emotion.

"I can't be the Akaran. I hoped you could help me be rid of this power and avenge my family."

Her hair turned a light shade of red. So fey eyes and hair could change colour depending on their emotions. His mother's stories had been right.

"My aim here is for all races to be free, and for that, we must all learn to work together," Niara said. "I don't understand why you want to waste your gift."

Drake's lip curled. "Gift?" he scoffed. "My family is dead; my brother disowned me because of this power. Can you take it or not?"

Niara's lips curved into a smile. "I lost someone once too—my mother. I blamed myself, cursed my power, but why not use your gift to bring justice for your family?"

His eyes narrowed. "How?"

"I'm creating a new order here as I try to get the leaders of each race to work together." She glided over to the window as she spoke. "But I cannot be everywhere nor do everything alone. In exchange for a home here and anonymity, I'd like you to work for me."

Drake's brow creased, "You want me to join your order? I'm no diplomat, nor do I give a damn about politics."

"No, Drakon. You would be working in secret as my eyes and ears. You can travel places, talk to people in a way I never can, especially among Demonkind."

"You want me to become your spy," he realised. "Why? I'm no one."

"You are the most powerful of all Demonkind, you can use your power to help me bring peace here in Britannia. In return, I'll teach you and train you on how to use your powers."

He shook his head. "I can't let my family's deaths go unpunished. I need to find those responsible."

"I can help you do that, but I warn you, revenge won't take away your pain." Niara played with a strand of her hair. "Will you join me?"

Drake glanced out onto the ocean outside, glistening like diamonds. What choice did he have? Spy or fugitive? Forever on the run.

"Not a spy," Niara said, somehow reading his thoughts. "In time you will teach others your skills, form an alliance against the Covenant and those who seek to hurt other Magickind."

"You truly believe that's possible?"

She only smiled. "It won't be easy and will take centuries but yes, I believe that."

Drake scowled at the thought of the Covenant. "Don't the witches predict one of their kind will bring them down?"

"Indeed, but there are other evils in this world that don't include the Covenant."

"Fine, I'm your demon. I'll do whatever it takes to avenge my family."

The memory faded as Drake walked into the hall and his senses tingled. Out of the shadows came his brother Daron who stood over six feet tall, his shaggy dark hair flopped over his washed-out blue eyes. His muscles looked saggy, his eyes dark.

Not the way Drake pictured his little brother to look.

Every demon in the room moved out of the way as the Akaran came over.

Drake's heart pounded as the familiar pain came back. Losing their family had torn them apart.

"Hello, brother." Daron smiled. "Welcome home."

Drake stared at Daron, waited for a reaction. After so long, he expected something more than a faint smile. Or had Daron forgiven him? Realised Drake had ever been involved?

"Brother," Drake replied. "You called me home, why?"

Daron smile widened as he turned away from Drake. "Guards, put him to death."

CHAPTER 10

Charlie's heart skipped a beat at Daron's words. She saw the guards move towards them. She felt her inner demon clawing its way to surface, demanding to get out. She wanted to let it go psycho on them as it had done in the past.

No, Drake told her. *Don't. You can't let them see your power.*

"Hey!" she snapped, dragging Drake backwards. "He's not going anywhere until I get my bounty. No money, no demon."

Daron's eyes narrowed. "Who are you? You dare challenge me, imp?"

Imp? Do I look like an imp? Imps are small creepy demons. And yes, I do damn well challenge you, she thought, raising her chin and opened her mouth to speak.

Charlotte, Drake warned.

Her eyes flashed. *I'm not going to watch you die.*

"Bounty hunter, Charlie Donovan," she said, tightening her hold on Drake's restraints. "Like I said, no money; no goods."

Daron sputtered. The fake Akaran didn't look like he had people deny him anything.

Power flared to life as her inner demon fought for control, but Charlie kept it at bay. "I am a Zexen, you don't have authority over me," she pointed out. "My people's allegiance is to the Grand Mistress, the council and all that crap. Mine is to money, so pay up."

Charlotte, let me handle this.

She glowered at Drake then at his brother. "You're not killing him."

Drake pulled himself free of the cuffs. "Do you want me to tell everyone here the truth, brother?" The words sounded strange yet Charlie understood them. "You are an impostor. With one word, I could end you, brother."

Daron's eyes narrowed. "You dare challenge me, Drakon?"

"I killed those responsible for murdering our family. I'm not here to challenge your rule—you summoned me here," Drake snapped. "Did you call me home only to kill me?"

"Why should I believe you?" Daron crossed his arms.

"I vowed to you I would avenge them; I wouldn't have come back if I hadn't."

"I want to believe you, brother." Daron's jaw clenched.

"It's time to put the past behind us. I'm not your enemy, nor do I have any desire to rule."

A muscle in Daron's jaw ticked. "Guards, stand down. I know now my brother is innocent. I absolve him of any past wrongs." He clapped an arm around Drake. "Welcome home, Drakon."

Drake hugged his brother, relief on his face. Charlie frowned. How could anyone forgive and forget so easily? It was like someone had flipped a switch and turned Daron into nice brother now.

"Everyone, we welcome home our brother Drake. Have a feast prepared."

Kaz and Nigel looked confused too, looking to Charlie for guidance.

"Did we miss something?" Kaz whispered, leaning close to Charlie.

Charlie shrugged. *No idea.* How the heck has she understood that strange language?

"What of these bounty hunters?" Seth asked, motioning to Charlie and the others.

"Let them be welcome. They're friends and treated me well," Drake replied. "At least let them stay for the feast tonight."

"Fine, but the bounty hunters must leave the castle now. I don't like inferior Magickind wandering around my halls." Daron raised a hand in dismissal.

Charlie opened her mouth to protest but Drake caught hold of her wrist.

Drake dragged Charlie off and she made a show of been disgusted by him. He said nothing as he led her into another room while Kaz and Nigel had left to go and find somewhere to stay in the city.

"Why didn't you insist on the others staying?" she asked when he shut the door behind them.

"I couldn't risk it. It's easier just to have you here. Plus, they can keep an eye on things outside the city," Drake said. "There's unease here; I can sense it."

A huge four-poster bed draped with heavy linens, along with a desk and rows of bookcases, sat in the room. Tapestries of a hunting scene and huge horned beasts covered the stone walls.

"Judging by how no one protested to you dragging me off, do you whisk all your conquests off to your room a lot?" she remarked.

His lips curved as he caressed her cheek. "Only the short ones."

"I'm serious, how many she-demons am I gonna have to fight off while we here?"

"No she-demons. I only want you."

Charlie bit her lip. "What language did you speak to Daron in?"

"Old Amargen, the language used by our ancestors—only he and I would understand it."

"I did too."

He frowned. "How?"

"No idea. Why does he want you back?" She dropped her bag on the floor and sat on the edge of the bed.

Drake dropped his bag on the floor, leant back against the chest of drawers. "I don't know. I couldn't touch his mind—it felt fragmented somehow."

"Maybe because he's batshit crazy from the looks of it."

"I don't believe that."

"You know immortals can lose their minds over time, especially if they don't have mates. You said demons need mates to anchor them."

"Yes, but it's rare for demons to find their true mates too," Drake said. "I need to stay and find out why he called me home. He put on a show back there for everyone, I know there's more to it than that."

"Meanwhile we need to figure out what Goodridge's next move is." She pulled her pack onto the bed. "Will Daron let me stay here long?"

"I'll make sure of it." Drake ran a hand through his hair. "There's so few of my clan left here. I thought…" He sighed. "The clans must be turning against each other. I need to see what else is going on."

"Okay, I'll find others, see what we can turn up." Charlie turned to go but Drake wrapped his arms around her.

"I can't have everyone thinking I'm a lousy lover for this to be over so fast."

She laced her arms around his neck. "I wouldn't know, thanks to your 'we must wait' motto."

"I saw the way my brother looked at you."

"Like he wanted to wring my neck." She laughed.

"No, like he wanted you in his bed."

Charlie snorted. "I'd cut body parts of him before I'd ever let him touch me. You're the only demon I want."

He captured her mouth in a hungry kiss.

Charlie felt herself melt against him. "You don't belong with the Akaran," the voice had said.

Yeah right! Nothing felt better than being in her demon's arms. They were both breathing hard when they pulled apart.

"How did I know your language?" Charlie asked.

Drake shrugged. "Our connection must be stronger."

"Like a bond." She grinned. "You better seal the deal soon, Vlad. I might get tired and move on to hunkier demons."

Drake let out a low growl. "I won't share you with anyone so forget that."

Charlie laughed. "You're cute when you're jealous. Go find out what your brother is up to."

Charlie headed out to the city among the hustle and bustle of street vendors trying to flog everything from livestock to magical goods as she searched for the others. The city seemed very old world like Setara which was filled with colour and a lot of tech. This place felt more rugged with rough stone walls and buildings, unlike the elegant architecture of Setara. She wondered if she'd be able to find out more of her own heritage while staying here.

Had Kaz and Nigel gotten lost?

She scanned the crowd of demons all dressed in a mix of tunics and hose whilst others wore more modern clothing like jeans and t-shirts. Strangely she didn't feel so out of place here. She missed her gear but knew she couldn't risk using it. She missed Drake more, leaving him alone made her uneasy even if he could take care of himself. But he'd wanted to talk to Daron alone and she didn't want to be around his creepy brother any more than she had to.

"Nice to fit in, isn't it?" asked a familiar voice.

Charlie spun around to see Helga sitting at a table inside a purple tent with a crystal ball on a round table in front of her. *Unbelievable!* "What the hell are you doing here?" Charlie hissed as she stormed inside. "Are you trying to blow my cover?"

The crone cackled. "I'm free to come and go as I please, girl. I enjoy telling fortunes at times. It makes life interesting," she said, rubbing the crystal. "Demons are a superstitious bunch."

Charlie pulled the tent flap closed, hoping no one had seen them together. "Look, I'm working here and I thought you didn't interfere with magical affairs?"

"Oh, I don't, but I am interested to see what happens given the war brewing between the demon clans. It amuses me." She gave a toothy grin.

"Sometimes I think you're mental." Charlie rolled her eyes.

Helga laughed harder. "Perhaps I am."

Charlie crossed her arms. "I know you were around when Cate was in transition and she and Jason first got together. You better not be here because I'm in transition now too."

Helga's lips thinned. "You're not in transition. I'm only here to watch what happens. When you've been alive for fifty thousand years you need to find amusements when you can."

Charlie's mouth fell open. "What? Of course I'm in transition. My powers are stronger, my senses are heightened. Denais go into transition in their mid to late twenties." She had to be in transition, it was the only thing that explained why her demon side and strange new abilities had started emerging. Having demon blood wouldn't stop the transition. Cate was half Ashrali and Charlie's stepmother Jade was a shifter, they had both transitioned.

"You're not just a witch, you're more than that."

"Right, I'm half whatever the hell my mother was." She sighed. "Why am I even talking to you? You never helped me to find Drake."

"You found him, didn't you?" Helga made another stool appear. "Just as I foretold."

Charlie snorted. "Like you'd ever give me a straight answer. Plus, you said I'm shielded from your visions."

"I can still tell you of events to come. Aren't you curious to learn more of those shadow figures?"

Charlie's eyes narrowed. "What do you know about them?"

Helga rubbed her crystal ball. "A little of this, a little of that."

Again with the riddles! Charlie slumped onto the stool. "They said Drake and I aren't meant to be together." She had no idea why, of all people, she was telling Helga this. She didn't even trust her, yet here she was babbling. Charlie rested her chin on her hand. "So all-knowing one, tell me my fortune. Tell me what else the future has in store."

Helga's eyes flashed white. "Your path is divided. Which way you choose will determine the rest of your life. Look to those who walk among the shadows; beware the traitor. Only you can save him."

The form of the girl flashed in Helga's place with her long dark curly blowing behind her and her white robe shimmering like moonlight.

"You," Charlie gasped, getting to her feet. "What are you doing here? What have you done to Helga?"

"Only you can save him," the girl repeated and pointed off into the distance where the golden walls of the citadel rose up. "Beware the traitor. Look to the shadows, but do not let them lead you astray."

"What traitor? Who I supposed to save?" Charlie made a grab for the girl, but instead found herself with her fingers around Helga's throat.

The crone's eyes widened in shock as she gasped for breath. "Shit! I'm so sorry." Charlie backed away, feeling a sharp pang of guilt. "There was a girl—I've seen her before. Goddess, what does this all mean?"

Helga laughed. "That wasn't me. I felt another presence. It used my power." She rubbed her throat. "Blessed spirits, that's not possible. I have shields in place to protect any outside force from using my gift."

"What the fuck is going on?" Charlie demanded. "I keep seeing that girl and creepy spirit people keep following me. Is this Goodridge's new way of trying to steal the Srimtar?"

Helga's hand shook as she conjured a cup and gulped down its contents. "I can't answer that. My sight is so clouded but I sensed they're connected to you."

"I need to figure out what this all means and I will." She paused.

"I didn't hurt you, did I?"

"No. I'm going to enjoy watching this all play out."

Both Helga and her tent vanished in a burst of light.

CHAPTER 11

Drake kept his senses alert as he headed into his brother's chamber that night. Everyone seemed to be enjoying the feast but he kept his attention on Daron. There had to be a reason why Daron had called him back after almost eight thousand years of silence and Drake couldn't figure out why.

Daron sat with a blonde woman on his lap. "Drake, come in. Want to share Dantalia's delights with me?"

Drake put on his business face, the one that showed no emotion. He didn't give a damn about the whore, nor could she interest him. The only woman who stirred any emotion in him was Charlie. "Leave us," he ordered.

The blue-eyed demon pouted. "Come, Drake, I remember when we—"

"Out!" His eyes turned black as his inner demon emerged. He had no patience for this. "Now." He grabbed her wrist and shoved her across the room. Dantalia yelped, grabbed the hem of her flimsy robe and fled.

Daron scowled. "What did you do that for? I remember when we both enjoyed her pleasures."

"That was lifetimes ago. I'm not the boy who fled from this place."

"No, my guards tell me you've been enjoying the imp. Perhaps I'll try her myself."

Drake snorted. "You wouldn't be able to handle her; she's a wily wench," he said. "I didn't come to discuss women. Why did you summon me?"

Daron gulped down a glass of wine, downing it one go. "I thought it time we made peace."

"Bollocks!" Drake pulled out a chair and sat. "Why now? You

168

called me here because you want something. If it's my power, forget it."

Daron sneered. "Have you not seen how few of our clan left? The clans look to me for leadership and we're being torn apart."

"Maybe if you brought them together, negotiated peace, they wouldn't be."

He'd kept close watch over the clans for centuries, watched them fight and kill for power. Demons hadn't always been warmongers. All that had changed after Oberoth had come with his vision of a better future, what good had it done them?

None. Most had fallen into slavery. Demons had become lesser races, the lowest of the low. Inferior to all of Magickind. Thought to be evil, soulless, a plague among the immortals and even shunned by the lesser races who weren't immortal.

Drake hated it but he'd been forced to work and live in the shadows for so long. *It's not my place to question,* he reminded himself. *He's the Akaran here.*

"You banished me for something I never did." He didn't keep the bitterness of his voice. Being back brought pain he long thought buried.

"I realise that. Papa wouldn't want us to fight, I see that now." Daron rose, put a hand on Drake's shoulder. "I brought you home because I know together we can save our clan."

"How?" Drake wanted to believe it but he knew Daron. His brother had lusted for power even before their family's death.

"Different clans have been challenging me. I've had no choice but to fight." Daron pulled off his shirt, revealing jagged scars and burns covering his chest and torso. "I can't keep fighting them by myself."

"You're the Akaran, you have to defend your throne and territory—Father always said that."

"That's why I need you here."

Drake stood up, anger rising as his inner demon rose again. "If you want my power, forget it. I can't rid myself of it even if I tried to." He'd tried to once, in the depths of despair and it had almost killed him. Arya's words and the need for revenge had kept him going.

"No, but I want you to fight by my side. We can bring the clans together just as Papa did."

"I'll help if I can but I'm not here to stay. I have my own life and responsibilities."

Daron laughed. "Running taverns? Yes, I heard about that."

His businesses were just a cover. His true responsibility had been to the Alliance and training Division agents. He was good at it, too. Despite the loneliness, he felt proud of everything he'd accomplished. Now he had Charlie to think of. No kinship to his brother would ever take him away from her. "I had nothing after I left here, I had to make my way in a strange country where demons are outcasts."

"Let's not dwell on the past. The real threat is the mist walkers."

"Mist walkers?" Drake scoffed. "Impossible. They're extinct—I killed them all myself."

Mist walkers had murdered his family so Drake had wiped out every last one of them—even Daron had killed many of them from what Drake had heard.

"These are different from the one we've encountered in the past. They're strong, fast. They move in shadow like Zexens. I'd think them Zexens too if those bastards weren't enslaved to the Grand Witch Bitch."

"Grand Mistress," Drake corrected. "Zexens aren't bound to her as they once were. The current GM released them of their pledge."

"But they still remain loyal to her and that damned council!" Daron cursed. "All demons should be loyal to the Akaran—me. That's the way it should be."

Drake bit back a smile. Daron was stuck in the past to think that way. One leader couldn't have all the power. That gave them too much opportunity to abuse their authority. "I'll look into it."

"We should be in this together, brother."

"As I said, I have my own responsibilities." Drake turned to leave.

"Stay, have a drink. We have a lot to discuss."

Drake forced himself to stay and listen to Daron's ramblings but he drank nothing. By midnight, he felt weary. His inner fury building over the things he'd learnt. Daron had lost half of their family's lands.

He stalked back to his room to find the bed empty. Panic filled him. The dread he felt of losing Charlie again made his heart ache. *Get a grip,* he told himself. *Damned link.*

Or was it more than that now? He thought the link had started to become a bond like true life mates had.

"Charlie?" he called. Maybe she'd stayed with the others at the local inn where he secured rooms for them.

Drake waited, sending out his senses into the universe to search for her. A bond wasn't something he could afford to worry about now. It would make them both too vulnerable.

Charlie, where are you? His claws came out as fury burned hotter. Damn it, he hadn't lost control like this since before he'd become the Akaran.

Light blurred as Charlie shimmered in. "Hey." She grinned when she saw him.

Drake tugged her tight against his chest, breathing in her familiar scent of chocolate mixed with citrus.

"Hey, what's wrong?" She wrapped her arms around him and stared up, her deep brown eyes shimmering to blue.

"Nothing." Drake buried his face against her shoulder. Her nearness soothed him, all rage fading as he held her.

"Clearly it's not nothing. Your eyes were black again. So, what's up?"

Drake shook his head. Nothing seemed to matter when she was around. "I panicked when I couldn't sense—I thought you disappeared again." He stroked her hair. "Did you phase out again?"

Charlie bit her lip. She did that when she held things back. "I don't know. The whole thing felt weird."

His eyes narrowed. "What?"

"You first," Charlie challenged.

He told her what had happened with Daron and she mentioned what had happened at the market.

"Is the spirit a threat?" He rubbed his chin. Only a very powerful entity could have possessed an immortal as old and strong as Helga.

Charlie shrugged. "I didn't feel threatened but I have no idea who she wants me to save." She settled on the bed beside him. "I think she's warning me about the shadow people." She'd admitted she'd seen them when she'd vanished before.

Drake tensed. "Stay away from them."

"What are they?"

"We call them mist walkers since they come and go like mist. They're hard to kill and can't be trusted." His jaw clenched. "They killed my family too. I thought I'd wiped them all out."

"Why come after me?"

"Perhaps they know you're mine. My people have feuded with

them for as long as I can remember and all Demonkind despise them," he said. "They're a blight on our race. They're—never mind. Just stay away from them."

"What are you gonna do about Daron?"

Drake sighed. "I can't help but feel this is my fault."

"He banished you and accused you of a crime you didn't commit." Charlie's eyes flashed red. "He's the one to blame for things here, not you. You shouldn't have to dig him out of this mess."

My little fire brand. He smiled. "If I hadn't walked away, this wouldn't be happening."

"He forced you to!" Charlie's eyes flashed.

Drake sighed. "I could've fought harder, fought for my place as Akaran. Instead I—"

"Instead you became a stronger leader. The Alliance wouldn't be around if it weren't for you. Think of all the people you've helped." She reached out and clutched his hand.

"I can't help but think of all the people who've been lost." He shook his head.

"Drake, don't let him do this to you. You know you did the right thing."

He pulled her close. "I can't leave, I have to be here."

She let out a breath. "I know so do I. I feel like I can find answers here too."

Drake slumped back onto the bed, snaking an arm around her waist as he pulled her close. "What did I do to deserve you?"

She laughed and rested her head against his chest. "You've nearly gotten blown up several times because of me. I'd say I'm bad luck."

"No, I'd go through all that again if I meant I have you."

Charlie snuggled closer to him. "I'm not tired. Come on, let's go for a look around. I want to see the place you grew up in."

CHAPTER 12

Charlie woke to find Drake gone, and scowled. She liked waking up next to him. Having a quick shower, she dressed in her usual jeans and t-shirt. She tried calling Kaz and Nigel but neither answered their phones. Strange. They had agreed to keep in contact at least twice a day. She guessed Drake must be off with Daron or some of the other demons.

Time to walk around Demon Town some more, especially around the citadel. It felt odd wandering around without Drake or Kaz and Nigel. Even among Demonkind she felt out of place. The demons either glared or looked suspicious of her. She noticed that growing up too—even when she hadn't known about her demon heritage. Wandering through the market she found no sign of Helga. Typical, she wanted to ask the crone more about what she'd seen in her vision. And when she needed her, Helga was nowhere to be found.

Checking her phone, Charlie still found no messages from the others. Without Drake around, she didn't have much to do so she decided to look around more on the outskirts of the city. She needed seclusion before trying to contact any spirits. She suspected the girl spirit might still be hanging around somewhere, Charlie hoped she'd be able to make contact and get some real answers using her medium powers. Maybe even the Srimtar might offer help too—and she couldn't risk anyone seeing that.

Charlie moved towards the city gates when she felt someone following her. Did Daron have people spying on her now? If so, she'd lose them soon enough.

Her alias made sense and Drake had made a show of keeping her around as a "plaything". Unless they didn't want her to escape. She thought about staying with the others but she needed to keep an eye on things to report back to the Alliance. Drake needed her too.

He'd found it hard to control his inner demon since his kidnapping. Charlie prayed she could convince him to become bonded soon. They'd both be safer but she wanted to bond with him, spend her life with him. He was it for her. No point in trying to deny it anymore.

She was crazy about that demon.

Charlie ducked around a corner, phased into a wall, and hovered there as a man stood looking around for her.

Seth.

"Why are you following me?" Charlie came out of the wall, frowning. She'd phase back out if she needed to. Although she'd promised Drake she wouldn't phase anymore her powers felt controllable.

Seth's eyes widened. "How did you do that?"

"Answer my question." She folded her arms. "My powers are none of your business."

Seth sighed. "I came to talk to you, but I can't risk us been seen together."

Her eyes narrowed. "Why?"

"Not here." He shook his head. "Daron has spies everywhere."

Charlie grabbed his arm, pulled him through the wall. They reappeared a couple of miles away in some ruins she'd spotted on the way there. "Talk," she said.

Seth glanced around, bewildered. "You're not a Zexen, are you?"

Charlie shrugged. "What do you want to talk about?" She sensed no threat from him, but she wouldn't let her guard down.

"You're Drake's mate."

Her mouth fell open and she started to protest. "No—" Goddess, how the heck had he known that? She'd thought she and Drake had done a good job hiding their relationship. Pretending to be lovers was one thing but that didn't make them life mates—or at least she hoped it appeared they weren't.

"Don't lie, I'm on your side. Daron is unstable. He kept us at war throughout his reign," Seth said. "I came to ask for your help."

"My help?" Charlie touched her chest. "Why?"

"Because Daron needs to be stopped. I know Drake is the true Akaran—you must convince him to kill Daron before it's too late."

"Whoa, back up." Charlie raised her hands. "How the hell do you know that?"

Seth ran a hand through his hair. "I overheard them arguing the day their parents were killed. Daron forced him out."

"Yeah, so why haven't you said anything before now?"

"I couldn't." Seth rubbed his chin. "No one questions the will of the Akaran, not without real evidence. Daron lusted for power even as a boy."

"If you were there that day, did you see who killed the family?"

"No, Daron said it was a sworn enemy—the mist walkers. That's the tale he's told."

"But you don't think it's true."

"I don't know. It's possible—they did try before and have surprised us with sneak attacks over the centuries," he admitted. "They're wily, they can come and go like mist but they do have some weaknesses. Light can make them visible. You're his mate, you must convince Drake to—"

"I'm not his anything." But she could tell he didn't look convinced by the lie.

Seth snorted. "You're his mate, I saw how he looked at you, how you look at each other. He wouldn't have kept you around if you weren't his."

Charlie groaned. "Even if I am, I can't ask him to kill his own brother. Part of him never got over losing his family," she said. "Like you said, we need proof."

"Then I'll help you get it. We must stop Daron before he can start another war."

"Why did Daron call Drake back here?"

Seth bared his teeth. "Because the clans questioned him. Though we hate the mist walkers, some of us are tired of war. More demons want to venture out of Kyral, but Daron has ordered a lockdown forbidding anyone to leave the country."

"Drake and I will do all we can but I can't make any promises."

"You're a witch too, aren't you?"

"So what?" Her eyes narrowed. She wouldn't be so quick to trust him.

"You can't let Daron know that; he despises witches. He'll be even more suspicious if he found out you're kin to the Grand Mistress and the Serenity."

"How the hell do you know that?" She gaped at him.

Seth pulled a piece of paper. On it read: *Grand Mistress and family celebrate in style.* The pictures showed Cate, Charlie, Niara and the rest of the family together at a party the year before.

Damned media! Charlie had thought no one would notice her there.

"Most people here ignore the affairs of the other races, I like to know what happens," he said.

"I'll do what I can be you should go now. I have my own reasons for coming here."

Seth nodded. "Be careful, Kyral isn't safe for you either." He shimmered away.

Charlie moved through the broken rooms of what looked like a castle. She loved ruins. It felt like touching history. The only downside was that spirits often hung out in them too. She cast her senses out, searching for any lingering signs of unwanted presences but found none.

Settling on the edge of a broken wall, Charlie closed her eyes. *Come on, I know you're around here somewhere.* She wished she knew the girl's name. Names made it easier to summon people.

Charlie waited but no presence came to her. Were her powers weak from transition?

Strange. She still felt no different. Every Denai knew when they were going through transition. Their powers and emotions heightened, yet Charlie felt normal. In control of everything, well, except when her phasing took her to strange places.

She sat on the floor. She didn't like meeting ghosts in the spirit realm unless she had to since they were stronger there but maybe it would be easier.

Charlie closed her eyes and felt the world around her fade as a spirit passed over to the next world. She could have gone there in body but both ways had risks.

Mist swirled around her, the walls of the ruins flashed in and out of focus.

"Hello?" she called. "I know you're here somewhere. Come out, I need to talk to you." She waited. "Please, come here. Tell me who you need me to save."

A figure moved out of the shadows. Myles Goodridge. A tall, muscular man with piercing purple eyes and short curly brown hair. Power rolled off him in waves.

Weird; she could never sense what Magickind he was, but his vibe felt familiar somehow.

Charlie gasped, realising he too had entered the spirit realm. Impossible. No one she knew could do that, except maybe Cate, but even she couldn't move in and out like Charlie did.

Charlie knew she had to get back to her body. Fast. "Wow, you didn't send any of your lackeys this time. How sweet." She smirked.

"Where's the Srimtar?"

"Safe and somewhere you'll never find it." She backed away, forced her spirit to go back. Nothing happened. *What the hell?*

"I know it's hidden somewhere here in the spirit realm. Bravo for that," Myles said. "But you see, you're not the mistress of this world, you can't control it the way I can."

Charlie closed her eyes, willing her power to reconnect her with her body. The longer she stayed disconnected, the more toll it would take on her body. She would die if body and spirit stayed apart too long. "You're not getting the orb. It isn't meant for you."

Myles snorted. "And you think it's for you? Ha!" He grabbed her by the throat in a vice-like grip.

Even in spirit, her lungs felt like they were burning.

"Listen to me, there's a war coming and nothing you can do to stop it. Your council and the Alliance will be no more."

Charlie raised her hand, trying to use her powers but they didn't work either. "You'll never bring them down," she hissed. "They're strong. You're just gang lord trying to take control of the underworld."

"Oh, that is only one of my visible forces. I control more than you can ever imagine. Strange, I thought you'd be powerful, but you're nothing, are you?" Myles laughed. "You need the Akaran to protect you. Stop running around in a world you don't understand, little girl."

Charlie fell power rise inside her as her eyes turned azure. Lightning shot from her hand as she sent Myles staggering.

Power hummed through her, she recognised it as her inner demon. She expected it to take control like before but it didn't. She remained in control. "I'm not powerless and this is my turf, not yours," she snarled. "Get out!" She waved her hand, sending a current of blue lightning straight at him.

Myles blurred, and then dodged it. In a blink, he grabbed her by the throat again.

Charlie punched, kicked and blasted him again. *Come on, demon.*

Now would be a good time to come out and go psycho on this bastard.

No response.

The Srimtar's in danger.

Still nothing.

Charlie dodged the blow, trying again to go back to her body. Still nothing.

Myles moved with the speed and skill of an old immortal. His powers were stronger but hell, Charlie was an enforcer. She used every bit of her training as she blocked his blows and hurled another bolt of lightning.

A wave of dizziness washed over her, the more she fought, the more toll it took on her body. Goddess, she couldn't risk coming close to death or she risked triggering the ascension.

"This is our realm, Charlie. Remember that," said a voice. "We control who comes and goes from the space."

Charlie blinked to the strange echo of memory. Who the hell had that been?

"This is my space. Get out!" She raised her hands, pushing at the fabric of the spirit realm, using all her strength to pushing back.

Myles laughed. "You can't push me out. You're too weak, too untrained."

Untrained? She was damn good at her job as an enforcer and witch. Or did he mean her demon side? Was Goodridge the same type of demon as her?"

Charlie's vision darkened, power falling away. Her heart thundered in her ears as the mists around her started to blur in and out of focus.

I'm dying, she thought.

CHAPTER 13

Drake cradled Charlie in his lap as Kaz felt for a pulse. He'd felt the soul tearing pain, signalling she'd stopped breathing.

"Her heart isn't beating." Kaz stared at him, wide-eyed. "We need to shock her; can you conjure electricity?"

Drake shook his head. "That's not my power. I'll shimmer her to—"

Charlie's eyes flew open as she gasped for breath.

"Thank the gods." Drake breathed, cupping her face. "Are you alright, little witch?"

Charlie sat up, breathing hard. Drake froze Kaz and Nigel. "Was it the mist walkers?"

"No, Goodridge—he attacked me in the spirit realm. How the fuck can he do that?"

Drake kissed her, not wanting to let go. In that instant he didn't give a damn about Goodridge, just felt relieved she'd come back to him. "How do you feel? Has the ascension started?"

"Drake, Goodridge fucking attacked me!" she snapped. "Now's not the time to worry about my ascension!"

Drake's expression darkened. "Your heart stopped; we need to focus on the ascension. We'll worry about Goodridge later."

Charlie rose, eyes flashing amber. "I feel fine."

Drake sent his senses out, scanning her body with his mind. Her aura hummed with energy, but nothing like the chaotic energy that came from the ascension. He breathed a sigh of relief. "Gods, woman, you're taking centuries off me. Why did you even come here?"

She snorted. "Oh, please, you'd be bored without me."

Despite the terror he felt, he laughed. "Indeed I would, little witch."

She explained what she'd come there and what she'd seen including the conversation with Seth.

"Do you think we can trust Seth?" she asked, brushing her hair back.

"I think so. I already had my suspicions about Daron but I can handle him," Drake said. "As for Goodridge, I have no idea how he could enter the spirit realm. Demons can't control spirits."

"I don't think he's a demon. I can't sense what he is." Charlie bit her lip. "What if he's like me?"

Drake's brow creased. "What do you mean?"

"He has powers like me. Maybe he's the same type of demon as I am."

"I'm starting to wonder if you're a demon," he said, rubbing the back of his neck.

Charlie winced. "What am I then?" She touched the small seven-pointed pendant at her throat, which showed the symbol of the Denai.

"I don't know. Your powers are unlike any demon's I've known. Plus, I can control demons—even half breeds, but my powers don't work on you."

She smirked. "You could never control me, Vlad."

"Nor do I want to. I love how I never know what to expect with you."

Her smile fell. "If I'm not a demon, what am I?"

The woman I love, he thought, but he couldn't say the words. Not yet. He didn't want to blow it because he'd almost lost her. Again. "We'll figure it out."

Charlie sighed, resting her head against his chest. "I thought I'd find that spirit again. I need to know who I'm supposed to save."

"Come, let's get out of here." He took her hand. "I need to find out if the mist walkers are planning an attack. There's only one place I can do that."

She arched an eyebrow. "How? I thought they were invisible?"

"I've learnt a thing or two in my years as a spy. I have intel that says they have an encampment on Mount Marlowe. We can shimmer to the base but we'll have to climb the rest of the way up. It's too dangerous to shimmer to the top."

Charlie brightened. "Brilliant, I love rock climbing."

Drake tried not to shudder as he looked up at the massive

mountain covered in a blanket of white with dark patches showing trees. Charlie seemed thrilled by the idea. "Maybe we should have asked the others to come with us," he mused.

"They're keeping an eye on things in Kyral," Charlie replied. "Besides it will be nice to have some time alone together. Mountains are romantic."

"I wouldn't call it that," he muttered.

"I forgot you're scared of heights," Charlie remarked. "Don't worry, I'll hold your hand."

He scowled at her. "I'm not afraid of heights. I just don't like them."

"Right, that's why you never go out on the balcony at home."

Drake shook his head. "I prefer my feet on the ground." He paused. She'd said "home", meaning his house back in Setara. "You stayed at the house while I was gone."

Charlie bit her lip. "You never said I had to leave during that bullshit speech when you said I should be with Scott," she said. "Did you want me to move out?"

He chuckled. "No, little witch. I want to be with you always." He gave her a quick kiss. "Anything of mine is yours now, including my homes."

"Homes?" She frowned. "How many homes do you have?"

"I have ten houses, a couple of estates and one or two castles." He laughed at her open-mouthed expression. "They're only places I use when travelling. I can't say any place was like a true home— except when I'm with you. You're my home."

"Good, because you're stuck with me. If you leave again I'll just follow you everywhere." She wrapped her arms around his neck.

"Likewise, little witch. Never let you go." He kissed her again, then led the way up the steep incline, still clutching her hand.

"What happens after our mission in Kyral?" she asked.

Drake shrugged. "It depends. I don't know how long we'll have to stay here."

"I miss Setara," Charlie admitted. "But if we have to stay here, I would, as long as we're together. I moved around so much after I left the academy it'd be nice if I could put down roots somewhere and have a real home together."

"I'd like that too."

"I'm glad you became my partner—I can't imagine working with anyone else now. When this mission is over, I want us to seal our bond too."

Drake hesitated. He'd wanted all of that ever since he'd first met her. Part of him had always wanted to settle down, have a family and home with his life mate but he felt things would change now he was back in Kyral. Perhaps not for the better.

He opened his mouth to speak but found he couldn't promise what she wanted to hear.

"You don't have to say anything we've got time to talk about the future—lots of time." She kissed him.

I hope so.

They moved on. Drake kept his senses on alert to detect any presence or surprise attacks and because he feared the mountain crumbling beneath them.

He avoided looking down whenever possible but Charlie seemed in awe of the view, peering over the edge.

"I wonder what phasing through a mountain feels like," she mused.

"We're not going to find out." Drake gripped her hand tighter. "We can't use our powers up here unless we have to—it'll give away our presence. We need the element of surprise."

They moved higher, the air growing thinner. Charlie kept pace with him, not complaining once.

We should go hiking and mountain climbing more often. Her thoughts echoed through his mind.

Strange, they only had a psychic link. It didn't and shouldn't allow them to hear each other's thoughts—that didn't come until the second stage of the bond. They either had to sleep together or admit they loved each other to do that for that to be complete.

Drake stopped, did that mean she loved him? He hadn't thought that possible given how she'd resisted them having any sort of relationship. That had changed over the past few months but he'd never dared hope she'd love him back.

Charlie frowned. "What are you staring at, Vlad?"

He shook his head, smiled. "Nothing."

"Oh yeah, your eyes are shifting between blue and black so you must be feeling some strong emotions."

"Your eyes change too, little witch." He stroked her cheek. "I thought how lovely you are."

"Yeah right," she scoffed.

"I'm being serious, Charlotte. You are beautiful; why don't you see that about yourself?"

She shrugged. "I'm okay, I don't care how I look most the time." She moved past him as rocks gave way.

Drake grabbed hold of her, wrapping his arms around her waist as he pulled her back. "Now you see why I hate mountains!"

"It's just a few rocks, I would have been fine."

Daft demon, she thought. *He's sweet though. I love it when he looks at me like that.*

"Like what?" He blurted out without thinking.

Charlie frowned. "I didn't say anything."

"Never mind. Let's keep moving. I want to reach the summit before nightfall."

Charlie gripped his wrist. "Are you listening in on my thoughts?"

He ran a hand through his hair. "It wasn't intentional."

"You said we couldn't do that."

He shrugged. "Bonds can form naturally. Maybe it's because I took your blood—I don't know how it all works," he told her. "Our relationship is nothing like I expected it to be."

"I don't mind if a true bond is forming, hell, I'd welcome it. Would you?" Charlie looked him straight in the eye.

"Of course. Why wouldn't I?"

"Because ever since you left I feel like you're holding back. One minute you wanted to be with me, now you don't."

"That's not true. The ascension—"

"The ascension didn't matter as much when we were in Setara. We almost slept together, now you don't want to. Why?" She folded her arms, raising her chin in her defiant way.

He couldn't keep secrets, not from her. No matter how he tried. "I'm afraid," he admitted. "Not of the bond but what might happen to you. I have a feeling I'm going to lose you and it won't go away. If I lost you—" Drake shook his head. "I would lose my soul. You anchor me, you're my heart."

Charlie reached up and kissed him. "Like I said, you're stuck with me. Nothing is going to part again—not even you."

CHAPTER 14

Charlie loved the view as they reached the top of the mountain. Vast fields, houses and the entire city of Kyral were visible from the summit. "This is gorgeous," she breathed, squeezing Drake's hand. She felt him tense as he looked down, uneasiness running off him.

Drake wrapped his arms around her, hugging her from behind. "Daron, Arya and I climbed up here when we were children. My sister loved it too."

"I'm sorry about your sister." She kissed his cheek. "She'd be proud of what you've become now." She smiled and returned the hug, glad for the warmth of his embrace. "Don't worry, I'll catch you if you fall."

He chuckled. "That makes me feel so much better, little witch."

"What are we looking for?" She glanced around the vast sea of white, her breath coming out as cool mist. "Is there a village made of mist up here?"

"I wish, but no. I'm hoping I'll sense something. An Akaran can sense all demons—just as they can sense me if I don't cloak myself."

They moved on, snow crunching underneath their feet.

"Can they sense you if you scan for them?"

He shook his head. "No, although it's hard to tell. They're an elusive bunch."

Charlie felt him cast his senses out, scanning the area in front of them. Her senses tingled at the feel of something else. Light flashed, colour swam in front of her eyes as an opening to the spirit realm. "Drake!" She grabbed his arm, pulling him away from it.

He blinked, surprised. "What?"

"Portal." She motioned to it. "Weird, spirit portals are rare and someone must've left it open. Maybe I should—"

"No, no magic, remember?" Drake clutched her hand. "Let's keep moving."

He led her back up the steep track.

Something blurred out the corner of her eye. Goodridge and two demons blocked their path.

"Ah hell," she muttered. So much for no magic.

Damn it! Drake cursed.

"Wow, you must really be getting desperate, Myles," Charlie remarked.

"Hand over the Srimtar or all the mist walkers on this mountain will find out you're here," said Myles. "They won't act kindly to the Akaran's presence, believe me."

"Not happening," Drake replied, fire forming in his palm.

I thought you said no magic? Charlie tensed, scanning for any more oncoming demons.

I did, but the bastard almost killed you.

You can't kill him, he's too strong, we don't know what he is.

Three more demons appeared behind them.

Can't you command them not to attack? Charlie asked.

I could but I sense blocks in their minds. My power may not work.

We can't blow our cover, let's... Charlie ducked as an energy ball flew at her head.

"One way or another I will get what I came for." Myles grinned.

She raised her hand, flinging one demon straight over the side of the mountain. Drake hurled fireballs, killing one and wounding another. Charlie blocked, kicked and knocked another to the ground. Myles stood there watching but didn't move.

Bastard, he knows this will only slow us down. She resisted the urge to phase, afraid Myles would pull her back into the spirit realm. She needed to stay in the physical world. She dodged another fireball, kicked the demon's legs out from under him and grabbed him by the throat. Her eyes bled to black as she unleashed her touch.

The demon laughed. "Your power won't work on me, witch."

Charlie felt the ground beneath her trembling as light shimmered around her. *No!* Her eyes fixed on Goodridge but he looked just as alarmed as she fell. Someone had opened a portal and it began to suck them in.

Drake! She reached up for him as he lay on the ground, held down by an invisible force.

Tendrils of energy seem to wrap around her, pulling her down.

Myles and his two remaining demons sank to their knees as a vortex began to form. "What's happening?" one of the demons cried.

Charlie took a breath, body incorporeal as she broke free of the strange force. She grabbed hold of Drake and shimmered out.

Charlie and Drake fell onto the glassy floor of the spirit world room. They landed in a tangle of limbs with her on top of him. "What the hell was that?" she asked.

Drake let out a low growl. "I sensed another presence. Someone tried to drag all of us into the spirit realm." He scrambled up, pulling her to her feet. "Impossible. No one has control over this world." He glanced around. "Except you."

Charlie shook her head. "I can't manipulate this world or open portals like that. I move in and out myself, but that was off the scale power. Weird, Myles looked just as surprised as we were."

"Indeed." Drake rubbed his chin. "If only I could have sensed more, I might have been able—"

"At least we're safe here. No one can enter this place but me."

Drake glanced around. "Did you create this place?"

She shook her head. "No, I just found it one day and it became my place. I come here when I need to single be alone," she said. "I must've brought you here in dreams too. I've never shown it to anyone. It's my secret place." She walked over to the Srimtar that sat shimmering on the table. It flashed as she neared it but the invisible walled sheet set around it still held. "Phew, at least this safe. What about the mist walkers?"

"I doubt there's much point in going back now. They will have scattered."

"Do you think they could be the ones who open the vortex?"

"No, they're masters of illusion. They have no power over realms." Drake frowned. "I can't sense time here."

"That's because time stops here—no idea how it works but time doesn't affect it," Charlie told him. "It keeps moving on the outside though. Back to Kyral then?"

"Not yet. Kaz and Nigel are keeping an eye on things. I hoped we'd have some time together before everything went to hell."

Charlie wrapped her arms around his neck and kissed him.

***

Drake glanced around, keeping one arm wrapped around Charlie as they reappeared on the mountaintop. After spending a few hours in Charlie's secret room, they decided to go back to the mountain. He needed to find out anything related to the mist walkers, even if it meant hunting around the mountain for the next few days. They could see in the dark and had the faint glow stars twinkling above them. Still, the thought of wandering around in the dark made him even more uneasy.

"Do you think it's worth coming back here? They must have all scattered by now," Charlie remarked.

They moved through dense forest. Drake scanned every inch of the mountaintop. They had to be there somewhere.

"Maybe we should get some sleep. It'll be dawn in a few hours." Charlie pulled her jacket tighter, shivering.

He'd forgotten about the cold. Weather didn't affect him as his body always stayed warm so he wrapped an arm around her. "There are caves a few metres away, my siblings and I used to camp there. We can shelter inside." Once inside the cave he started a fire and wrapped his jacket around her. "Get some sleep, I'll keep watch."

He cast a protective ward around them. Charlie snuggled against him as she slept. He couldn't remember ever feeling so content as he brushed her hair off her face. "I love you, little witch."

"Drakon…" a voice whispered.

His head shot up to see the glowing form of a girl with curly black hair and his gut twisted. "Arya? How—"

Arya held out her hand as she tried to reach for him, but a swirling mist whirled around her, making her form waver.

"No, Arya!" His hand met empty air when he tried to grab her. Then she vanished in a blur of light. "Come back!"

Something moved in the shadows, sending his senses reeling. Drake let go of Charlie, shot his feet, flames forming in his palm. Hands grabbed him, wrenching his arms back as someone shoved him to the ground. A woman with long blonde hair, covered in blue markings appeared. "I wouldn't bother fighting, Akaran. You're no match for us."

A man appeared and picked Charlie up, jabbing something in her neck. She slumped against him.

Drake snarled. "You!" He recognised Scott, Charlie's former lover, in an instant. "You're one of them!" The blue tribal markings showed Scott to be a mist walker too as he grinned. "What did you do to her?" Drake pulled but the invisible bonds held him in place. "If you hurt her—"

"I'd never hurt her," Scott snapped. "We came here to save her from you."

Drake reached for the full depth of his power. He didn't care of all Demonkind found out what he was; he wouldn't let them take his mate. "She's mine!"

The woman laughed. "Funny, it almost sounds like you care for her."

Care? She was his life now. Power built up, his eyes turning to black, fangs extending. "If you take her from me, I'll rip this world apart until I kill every last one of you."

"You're fighting a war you can't win, Akaran. You and your brother have murdered enough of my kind," the woman retorted.

"Can you blame me after you killed my family?"

"That wasn't us. We don't kill unless we have to."

Drake gave a harsh laugh. "Why should I believe you?"

"You don't have to believe anything," she said. "Let's go."

Scott and Charlie vanished in a blur of light.

"No!" Drake roared. "Bring her back. Do you what you want to me, just let her go." He called up the full force of his power and grabbed the woman by the throat as he broke free of his bonds. "Return her to me or I will kill you."

"How do you think she'll feel when she finds out you killed her mother?"

Drake's eyes narrowed. "Impossible, her mother died in childbirth."

Her lips curved. "I faked my death well. Now I have my daughter back and you'll never see her again."

Both the woman and the shadows vanished.

Drake let out a bellow of fury, the whole mountain trembled from the force. "If you want a war, I'll give you one."

EPILOGUE

Charlie's head pounded as she woke. She had the sensation of being carried around, followed by a soul gripping pain that made her blackout as she laid in what looked like a circle of light. She forced her eyes to open, ignoring the wave of nausea. "Drake?" she called.

She lay on a soft bed. Light poured in through the windows. With cream walls and a flagstone floor, the room looked bare, with only a chest of drawers, a table and a wooden chair. It didn't look like the room she'd shared with Drake at the castle.

"Drake, where are you?" She reached out to him with her mind but felt nothing. Her heart skipped a beat. Charlie sat up, the room around her started spinning as bile rose in her throat. *Where the hell am I?*

The door opened with a man walked in. He was skinny and blonde. It took her a moment to place him.

"Scott? Am I hallucinating now?" She hadn't seen her ex-boyfriend since the night she told him she'd wanted to be with Drake and ended their relationship for good.

Scott gave her his goofy grin. "Hey, Char, how are you feeling?"

"Where am I?" she demanded. "How did I get here?"

"It's okay, you're safe now." He squeezed her shoulder. "You're in Alanon. We brought you here."

"Who's 'we'? Where's Drake?" The last thing she remembered she'd fallen asleep next to him in that cave. "Why can't I sense him?" Her heart beat faster as her panic rose. She wanted nothing more than to get back to him.

"All that matters is you're safe. Drake can't hurt you anymore." He tried to reach for her again, but Charlie shrugged him off.

"Drake would never hurt me, I'm his mate." She shoved his hand away. "Tell me what's going on right now."

His smile faded. "I'm not the best person to answer your questions."

"What does—"

The door opened as a beautiful blonde woman walked in. The stranger she'd seen in the mist.

"You need to tell me what the fuck you've done." Charlie crossed her arms.

"Charlie, it's good to have you here with us." The woman smiled. "I've longed for this day."

Charlie glowered at Scott. "I want answers. Now! So cut the crap."

"I'm Irina, I'm your mother and leader of the Illuminari," Irina said. "Illuminari are sometimes called mist walkers."

Charlie burst out laughing. "Okay, lady. I don't know what kind of game you're playing but my mum died twenty-four years ago," she said. "And you're not her."

"Helena was one of my many aliases. I know I look different—this is my true form but I am your mother, Charlotte," Irina said. "I brought you here to save you. It's a good thing the fake Akaran contacted us when he did."

Fake Akaran? Daron, I should've known he had something to do with this. "From what?" she demanded, eyes flashing.

"From Drake," Scott answered. "You were never his life mate. When you almost died six years ago he cast a spell that bound you to him. He knows what you are, now you can't use—"

"This is some messed up shit!" Charlie raised her hands. "First you kidnap me, now my dead mother is supposedly alive. Is this some kind twisted plan to get me back?"

"Scott is telling the truth. The Akaran isn't your mate, demons have no soul mate," Irena told her. "Your powers have been growing, I knew it was time to begin your training myself."

Okay, more lies. What do these idiots think they're playing at? Charlie backed away. "Okay, enough already, I'm leaving." She tried shimmer. Nothing happened. "What have you done to my powers?" She noticed a silver bracelet on her left wrist. She'd seen similar tech before. "You bound me? Are you serious?"

"It just a precaution—your powers are—" Irina said.

"You're not my mother," she snarled the woman. She turned to glare at Scott. "You bastard. If you cared about me you wouldn't kidnap me and hold me prisoner."

"You're not a prisoner, Char. We saved you. Drake and his brother were going to use you to start a war," Scott insisted.

"Drake cares about me and he'll go ballistic unless I go back right now." She shoved Irina aside, punched Scott in the face and then stormed into a long corridor.

The winding corridor of sandstone walls and flagstones stretched out. There were no doors, no paintings, nothing as she ran, turning in different directions.

"Charlie." Scott appeared behind her.

"Stay away from me," she warned, backing away.

"You can't leave this place without magic; it's spelled." He held out his hand. "Just come with me. Irina and I will explain everything. I know you're scared, but this is where you're meant to be. We brought you here so you could learn about who and what you really are."

Charlie backed away, feeling a void within her soul. Her connection to Drake had gone.

Looking all around, she knew there was no way out. She was on her own now.

SHADOW GUARDIAN

CHAPTER 1

Focus, Charlotte," Irina snapped.

Charlie McCray scowled at her mother as they sat together on the floor of the ancient temple. But hell. at least they'd left the Illuminari's compound for once. *I am bloody focusing. If I focus any more I'll pass out.* She kept her mental shields in place. The last thing she needed was for Irina to hear her true thoughts. After spending the past few weeks in the mist walker's hidden compound, she grew weary of being there. She'd made it her mission to find out everything she could about them and her mysterious mother who'd been thought dead for the past twenty-four years.

The mist walkers, or Illuminari as they called themselves, were a secretive bunch who spied on the rest of Magickind after being hunted almost to extinction by the other races. They called themselves resistance fighters, but Charlie thought of them more as rebels. If they really wanted to become a known race and be accepted, why the hell didn't they stop hiding in the shadows?

"All Illuminari inherit the knowledge about our people from birth," Irina said. "You just have to unlock it."

The only good thing about being out of the Illuminari compound was Irina had done something to the bracelet which had been blocking Charlie's powers for the past month. Irina had somehow configured it so Charlie could use her powers again. *About bloody time too!*

Vines covered the temple's grey stone walls and patches of coloured light covered the floor as the sun shone through the broken stained-glass window. Charlie didn't know why Irina had chosen this location of all places to practise learning to use her full demon powers. It made little sense because the Illuminaris had a whole fortress to use back in their hidden compound.

Charlie rose, brushing her long brown hair off her face and turned to her mother. "I've been trying to unlock it for over a month and I've not remembered anything. Maybe I'm not like you." She crossed her arms, scowling down at the blue dress she wore. Goddess, she missed real clothes!

Irina sighed. "Still so resistant. I keep telling you your place is here. All Illuminari are sworn to help our people."

"Guess I'm not as shadow sworn as you lot." *My place is with Drake, the love of my life. Instead of being with him, I'm stuck with you, my ex and a bunch of—*

The walls trembled, sending dust flying through the air.

"What was that?" Charlie frowned, casting her senses out.

Irina's azure eyes widened in shock. "We're under attack. Hurry, we must…"

Light blurred as Myles Goodridge shimmered in beside them.

Oh shit! Charlie raised her hand, blasting him with a bolt of blue lightning. *Hell, at least that's one demon power I can kind of control.*

He raised his hand and it fizzled out.

Well, mummy dearest. You did a lousy job teaching me that. She gritted her teeth.

Myles raised his hand, sending Irina staggering backwards, her body flicking in and out of existence. "You're the one I came for," he said to Charlie.

Charlie grinned. "Good, I need some fun after being stuck in this place so long." She flew at him.

He phased, her hand passing right through his body when she tried to hit him, his own hand solidified as he punched her in the stomach. "Don't think any realm is free from me. I can walk between worlds as easily as breathing."

Charlie grunted from the blow, then phased out as he fired a bolt at her.

He wanted one thing—the Srimtar. An ancient orb with immense power that had unknown abilities. As the orb's guardian, she knew she could never let him get his hands on it.

She blocked his next blow. Goddess, this guy was stronger and much more well-versed in his powers than her. Where was the so-called knowledge Irina kept harping on about? How could she stop him?

Charlie hurled another lightning bolt. *Think,* she told herself. *Stay alive.*

She couldn't outmatch him in strength but there was one place she could be stronger. One place only she could enter, her space between worlds. Light blurred around her as she started to shimmer and the room around her faded, replaced by glowing purple walls that shimmered like mist as she reappeared in her secret place.

The small opaque orb sat on the table made from the same misty substance. It burned bright red as it did when it sensed a threat.

Charlie grabbed it, clutching it in her palm. She let out a breath she didn't know she'd been holding. She hated running away but the orb was her number one priority. In the wrong hands, it could kill hundreds, even thousands, of people since it only seemed to let her touch her. Anyone else who tried using it ended up dead. As its guardian, only she could withstand its power. "Phew! You're more trouble than you're worth sometimes."

The walls around her trembled. *Now what?*

Another blast made the walls flash. Goodridge had tried to follow her and now tried to take down her walls. The walls around her shook even more, vibrating from the onslaught of energy. Charlie backed away, unsure of what to do. Just because she'd found this space, didn't mean she knew how to control it. She glanced down at the Srimtar. She'd used strange magic to protect it before—or maybe it had been shadow magic—could she again?

She raised her hand, sending out a bolt blue of light that rippled over the flashing walls. The orb flared between her fingers, pulsing with energy. Charlie's eyes snapped shut as a vision dragged her in. A woman lay on the floor, her long blonde hair plastered against her face, holding a screaming baby wrapped in blankets as she stood, tears streaming down her cheeks.

Charlie froze, seeing the woman was Irina.

"Forgive me, daughter," Irina said. "I'd keep you if I could. It wasn't supposed to be like this." She glanced around; eyes wide. "He'll kill you if he ever found out. Please forgive me. One day you'll remember where you came from. Remember you are loved."

Gold light flashed as Niara appeared, frowning. "Helena, where have you been?" she asked. "Stephen said—"

Whoa, what's my great-grandma doing here? Charlie wondered. *That baby must be me. Weird, I thought she never even got to hold me.* She'd always wondered what it would've been like growing up with a mother, but the reality of having Irina around now paled in comparison to her dreams.

"Serenity, you must take my child." Irina shoved the baby into Niara's arms. "Please take her back to Steve. I know he'll look after her. He's so excited about becoming a father."

Niara clutched the baby. "What are you talking about?" she demanded as Irina backed away.

Irina shook her head. "Tell Steve—tell everyone—I died in childbirth. No one must know the truth."

Niara's eyes narrowed. "I knew you were never a witch, but you can't just abandon your child like this."

"If I don't, she'll die. There are worse things in this world than even Raven or the Covenant. Please, if you care for her, do the right thing and let me go. No questions asked."

"I don't know what you're running from, but I promise she'll be loved and cherished by our family." Niara looked down at the baby and clutched her to her chest.

Irina nodded, sniffed. "I know."

"Steve will be devastated."

"It's safer for everyone this way. He has a daughter; she'll bring him more joy than I ever could." She turned to go but hesitated. "Her name is Charlotte. Steve wanted her name to begin with a C or K like the McCray family tradition—we argued about it."

Niara smiled at the baby as Irina shimmered away.

Charlie blinked as the vision faded, still gripping the Srimtar and felt Goodridge trying to break through the room's defences. She shimmered out, reappearing back in at the temple. She grabbed her mother's hand. "He'll be coming back. We need to get out of here."

Irina clutched her bleeding shoulder. "He's too strong. I can't force him out."

"Come on, we aren't called mist walkers for nothing. Tell me what to do. I'm not letting him take my orb."

Irina gripped her hand. "I can't shimmer from here. Let's get outside and make a run for it. I can't risk him following us."

CHAPTER 2

"Ah, hell." Charlie muttered as she and Irina stepped outside and said, "What are you doing here?"

Myles Goodridge, gang leader and murderer, stood along with a group of his men surrounding them. He looked just as Charlie remembered, with the same mop of dark hair curly hair and cool purple eyes.

She scanned the crowd of men, and then glanced at her mother, who just stood there, unmoving.

"You can't be here," Irina said. "You..."

Myles grabbed Irina, cuffing her with bonds that bound her powers. "Now, hand over the Srimtar or she dies."

Charlie clutched the orb, feeling torn. Irina shook her head, eyes wide. She didn't want to watch Irina die but she knew she couldn't let go of the orb either. It was too dangerous for anyone to have. "It's mine. You'll have to kill me before I let you take it."

"So be it." Myles raised his hand.

Shots rang out, bullets ripped through the air, hitting Myles and his men in the chest. Myles staggered and Irina pulled free of his grasp.

Charlie grinned when she saw Scott, Irina's lieutenant, standing there. Scott grabbed Irina, pulling her out of the line of fire. "About bloody time!" Charlie muttered and threw an energy ball at Goodridge.

Myles's men grabbed Scott and Irina, cutting off their escape. Myles blurred, grabbing Charlie's arm. "One thing you need to learn about me," he hissed. "Is that your power will never be a match for mine."

Power jolted through her, their bodies fading in and out of existence. Charlie screamed as the netherworld's energy rushed against them. Myles gripped her arms. "Give me the orb."

Charlie tried to move but the force of the colliding worlds made it impossible for her limbs to comply. *Let go of me!* She tried to draw magic, but Myles seemed to have a hold on that too. She hoped her inner demon would take control, then realised it wouldn't. She'd come to accept that part of herself. She'd be damned if she'd go down without a fight.

The orb pulsed and vibrated as she clutched it tight, her knuckles turning white. How much longer could they both withstand this?

Charlie knew she couldn't keep hold of the orb, nor could she let Myles have it. So she did the only thing she could; she threw it into the netherworld, sending it back to its secret hiding place. *Go, protect yourself.*

The orb flashed then blue light exploded ripping both the physical and spiritual planes.

"No!" Myles cried just as the blast threw them apart.

Charlie closed her eyes, braced herself the inevitable. She'd cheated death many times over the past few years. Now would be the last time to face it. *Forgive me, Drake. I wish we could've been together.* She felt herself falling into oblivion. No pain, just floating through emptiness. When she opened her eyes, she found herself standing in the spirit world, surrounded by a haze of mist and dancing lights. The dark-haired girl she'd encountered weeks before stood waiting for her. She'd wondered what had happened to the strange spirit but had thought it had given up in its quest to get Charlie to help her.

"Let me guess, I didn't save whoever was supposed to say before I died." Charlie sighed.

"You're not dead. You are a shadow walker and a medium. You can walk between life and death the way other immortals can't."

"I'm not immortal." Charlie frowned. "Wait, did I ascend? I thought I'd remember that." She reached for her magic, expecting it to feel stronger but it felt the same. Denais were supposed to come into their full powers when they ascended. She should have felt something.

"You didn't need to. You transitioned into a true immortal the day you first almost died."

Charlie ran her fingers through her hair. "You mean when Drake saved me six years ago."

"Yes, your bond triggered your immortality. You didn't need to ascend the way other witches do because of your demon powers."

"Wait, what bond? Drake and I aren't bonded. We never even slept together."

The girl smiled. "Your bond has been there long before either of you knew about it. It's kept you both alive, but it's weak because you both choose to block it out."

Charlie stared at the girl and recognised the cool blue eyes. "You're Drake's sister Arya," she gasped.

Arya nodded. "Yes, I am."

"Why have you been following me? Who am I supposed to save?"

"I needed to be sure you and my brother were both safe. The Armargens and the Illuminari will kill each other given the chance," she replied. "Drake needs you. You're his light. His power will consume him if you're not there to anchor him."

She glanced around at the spectrums of purple light and shivered. "Can I go back?"

"You can, but I have something to show you first." Arya held out her hand.

Charlie took it without hesitation. The girl had never been a threat to her; she'd only meant to help.

A swirling vortex spun around them, making Charlie's stomach do flip flops. When she opened her eyes, she stood in another room. Smoke filled the air; tapestries covered the walls and wingback chairs surrounded the fire.

"Arya?" she called. "Where are you?"

Arya? she called out in thought, casting her senses out to try and find her. But the girl was nowhere to be found.

A dark stain began to spill across the floor and a coppery tang filled the air. Blood. Charlie moved around the chair and found a woman lying there next to a man. Both had been stabbed numerous times.

"Shit." She fell to her knees by the woman, seeing her chest still moving. "Hold on." She pulled a blanket off the chair, pressed against the wound. "I'll get some help."

The woman said to her, "My children, please you have to save my children. Drake, Arya, they won't be safe."

"Drake? Goddess, you're his mother. I've come back in time," she rambled. Judging by the tapestries room she guessed they were in Drake's family home in Kyral.

"Please find my children…" the woman rasped, then her eyes glazed over.

Shit! Why the hell had Arya bought her back in time to when Drake's family had been murdered? It made no sense.

The body of a huge muscular man lay there, his eyes already empty. Charlie guessed he'd be Drake's father, the former Akaran and leader of all demons.

The sound of running footsteps made her heart beat faster. Charlie phased, vanishing into a wall as a lanky young man came in. "Mama? Papa?" he said.

Charlie froze. Drake. He looked younger, skinnier, but she'd recognise him anywhere. She had to stay hidden, she couldn't risk being seen by anyone or she'd screw up their entire future.

"No, Mama. Wake up, you can't leave." He shook her shoulder. "Please." He glanced over at his father then hurried out of the room. "Arya!"

Charlie hurried after him, jumping from wall to wall as she went. She had no idea why Arya would have brought her back here but guessed it had something to do with Drake.

"Arya?" he bellowed, running from room to room.

Charlie hoped she could stay incorporeal. She didn't dare risk anyone seeing her, especially Drake. It risked changing their entire future together if they saw each other before they met in the present.

"Wake up, little sister." Drake fell to his knees, clutching his sister to his chest.

Charlie moved out of the wall on instinct and saw Arya's eyes flutter open. Was this what she had wanted to show her?

"You can't give up. You must find your mate," Arya rasped. Her blue eyes fixed on Charlie who froze. "She walks in shadow."

Arya could see her! Maybe because she was close to death, Charlie didn't know.

"What? I don't have a mate," Drake insisted as he picked her up. "I'll find a healer. Stop talking, save your strength."

"It will take centuries, but she'll help you control your power," Arya whispered, then her body went limp.

"No, little sister. You can't leave me." Tears spilled down Drake's cheeks. "No!" he moaned.

Without thinking, Charlie wrapped her arms around him, hugging him from behind. "I'm so sorry, Drake," she murmured. "I had no idea." She rested her head against his back.

He tensed then reached up to grasp her hand as she became solid.

Charlie saw movement, turned as Daron came at them with the sword. She gasped. "Behind you!"

So this is the killer.

Drake didn't seem to hear as the sword came down on him.

Light blurred around the room as Charlie's body shifted between corporeal and incorporeal. She hadn't stayed incorporeal for this long before it had taken its toll. Damn it, she couldn't be seen. The fight with Myles had already drained her of a lot of energy. She dove into the nearest energy source she could find, Drake.

Whoa, weird, she thought as she settled inside him. She now had complete control over his body. She dodged the blow. "Why you are doing this?" she demanded in Drake's voice, dodging again.

"Because I'm tired of waiting for power," Daron snarled, swinging the sword again.

Okay, you are so going down. She blocked his blow, grabbed the sword, then flipped it so she held the blade then hit him on the back of the head with the hilt. *I should kill you, you bastard!* Lightning flashed as a strange mist filled the air. *Now what's happening?*

Charlie leapt from Drake's body as the bolt hit him in the chest, a massive surge of power jolting through him.

He's become the Akaran, she realised.

Drake blinked, bewildered as he stared at his bloodied hands. "What have I done?" he muttered. "Did I do this? Gods, Arya." He gathered her up in his arms.

Daron groaned, glanced between Drake and the fallen sword.

"Daron, what happened?" Drake asked. "I don't remember. Who did this?"

Daron blinked and then his lip curled as he scrambled up. "You did this."

"What?" Drake gaped to him. "No, no. I'd never hurt them. You know I wouldn't." He let go of Arya, fire forming in his palm.

"You're the Akaran," Daron snarled. "You killed Papa for his power."

"No!" Drake bellowed, the walls around shaking so hard Charlie almost fell out of her hiding place. "If I did, why would I kill Mama and Arya?"

Heavy footsteps thundered down the hall.

"Get out," Daron hissed. "You have no right to Papa's throne. Leave. I'll take the throne; it is my right. You're never to return here."

Stunned, Drake staggered back. "But I didn't—"

"Go, Drake. Before I tell everyone what you did."

Drake stood there, the look on his face threatening to break Charlie's heart. Arya had told her to save him so she'd do just that. She dove inside his body and the feel of power intensified, replenishing her own strength. She felt it then, the soul bond between them as the Akaran's power settled into its new host.

"You know damn well I didn't do this," she snapped in Drake's voice. "I'll prove my innocence. Remember, brother, I'm the one with the real power now."

She used Drake's powers to shimmer out. He collapsed onto the hot desert sand, pain threatening to overwhelm him. *I can't do this,* he thought. *I don't deserve to live.*

His grief made Charlie ache for him as she phased out of his body. "You can't give up," she snapped. "You have to fight."

Drake blinked, seeming to hear her.

"You can't give up. You're the Akaran, think of the good you can do," she continued. "Fight, fight for me. You have to stay alive. For me, for us." She touched his cheek.

He stiffened. "What am I supposed to do now?" he murmured.

Charlie thought fast. "Go to Elaris, to the Serenity," she blurted out without thinking. "She can help you to control your power." But she knew Niara would have been the only one able to help. "Remember Arya's words. Remember your life mate. She's out there waiting for you. You have to find her."

Drake wiped his eyes and said nothing.

"Don't give up," Charlie said. "Remember not to give up. You can become a great man. Don't give up on your mate either, no matter what."

The desert and Drake faded as Charlie appeared back in the spirit realm, holding Arya's hand.

She wiped tears from her eyes. "Why did you do that?"

Arya gave a sad smile. "He needed to be shown the way and you had to see the truth."

"Daron killed you and your parents. You've been stuck in limbo ever since."

"I had to watch over my brother until he found you."

Charlie laughed. "I haven't made things easy for him either." She stared at the girl, stuck somewhere between a child and a woman. "I have to go back."

"He'll need you by his side."

She sniffed. "He has me, even if he doesn't realise that." She hesitated as she went to leave. "What about you? You can't stay here. You have to move on; it's not natural for spirits to stay behind."

"I think I'm ready to move on now. I know you'll take care of him."

Charlie gave the girl a quick hug. "Thanks for what you did. Go now, be at peace." She watched as Arya shimmered with white light then faded.

CHAPTER 3

Drake stood inside the cave where he last saw Charlie. He still felt the lingering trace of her presence there. He pictured her lying there asleep in his arms, almost as though he could reach out and touch her. It made his heart ache and the familiar anger rose.

He'd spent the past few days scouring every inch of Mount Marlowe trying to sense her and find a trace of those he had taken her. The Illuminari leader Irina Devereux claimed to be Charlie's mother, who'd been thought to have died giving birth to her.

Drake still couldn't believe the very clan who'd murdered his parents and sister were Charlie's own demon clan. Still, it would never change his feelings for Charlie.

Kaz and Nigel, two enforcers who worked with Charlie and on their unofficial team, had been helping with his search too.

"Drake, I don't think we're going to find anything up here." Kaz touched his shoulder and gave it a squeeze.

He shrugged her off, scowling. "Don't say that," he growled. "She must be somewhere, and I won't rest until I get her back." He stalked outside, the icy air hitting his face. The cold didn't bother him. He was immune to all changes in temperature.

"Hey, I know you miss her—we all do—but at least we know they won't hurt her." Kaz followed him out, pulling her pink hat down over her red hair.

"Do we? That clan is responsible for killing my family. I won't just let this go until I get her back."

"Charlie wouldn't want you starting a war for her, hell, she'd be pissed off." She crossed her arms. "Nigel has ears; we know what you and Daron have been talking about. You want to find the Illuminaris and go to war against them."

"They took my mate; I have every right to wipe them off the face

204

of the earth." Hell, he thought he'd done just that centuries ago. But they were a wily bunch.

"How do you think Charlie will feel if you hurt her mother?"

Drake winced. He knew Charlie; she wouldn't be happy by her mother's sudden reappearance. Plus, she needed him to find her and get her away from them. They had to be holding her against her will or else she would have come back to him by now. He knew she would.

"We still have Goodridge to worry about, why does everyone seem to have forgotten about that?" Kaz asked.

Because finding Charlie is much more important than worrying about Goodridge. I'll deal with him later.

Kaz sighed. "I'll go find Nigel and have another look around. Stay in contact."

Drake waved her away without saying another word.

He reached out to Charlie with his mind but the ever-present link that had existed between them seemed to have vanished along with her. He didn't understand it. They were life mates even though they weren't bonded yet. That link wouldn't just break without killing one, or both, of them. In his soul, Drake knew Charlie still lived. He'd know if she were gone. But then, where was she?

He moved along with the path, snow crunching under his feet as a blanket of white stretched out over the mountaintop, disappearing into the clouds. He ignored his fear of heights as he climbed higher. Tired of the steep climb, he shimmered until he finally reached the mountain's peak. Despite his fear, being up there gave him a strange kind of peace.

Where are you, Charlie? He closed his eyes, dropped his mental shields and let his power roam free as despair threatened to overwhelm him. He let out an anguished moan, a demon crying out for his mate.

His power shot out, shaking the very mountain. His inner demon clawed at his mind as the part of himself he'd fought to rein in for so long tried to take control.

More power leaked out of him; stone groaned as the mountain continued to shake but he didn't care. He could feel his soul slipping away into darkness. Demons needed their life mates, the bond tethered them. As the most powerful of all Demonkind, Drake had spent over eight thousand years keeping his power and his true nature under control. He'd been good at it too. That had changed six years earlier when he'd found Charlie when she'd been only eighteen. Since then he'd come to know her, love her, even. That had all ended the night they'd taken her away. He hoped they wouldn't harm her but…

Rage quickly replaced the emptiness, he wanted blood now, revenge on every Illuminari. They may have killed his family, but he wouldn't lose his mate too.

His eyes bled to black when he opened them, his fangs came out as power hummed through his veins. *I am the Akaran, I am power. No demon is free from me. Now where are those fucking Illuminari!*

The mountain groaned and twisted beneath him. The Akaran had a mystical connection to his realm too. He could control every inch of Kyral. One way or another he would use it to find Charlie.

"Drake, what the hell are you doing?" Kaz yelled through the commlink in his ear.

"Leave." His voice came out low and guttural. The sound of a true demon. "Now."

"But what's happening to the—" He waved his hand, Kaz and Nigel's presences vanished from his mind as he sent them back to Setara. They'd be safer there.

Drake raised his hand, as power extended out every inch of Kyral. The earth pulsed and breathed as if they were one being. He sensed the presence of every demon in his realm and beyond as he scanned their minds. He'd keep looking until he found a trace of his mate.

Drakon, what are you doing? Daron demanded. *The ground is shaking, and people know I'm not the one doing it. Are you trying to ruin everything I've worked for?*

He muted out his brother's voice. He didn't care if anyone found out the truth. He'd never wanted to reveal his true nature, instead preferring to let Demonkind believe Daron was the Akaran while he remained in the shadows.

They no longer mattered.

Charlotte! he cried. *Where are you?*

Around him, rocks and heavy boulders fell away as the mountain began to crumble beneath his feet. He remained in place, held there by his power.

He clenched his fists as a pool of molten lava rose from the ground, filling the air with a heavy odour. He liked to heat, hell, he didn't like mountains anyway. With a single thought, it crumbled around him, leaving ash in its wake as the lava consumed all of it. The Illuminari had been there, it had been one of their bases once. Perhaps it wiped some of them out in the process.

Drake landed on solid ground, the earth trembling beneath him. The thrill of power filled some of the emptiness inside him. *I'll take this place apart bit by bit until I find her.* He grinned at the thought. Hell, if Charlie hadn't come there they might never have found her. He pulled out the comm link, incinerating it. He didn't want to listen to reason. The time for that had ended.

Now it's time for blood and war.

Drake shimmered in and out of the different planes of existence, drunk on power as he searched for the Illuminaris. He'd already shimmered to half a dozen different places; a couple of demons had tried to challenge him as the earthquakes had already brought down several buildings. But he killed them without a hint of remorse.

Nothing mattered now.

The sun beat down on him as he moved over the hot desert sands, stalking through it. *Where are you, Illuminaris? Come out! I will find you. No demons—not even you—are safe from me.*

A swirling blue vortex formed around him—just like the ones he'd seen those bastards use. Finally, he had them. Drake raised his hand, trying to get control of the vortex. Light flashed as his power bounced off and the portal swallowed him up. He felt like he was being sucked through a vacuum as the portal tossed him around then spat him back out again.

Drake growled as he landed on the floor that looked like it had been made from purple glass. Purple-blue mist made up the walls that shimmered faintly in the low light. He frowned; he knew this place. "Charlie," he managed to choke out, jumping to his feet.

"Drake, what have you done?"

He spun around. There she was, his little witch, with her long brown locks tied into a knot, her dark brown eyes and her luscious curves. She looked just as he remembered. His heart twisted at the sight of her.

She held up her hand. On it, she wore a black gold ring encrusted with a huge amethyst stone. It could control both him and the power inside him. "Do I need to use this?" she asked. "Please don't make me, I don't want to hurt you."

Drake hesitated, part of him wanted nothing more than to wrap his arms around her, the other wanted to continue the hunt for those who'd taken her.

"Drake." She reached up, cupping his face. "Stop, this isn't you."

All at once the power retreated, his fangs retracted, making him gasp. "Charlotte…" He touched her cheek, his hand making contact with solid flesh. "Gods, I thought I lost you." He pulled her into his arms, burying his face against her shoulder.

She sighed and clung to him. "I'm okay. They haven't hurt me."

He kissed her long and hard, not wanting to let her go. "Our link." He felt her there now at the edge of his mind. That Illuminari bitch hadn't broken it after all.

"I thought it had gone too. Irina used magic to try and break it, but it didn't work." She kissed him again. "Listen, we don't have much time before I have to go back. It's a good thing I found you before you lost complete control."

He gripped her shoulders. "I'm not letting you out of my sight again," he growled. "I may have let my powers get the best of me for a moment there, but I have every right to rip every Illuminari limb from limb."

"Irina is my mother—biologically at least. You can't kill her or them."

Drake snarled, "They kidnapped you! You can't expect me to do nothing."

"Please promise me you won't start a war over this," Charlie begged, taking his hands in hers.

He pulled away and ran a hand through his hair. "You don't know what you're asking of me. They killed my family." His hands balled into fists.

The ring flashed on her finger. "Please don't make me use this," she said again.

"Fine; tell me why you won't come back with me right now."

She told him what she'd seen in the past. "You don't remember, do you?"

"Remember what?"

Charlie bit her lip. "The girl I kept seeing was your sister Arya." She clutched his hand. "She stayed in limbo watching over you. She took me back—well, I'm not sure if that was her or me—but I went back in time," she explained, putting her arms around him. "Drake, Daron killed your family, not the Illuminari. That's why he banished you so he could be the Akaran instead."

Drake pulled away from her, shaking his head. "No, he wouldn't do that. My brother is a lot of things, but…"

"You know I wouldn't lie to you."

"Did you see him physically do it?" He didn't want to believe it, didn't even want to consider the possibility.

"No, but he had the sword in his hand and he tried to kill you too. He might have done so if I hadn't been there."

"I don't remember any of it and I've been relieving it for centuries." He wracked his brain, trying to remember what she'd said, but most of what happened after his family's deaths remained a blur until he'd found his way to Elaris.

Charlie hesitated. "I was weak from being incorporeal for too long so I kind of possessed you and fought back. That's why you don't remember much of it."

Drake turned away from her. "I can't believe this. I won't." She tried to hug him, but he shrugged off her embrace. His hands clenched so hard he could feel the bones popping. "Daron wouldn't…" His voice trailed off. He knew she wouldn't lie to him and his eyes bled to black as the rage returned. "I'll kill him for this."

"No, you won't."

He gaped at her. "He has to pay for his crimes." He started to shimmer out, but something held him in place.

The ring on Charlie's finger flashed. "Look, I know you're angry right now, but you can't go rushing off to confront Daron."

"Why the fuck not?" he demanded.

"Because he wants you to lose control. If you kill him, other Demonkind might turn against you too."

Drake's jaw clenched. She had a point. After his earlier stunt, killing Daron outright wouldn't win him any favours. "I've never desired to be the Akaran and I never will."

"But it's what you are. You can't…"

"I can't ignore this, little witch." He touched her cheek. "He took my family from me."

"I'm not asking you to." Charlie sighed. "The reason I haven't come back is because I think Goodridge might be an Illuminari too. If I stay there and learn to control my demon powers maybe we'll have a chance of defeating him." Then she'd finally have justice for her teammates, she'd no longer be hunted by Goodridge and perhaps the Srimtar would stay safe.

I need you with me, he thought but didn't say it aloud. "I could kill him just for his involvement in handing you over to them." Drake ran a hand through his hair and frowned. "He knew I'd lose control once I lost you. He planned this." He started to pace. "He would have guessed the power would get the best of me. Like how I crushed the mountain."

"I liked that mountain," she muttered. "Irina doesn't know I'm here. I can carry on staying with them, to see what I can find out."

"I'll play along with Daron if I must, then. But I'll need the other demons on my side," he said. "Daron might challenge me for the right to rule. I'll be ready for that." He stared at her. "We'll have to remain apart then."

Charlie wrapped her arms around his neck and kissed him. "We've been apart before and we always find our way back to each other."

"It's different now. I need you by my side. Plus, Scott—"

Charlie snorted. "You're not worried about Scott, are you?"

"Should I be?" He arched a brow.

"I love you, not him. Never forget that."

"I love you too, little witch." Drake kissed her again, never wanting to let her go.

"When you need me you know where to find me." She smiled.

"When this is over, I'm sealing our bond and tying you to my bed for the foreseeable future."

"Promises, promises." She laughed and cupped his face. "You should go now. I'll have to get back before I'm missed."

"You know how to call me too—if you need me." He squeezed her hand and kissed it, touching the ring. "Don't lose this."

"I won't."

CHAPTER 4

Charlie reappeared in her room at the Illuminari's base, feeling the familiar ache in her chest. It hurt to be apart from Drake now, too. She resented Irina for dragging her into this but knew she had to stay. For now, at least.

Scott sat waiting in a chair, frowning. "Where have you been? Irina said you didn't come back with her," he asked. "How did you get out?"

Charlie put hands on her hips. "I'm Illuminari too, remember? I can come and go thanks to mummy dearest taking that damn bracelet off me a few days ago," she said. "Where I've been isn't your business."

"If Goodridge sensed you—which he can more easily now your Illuminari powers are stronger—you..." His jaw set. "You went to see Drake."

She crossed her arms. "I told you this wouldn't break us up. I love him, he's my life mate. No hocus-pocus is going to change that."

Scott sighed, running a hand through his short blond hair. "You're never going to accept that we are just trying to help you, are you?"

"Fine, so help," she snapped. She wanted nothing more than to run back into her demon's arms but knew she didn't stand much chance against Goodridge. He badly wanted the Srimtar and she doubted she'd be able to thwart his attempts for much longer unless she learnt to control her demon side.

Scott motioned for her to follow. He led her down to a small cobblestone courtyard. The keep's stone walls surrounded it on all sides.

Charlie thought she sensed other people close by but saw no one. "Aren't there other demons around here?"

Scott nodded. "Yeah, but I wouldn't call them demons if I were

211

you."

"Why haven't I seen them?"

Hell, seeing other people aside from Scott and her irksome mother would have eased some of the boredom of the past weeks. Maybe she'd learn something too.

Scott bit his lip. "The others are wary of outsiders. We're so used to our own company."

Or maybe you just don't trust me.

"What are we doing out here then?" Charlie fiddled with the hem of her dress. *Goddess, I'd kill for some jeans and a t-shirt. Or any real clothes rather than this crap.*

"Since you've been so resistant to Irina I thought I'd show you some techniques," he said, rubbing the back of his neck. "Bear with me though. Most Illuminari inherit our genetic knowledge."

"How does that even work? No Magickind can do that." She thought back to all the lessons she'd enjoyed growing up as a Denai. Magickind history was one essential element of their education.

Scott shrugged. "It's part of our nature. We are one of the elder races. Irina thinks we're way more advanced than the others."

Charlie made a rude sound. "Okay, get teaching then."

"Close your eyes. Try to phase."

"You first," she challenged.

Scott's body blurred as he phased then turned into pure white energy. "We can become incorporeal at will. There are no limitations to what we can pass through, even different planes of existence."

"Like Goodridge can." Charlie frowned. "Is he one of you too?" She'd considered the possibility, but Goodridge had power that went way beyond an Illuminari's.

He fiddled with his shirt, something he always did when he got nervous.

Charlie wondered why he wouldn't just tell her what he knew about Goodridge. "Scott, you never were good at lying—scratch that, you were damn good. You lied to me all through our relationship."

"I don't know much about Goodridge. If I did I'd tell you." He avoided her gaze.

Charlie arched an eyebrow. Would he? He'd proven very loyal to Irina and Charlie guessed he'd do anything for the Illuminari leader. All she had was his word to go on.

"I already know how to phase," she pointed out. "Been doing it for as long as I can remember."

"Yes, but you can't phase for long—only as long as you can hold your breath."

Yeah, that's how it works.

"We can stay incorporeal for much longer. It just takes time and practice. Irina can stay incorporeal for up to an hour," Scott said. "Try it."

Well, wouldn't want to disappoint mummy dearest, would we?

"Fine." Charlie drew in a breath.

"Try not to do it that way. Magic should flow easily as you breathe. You shouldn't have to do it consciously."

She tried not to roll her eyes and then tried to phase. Nothing. She tried again. Still nothing. "I can't use my power like this. Maybe it works different from yours since I'm only half demon."

They continued on for the next hour. Charlie felt her patience wearing thin. "It's not working." She sighed. "Maybe I'm just not one of you."

"You can leave if you want to. But Goodridge isn't just a threat to us or you, but to all of Magickind."

She frowned. "You didn't bring me here to get me away from Drake." She realised, seeing the fear in his eyes. "You're scared of Goodridge."

Scott snorted. "No, we're—"

Charlie put her hands on her hips. "Now you're lying. I know you better than you think, mister."

He smiled. "I miss this."

She scowled and couldn't help wondering if any part of their relationship had been real. Even when they'd been friends as kids.

Irina suddenly appeared. "Charlotte, you're late for our lesson."

Right, more lessons.

Charlie waited until nightfall before slipping out of her room. She needed more than a few scraps of info, needed to know if these people could really be trusted. As she crept along the hall, the flagstones felt cold under her feet. There were no torches, lamps or anything lighting the corridor, she'd noticed neither Scott nor Irina seemed too fond of light at night-time. Charlie suspected light might possibly make them partially visible when they were incorporeal but hadn't had a chance to test the theory yet. She wondered how they turned into strange mist too but guessed she might not be able to do that herself.

Charlie kept her senses on alert she moved through the corridor, careful not to disturb any of the rich tapestries lining the walls. Now she had that damned band off which had restricted her powers, she hoped she'd be able to move around more freely. The murmur of voices echoed down the hall.

Finally, maybe I'll get to see more Illuminaris now. She moved out onto a landing.

Below Irina and Scott sat with two other Illuminaris, a man and woman. Both had sandy blonde hair and blue tattoos that shimmered in the low light. Another sign Charlie wasn't one of them, she thought as she ran her hand through her brown locks. She crouched down so they wouldn't see her, crawling along the landing so she could listen in.

"Our base close to Elaris has been wiped out," said the man. "It was Goodridge. He is hell-bent on wiping us all out."

Irina ran a hand through her hair. "Are you sure it was him and not the Akaran?" she asked. "He swore revenge on us because he believes we're responsible for his family's murders."

"We're certain," said the woman. "We saw Goodridge ourselves. He seemed to enjoy the carnage, though it looked like he was looking for something."

No doubt me and the Srimtar, Charlie thought. *Is that why they want me here?*

Irina and Scott glanced at each other.

"Maybe we should take Charlie somewhere else," Scott suggested. "If this place becomes compromised we won't be able to shield her."

"No, she's safe from him," Irina insisted.

"Has she started mastering her powers yet?" the woman asked.

Charlie frowned. Why the hell would they be interested in her powers?

Irina shook her head. "She is… resistant. She's still loyal to her father's family and I suspect to the Akaran," she said. "I left it too long. I should have brought her here before Goodridge ever found her."

Maybe mummy dearest is not lying about the protection thing. Still, she's not truthful either.

"We need her on her our side," the man said. "As guardian of the

Srimtar, she's the only one who can save our people."

Charlie gasped then covered her mouth to stifle the sound. *I knew there was more to it!* Her fists clenched.

"That's an old prophecy," Scott remarked dismissively. "It might not even be true."

"Given to us by the witches, they're very good at foretelling accurate prophecies."

Charlie sat there listening as they continued talking about her and Goodridge. She wanted to storm down and confront Irina but forced herself to wait until the meeting finally ended. She rested her head against the wall, thoughts racing with unanswered questions. Finally, the man and woman said goodbye and left.

"You can come down now, Charlie," Irina called.

She flinched. Irina had known she was there the whole time. *Big of you to let me eavesdrop!* She rose and stormed down the steps, feeling the rough stone biting into her bare feet. "Why did you bring me here?" Charlie demanded, hands on hips. "Tell the truth. Right now." She wondered if her Denai ability to sense the truth really worked on the living. Hell, Scott had fooled her for years without her suspecting him.

Scott said, "Char—"

Her eyes flashed. "You stay out of this. Better yet get the hell out. This doesn't concern you."

Scott glanced at Irina, who said, "Good night, Scott." He left the room without another word.

Irina sighed. "I brought you here so you can learn to control your demon powers. I didn't lie about that," she said. "And keep you safe from Goodridge."

"And?" Charlie demanded, eyes flashing red. "Why were those people acting like I'm some kind of saviour?"

"Because there's a prophecy. Like your aunt was predicted to stop the Covenant, there's another prophecy about you," Irina told her. "As a race, our people are dying out. We rarely have children and Goodridge hates us enough to want us all gone. Prophecy says a witch who walks in shadow will bring us into the light and save us."

Charlie scoffed. "How? I'm no saviour and I'm not Cate either." Cate had always known her destiny and given her phenomenal powers, had it fulfilled too.

"But you are half witch and half Illuminari." Irina reached out and took her hands. "We believe the Srimtar is part of it too. With it, you can stop Goodridge once and for all."

"The Srimtar isn't a weapon." Hell, she still hadn't figured out what it was but didn't think it had been designed to hurt others. Charlie pulled her hands away. "I get that Goodridge is a threat, but I still don't understand why you didn't just tell me all this instead of dragging me here against my will."

"That night on the mountain Goodridge planned to come for you. If we hadn't taken you then, he would have."

"I've fought him before and escaped," Charlie snapped. "You should have told me all this before now. Why did you try to break my link to Drake?"

"The Akaran is a danger too. So many of them go mad from the power they wield. His father and brother slaughtered us. I couldn't risk you getting hurt when Drake's power destroys him."

"Sounds like you're still living in the past," Charlie said. "You can't force me to stay here."

"I haven't, and I won't. Leave if you want to but heed my words, you won't stand a chance against Myles. He's toyed with you, testing your connection to the orb. He won't be so lenient when he comes to claim it."

Charlie turned away. "I need some space to think about all this." She turned and hurried out of the room.

Grabbing a pair of shoes and the bracelet that prevented anyone from sensing her, Charlie shimmered out. After some goading, Scott had revealed that the bracelet didn't just block her powers. The gems on it had other uses which meant she could turn off the power blocker element. At first, she thought about shimmering to Drake, she ached to see him again but instead found herself stomping through the woods as she made her way towards Helga's tree. She had no idea why she picked this of all places yet it felt peaceful there.

It seemed like a good enough place to think. She hadn't seen Helga for a couple of weeks and it felt strange not having the crone pop up to spy on her.

She found a fallen tree stump, sat down on it and ran her hands through her hair. Above her stars twinkled like tiny diamonds in an ocean of blackness. She hoped the bracelet would shield her from Helga too since she didn't feel like more of the crone's riddles.

Maybe Drake would be looking up at the sky too, thinking of her.

Blue light flashed as the Srimtar appeared in her hand. She rolled the orb between her fingers. *What are you?* She wondered. *Why did you drag me into all of this mess?*

"Are you coming in then?" The sound of Helga's voice made Charlie fall off the stump, almost dropping the Srimtar.

"Why do you have to do that?" she growled, clutching the orb to her chest. "Jeez, you could frighten someone to death!"

Helga cackled, stroking the eagle perched on her shoulder. "Ah, so young, Seamus." She ruffled his feathers. "Youth is so amusing."

The eagle is called Seamus? Weird! "Ha ha, very funny." Charlie scowled as she scrambled up. "No, I wanted some solitude."

"Couldn't you have that in your place between the worlds?"

Charlie's eyes narrowed. "How do you—never mind. I doubt anything gets past you." She reminded herself not to be surprised by anything Helga said anymore.

"Are you coming in then?" Helga waved her walking stick towards her house. "I have tea brewing."

She bit her lip. "Fine, but no riddles or cryptic crap, okay?"

Helga only cackled as she hobbled back towards her home. The house had been carved out of the tree itself. Bark and leaves covered the walls in places, and roots lined themselves across the low ceilings. Charlie wondered how there could be so much room inside a tree but didn't ask any questions about it.

A fire crackled in the hearth and a small kettle hung above it bubbling with smoke. Helga's eagle flew across the room, landing to perch on top of Helga's chair.

Seriously, who keeps a bloody eagle inside their house? Weird choice of pet, if you ask me.

"I didn't ask you and he's more than a pet. He is a... familiar if you like," Helga said, picking up the kettle and pouring out two cups.

Charlie didn't know much about familiars, had heard they were some kind of spirit animal but were thought to just be a myth. "Stay out of my head." She slumped into a second wingback chair. "It's rude to eavesdrop."

"You shouldn't broadcast your thoughts so loudly then," Helga replied. "Plus you eavesdropped on your mother earlier."

"She's not my mother," she insisted. "She's—hell, I don't know what she is to me."

"I'm surprised you're not with your handsome demon lover. Life mates find it difficult being separated, especially now your bond is growing."

"Drake isn't…" She shook her head. She and Drake weren't lovers. Hell, every time they drew close something always seemed to part them. Be it fate or they themselves. "Drake's not the problem." Things had been so much simpler a few months ago when all she had to worry about was his belief they were meant to be together. She resisted the idea for over six years, even dating Scott in the meantime, but she'd fallen hard for Drake once she'd gotten to know him. She'd dragged him into all this when the Srimtar's protective magic had killed her enforcer teammates and Drake had come to save her from Goodridge.

"Everything happens for a reason," Helga murmured, petting Seamus.

Charlie took the cup from her. It was a roughly made clay mug, nothing like fine china Niara used. She winced, realising she missed her home in Setara too. Despite the message she'd sent them telling them she was fine her family would no doubt be worried about her.

"My other great-grandma, Seline, used to say that," Charlie mused and frowned at the crone. "Come on, start imparting the cryptic mumbo-jumbo then."

Helga laughed, flashing yellow teeth. "Ah, I like you, little Denai. You're spirited." She paused, staring into the flames.

Charlie leaned forward. "Is there a prophecy about me too?"

"There are many prophecies. Some are remembered, others forgotten."

Now this sounded like the Helga she knew. "I'll take that as a yes." She blew her hair off her face, sipped the tea, wishing it was something stronger.

"Let me tell you a story, then perhaps you will understand things better," Helga said.

Charlie arched an eyebrow. Wow, Helga had never been one for stories.

"Back during the beginning times, several races lived in different lands. For the most part, they existed harmoniously together. Neither race or power mattered, nor did any one leader rank higher than the other," Helga said. "Their desire was to find true spiritual enlightenment and pass our knowledge onto future generations."

Charlie stayed silent. Weird, Helga never spoke about the days of what she guessed were the five elder races.

"They lived that way, side-by-side, for millennia. As their power and technology advanced so did some people's desire for more," Helga continued. "Then came the dark times when the races started to fight and overpower each other—this came much later but those older beings left this world when they grew weary of it all. Some chose to stay watch over their descendants and the other races that came from them.

"The leaders came together to end the dark times and were forced to stop one of their descendants who tried to climb ultimate power. He was stripped of that power and the old alliance agreed they'd never again interfere in the ways of Magickind." Helga stroked her eagle. "A few leaders passed from this world, some remained. Eventually, the dark times passed—for a while, at least."

Charlie sipped her tea, surprised it didn't taste too bad. She didn't like tea at the best of times. "What happened to the others? The first immortals?"

"Most of them were either killed during the war, some chose death. Living for centuries can be tough for some of us," Helga answered. "One of the strongest of our descendants craved the elders' power, decided the other races were inferior."

Charlie choked on her next mouthful of tea. "Whoa, do you mean Oberoth?" She hadn't thought much of Niara's ex-husband—her great-grandfather—much over the past six years. He'd been killed during the revolution of Setara, ending his ten-thousand-year rule of murder and bloodshed.

Helga nodded. "He plummeted the world into darkness. We all wondered if it would ever end."

"You were part of the elder races, weren't you?" Charlie asked. She'd guessed it previously but hadn't been entirely sure.

Helga shook her head. "I was one of the first. I lived in that wonderful time so long ago," she said, running a hand through her straggly hair. "There came a point when almost all races were wiped out. The traitor wanted to go back, to change what was. He took and stole power from many of the others until he had power greater than any of us could imagine." Helga rose and pulled an hourglass from her shelf. "Your grandfather is the Tempus so you must know of time travel and its risks."

Charlie nodded. "A little. Grandpa always lectured us about the dangers, but I can't walk through time like Cate can." Time travel was meant for observation only. Time itself couldn't be changed unless it was meant to be. No one had ever managed to overcome that. Anyone who tried suffered devastating consequences.

Helga flipped the hourglass over so that the sand started pouring down. "Time is a precious thing even for immortals. We often forget someone we love can be gone in an instant."

Charlie gulped down more tea as it started to grow cold. She had no idea where this story was headed but still felt compelled to carry on listening.

"Time can't be changed not without serious repercussions. Even then, time has a way of righting itself. Destiny always has its own way."

She nodded. "Right."

"The traitor shifted and warped his terrible power, tried to use it to go back, to change history…"

Charlie leaned forward, eager to hear the ending. "And?"

"The others—an alliance of the first races came together, stopped him. But no one knows what happened to the power he wielded. Some say he warped it into an object so he could one day reclaim it."

Helga fell silent as she started sipping her tea again.

"What made you stay here?"

"I could have ascended, moved on to a higher plane like my kin did. But I wanted to stay here so the others let me. I couldn't leave my daughter behind."

Charlie gasped. "You had a daughter? Wow!"

Helga nodded and smiled. "She was strong, wilful." She laughed. "Stubborn too. The most beautiful girl with hair like sunshine."

"What happened to her?"

A tear dripped down Helga's cheek. "She's gone from this world now but her memory lives on in her descendants."

"I'm sorry." Charlie reached over and squeezed Helga's gnarled hand. "Thanks for telling me the story. I guess absolute power really does destroy everything." She rose and set the mug down. "Thanks again. It's put a lot of things in perspective for me."

Charlie turned and walked out. She had to stay with the Illuminari and learn what she could.

Goodridge had to be stopped before it was too late.

CHAPTER 5

Drake strode into the great hall, wondering what the hell Daron had summoned him for now. Every time he looked at his brother he wanted to tear him apart, remembering the images of seeing their parents and little sister lying on the floor dead.

He hadn't heard much from Charlie the past few days and it made him more uneasy. He hoped she found whatever she was looking for there and came back to him soon. Seeing her every night made the separation easier, but he still hated not being near her.

Daron sat on their father's throne, Drake wouldn't think of it as Daron's or his own.

Other demons gathered around the hall.

Now what? He grew weary of being stuck in Kyral and longed to go back to Setara, but the Alliance wanted him to keep an eye on Daron to find out what his next move was.

"Everyone gather around. As you know it will be ascendance day in two days' time," Daron said. "Traditionally the day when all Demonkind come together to celebrate the blood moon. A time of great power for all of us. We'll be hosting a feast of course and every leader of each clan will be here for the festivities."

"Those of you who'd like to take place in the fights will need to be signed up," said Arvin, Daron's lieutenant.

Drake joined his brother on the dais. "Why did you summon me?" he hissed, leaning close to Daron. "I already know about the planned festivities."

"When I said I invited everyone, I meant everyone—even the leader of the Illuminari will be there."

Drake frowned. "Why would you do that? We—"

"I thought you'd be pleased, brother. No doubt your imp will be there, too."

He shrugged. "Why would I care about her? She was just a plaything." He kept his expression neutral, not wanting to give away his true feelings about Charlie. He couldn't fathom why Daron would want to invite the Illuminaris to the celebrations. They'd spent the last month talking about destroying the entire clan. What had changed? He knew his brother well enough to know Daron did nothing without careful consideration first. Although Daron hadn't exactly seemed in his right mind recently.

If Daron had invited the Illuminari, he no doubt had something big planned. Drake knew he had to warn Charlie.

Drake headed out after unsuccessfully trying to contact Charlie. Daron hadn't been happy when he'd heard Drake had been doing Alliance business. In truth, Drake had still been searching for leads on Goodridge and out talking to the different clan leaders. Plus it gave him the chance to check on things in Setara whilst he was there. Drake had to be careful and had even resorted to placing compulsions on those he'd already spoken to, for the fear word would get back to Daron.

It was only a matter of time before Daron tried to challenge him. He was already losing face and respect among the other clan leaders. Something had to change and soon. Daron needed the power of a true Akaran, he could no longer fake his way through pretending to be it. He blamed the lack of power on keeping Kyral safe by using the lands protective wards to keep other Magickind out. He'd done a good job at faking it all these centuries, but people now questioned him.

Drake headed out to talk to the next clan leader, a demon called Rubin of the mercury demons. They were a vicious, angry bunch who were fearsome warriors and spent most of their time warring with other clans. This visit would serve two purposes, one to question them about Goodridge and to find out if they'd side with him or Daron.

He reappeared outside a large hut. Sand stung his face and he sensed a storm brewing. He headed inside and two guards wearing leather armour and holding battle axes blocked his way. *Axes? Gods, I need to introduce these people to some real technology.*

"State your business," one of the guards barked.

"Drakon Damrus, of the clan Amargen, here to see Rubin." He

scanned the thoughts in case they tried to attack him.

"Let him pass," boomed a rough voice.

The guards moved aside, and Drake stalked through the tent. A huge man with flaming red hair and a long beard sat dressed in leather armour, a battle axe by his side. "The Akaran's brother." He acknowledged Drake's presence. "I'm surprised to see you here," Rubin remarked. "Especially given how I oppose the Akaran."

"Yes, I heard you and the others are planning to overthrow Daron."

"So the little whelp sent you to dispatch me instead of coming himself?" Rubin said. "That sounds like something he'd do." His chest heaved with laughter.

"Not exactly." Drake leaned forward, his eyes bleeding to black and flames flashing there.

Rubin drew back, flinching. "Impossible. If you challenged Daron, I'd—"

"Fool, I became the Akaran after my brother murdered her parents. I've always had the power," he growled. "My brother has remained in power long enough. It's time for his reign to end. I suspect Daron will challenge me during the night of the blood moon. I want to know who I could trust to support me when the time comes."

Rubin rubbed his beard. "Have a seat."

They briefly talked about what would happen when the time came. But Drake couldn't tell yet if Rubin would prove to be an ally. Rubin could talk the talk but that didn't mean he would take action when the time came. Drake needed reliable allies for his plan to work.

"It's about time we had a true Akaran to lead us," Rubin said. "You can—"

"Make no mistake, I won't be ruling the way my father did. My loyalty is to the Alliance, only under them and the council will we be able to end my brother's madness."

Rubin's mouth fell open. "You want us to pledge loyalty to the Alliance and the council? Why would we do that?"

Drake tried not to sigh, yet he knew bringing all the clans around to his way of thinking would take time and effort. He had to choose his allies carefully or risk all the clans taking his brother's side.

"Because only with them do we have a chance of moving forward. I'll still act as your leader, yes, but the old ways no longer serve us.

Aren't you tired of the endless in-fighting among the clans?"

"We'll see who wins but for now I need time to consider your proposal."

"Very well." Drake grasped Rubin's forearm. "See you at the feast."

Drake slumped into his seat at the table in the Alliance's HQ. The Alliance was made up of five different leaders of Magickind. They had come together several years ago to be a separate organisation from the United Magickind Council. They worked in the way much as enforcers did but on a much higher-level ensuring justice for all of Magickind. Drake represented all demons, McNabb, a wiry-looking man represented the Ashrali, Jason, a tall dark-haired man with silver eyes represented the elementals, Cate the witches and Lana the Phoenix elementals. They represented each of the five elder races.

"What news do we have on the Goodridge investigation?" asked Lana. With her willowy figure and long silver-blonde hair, she looked her usual gorgeous self. Drake noticed her sending glances his way with her usual seductive smiles and tried not to roll his eyes. He was in no mood for her usual flirtations.

"I've been investigating more leads. With the help of Agents Monroe and Snowden and my own contacts, I've discovered Goodridge has been bringing together groups of different Magickind the secret meetings. What the meetings are for I have yet to discover but Goodridge seems to be planning something large. His only ventures have been gangs, smuggling and illegals so far. This feels different."

McNabb stared at the screen. "All of these names are on our watch list. They're either known criminals, former Covenant connections, or oppose the council and the Alliance," he observed.

Cate gave Drake a hard look. "What about Charlie?" she demanded, her sapphire eyes flashing. "She hasn't returned any of my calls and I can't sense where she is either."

Drake winced. He hadn't expected her to bring up Charlie in the middle of the meeting but then Charlie was just as much a part of this case as he was. "I already told you, she left a month ago. I haven't seen or heard from her since," he replied, crossing his arms. "She said she wanted to time with her mother."

"Right, her dead mother who's been gone for almost twenty-five years."

"The GM has a point," Lana agreed. "Why would your life mate leave? Mates find it unbearable being apart."

As if you would know anything about having a life mate. You change lovers as often as I change suits.

"Shall we get back to the case?" Jason suggested, which earned him a glare from Cate.

"Should we be worried about the mist walkers now?" McNabb wanted to know. "They're almost as feared as Nulls. They may not be able to neutralise magic like Nulls can but they can possess people."

"They're not a threat," Drake insisted. "There is only a handful of them left. We should focus on the threat from Goodridge."

"I suggest you find one of those meetings and get inside," Jason said.

"I'm working on it," Drake answered. "I have another contact I'm meeting later today."

"What about the situation with your brother?" asked Lana. "Have you removed him from power yet?"

Drake pursued his lips. "My brother isn't a problem. I've been keeping a close eye on him." Plus, Seth would watch Daron whilst Drake wasn't around.

"Very well, we'll meet again in a week—or before if you have any news to tell us," said Cate. "This meeting is over."

McNab left and Lana sauntered off, but Cate and Jason remained.

"I didn't appreciate you showing me up like that," Drake snapped.

Cate stared daggers at him. "My niece has gone gallivanting goddess knows where with her supposedly dead mother, I expected you to be a bit more worried," she snapped back. "All I have is your word to go and a short text message from Charlie. What if she's in trouble?"

Drake's hands balled into fists "She chose to go," he snarled. "Now if you don't mind, I have to get back to work."

"You really are a bastard. No wonder Charlie never wanted to be with you." Cate stormed out of the room.

Drake hissed out a breath, anger heating his blood.

"Sorry about that." Jason winced as the door slammed shut. "We're all concerned about Charlie."

"And you think I'm not?"

"I think you don't know how to deal with it," Jason remarked.

Drake scowled at his best friend. "I'm fine."

"Well, you know where I am if you need me."

Drake stalked down the hall. He wanted to break something, strangle someone or both.

He shimmered back to his home office, and there found Lana there naked except for her silky long blonde hair covering her lithe body. She draped herself over his desk, smirking.

Her desire filled the room like a sweet perfume which only made him even more pissed off. "What are you doing?" he growled.

"You seemed so tense. I thought I'd come to relax you."

"We only had one night together, and it was decades ago."

Her lips curved. "That was the best night of our lives. Admit it. That little witch could never dream of the things I could do to you."

He bared his teeth. "Don't speak of her."

"She's made you like this. Honestly, darling, demons aren't meant to be bound, especially not you."

He snorted. "What am I meant to be, then?" he demanded.

"Free, wild. unrestrained." Lana laced her arms around his neck. "We were incredible together—we still can be."

Drake's lips thinned. "Women only come to my bed when they want something from me—or I want something from them."

"I want nothing from you," she purred. "You need me. When was the last time you lost control?"

Lana didn't stir anything in him as he stared at her. The demon in him had become stronger as instinct had taken over from emotion. Since Charlie had been in his life again, everything had seemed brighter. Now, without her, it all turned to black and white again, grey even.

Lana tilted her head back to try and kiss him. "Do it," she demanded. "You know you want to."

Drake backed away, yanked his jacket off and tossed it at her. "Go," he growled. "Get out!"

Lana threw it back at him. "That witch really has you under her spell," she snapped. "You'll regret this. No one says no to me."

"That shows how easy you are." He laughed.

She slapped him hard across the face. "You bastard!" she hissed. "I'll have you out of the Alliance, I'll—"

"Save your words. You can't touch me and you know it. Now get the fuck out of my house!"

Lana vanished in a flash of silver fire after hurling a fireball at his head. Drake dodged it and chuckled. Oh yes, he felt better already. Now for work.

Drake glanced at his PDA for the intel he had on his contact Lucas Perry, a low-level demon hybrid. Perry liked to hang around with people of power and influence, including Goodridge.

It was an odd country, Rosevergn. Magickind appeared free but the laws there were much harsher.

Perry had insisted on meeting at the hotel's bar. Now all Drake had to do was wait.

He settled on an overstuffed armchair in the hotel's lobby, reading the news on his PDA and sipping their poor excuse for coffee. How the place rated three stars he couldn't fathom.

His inner demon yearned for action, but Drake hoped the meeting would go as planned. Then what? Back to work? Even that didn't fill the void the way it used to.

He checked his phone again. No calls. Charlie's smiling face stared back at him on the screen, making his chest tighten. Cate had been wrong. He worried about Charlie every second she remained gone.

Lucas Perry came in, glancing around as he did so.

Showtime. Drake straightened, shoved his PDA into his jacket and rose. He knew this role well, knew how to play the part. His expression smoothed and showed no emotion. "Perry."

"Drake." Perry glanced around. "Not here. It's too public. We need somewhere more private."

Drake arched an eyebrow. He needed answers now. Changing venues wasn't part of their deal. "I know a place."

CHAPTER 6

Someone tapped on the door of Charlie's chamber. Charlie's head shot up and she quickly gathered up the pieces of paper and other files that she had strewn across the flagstone floor. Bundling everything together, she sent it off to her room in the spirit world and then got up to stand by the window. "Come in." She sighed.

The door opened and Scott peered in. "Ready for breakfast?"

"Sure, just drop the tray on the table." She resumed pacing, mind racing over what her next move would be. No training had taught her how to deal with spying on her mother. Did they even have a program for that?

Scott held up a small picnic basket. "I thought we could go for a walk and have breakfast together."

Her eyes narrowed. "I already told you, we're just friends now. I'm still with Drake. That will never change."

"I'm not asking you on a date, Char. I just wanted to show you around the base. I thought you'd be sick of being cooped up in here."

"Oh." She bit her lip. "Okay then." Maybe getting some air would do her good and help clear her head. It was about time she got to see more of the place after being there for so long.

She followed him outside. The Illuminari's base had been set up in the ruins of an old fort close to the border of Kyral. Some of it had fallen into ruin but Charlie guessed they'd fixed the place up since some of it had been rebuilt. Only a few members of the clan lived there. Charlie knew this would be the perfect opportunity to find out more about them.

Scott led her up a set of spiral steps to the roof. It looked out onto a breath-taking view. In the distance, she saw the golden sands of Kyral, on the other were the lush green hills of Rosevergn, one of the countries that made up an area called the Middle Kingdom.

It felt like being caught between two worlds.

Kind of like me and the Illuminari.

"Wow, it's beautiful," Charlie breathed. One of the things she'd loved about Setara was its rugged landscapes. She'd always loved hiking and rock climbing, but Scott had never been a fan of adventurous activities during their brief relationship. He'd preferred to stay indoors.

"Yeah, it is."

"So, do you really hate the outdoors or was that just part of your cover story too?"

Scott winced. "Not everything about me was a lie. Everything except my real identity was true. I'm sorry…"

She waved her hand dismissively. "Don't. I'm over it. Look, we had fun back in school and when we got back together last year, but it's nothing compared to what I have with Drake."

He scowled. "Don't you mean had with Drake? You broke up with him, remember?"

She bit her lip again. One way of proving her loyalty to them had been to tell them she'd broken up with Drake. The lie still tasted bitter in her mouth. As if she would ever break up with him. Hell, Drake had tried that once when he'd thought he'd been protecting her, but she'd just followed him and showed him they could work together, no matter what fate threw at them.

She felt the familiar ache in her chest and the emptiness that came with it. The longer she and Drake stayed apart, the worse it became. She wanted to try calling him in thought but had been too afraid Irina would sense their connection.

"I love him, Scott. That's never gonna change," she said. "He's the one, my soul mate, life mate—whatever you want to call it."

"It's wasn't real. He's the Akaran. The very fact of what he is means he can't love you or anyone else."

Charlie looked away, digging her nails into her palms to try and control her anger. "Let's not talk about Drake," she muttered. "Where's the breakfast you promised?"

Scott grinned, then he pulled out a basket filled with bread, fruit and a bottle of orange juice. They sat down to eat.

"So how old are you really?" she asked.

"I'm just over two hundred, pretty young for an immortal."

"Have you been a spy all that time?" She bit into her apple.

Scott shrugged. "It's all I've ever known. We've been hunted for millennia. The Covenant used us, and Drake's father banished us, saying we weren't true Demonkind."

"I'm sorry, I had no idea." As a Denai, Charlie had grown up learning all of the races of Magickind, but demons were the least understood.

"We took it as a blessing, we don't consider ourselves demons either. We're not cold and power-hungry like them. We use our powers for the good of our people," he told her. "All of Magickind ostracised us, even the Ashrali. We're not fey but we're not demons either. So we choose to be our own race, unconnected and unaligned to anyone but ourselves. Our stealth powers make it easy for us to blend in when we need to."

"Don't you all hate not being able to live like your real selves? To live free?"

"Of course, that's why we have safe havens like this where we go when we're not on missions. We get to live with our own people, be our true selves—they never last long," Scott said. "Demons fear us and the rest of Magickind aren't much better. We're considered a threat so we might as well be dead to them."

"Kind of like the Nuardans when they were enslaved by Oberoth," she mused.

"The Nuardans were forced into slavery, we are not slaves to anyone. It's impossible for us to settle down and have families, but the work we do is important."

"So you play both sides." Charlie mused. "Like between the Covenant and the rest of Magickind?"

"Something like that, but we're certainly on our own side. We play the side that benefits us most."

"Haven't you tried talking to the council? I mean Niara could—"

"Like I said, we're separate from any form of government." Scott closed the basket. "Your mother will be waiting for you."

"Right, time for more lessons to begin."

Charlie met Irina in one of the empty rooms. Although she'd felt the presence of others at the keep, she hadn't seen anyone else yet except for the two speaking with Irina a few nights ago. It still felt weird seeing the mother she'd thought had been dead for so long. She still wondered how Irina had been able to fake being a spirit too.

Charlie had even previously summoned her several times over the years and hadn't sensed the deception.

"So can you show me how to use my powers now?" Charlie asked.

"As I said before all Illuminari knowledge is passed down through our blood. You just need to learn to access it."

"Yeah, I know but you still haven't shown me how to. And I've been stuck here six weeks now."

"It's not something that can be taught. It's instinctual." Irina explained. "Illuminari children access it when they come of age—it's something that comes naturally."

"Well, like I said before, I'm a witch." She crossed her arms.

"You're still my daughter, Charlotte. You have my powers too. How else do you think you pass in and out between the worlds?"

"You mean phasing?" Charlie shrugged. "I always assumed it came from my medium powers."

"It doesn't. We can pass through anything including different realms. It makes it much harder for anyone to find us that way."

"Goodridge can pass through the worlds too."

Irina nodded. "Which is why you need to learn your abilities quickly," she said. "Close your eyes."

Charlie did so, trying to curb her impatience. She wanted to find out what the hell they had planned.

"Feel power rise up from that place inside you," Irina continued.

Charlie drew magic. *Come on, show me what the hell these people can do.* She felt her body flicker in and out as she phased. When she opened her eyes, she found herself in her secret place between the worlds. "Ah, crap," she muttered. The last thing she needed was Irina, or anyone else, to find out about this place. But she couldn't deny the feeling of coming home it brought being back here. Charlie grabbed her phone and called Kaz.

"Charlie? Gods, it's about time," Kaz answered on the first ring. "Where the hell are you?"

"Listen, I can't talk long. I'm just checking in. How is the case going?"

"Goodridge himself has been quiet for a while. The Tears have been up to the usual weapons deals so not much on the case is moving forward," her friend replied. "Are you okay?"

"If you mean how I'm feeling hanging out with my ex and my

supposedly dead mother, yeah I'm great," she said and sighed. "I'm not getting much from either of them. I can't figure out how to use my demon powers like they can."

"Aren't you going to ask about Drake?"

She winced. "How is he?"

"Now we're back in Setara we haven't seen much of him. He's been working with the Alliance more and he seems pretty miserable. He misses you."

"I miss him too," she admitted. "I'd better go; I'll call you again when I can."

Charlie phased back to find Irina pacing.

"Blessed spirits, where did you disappear to?" her mother demanded, hands on hips. "I thought…"

Charlie shrugged. "I went into the spirit world and came back again. No big deal."

"You can't just go wandering around the worlds. It's dangerous when you don't know how to protect yourself."

Charlie snorted. "I've been protecting myself just fine for years. Now this meditation stuff isn't helping. Maybe there's not much point in staying here." She saw something flicker in Irina's eyes.

"Maybe we could try something else that will take me a few hours to set up. In the meantime go with Scott. He wants to show you around the local town," Irina said. "Remember to wear your bracelet."

Charlie rolled her eyes. Irina might not have been around to be a mother to her, but she certainly knew how to boss her around like one.

CHAPTER 7

Rosevergn reminded Charlie of Setara with its street vendors and old-world beauty of stone houses mixed with modern tech.

"Beautiful, isn't it?" Scott remarked.

"Yeah," she breathed.

"This is my favourite place. I always try to come here when I can," he told her. "I always dreamed of bringing you here too. Had the whole trip planned out."

Charlie sighed. *Not this again!* "There was always something between Drake and me. I felt it when I first met him—I just didn't understand it then." She tucked her hair behind her ear. "I'm sorry, Scott."

Scott looked away. "Me too. I knew it, even then. I never wanted to see it though."

Charlie squeezed his hand. "Enough of the heavy stuff. We are supposed to be digging up intel on Goodridge, remember?"

"Right. Just don't let your mum find out that we're doing it."

Scott had offered to hook her up with a contact of his called Lucas Perry. Charlie hoped Perry would be able to give her information on what Goodridge was planning next. Goodridge wouldn't just stop looking for her or the Srimtar. It seemed strange he'd gone quiet since her stay with Irina and the Illuminaris. Irina's shielding her wouldn't last forever, not from someone as powerful as Goodridge. She had to find out what the guy was up to. The time for playing nice with her demon clan was over, now it was time to get back to work and back to business.

"So where are we meeting this guy?" she asked.

"It's not exactly arranged. I know where he likes to hang out but there might be only one way for you to get there. And you're not gonna like it."

"There's a lot I would do to bring down the bad guys, but this bites the bullet." Charlie frowned at her black push-up bra and miniskirt that might as well have been a belt. She tied her hair back in a half ponytail, plastered her lips with fiery red lipstick. "You so owe me for this."

Scott peered around the curtain. "Perry is here," he hissed, then on seeing Charlie's get up properly, his eyes went wide. "Wow."

"Yeah, wow just about covers it." She fiddled with the uncomfortable bra. "This contact better have some fucking good intel."

Scott grinned. "Seeing you like that I'm sure he'll sing like a canary."

"Right, so I dress like a whore, play nice with Perry. But I swear if anyone touches me I'll phase off their balls and then feed it to them."

Scott stifled a laugh. "No one will touch you. You just have to look good and chat with Perry," he said. "Good luck, Char."

Charlie headed out. She'd never had a problem with her body but she'd never displayed this much skin in public before. But the girls around her all wore similarly skimpy outfits. Some of them sat around the bar area, whilst others danced around on poles as lights flashed around them.

This what I get for hanging with a bunch of spy demons. She plastered a smile on her face and grabbed a tray of beers. The place stank of stale sex and cheap perfume. She'd stashed her stuff away in one of the walls, one good thing about hanging out with Illuminaris she had figured out to make objects stay incorporeal too.

Scott had already described what Perry looked like. Lanky, blonde with a short beard. She hadn't seen anyone by that description yet.

Another waitress frowned at her. "Haven't seen you here before."

"I'm new," she muttered.

"I'm Tara. A little thing like you will—"

"I'm busy," Charlie said.

Along with the bar, there were private rooms too. Tired of the uncomfortable getup, Charlie phased into one of the walls, saw a couple going at it and hurried to the next room. There sat a blond man, tapping his foot as another woman walked in. She was tall with mocha-coloured skin and breasts almost spilling out of her skimpy bra.

"What do you want?" the woman asked him. "I have many girls."

The man sighed. "Get me another drink. My friend will be joining us soon."

Charlie's heart beat faster. She wouldn't have long. Good thing Perry didn't seem interested in the madam herself.

"Maybe your friend would like some company."

Perry laughed. "Yeah, he's a tight arse. Send a girl to him to loosen him up before he comes in here. I want something young, pretty but not too flashy."

Charlie slid out of the wall and grabbed a tray off the table whilst she made sure no one had seen her.

The madam gave her a questioning look as she came out. Charlie gave her the "don't mess with me I'm a Denai" look and the woman left with a glare.

Okay, show time. I'm a slut. Think slutty. Jeez, maybe I should have gone undercover as a slut back in Setara and got some experience with this kind of thing instead of working in Major Crimes.

"Hey, baby, fancy a drink?" She smirked.

Perry brightened. "Well, you're not like the usual girls around here."

Yeah, arsehole, I'm not a whore. Real men don't have to pay for sex. But her smile never faltered. "I am what you'd call extra special. I serve only the best clients."

Seducing men had never been her strong suit. She could turn it on when she needed to but had never done anything like this.

"I bet you are." Perry rose, grabbing the tray. "Fuck, you're gorgeous."

She ran a hand down his cheek. "So what do you like?"

"Just you." He made a grab for her.

Charlie sidestepped him. *Okay, matey, don't get too grabby or I will start phasing off different body parts.* "Don't you have a friend coming?"

"Yeah," he scoffed. "He can wait."

"See, I have rules too," she added. "When I'm with a client, I don't like interruptions." She ran a finger down her chest. "Make sure we don't get interrupted, then I'm all yours."

The sound of loud voices came from outside then someone barged into the room. Her senses tingled, alerting her to a familiar presence and she froze.

Drake.

Charlie felt all the blood drain from her face. Holy shit! His blue eyes turned black and widened when he saw her too. Even under the heavy makeup, he'd still know her. She stood there frozen as they stared at each other. Charlie forced her brain to work again, sidled up to Perry. "Shouldn't we have some privacy?"

Perry squeezed her arse in response. "Drake, I'm busy. Go away at the bar for a few minutes," he snapped. Drake looked ready to murder someone. She guessed it to be Perry rather than her.

Charlotte, get out of here, Drake growled.

No way, you get out! I'm working. "Yeah, we're busy." She snuggled into Perry.

Drake's eyes turned pitch black, power seemed to charge the air around them. Charlie felt the hairs on her arm stand on end. She knew she'd made a big mistake. Demons were very possessive of their mates and killed anyone who got between them. Drake may have ignored the six years when she dated others, but Charlie doubted he'd have so much restraint now.

"Drake, for fuck sake, man, let me have some fun. I'll tell you what you want to know later," Perry said.

Charlie pulled away from Perry, placed her hands on Drake's chest and shoved him backwards. "Go!" she snapped. "I have a job to do here."

Drake, snap out of it! Don't you dare ruin this, she warned. *Just let me talk to him. It's not like I'm going to do anything with him.* He stumbled back but it didn't seem to deter him. Charlie thought fast trying to think of a way to break him out of the uncontrollable rage. *If you love me, you won't do this.*

Drake's head snapped back. His eyes returned to their normal blue. Pain shone there now instead of fury. Charlie's heart ached at the sight. She wanted to throw her arms around him, tell him how sorry she was. But Drake only walked away, not looking at her as he slammed the door shut.

"Where were we?" Perry cupped her breasts.

Charlie grabbed the tray and hit him on the head. "You know I'm not this slutty." She grabbed her gun from the wall, aimed it at his head. "So tell me where Goodridge's next meeting will be."

Perry yelped, clutching his forehead. "You bitch!" he spat.

"Damned right about that part." She grinned. "Now tell me where the meeting is." She aimed the gun at his groin. "Or I'll—" She motioned and turned the gun's safety off.

Perry raised his hands. "Party, at the Grand. That's all I know."

"When?"

He shook his head, keeping his hands raised. "That's all I know, I swear."

"Good boy." Charlie hit him over the head with the beer tray and then phased through the nearest wall. Once she grabbed her clothes she'd planned to get back to Scott, but she couldn't just leave Drake. She had to make sure he was okay first.

She passed through the walls until she reached the room where she'd stashed her stuff. She pulled off the crappy skirt then heard shouts. She grabbed her clothes and made a dash for the wall.

Drake appeared in front of her.

She froze as his eyes—now dark again—roamed over her. Her cheeks flushed. "Drake, I have to go. We..."

"Back to Scott. I can smell him on you, mixed with that bastard Perry."

She sighed. "I came here for intel, just like you," she said. "I'm sorry for what I said. I really am but—"

He put a hand around her nape, he crushed his mouth to hers, thrusting his tongue inside. Charlie gasped, taking him deeper as she wrapped her arms around him. She moaned, yanking him closer. This was the only man she wanted to touch.

His grip tightened as his hands clamped around her waist. He was losing control again. "Need you," he ground out.

Damn it, he'd go ballistic if anyone tried coming between them again. Grabbing his hand, Charlie pulled them through the wall.

"Fuck!" Drake gasped, eyes changing back to normal.

Charlie felt it too. They were in a void. A place where no magic existed. They had no powers and were now trapped.

CHAPTER 8

Drake tried to think of something, seeing only a door without a handle. He raised his hand, but his power had already diminished.

"Why would they have a void in a brothel?" Charlie asked and cringed. "Never mind, I don't want to know."

Drake leant against the wall, taking a deep breath. "Sorry I lost control again. I just couldn't stand the thought of him touching you."

"It was only acting," Charlie said. "I didn't want him pawing at me any more than you did. Come on, we need to find a way out of here. We don't stand much of a chance without our powers."

He pulled off his jacket and grinned. "Not that I mind the way you're dressed, but here." He held out her.

She took it and slipped it on. "Some void rooms have areas where they end and magic can exist. Help me look." Charlie ran her hands along the wall.

He tried remembering the void at Cate's house that they had used once to interrogate a prisoner not long before *Denai Storm*. That had had weaknesses, but they were almost impossible to find unless you knew where to look. "Are you going back to the Illuminari base after this?" he asked, checking the walls and floor but feeling no sign of his powers returning.

Charlie shook her head. "I'm not getting anywhere with them. I'm still no closer to figuring out my powers and I know I'll have to face Goodridge sooner or later. Irina says she's been shielding me from him—I'm starting to think she's telling the truth."

They both searched the entire space, finding nothing.

Charlie let out a breath. "I guess we'd better be ready." She picked up her gun from the floor. "I don't suppose you have any weapons on you, do you?"

"I prefer to use my wits and my own strength to fight my battles."

Drake pushed his weight against the door. "It's reinforced Silveron. I won't be able to get through it without magic."

"Stand back." She raised her gun, but Drake caught hold of her wrist.

"I wouldn't do that, little witch. It will just bounce off and injure us instead."

"We can't just sit here and do nothing." She slumped against the wall.

"Perry will think us long gone knowing him. He won't think we're still here." Drake wrapped an arm around her. "At least we're together."

"How can you be so calm?" Charlie sighed.

"I'm with you. You calm the darkness in me that comes with being the Akaran," he said. "I used to think I had to rein it in, never let it out. Now I know I can control it."

Charlie rested her head against his chest as she hugged him. "Ever since we met it feels like one big uphill battle."

He smiled and touched her cheek. "I wouldn't have any other way."

She looked up into his eyes. "Why haven't you sealed our bond yet? We already have a partial bond; we should have sealed it by now."

He smiled. "Because I never wanted to force on you. I wanted you to have a choice."

"I do want it, I want you. Hell, I just wanna go home with you. No more demon stuff or worrying about the Srimtar."

Drake leaned down and captured her mouth in a soft kiss. "I love you," he breathed and deepened the kiss. He felt power spark between them and pulled back, frowning. "Did you feel that?"

Charlie nodded. "Yeah, maybe we do still have power." She pulled his head down for another kiss. More energy sparked between them. Charlie tugged at his shirt, her hands roaming over his chest.

Drake tensed when he heard the sound of voices outside. He pulled away. "I think they're coming. Stay…"

"Drake, if there's one thing I've learnt whilst being stuck with my mother is you're my partner. We need to work together if we going to make this work between us."

He squeezed her hand. "I meant stay behind me whilst I draw their attention then you can blow their heads off." Drake rolled up his sleeves. "We're not dying here today."

She gripped his hand in return and said something that stunned him. The first part of the joining vows. Energy jolted between them, creeping into his very soul. The next stage of their bond was now sealed.

Charlie smiled. "I know you wanted it to be the perfect moment but I'm tired of waiting. So you're stuck with me now."

"When we get out of here, I am making love to you and sealing the final part of our bond." He pulled her into a deep, searing kiss. "I'll just have to make sure we get out of here alive."

"You better!"

They stood, ready for whatever came at them as the door creaked open.

Drake felt his power slowly returning as he and Charlie stumbled outside into the hallway.

"Ah, hell!" Charlie muttered.

Goodridge himself stood a few feet away. "How nice to see you both again. Here's me thinking you'd broken up," he said. "Kind of disappointing. You both make each other weak, I thought you would've learnt that by now."

Drake felt sweat running down his brow. Being stuck in a void for so long had taken its toll on him and Charlie looked pale too. Had the joining vows not worked? He thought they had but being in a void might mean the next stage of the bond hadn't fully formed due to their lack of power.

"I thought you would have given up too," Charlie remarked, keeping an arm wrapped around Drake. "You won't find the orb."

Drake closed his eyes, feeling his senses stir, but they still felt weak. *Come on,* he thought. *I need power.* For once in his life, he wanted to feel the power he'd spent so long hiding. If only they were in Kyral, the land itself would give him energy.

I can't shimmer, Charlie said.

I doubt I can either, Drake replied.

"No more hiding or running away, I will have my orb." Myles raised his hand.

The ground beneath their feet trembled. Charlie clung to Drake. *He's trying to open a portal.*

Then let him.

Charlie pulled away, her hands flaring with light. *I'll work on the portal. You distract him.*

He smirked. *Gladly.*

Goodridge sent a bolt of blue lightning at him.

Drake raised his hand, deflecting it. Despite his weakened state, he wouldn't die here or let Myles harm his mate.

Goodridge grinned. "I wondered when you'd start acting like a real Akaran." He fired another bolt.

Drake let the energy wash over him, feeling it strengthen him. His eyes bled to black as his inner demon came out, fangs protruding. He was Akaran, strong, hard. The true leader of Demonkind. It felt good to embrace it.

The ground trembled and writhed as a glowing vortex appeared, swirling like a whirlpool of energy.

I don't know how much longer I can hold him off! Charlie said. *If he opens a portal, we'll be on his turf. He'll have the upper hand.*

Drake raised his hand again, as Akaran he could control any demon who'd sworn allegiance to him. The Illuminaris hadn't done so but Drake suspected he could use that control to at least slow Myles down. He dropped his shields, letting his power roam free. Still weak but still there as he clenched his fist. *Stop!* He gave the mental command.

Myles's eyes widened then flashed. "You'll never control me, demon."

Charlie flung out her arm, sending Myles skidding to the ground and disappearing through the open portal. *Drake, let's go!* She wrapped her arms around him. *He won't stay gone for long.*

Drake felt her magic wrap around them as she shimmered them out. They reappeared a few feet down the corridor in a heap.

Bullets zipped through the air as two of Goodridge's men appeared. Drake shoved Charlie down, covering her body with his own as heat seared his back. Gripping Charlie's arm, he pulled her around the corner.

"We've got to get out of here," Charlie said.

Drake winced from the pain; without his full power, the wounds wouldn't heal. He straightened "I'll go; you follow and make your escape."

Her dark eyes narrowed. "No, not without you."

"I'll be fine."

"You've already taken hits."

"It's just a few grazes."

"Oh, yeah?" She motioned to his shoulder.

He glared down, feeling the sting of metal as more blood seeped out. "Just go, I'll be right behind you."

"No, I can't lose you again." She cupped his face and kissed him.

His lips curved into a smile. "I'm not losing you either, little witch. I won't die here today, I promise you that. Follow close behind me then they won't see you."

"Then we'll both shimmer out."

"To where?" he asked. "Our powers will still be weakened."

Charlie handed him her gun. "Once we're outside we can find Scott..."

"I dislike this plan already," he growled.

Charlie rolled her eyes. "You really need to get over that."

Drake's jaw clenched. "My house is less than a mile away. We can go there."

She hesitated then nodded. Drake yanked the door open. A hail of bullets came through as he stood back with Charlie close behind him. He glanced around the corner. Shots ripped through the air as he fired. The gunmen ducked for cover. Drake hurried into the passage, feeling power flood through his veins. Charlie wrapped her arms around him, phasing as more bullets came at them.

He shimmered, feeling a searing pain tear through his back.

***

Drake and Charlie landed on the floor they materialised in the foyer of his house. He grunted from the pain.

"Oh, thank the goddess!" Charlie breathed. "Wait, what if he can sense me here? I lost Irina's bracelet. Oh, shit!"

Drake got up and stumbled, blood seeping from his shoulder.

"Come on, that needs tending to." She pushed her hair off her face and wrapped an arm around him, helping him up. "I thought being bonded would feel different," she admitted. "Cate said it felt amazing when she sealed her bond with Jason." Cate may have added a few more unnecessary details about what had happened after they sealed her bond, but Charlie had been too grossed out to listen. "Ready to fully seal our bond yet?"

"Later," Drake told her, as they staggered together down the hall. "If Goodridge comes, let him. But we should be safe here. My house is warded tighter than Stanhold prison."

"I just thought we'd have more energy now we're past the next stage. But I guess being stuck in a void and blocking a portal between the worlds will do that." She grinned.

"You're beautiful, little witch." His lips trailed down her neck, making her giggle.

She gave him a playful shove and rose, using the house's computer screen to figure out where they were and gasped. "Hey, we're home. You said…"

"I missed home too. So I used what strength I had to get here."

Charlie helped him to into the kitchen where she washed off the blood as best she could. As he sat she noticed his colour returning and she felt a little better herself. "It feels like forever since we were last here," she murmured. "Rather than just three months ago."

"I still have to return to Kyral. It's the night of the blood moon tonight." Drake rubbed his shoulder. "Daron will no doubt make his move then. I'll have to fight him, make a show of strength to prove myself as the Akaran in my people's eyes."

"What happens after that?" Although she'd known he was the Akaran, him actually taking place as leader of Demonkind had seemed impossible. He hadn't wanted the position, but he couldn't deny what he was anymore. Just as she couldn't deny about being an Illuminari either. No, she didn't like that term, Denai Illuminari, or demon witch didn't seem to fit. *I'm a shadow walker. I walk in shadow and I'm sworn to protect the innocent and keep the Srimtar safe.*

"All of your case files and things are where you left them. I had your stuff brought back from Kyral too," Drake told her.

"I love you." Charlie threw her arms around him and gave him a passionate kiss.

Warmth swelled in her chest as she felt the link that now bound them together more strongly than ever. Yet it wasn't just the bond. He'd always been there for her even when she'd been a headstrong kid and during the years they'd been apart. She'd always felt him there with her, even during the horrific day when the Srimtar had killed her teammates he'd been there with her every step of the way.

Drake ran a hand through his hair. "I think we're strong enough to make it upstairs now. Are you coming?" He held a hand to her. "No doubt you'll want to work."

Charlie took it, smiling. "Work can wait a little longer." She tugged him inside the lift. "You sure you're alright now?"

"Never better, little witch." He pulled her in for another kiss, this time slow and deep. "I need you." His eyes darkened again, this time with the lust, not power.

Charlie pressed a button, making the lift shutdown. She was sick of waiting so she shoved him back against the wall. Damn it, she needed him too. Needed to feel close to him. She didn't know if it was the strengthened bond or because they'd been apart for so long. Nor did she care as she wrapped her arms around him, wanting to be as close as she could get.

Drake pulled her bra off, breaking it with a snap before pushing her against the wall, devouring her mouth as he kissed her.

She tugged off the skimpy skirt and underwear as she pulled back, glad to be rid of them. Her hands roamed over his chest.

She fought to get his trousers undone. He kicked them off, picking her up. She felt the cold steel of the wall behind her but didn't care. She wrapped her legs around his waist, moaning as he thrust inside of her for the first time.

His hand gripped her hips with almost savage strength as he slammed into her again with one swift stroke.

Charlie gasped as she adjusted to the feel of him inside her. It felt like pure elation. She met him thrust for thrust, her nails grazing his shoulders.

The air grew steamy as they devoured each other. She cried out as shock waves of pleasure wracked through her body.

Drake gasped her name as they came together in a crash of emotions and power.

CHAPTER 9

Drake scowled at the breaches, shirt and tunic he was required to wear for the night's festivities. He much preferred a good suit, but he had to play the part of the Akaran's brother for the time being.

Not long now until he'd see Charlie again too. Although part of him wanted to keep her away he knew she'd come anyway. The thought made him smile as a knock sounded on the door.

Flames flashed around him as he changed into the clothes. Seth, already clad in his dress uniform, bowed when Drake opened the door. "Everything is ready," Seth told him.

In the great hall, decorations covered the walls and ceiling. Dozens of demons had already gathered dressed in their finest. Drake took his seat beside Daron and greeted some of the guests. Music started playing as more people flocked inside. Yet Drake felt the unspoken tension in the atmosphere. He scanned the crowd but found no sign of the Illuminaris yet.

Come on, Charlie, where are you?

"It's going to be a memorable night, brother." Daron grinned, raising his goblet.

"Indeed it is."

A hushed silence descended as a blonde woman dressed in a flowing silver gown came in her blue tattoos glittering with her dress.

"Excuse me." Drake leapt from the dais and stalked through the crowd. He found Charlie dressed in a long silver evening gown with her hair tied back and silver tingeing in her eyes. Drake ignored Scott by her side and pulled her into his arms, kissing her long and hard. He didn't care who saw them, she was the only thing that mattered to him.

"Hello, stranger," she murmured against his lips.

"I missed you."

"You only saw me a few hours ago." She grinned.

"A few hours too long." He wrapped an arm around her waist and led her across the room.

Has Daron done anything yet? she asked.

Not yet. He'll wait until the moon is at its highest point no doubt.

I still don't like this idea, Charlie said. *If Daron becomes stronger too... What if something goes wrong and he overpowers you? I know I have your ring but—*

But you mustn't use it. Remember, Charlotte, you're not allowed to interfere with the fight.

Why do you have to fight him at all? We have enough evidence.

I have to do this, little witch. It's the only way. He touched her cheek.

He turned to Daron, Charlie glued to his side. "Brother, you remember Charlotte, don't you? My life mate." Drake felt her tense as he wrapped an arm around her shoulders.

"Daron." She gave him a smile that showed too much teeth. "Long time no see."

Why the hell are you telling him I'm your life mate? You said you didn't want anyone to know I'm your weakness, she said to Drake.

You're not my weakness. You're my strength, he assured her.

"Hello, Charlotte." Daron rose and kissed her cheek. "Nice to see you again. Please enjoy the festivities."

"Remind me to scrub my face later," she muttered once Daron had moved on.

Drake chuckled. "Come on, let's dance."

Charlie grabbed his hand and didn't stop until they were outside in the courtyard. "How can you be so calm right now?" she demanded. "What if something goes wrong?"

"It won't."

"Drake, your confidence is one of the things I love about you, but now is not the time to get cocky."

"I'm never cocky," he assured her and grinned.

She jabbed him in the ribs. "Will you please—"

He cut her off with a kiss. "Relax, love. We'll get through this together."

She wrapped her arms around him, resting her head against his chest. "Good, because if you die on me I will kick your arse."

"Let's just enjoy ourselves. I want to dance with you."

She bit her lip. "I don't dance. I'm not very good at it."

"Lucky for you I am." He took her hand wrapped his other arm around her waist. Together they danced under the glowing red moon and Drake waited for the inevitable to come.

When the moon became steadily full, they headed back inside the great hall. Drake stalked across the room towards Daron. Charlie feared what he might do. As if she didn't have enough to worry about already. But she couldn't lose him again.

Daron rose when they came in. "Ah, the imp is still here."

"I'm not an imp." She crossed her arms. "I'm a witch demon; actually I like the term shadow walker best."

Drake raised his hand. Daron started to choke, clutching at his throat as he struggled for breath. "Did you kill Arya and our parents?"

"What—no!" Daron clutched his throat. "Stop!"

"Tell the truth." Drake's eyes bled to black.

Daron's eyes bulged as he struggled for breath. "Yes…"

"Why?" Drake let go, causing Daron to fall to the floor. "How could you?"

Daron sputtered. "Because Papa would've killed us. He wanted to join the Covenant, ally with the fey of all people! His reign needed to end, and I wanted his power."

"You never had to kill Mama to do that much less Arya."

Charlie snorted. "He would've killed you given the chance and would have too if I hadn't stopped him."

Daron glared at her. "I knew I recognised you from somewhere. Drake, can't you see? She's trying to turn you against me," he snapped. "How can you believe her over me? I would never have…"

"Because I trust her more than I've ever trusted anyone." Drake grabbed his brother by the throat.

"Drake, you can't kill him." Charlie touched his arm. "You're not a murderer."

"Don't be ridiculous, Charlotte. I've killed when I've had to. I'm no angel."

"I know that, but you're not a cold-blooded killer either." If he killed Daron, it might not be something he could come back from, and she couldn't lose him again. "He's still your brother; you can't kill him. Arya wouldn't want that either."

Drake punched Daron in the face, then muttered something in Demonish. "Your powers are now bound. I'll be sure everyone learns the truth now."

Drake kept hold of Daron as they shimmered to the great hall and he let out a loud roar made the walls around them vibrate. Charlie winced but knew he had to show everyone Daron's betrayal. She wanted to rush the dungeon to find her mother, but she stayed in place. She was a demon too and the Akaran had just called every demon in the city to appear before them. Dozens of male and female demons shimmered in, their eyes wide.

"For millennia, this man has ruled in my stead." Drake kept a firm hold on Daron. "But he is a deceiver. It is I who am the true Akaran. As your true leader, I'm here to tell you Daron is the one who killed Thaddeus, my father, and the last Akaran along with my mother and sister. For this, he will be punished."

A murmur rang through the crowd.

"How do we know this is true?" someone spoke up.

"I saw it, as did my mate, Charlotte."

Charlie tried not to flinch under their gazes.

"Daron, do you confess to your crimes?"

Daron glared daggers at Charlie. "Yes, but I did the right thing. My brother abandoned us the moment he came to power, why would you choose him over me?" he demanded. "Haven't I—"

"Hundreds of died because of you. We follow the true Akaran," someone yelled, and shouts rang out.

"Our law states he must be put to death," Seth spoke up.

"This isn't punishment enough from what he took from me," Drake said. "As Akaran I can choose his punishment. I say he should be judged by a Denai and have the touch used on him. That way he'll suffer the pain he's caused for eternity, even in death."

"Witches are forbidden in Kyral," another demon spoke up.

"That law is hereby abolished. The witches are our allies—my life mate is a Denai too."

Please don't drag me into this, she told him as more glares came her way.

"Yes, she's a witch. She's turned…" Daron said.

"Anyone who dares harm my mate will suffer at my hand," Drake growled. "Daron will be locked up until—"

"I'll do it," Charlie blurted out the words before she could stop herself.

The room fell silent.

Charlie, what are you doing? Drake snapped.

You need a Denai to pass judgement on him. I'll do it. She walked over to them.

No, I'll call Cate or your grandmother Ceri.

It would take too long for them to get here and I'm the only other Denai who can compel demons.

Charlotte, I can't let you kill him.

I'm not. He's done that himself.

The other demons muttered between themselves as Daron struggled against Drake's grip. "You can't let her touch me. I deserve an honourable death."

"You deserve nothing," Drake snarled, forcing Daron to his knees.

Daron glared at her. "I knew you were nothing but trouble, imp."

Charlie grinned, feeling a sense of calm come over her as her Denai training kicked in. "That's why you teamed up with my mother, too. You knew you'd get rid of me and get the Illuminari leader all in one go," she said. "For the record, I'm all witch." She wrapped her fingers around his throat, Daron's eyes turning black as she unleashed the power of her touch.

Denais punished the guilty by forcing them to suffer all the pain they caused others. It crippled them, and they would suffer it even in death. Charlie had never used her touch on the living before—only a couple of times on spirits. Death by the touch was considered a fate worse than death and only used on the worst kind of criminals.

Charlie felt her power jolt from her into Daron, shaking the air around them like thunder without sound. She pulled back, knowing she wouldn't have long before the deadly magic killed him. "Did you murder your parents and sister?"

The touched person could never lie once under a witch's control. Daron nodded. "Yes, I wanted the power of the Akaran. I tried to kill Drake too, but you stopped me."

"Did you team up with my mother Irina?"

"Yes, I wanted you gone. Plus, I learnt their location." Daron tried to reach for her. "Please, my lady, forgive me."

Charlie shoved his hand away in disgust. "It's just the magic. You don't truly feel guilty for anything."

Daron screamed as blood dripped from his nose then he slumped to the floor, dead. Drake incinerated the body with a fireball, then took her hand. "Call the meeting. I want to talk to every leader of every clan. Any who refuse, I'll summon by force. We'll meet tomorrow morning."

Charlie felt numb as Drake led her out into an empty hall.

"Are you alright?" He placed his hands on her shoulders. "You shouldn't have had to do that."

She let out a breath. "Yes, I did. I saw what he did too, and I had to be the one to pass judgement." She rested her head against him as he pulled her in for a hug. "What happens now?"

"I have to talk to all the leaders. Tell them to become part of the Alliance. I doubt many will object," he said. "Then we're leaving."

Her eyes widened. "You're the Akaran, you belong here."

"No, my place is with the Alliance. I'll choose someone to be my representative here. This hasn't been my place for a long time." He stroked her cheek. "I promise I'll do what I can for your mother."

CHAPTER 10

The next morning after learning Daron had had Irina arrested Drake and Charlie headed straight for the dungeons to see her. In the chaos that had followed after Daron's demise, they'd both forgotten about Irina. The Illuminari leader sat on a steel bunk, the blue markings covering her arms and legs looked black in the dim light. Drake had wanted to keep her there a while longer but knew Charlie wouldn't let him. He thought it might give the Illuminari some time to think on some of her past mistakes.

"Charlie." Irina shot to her feet and came over to the bars. "Please let me out of here." Irina looked at Drake. "You know now my people and I had nothing to do with your family's deaths."

Drake scowled. "Yes, but you still tried to split us up and break our link."

Charlie waved a hand. "She couldn't though because we already have a partial bond."

Drake wrapped an arm around her. He couldn't believe they'd been connected for so long. He knew it must've kept him grounded when he'd almost lost himself to darkness over the last few centuries of misery. "I can't release you, Irina, even if I wanted to. The Grand Mistress has ordered you be brought to Setara to face judgement for several crimes."

Charlie gaped at him. "Why didn't you mention that?" she hissed.

He rubbed the back of his head, feeling at a loss for words. He hadn't wanted to mention it but knew he wouldn't have been able to keep it a secret long. *Because I've been trying to figure a way out of it.*

"There is something that might help your cause," he said to Irina. "Which is?"

"Come with me to my meeting. Swear allegiance to me and the Alliance. Your people won't have to be hunted or outcasts anymore.

You'll be recognised as a true demon clan."

Irina's eyes narrowed. "Why would I do that?"

"Because it's the right thing to do." Charlie squeezed Drake's hand. "I'll always be loyal to my family and Drake's part of that. I'd like you to be part of my life too, but you need to start proving you're trustworthy to everyone first."

Irina shook her head and glowered at Drake, pointing. "His people have—"

"Both sides carry blame," Drake said. "I'm asking you to let go of the past and forge a new future. One of peace. Your people are dying out; don't you want to live in the open?"

Irina gave him a hard look. "You truly love her, don't you? You must do to consider peace with my people."

Drake wrapped an arm around Charlie. "More than life. She's already proved how strong she is. Time for you to do the same."

Irina paced. "You don't know what you're asking of me."

"We're asking you to do the right thing for once," Charlie snapped. "Look, you're never going to be the kind of mother I want but you could at least do this one thing for me. You owe me that much."

"I tried to save you, didn't I?" Irina demanded. "I would've shown you how to use your powers, to be a true Illuminari."

"No, you tried taking me away from the love of my life and made me stay in Alanon without even asking me how I felt about it!"

Drake bit back a smile. He loved her fire.

"It won't get me out of prison, will it?" Irina asked, crossing her arms.

"No, but it would look good in front of the council and the Grand Mistress," he said. "You spied on Seline McCray and other council leaders; your fate lies with the current Grand Mistress now."

Irina gave a harsh laugh. "I gave them my only daughter; you'd think that would be enough." She pouted. "Fine, I'll go to your meeting."

Drake felt his heart pounding as he waited for every demon leader to convene in the meeting hall. He hadn't played any part in politics before, even working for Niara had excluded him from that, and he only had a vague recollection of his father bringing the clans together. Still, Charlie had come back to him; having her there gave him

253

strength.

Twelve men and women gathered around the huge round table. Was this all that remained of the clan leaders? No, he sensed there were a few more. There had been over fifty demon clans back in his father's day.

So few clans, so much animosity. Demons weren't a peaceful bunch, but they'd never been so bloodthirsty before the first great war. Would he really be able to get them to swear loyalty to the Alliance?

"Thank you all for coming." He kept his expression neutral. An Akaran never showed true emotion in situations like this or it'd be seen as a sign of weakness. "I called you all here to—"

"You want us all to swear loyalty to the fucking Alliance." Garth, leader of the rage demons spoke up. "You're out of your mind, Drakon. Just as you're mad for bedding a witch."

Drake gripped the table, forcing himself to remain calm. "That witch is my life mate, and no, I'm not mad. Demonkind are scattered, divided. It's time we all joined together."

"Why can't you do that?" asked Roan, leader of the sage demons. "Isn't it the Akaran's job to do just that?"

"Yes, but it's also my job to lead our people out of obscurity. Look at us." Drake waved a hand. "My brother forced most of you to remain in this country, those here don't live in the modern world with tech and advancement. I've seen very little of that during my time here."

"Demons are still treated like scum," Dalia, another leader spoke up. "Even you."

"Am I?" Drake arched an eyebrow. "I've worked with the council and the Alliance almost all my life. I created a division where races work together to keep the peace—more than even enforcers do. Let's show the other races we deserve a place among them."

"Fine words for a man who's worked for the council for centuries—a council which excludes demons," said Garth.

"What of the witch?" asked Dalia. "She is Illuminari, why should we trust her?"

"My witch is kin to the Grand Mistress and the Serenity. She has no loyalty to her mother's people, but I do have someone already willing to sign." He unrolled a piece of parchment, a treaty to pledge loyalty to the Alliance and its allies.

The doors opened; Charlie came in leading Irina by her chains.

Many of the demons muttered curses, uneasy at the sight of the Illuminari leader. One of the very beings who had infiltrated the clans.

Irina held her head high. Drake knew if she were anything like her daughter she wouldn't cower before these people. "As leader of the Illuminari I pledge my loyalty and that of my people to the Alliance."

Garth scoffed. "You're only doing it because you'll be put to death soon."

"No, I'm doing the right thing." Irina met the other demon's gaze. "With this treaty, we'll be free and no longer hunted—that was the agreement. We and all demons—" Her lip curled. "Are equal and protected by this agreement."

"The treaty here signed has already been by my aunt and the leaders of the Phoenix, Ashrali, Nuardan and shifters." Charlie motioned to the table. "See for yourselves. The treaty is legal and binding. It can't be undone." She handed Irina her knife. All treaties had to be sealed by blood.

Drake didn't like the Illuminari having any kind of weapon. He braced himself in case she tried anything, but Irina pricked her finger and pressed it to the parchment before handing it back to Charlie. Drake glanced to the other faces in the room as everyone fell silent.

Garth step forward, drew a wicked-looking knife and signed. Slowly, the others followed suit.

CHAPTER 11

Drake leaned against the bar waiting for Silas, one of his demonic contacts, to appear. Charlie shifted on the stool next to him. "Remind me again why you're calling Silas of all people," she remarked.

"He's an old acquaintance."

She scowled. "Yeah, and he's a slippery bastard who wouldn't even tell me where you were when you went missing."

Drake said, "He'll never give you straight answers unless you have something valuable to offer."

She crossed her arms. "What you can offer him?" she asked. "Shouldn't we be getting ready for that party?"

"We will and that depends on what he has to say."

Silas appeared. With his pointy white beard, beady eyes and white hair that rose in two short tuffs, he gave Charlie the creeps. "Well, well, look who has finally outed himself as the Akaran." He gave a toothy smile, showing shrivelled gums. "And the witch is here too, wonders never cease."

"What do you know about Goodridge's meetings?" Drake got straight to the point. "What was he planning?"

Silas's lips thinned. "Why?" His eyes narrowed. "Goodridge is bad news. I thought you would know that by now."

"Oh, believe me, we do," Charlie muttered.

"Come now, Silas. You know something," Drake said.

"Price, boy. My intel comes with a price."

"Name it."

Silas cackled. "Fine, then I want your club."

Charlie snorted. "Why the hell would you want a club?"

"Done," Drake said without hesitation. "Now tell me what you know."

Why are you giving him the club? Charlie asked.

It's just a club. I have dozens more.

Kind of fond of this one.

"Fine." Silas dropped a small silver crystal disc into Drake's hand. "You'll need this to get into the party."

Charlie's eyes narrowed. "That's it?"

Silas sidled at her. "Would you be needing something, witch?"

"Nope, ever thought of seeing a dental hygienist? They can work miracles nowadays."

Drake stifled a laugh, then conjured a piece of paper. "Here is the deed to the club."

Silas grinned, grabbing it. "This is for a club in Lordan." He scowled. "What the hells?"

"You said a club, not *this* club. Besides this place is not only mine. Most of my businesses also now belong to Charlotte too." He took Charlie's hand, then glanced at the other demon. "Pleasure doing business with you, Silas."

Charlie gasped as they reappeared in their bedroom. "Why the hell didn't you tell me that you put me on the deeds to your businesses?"

"It hasn't all been processed yet." He shrugged. "I wanted to wait until it was settled."

She scowled. "No, I meant why would you put my name on there in the first place without asking me first?"

"You're my mate. Everything I have is equally yours."

Charlie let out a breath. "But I don't want them. They're yours."

He laughed. "You don't have to run them, little witch." He gave her a quick kiss. "I don't see the problem."

She rolled her eyes and muttered. "Demons!" Then she said, "Drake, we're supposed to talk about big stuff like this—not that anything about our relationship has ever been normal."

"Everything I have, everything I am, belongs to you now. That's what being life mates means." He stroked her cheek. "I thought you wanted us to have a life together?"

"I do, believe me. The business thing is just weird that's all." She smiled. "The forever thing I can deal with."

"Come, the party will start a few hours. We'll need to be prepared and ready."

"I still can't believe you gave him one of your clubs."

Drake waved a hand. "It's a seedy place. I'm glad to be rid of it," he told her. "Time to pick our aliases and disguises."

Drake straightened his tie, feeling the prickle of the chip he'd had placed under his skin to disguise his true appearance. His hair appeared longer, his jawline rougher and covered in stubble. His eyes now looked dark green, to match his alias—Johan, a lesser-known leader of a demon tribe. He just hoped the chips would be enough to disguise their true appearances when they met with Goodridge.

"I'll never get used to this part of the job." Charlie scowled at her reflection. She looked petite with curly blonde hair and blue eyes. She wore a plunging red gown that matched her fiery red lipstick.

I much prefer your true appearance. Drake wrapped his arms around her, kissing her neck.

She giggled. *I thought you liked blondes.*

What made you think that?

Lana's blonde; so is that woman in Kyral.

I never used to have a preference. As long as it was female and decent looking, I didn't care.

She rolled her eyes. *I feel so loved.*

"You should." He kissed her again. "You're the only one I've ever loved."

Charlie smiled, leaning into his embrace. "Good, because you're stuck with me now. I mean it. If you change your mind, I'll just follow you everywhere."

"Likewise, little demon."

Little witch sounds better, she said.

Remember, we get in, assess the situation with Goodridge, then get out.

I hope these chips really disguise us, she remarked. *Goodridge is powerful. He might see straight through us.*

Drake shook his head. *I've used this device countless times over the centuries. It will work, and I believe your father did a good job on the upgrade.*

Charlie grinned. *When this was all over, and we get to the orb back we should go and visit my family again. Tell them the news about us being bonded.*

We not fully bonded yet, he pointed out.

Right, we should do something about that.

We will soon, he promised.

Drake wanted to take the joining vows more than anything. But somehow he wanted it to be special, more meaningful. Most demons became fully bonded when they mated but he wanted it to be different. He had something big planned; he just needed it to be the right time.

Charlie frowned. "Why do I sense you're hiding something from me?"

He smirked. "It's a surprise."

"Never been a big fan of surprises."

"So I've noticed." He let go of her as the lift doors pinged open.

Charlie slipped her arm through his as they headed into a foyer.

Drake sensed a mass of demons throughout the building. Their energy signatures felt different which meant they hadn't sworn allegiance to him and he wouldn't be able to control them. At least not to the extent he could others. Drake spotted a giant standing guard in front of some double doors. With incredible strength, giants didn't have much in the way of magic except for a higher resistance to it.

Remember when we get in, watch the meeting then we get the hell out, Drake said. *Don't be tempted to go snooping.*

Charlie pouted. *As if I would.*

He stifled a laugh, dropping the disc into the giant's outstretched palm. The giant scanned it. Charlie gripped Drake's arm tighter. *Silas better have given us the right disc,* she remarked.

He will have if he knew what was good for him.

The scanner bleeped, and the giant motioned for them to follow. Charlie let out a breath, relieved they had made inside.

Relax, little witch. We have to look like we belong here.

Yeah, yeah. We're walking into the viper's den. You can't blame me for being a little nervous.

Inside, a dozen demons stood or sat around the grand ballroom. Chandeliers sparkled overhead; a rich red carpet covered the floor.

Are all these people demons? Charlie asked. *With so much energy in here, it's hard to tell who is what.*

Most. None of them have sworn allegiance to me. Must be why Goodridge invited them. He spotted a table near the front and sat down with Charlie beside him.

Time for the games to begin.

CHAPTER 12

Charlie shifted in her seat. She wanted the damned meeting to begin and find out what Goodridge was up to.

Drake clutched her hand underneath the table which relaxed her a little. Until her senses tingled. Wearing the usual grey tunic and trousers, Scott, with his Illuminari tattoos on full display, waltzed into the ballroom.

"Holy crap!" she muttered. *Drake!*

Drake's gaze shot to Scott too, eyes narrowing. *This could be a problem.*

Bugger, bugger! Maybe I should have called him again after going back to Setara. But she had her own problems to deal with. Now Irina had sworn the Illuminari's loyalty to Drake and the Alliance she thought she wouldn't have to worry about them for a while.

Great, just great.

Ignore him, Drake told her. *We have a job to do.*

Right, I'm Lila. A succubus, sex-crazed demon. Or, at least, my alias is.

"Mind if I sit here?" Scott came over to their table. Charlie grabbed her water glass and gulped some of it down.

"Please." Drake motioned to the seat opposite them.

Charlie scowled. *What are you doing?*

I can keep an eye on him this way.

She rolled her eyes. *You really need to get over the jealousy thing.*

I am over it, but that doesn't mean I trust him.

"I'm Scott, lieutenant to the lady of the Illuminari," Scott said.

"Johann, leader of the Amara tribe. My wife, Lila, leader of the succubae."

Charlie gave Scott a cold smile. "Pleasure."

Scott opened his mouth to speak, but everyone fell silent as the lights dimmed and Myles Goodridge appeared. "Thank you all for coming here today," Myles's voice boomed. "We gathered here because all of us are tired of the way Magickind overruled both here and throughout the world. The council and the Alliance's reach grows every day. Their power and influence govern dozens of races. Now even the Akaran himself has announced allegiance to them." Myles settled on the podium. "But I say that time needs to end."

Here we go. Charlie rested her chin on her palm. She knew there was a need for domination in there somewhere.

"Why should we believe you can bring about any type of change?" Drake prompted in the voice of his alias. "The Covenant spent millennia trying to change things and you only lead a gang of thugs."

A murmur rang out through the crowd. Some agreeing, others not.

Charlie bit back smile. *Go, demon.*

Myles's smile never faltered. "True, but the Covenant were wrong in their approach of attacking the other races head-on," he continued. "They never had the true power required for such an endeavour."

"And you do?" another demon asked.

"Yeah, do you?" a she-demon with claws spoke up. "The Covenant was always making empty promises and with or without the Alliance we're doing fine."

"Are we?" the first demon—Devin, Drake had said his name was—asked. "The last Akaran treated us like shit. I'd say we're better off without any leaders. We should all do our own thing."

Charlie saw Drake's lips twitch. If they only knew what he had done for them over the centuries.

"Agreed, I like things the way they are," the she-demon growled. "Why would we follow you anyway?"

"Because together we can prove unstoppable," Myles replied. His body shimmered as he passed in and out of existence. "Wouldn't you all like to be able to walk in and out of reality?" he asked. "To not be left out? The rest of Magickind treat demons as inferior. It's time we proved them wrong."

"How?" Drake demanded. "Your words may inspire but we need proof."

Myles pulled out a small crystal orb. It reminded Charlie of the Srimtar.

"This is an orb used by Oberoth to store some of the energy he amassed during his reign." Myles held it up. It turned red as a ball of energy shot upward, shattering the chandelier and plunging the room into heavy darkness.

Looks like he's building weapons of mass destruction, Charlie remarked.

It's like he's trying to build a new Covenant, Drake replied.

He can't—can he? It took Oberoth centuries and we have measures in place to prevent that.

Evil never goes away. It just changes forms.

"Bear in mind, that's just a taste of power," Myles told them. "Imagine what we could do with more of these."

Charlie let out a harsh laugh. "You really think you're going to bring down the council and the Alliance with that?" she snorted.

"I have more to show you later—but first enjoy yourselves," Myles said. "Eat, have wine." He moved off the podium and started talking to Devin.

I don't like this, said Charlie. *It doesn't feel right—none of it does.*

I'll stay here, see what else he has to say.

Good, I'm going to snoop around a bit.

Charlotte. He gave her a hard look.

Drake, Myles doesn't sit and chat. He's up to something and I'm going to find out what. You keep an eye on things here.

Fine, but be careful. Don't phase or he might sense it.

Yeah, yeah. You need to stop the protectiveness.

He gave her a smile.

She shook her head, rose and headed out the room. A giant step in front of her. At eight-foot-high, he made Charlie feel small in comparison as she stared up at him. "Where are the toilets around here?"

He grunted, pointing a finger behind him.

"Thanks." She totted off on her high heels, ducked inside, did a quick scan of the cubicles to make sure no one was there. Charlie peered out the door again, the giant still stood where she had left him, watching what was happening in the ballroom.

The door creaked as she slid it back open. She kicked off her shoes, dropped them into a bin, then snuck out the door. A camera sat one corner, she ducked to avoid it, wishing she could phase. But she didn't dare risk it.

Charlie crept down the corridor, watching the cameras and guards as she moved around. Spotting a door with a keypad, she pulled out a device she had clipped to the inside of her thigh, held it over the lock. It flashed green, she hurried inside. Charlie clipped the lock scrambler back on, glanced around the office. Another box sat there. She tried to pry open, to her surprise it opened easily. Inside were dozens of files each with pictures of the guests including mentions of their powers and backgrounds.

Someone's done their homework.

"Charlie?"

She stopped dead to find Scott tucking in behind her.

"Goddess, how the hell did you know it was me?" she hissed.

"I knew you'd come here so I managed to wrangle an invite."

"Go, I'm busy. Leave before someone comes looking for you."

"I need you to get Irina out of prison."

Her mouth fell open. "That's what you came here for? Are you serious?"

"That and to ask you to come back with me. You still haven't mastered your demon powers." He stuffed his hands into his pockets.

Charlie ran a hand through her fake blonde curls, missing the feel of her real hair. "Are you trying to get us killed?"

"Think about it." Scott turned to go. "Your mother keeps our people safe. We may not survive without her."

"Why are you really here?" she demanded.

He touched her cheek. "Because I want you back. We were starting to connect again. I know you felt it too."

"You're my friend, that's it." She shoved him towards the door. "I love Drake. End of discussion. Now go!"

The door swung open and the giant came in. Scott froze as something flashed.

"What—" Charlie started to ask and gasped when Scott fell forward, blood gurgling out of his mouth.

He'd been shot. "No, no, no. This can't be happening." She cradled his head in her lap. "Scott, just hold on."

I'm sorry, he told her.

Charlie looked up and saw the gun aimed at her. Scott shot up, trying to tackle the giant. Charlie kicked the gun out of the way. The giant growled, threw Scott across the room, then grabbed Charlie, punching her. She dodged the blow, kicked his shin and yelped as pain exploded in her barefoot. She wanted to use magic but didn't dare. The minute Myles sensed her; the game would be over. Instead, she grabbed the giant, about to use her witch powers on him.

The giant punched her in the face, making her vision blur as blood poured down her face.

"You'll pay for that," she mumbled, feeling power flow between her fingers. But the giant punched her again and everything went black.

CHAPTER 13

Drake tensed in his seat. *Charlie, where are you?* He felt her close by but couldn't sense her emotions as she seemed to be blocking him. They had agreed to do that during missions so they could focus on their own things and not worry about each other. But Drake hated the feeling of loss and familiarity that came with their deepening bond.

"Everyone please gather round," Myles motioned for them to gather around a circular table.

Charlie, answer me, he said. *You need to get back here, Myles is about to do something.*

He noticed Scott slip out of the room too, but he didn't feel jealous anymore. Jealousy seemed a useless emotion now. He knew Charlie loved him as much as he adored her. But worry filled him. If Scott interrupted her... But how could Scott have known Lila was Charlie?

"I have one more thing to show you all."

Myles had already given them another lecture about joining his cause. Drake could see the others starting to believe his tale.

Charlie? He called again. *You need to come back. Myles will notice you're gone. Why won't you answer me?*

No reply.

"Would you all please sit?" Myles added.

Drake moved over, keeping a watchful eye on Myles. This didn't feel right. Everyone sat down, Drake did the same to avoid any unwanted attention. *Charlie?*

Again, nothing. Could she just be ignoring him or was she in trouble?

Myles placed the orb in the centre of the table. "I'll now demonstrate another gift this can give us," he continued.

Drake sensed the hum of power in the air, then raised his mental shields and physical ones. *Charlie, damn it, where are you?*

The crackle of energy made it harder to concentrate. The orb pulsed with red lights, its vibration humming through the air. Splinters of energy shot out as tendrils of power wrapped around every person at the table.

Drake gasped, feeling invisible fingers clawing to get inside him, to get to his power. His eyes bled to black as his inner demon came out. He let out a growl, his fangs extending.

Screams echoed around the room as one by one each demon exploded in a burst of light.

No! Drake thought.

Energy reverberated outwards, sending Drake crashing across the room as glass shattered and wood splintered from the blast. The air left his lungs but his power remained in place. Anger soon replaced shock as only he and Myles remained in the shattered remains of the ballroom.

"Nice disguise." Myles smirked. "You almost had me fooled there."

Drake scrambled up. "What did you do?" he snarled.

"Simple. I stole and absorbed the power of every demon at the table," Myles explained. "Except yours, of course, but now..." Blue rippling energy formed in his palm. "Let's see if the Akaran is still the most powerful of all demons."

Drake shimmered out just as the blast came at him, then reappeared, the blast hitting the walls behind him, sending wood and plaster flying. Fire formed in Drake's hand, and he hurled it at Myles, who phased before it could reach him. This was pointless.

Myles threw another energy ball, but Drake didn't seem to think he was even trying to kill him.

"Why are we doing this?" he demanded. "This building is unstable—even if you bring it down, you know it won't kill me."

Myles laughed. "No, but it's fun," he replied. "I have what I came for. I'll be seeing you." He vanished in a blaze of light.

Drake froze. Charlie. He didn't sense her.

He blurred out of the room, stopped when he saw someone lying in the open doorway. "Scott?" Drake knelt beside him. "What happened? Where is Charlie?" He felt Scott's life force draining away.

Scott gasped. "Gone, giant stabbed her with something. Tried to…"

Drake held a hand over the wound and drew magic.

"Don't," Scott hissed. "We both know I'm dying. Go. Find her."

Drake hesitated, this man mattered to Charlie, but Scott was right. No magic could save him now. "I'm sorry I can't help you."

"Promise—promise you'll look after her. I loved her—even though I knew she wasn't mine."

He nodded. "I will."

Blood gurgled from Scott's mouth as he drew one last breath. Drake closed Scott's eyes, muttered a short prayer. He would send someone later to deal with the body.

Drake shimmered out, sending senses out into the universe where any trace of his mate but felt nothing. Damn, why hadn't he sealed their bond? Then he'd be able to sense her no matter what interfered. Knowing Goodridge, Charlie might not even be on the physical plane now.

When a deep scan revealed nothing, Drake knew there was only one person left to help him.

The wards of Stanhold prison flashed as glowing swirls of pink, green and red energy. It had been created to shield and prevent anyone from passing through them, but Drake used his full strength to shimmer straight into Irina's cell block.

The Illuminari leader looked up, frowning. "How did you get here?"

"Never mind. Goodridge took Charlie," he snapped. "I can't sense her location. You need to help me find her."

Irina arose from her cot, grabbed the bars. "Haven't you sealed the bond?"

"No." *Because I'm a bloody fool.*

Irina motioned to the collar around her neck. "I have no power."

Drake waved his hand and the cell door slid open. An alarm wailed, followed by the sound of heavy footsteps. The outer door burst open as two Zexen guards came in, with rifles aimed at Drake's head.

"Back away from the prisoner," the first guard yelled. "Put your hands…"

Drake rolled his eyes, waved his hand so the guns went flying. "Tell the Grand Mistress the Akaran needs to borrow her prisoner and will return her later." He grabbed Irina's arm and shimmered them out. They reappeared in his office back at his house in Setara City.

"I don't see how I can help," Irina remarked.

He pulled out a key from his desk drawer and unlocked the collar. "You're her mother. You need to sense her and tell me where he's taken Charlie."

Irina rubbed her neck. "I can't. Myles is very gifted. He insulated himself from everyone—even me."

Drake frowned. "What does that mean?" He gasped. "He's your son, isn't he?" He'd suspected Goodridge was Illuminari too but hadn't thought he'd be related to Charlie.

Irina nodded. "Yes, his father took him from me. I couldn't do anything to get him back."

"Why not?" Drake demanded. "You're not powerless."

"I was against one of the most powerful men in all of Magickind."

Drake shook his head. He didn't give a damn about Myles' history. "Focus on Charlie then. She has to be somewhere!" he snapped. "Myles will use her to get the orb and with the amount of power he accumulated earlier he might just find it."

Irina opened her mouth to protest and Drake slapped her. "Look, you might have given birth to her but you're no mother. No parent would abandon their child," he hissed. "I don't care what happens to you, just help me find her!" The walls vibrated from the force of his fury.

"She truly calms you, doesn't she? I never believed demons could have mates." She sighed and closed her eyes. "I'll try, but it would be easier if I could search the different planes myself."

"Fine, but I'm coming with you." He pulled out a pair of cuffs, slapped one onto her wrist then clipped the other bracelet onto his own. "Don't even think of trying to escape. Cate will be seething when she finds out what I've done."

Irina frowned, glancing around the room. "Won't she send the guards after me?"

He shrugged. "She won't, I already sent her a message. Let's go." He knew Cate would give him hell later for daring to go up against her, but she'd get over it when she knew it was for a good cause.

Irina shimmered out, dragging Drake into the unknown.

CHAPTER 14

Charlie's jaw throbbed as she opened her eyes. *Argh, not again! How did he knock me out this time?* She remembered the giant's fist coming towards her as she held Scott. *Goddess, Scott!* He'd been dying. She looked around the glowing lights of the lab. It reminded her of the places she'd seen in Setara after the revolution that the Deva's and her great-grandfather's people had used.

Silveron bonds held her wrists in place and her ankles. Her magic felt just beyond reach too.

Great, just great. Everything had been going well until Scott's distraction, but she couldn't feel angry with him. If he died she'd be losing someone she still cared about. Charlie sniffed, she couldn't fall apart, she had focus. Myles needed her to find the Srimtar's hideout. Maybe Drake would be able to save Scott.

Drake? She reached out to him with her mind to feel his presence. She pulled at the restraints, searching for any signs of weakness. But Myles could phase like her. He'd know how to keep an Illuminari in place.

She gritted her teeth. "Come on, I know you're lurking around his somewhere. So come out."

A door slid open. "Glad to see you are awake, sister," Goodridge snapped. "Given you're so eager to begin…" He pulled over a machine.

She frowned at him and glanced at the device. Another mind-reading device from the looks of it. "Haven't we established those things don't work on me?" she scoffed. "Why the hell are you calling me sister?"

He grinned. "She didn't tell you? Irina is my mother as well. I am half Illuminari too." Myles jabbed a wire into her arm. "This doesn't just read your mind." He jabbed something else into her other arm, blood began to filter out through the tube.

Charlie's mouth fell open. She had always suspected he was also Illuminari but hadn't imagined they'd share the same mother. "You're going to bleed me dry? Smart plan, brother."

"When a guardian nears death the orb becomes vulnerable too."

Charlie watched her blood flow freely, tried to phase away but the bonds held firm. "The orb isn't meant for you, why can't you understand that?"

Myles snorted. "Of course it's for me. It always has been and soon I'll finally fulfil my destiny."

"And what's that? To be a tyrannical maniac and try to control all Magickind? I'll be happy to spoil that for you."

"You won't spoil anything. I know Drake will come looking for you."

"Why do you want it so bad?" she asked. Since she'd be stuck here a while she figured she might as well get some answers. She'd never known why or what he wanted the Srimtar for.

"You'll be dead soon. The Srimtar has the power to right a wrong. To fix a past mistake."

Another man came out into the room and whispered something to Myles. Charlie heard Irina's name being mentioned, then the man left.

"Did she dump you at birth too?" Charlie prompted.

Myles scowled at her. "No, I lived with her for five years until my father rescued me from her and her band of outlaws." He glanced at the machine. "Don't worry, sister, within the hour it will all be over for you. It'll be a merciful death given all the trouble you've caused me."

Myles left the room; Charlie scanned the lab. She needed to get out of there. Her blood had already begun to fill the large container.

Think, she told herself. *Stay alive.*

Drake? She called again.

Damn, she would have given anything for him to bust in and help her free.

Irina? Hell, it was worth a try.

No response.

Come on, focus, McCray. Charlie noticed her watch and ring had gone. No weapons there then. A wave of dizziness washed over her. Shit, had she lost that much blood already?

Charlie's eyes drooped closed but she opened them again. *You must stay awake.* She had to get that tube out.

Charlie gritted her teeth, trying to twist her arm enough to get the tube out of her wrist but it was in too deep. Beside her, the machine whirred to life. Her eyes blurred and blackness dragged her under.

Charlie blinked as blackness gave way to a kaleidoscope of colours, reds, greens, blues and everything in between. *Did I die already?* She floated through the lights. Somehow she didn't think she was dead.

Where the hell am I? She landed on a floor of purple glass. It looked like her place between the worlds but felt different. Mist swirled around her, forming into images. Then she understood what it meant. These were the memories Irina had kept telling her about.

First, a group of people appeared—Illuminari demons. Lightning flashed, and she saw them disappearing into shadow. One Illuminari stood with five other people. A witch, a Nuardan, an Ashrali, a Phoenix elemental and a shifter. The five elder races. Not five, six, she realised.

Words and images rushed to her mind so fast she gasped. Now she knew what she was. The mist around her faded to fall into the glowing form of the Srimtar.

Another image appeared of the six people standing together. One man stepped forward and light began to drain away from the other figures, swirling into an orb. The Srimtar.

Helga's story came flooding back. This was it. The weapon that could warp time.

Charlie gasped as Myles's hand clamped around her throat, his eyes flashing azure. His power shot through her, exploding outwards, searching for the orb. She sucked in a breath, her body phasing for a second before she hit the floor. "You want to go back in time. That's why you need it."

"It's easy to find a way to witness the past if you have enough power. But I can't change it, no matter how hard I try." He grinned. "My father thought that. That's why he created the orb for me."

Charlie gulped. "You mean Oberoth? But he's dead."

Myles's expression hardened. "Yes, your precious family took him from me. But I always knew I'd be able to save him," he said. "To follow in his footsteps. He never got to retrieve the Srimtar for himself—the first alliance stopped him. They used their power to curse the orb and then Denai predicted you would be the one to protect it."

Denai? The Denai? As in the mother goddess the witches named themselves after?

Helga's story suddenly made sense. Denai was her daughter; Denai predicted that prophecy.

"Myles, the ancients cursed the orb with good reason. The past can't be changed—not unless it's meant to be." She'd only been able to save Drake because she was meant to. "You can't save Oberoth, and I'll be damned if I let you try."

Myles lunged at her, but she dodged him. Something clattered onto the floor as she called for it. The Srimtar rolled towards her. Myles froze mid-strike as Charlie grabbed it and its power suspended the room in time.

The orb pulsed and vibrated between her fingers, stars swirling inside of it. So many had died because of this thing, for the power held inside it, including her own teammates. She might be able to withstand it, but she couldn't use it. Time wasn't meant to be changed. You could only learn from the past, not change it to suit your own needs.

People wouldn't stop coming for it either. The lure of so much power would never go away.

Charlie knew what she had to do. She gripped the orb, called her power and the Srimtar phased between her fingers. Once incorporeal, she let the orb hover there a moment then squeezed it between her hands. She felt glass shatter. Light exploded outwards, knocking her and Myles to the floor. Energy reverberated through the air with a roar as the Srimtar broke and its power evaporated.

Charlie winced, feeling the energy wash over her.

"No!" Myles screamed from where he lay. "No! How could you do that? How could you throw away all that power?"

"That power wasn't meant to be used by anyone. People died to create that orb, even more died because of its existence." She scrambled up. "The cycle needs to end."

"No, that orb was mine! It was meant for me!" he cried.

Energy shot through the room as he opened a portal to the spirit realm.

Charlie stood her ground, letting the massive surge of ether wash over her. She felt stronger now; he wouldn't drag her in either. She threw a bolt of lightning, sending Myles hurtling across the room. She raised her hand, forcing the portal to close.

Drake and Irina appeared in a blaze of light.

"Myles, stop," Irina pleaded.

"You stay out of this," he snarled. "That orb was meant to be mine. I'd finally fulfil what my father tried to do. All Magickind would bow to me. I'd be unstoppable." He glared at Charlie. "You destroyed everything I worked for!" Myles shot up, raising his hand.

"Stop," Drake commanded, his eyes bleeding to black.

Myles froze, eyes widening. "How?" he hissed.

"I'm the Akaran and you're still a demon," Drake said. "Now that your mother has sworn allegiance to me, I can control you too."

"Myles, please. We can be a family now. Let go of this madness," said Irina.

Myles fought the compulsion and lunged at Charlie, then fell to the floor, dead.

Charlie let out a breath as Drake pulled her close. "Where's Scott?"

"I'm sorry, little witch. He's gone."

She hugged her demon, glad for the warmth of his embrace.

Irina stood staring at Myles.

Charlie went over to her and touched her shoulder. "I'm sorry it had to end like this."

Irina sniffed. "I lost him a long time ago. I hoped Oberoth wouldn't corrupt him, but—" She shook her head. "Take me back to Stanhold now, please. My trial begins in a few hours."

"No, I'll talk to Cate. With what I found, it should be enough to earn your pardon," Charlie replied. "Go home, we will see each other again soon."

Irina's eyes widened; she wrapped her arms around her daughter. "I hope we can be friends now."

"Me too." Charlie returned her hug.

Irina stared down as Drake disintegrated Myles's body then she vanished in a blur of light.

"I'll call Kaz and Nigel; they'll have a field day with this place," Charlie said. "Right now I want to go home, then we're taking a few weeks off. I think we've earned a holiday."

Drake grinned. "Mind if I fully seal our bond now?"

She kissed him. "You better. Like I said, you're stuck with me forever now."

If you enjoyed reading this book be sure to leave a review! For more news about my books sign up to my newsletter on tiffanyshand.com/newsletter

ALSO BY TIFFANY SHAND

ANDOVIA CHRONICLES

Dark Deeds Prequel

The Calling

ROGUES OF MAGIC SERIES

Bound By Blood

Archdruid

Bound By Fire

Old Magic

Dark Deception

Sins Of The Past

Reign Of Darkness

Rogues Of Magic Complete Box Set Books 1-7

EVERLIGHT ACADEMY TRILOGY

Everlight Academy, Book 1: Faeling

Everlight Academy Book 2: Fae Born

Hunted Guardian – An Everlight Academy Story

EXCALIBAR INVESTIGATIONS SERIES

Denai Touch

Denai Bound

Denai Storm

Excalibar Investigations Complete Box Set

SHADOW WALKER SERIES

Shadow Walker

Shadow Spy

Shadow Guardian

Shadow Walker Complete Box Set

THE AMARANTHINE CHRONICLES BOOK 1

Betrayed By Blood

Dark Revenge

The Final Battle

SHIFTER CLANS SERIES

The Alpha's Daughter

Alpha Ascending

The Alpha's Curse

The Shifter Clans Complete Box Set

TALES OF THE ITHEREAL

Fey Spy

Outcast Fey

Rogue Fey

Hunted Fey

Tales of the Ithereal Complete Box Set

THE FEY GUARDIAN SERIES

Memories Lost

Memories Awakened

Memories Found

The Fey Guardian Complete Series Box Set

THE ARKADIA SAGA

Chosen Avatar

Captive Avatar

Fallen Avatar

The Arkadia Saga Complete Series

ABOUT THE AUTHOR

Tiffany Shand is a writing mentor, professionally trained copy editor and copy writer who has been writing stories for as long as she can remember. Born in East Anglia, Tiffany still lives in the area, constantly guarding her work space from the two cats which she shares her home with.

She began using her pets as a writing inspiration when she was a child, before moving on to write her first novel after successful completion of a creative writing course. Nowadays, Tiffany writes urban fantasy and paranormal romance, as well as nonfiction books for other writers, all available through eBook stores and on her own website.

Tiffany's favourite quote is *'writing is an exploration. You start from nothing and learn as you go'* and it is armed with this that she hopes to be able to help, inspire and mentor many more aspiring authors.

When she has time to unwind, Tiffany enjoys photography, reading, and watching endless box sets. She also loves to get out and visit the vast number of castles and historic houses that England has to offer.